Christmas
Presents

Seasonal romances from three of our
best-loved Presents...™ authors!

GW00659767

Christmas Presents

HER CHRISTMAS FANTASY
by
Penny Jordan

A BABY FOR CHRISTMAS
by
Anne McAllister

CHRISTMAS NIGHTS
by
Sally Wentworth

MILLS & BOON®

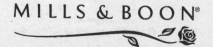

*MILLS & BOON and MILLS & BOON with the Rose Device
are registered trademarks of the publisher.*
*Harlequin Mills & Boon Limited,
Eton House, 18-24 Paradise Road, Richmond, Surrey, TW9 1SR*

CHRISTMAS PRESENTS
© by Harlequin Enterprises II B.V., 1999

Her Christmas Fantasy, A Baby for Christmas and *Christmas Nights*
were first published in Great Britain by Mills & Boon Limited
in separate, single volumes.

Her Christmas Fantasy © Penny Jordan 1996
A Baby for Christmas © Barbara Schenck 1995
Christmas Nights © Sally Wentworth 1996

ISBN 0 263 81544 7

05-9912

*Printed and bound in Spain
by Litografia Rosés S.A., Barcelona*

Born in Preston, Lancashire, **Penny Jordan** now lives with her husband in a beautiful fourteenth-century house in rural Cheshire. Penny has been writing for over ten years and now has over seventy novels to her name including the phenomenally successful TO LOVE, HONOUR AND BETRAY. With over thirty million copies of her books in print, and translations into seventeen languages, she has firmly established herself as a novelist of great scope.

HER CHRISTMAS FANTASY

by

PENNY JORDAN

CHAPTER ONE

LISA paused hesitantly outside the shop, studying the very obviously designer-label and expensive outfits in the window doubtfully.

She had been given the address by a friend who had told her that the shop was one of the most exclusive 'nearly new' designer-clothes outlets in the city, where outfits could be picked up for less than a third of their original price.

Lisa was no fashion victim—normally she was quite happy with her small wardrobe of good-quality chain-store clothes—but Henry had seemed so anxious that she create a good impression on his family and their friends, and most particularly his mother, during their Christmas visit to his parents' home in the north that Lisa had felt obliged to take the hints he had been dropping and add something rather more up-market to her wardrobe. Especially since Henry had already indicated that he wanted to put their relationship on a more formal basis, with an official announcement to his family of their plans to marry.

Lisa knew that many of her friends found Henry slightly stuffy and old-fashioned, but she liked those aspects of his personality. They indicated a reliability, a dependability in him which, so far as she was concerned, outweighed his admitted tendency to fuss and find fault over minor details.

When the more outspoken of her closest friends had

asked her what she saw in him she'd told them quietly that she saw a dependable husband and a good father.

'But what about romance?' they had asked her. 'What about falling desperately and passionately in love?'

Lisa had laughed, genuinely amused.

'I'm not the type of woman who falls desperately or passionately in love,' she had responded, 'and nor do I want to be!'

'But doesn't it annoy you that Henry's so chauvinistically old-fashioned?' Her friends had persisted. 'Look at the way he's fussing over you meeting his parents and family—telling you how he wants you to dress.'

'He's just anxious for me to make a good impression,' Lisa had argued back on Henry's behalf. 'He obviously values his parents' opinion and—'

'And he's still tied to his mother's apron strings,' one of her friends had scoffed. 'I know the type.' She had paused a little before adding more seriously, 'You know, don't you, that he was on the point of becoming engaged to someone else shortly before he met you and that he broke off the relationship because he wasn't sure that his family would approve of her? Apparently they're very old-fashioned and strait-laced, and Janey had been living with someone else when she'd first met Henry—'

'Yes, I do know,' Lisa had retorted firmly. 'But the reason that they broke up was not Janey's past history but that Henry realised that they didn't, simply *didn't* have enough in common.'

'And you and he do?' her friend had asked drily.

'We both want the same things out of life, yes,' Lisa had asserted defensively.

And it was, after all, true. She might not have fallen deeply in love with Henry the night they were introduced by a mutual friend, but she had certainly liked him enough to accept his invitation to dinner, and their relationship had grown steadily from that date to the point where they both felt that their future lay together.

She might not be entirely comfortable with Henry's insistence that she buy herself a new wardrobe in order to impress his wealthy parents and their circle of friends, but she could sympathise with the emotion which had led to him making such a suggestion.

Her own parents would, she knew, be slightly bemused by her choice of a husband; her mother was a gifted and acclaimed potter whose work was internationally praised, whilst her father's stylish, modern furniture designs meant that he was constantly in demand, not just as a designer but as a lecturer as well.

Both her parents were currently in Japan, and were not due to return for another two months.

It would have been a lonely Christmas for her this year if Henry had not invited her to go north with him to the Yorkshire Dales to visit his parents, Lisa acknowledged.

He had already warned her that his parents might consider her work as a PA to the owner of a small, London-based antique business rather too bohemian and arty. Had she worked in industry, been a teacher or a nurse, they would have found it more acceptable.

'In fact they'd probably prefer it if you didn't work at all,' he had told Lisa carefully when they had been discussing the subject.

'Not work? But that's—' Hastily she had bitten back the words she had been about to say, responding mildly instead, 'Most women these days expect to have a career.'

'My mother doesn't approve of married women working, especially when they have children,' Henry had told her stiffly.

Firmly suppressing her instinctive response that his

mother was very obviously rather out of touch with modern life, Lisa had said placatingly instead, 'A lot of women tend to put their career on hold or work part-time when their children are young.'

She had hesitated outside the shop for long enough, she decided now, pushing open the door and walking in.

The young girl who came forward to help her explained that she was actually standing in for the owner of the shop, who had been called away unexpectedly.

The clothes on offer were unexpectedly wearable, Lisa acknowledged, and not too over-the-top as she had half dreaded. One outfit in particular caught her eye—a trouser suit in fine cream wool crêpe which comprised trousers, waistcoat and jacket.

'It's an Armani,' the salesgirl enthused as Lisa picked it off the rail. 'A real bargain… I was tempted to buy it myself,' she admitted, 'but it's only a size ten and I take a twelve. It's this season's stock—a real bargain.'

'This season's.' A small frown puckered Lisa's forehead. Who on earth these days could afford to buy a designer outfit and then get rid of it within a few months of buying it—especially something like this in such a classical design that it wasn't going to date?

'If you like it, we've got several other things in from the same per…the same source,' the girl was telling her. 'Would you like to see them?'

Lisa paused and then smiled her agreement. She was beginning to enjoy this rather more than she had expected. The feel of the cream crêpe beneath her fingertips was sensuously luxurious. She had always loved fabrics, their textures, differing weights.

An hour later, her normally immaculate long bob of silky blonde hair slightly tousled from all her trying on, she grimaced ruefully at the pile of clothes that she had put to one side as impossible to resist.

What woman, having bought such a luxuriously expensive and elegantly wearable wardrobe, could bear to part with it after so short a period of time?

If she had been given free rein to choose from new herself, she could not have chosen better, Lisa recognised as she sighingly acknowledged that the buttermilk-coloured silk, wool and cashmere coat she had just tried on was an absolute must.

She was, she admitted ten minutes later as she took a deep breath and signed her credit-card bill, buying these clothes not so much for Henry and his family as for herself.

'You've got an absolute bargain,' the salesgirl told her unnecessarily as she carefully wrapped Lisa's purchases in tissue-paper and put them into several large, glossy carrier bags.

'I think these are the nicest things we've had in in a long time. Personally I don't think I could have brought myself to part with them… That coat…' She gave a small sigh and then told Lisa half enviously, 'They fitted you perfectly as well. I envy you being so tall and slim.'

'So tall.' Lisa winced slightly. She wasn't excessively tall, being five feet nine, but she was aware that with Henry being a rather stocky five feet ten or so he preferred her not to wear high-heeled shoes, and he had on occasion made rather irritated comments to her about her height.

She was just on her way out of the shop when a car drew up outside, its owner double parking in flagrant disregard for the law.

He looked extremely irritable and ill-tempered, Lisa decided as she watched him stride towards the shop, and wondered idly who he was.

Not a prospective customer, even on behalf of a woman friend. No, he was quite definitely the type who, if he did buy clothes for a woman, would not need to exercise financial restraint by buying them second-hand.

Lisa was aware of his frown deepening as he glanced almost dismissively at her.

Well, she was equally unimpressed by him, she decided critically. Stunningly, almost overpoweringly male he might look, with that tall, broad-shouldered body and that hawkish, arrogant profile, but he was simply not her type.

She had no doubt that the more romantic of her friends would consider him ideal 'swoon over' material, with those frowning, overtly sexual, strongly drawn male features and his dominant masterful manner. But she merely thought him arrogantly over-confident. Look at the way he had dismissed her with the briefest of irritable glances, stalking past her. Even the silky gleam of his thick dark hair possessed a strong air of male sexuality.

He would be the kind of man who looked almost too hirsute with his clothes off, she decided unkindly, sternly suppressing the impish little demon of rebellion within her that immediately produced a very clear and highly erotic mental image of him thus unclad and, to her exasperation, not overly hirsute at all... In fact...

Stop it, she warned herself as she flagged down a cruising taxi and gave the driver the address of the friend who had recommended the shop to her.

She had promised her that she would call round and let her know how she had fared, but for some reason, once her purchases had been duly displayed and enviously approved, she discovered that Alison was more interested in hearing about the man she had passed in the street than discussing the likelihood of her forthcoming introduction to Henry's parents' going well.

'He wasn't my type at all,' she declared firmly to Alison. 'He was far too arrogant. I don't imagine he would have the first idea of how to treat a modern woman—'

'You mean that Henry does…?' Alison asked drily, stopping Lisa in her tracks for a moment before she valiantly responded.

'Of course he does.'

'You just wait,' Alison warned her. 'The moment he gets that ring on your finger, he's going to start nagging you to conform. He'll want you to stop working, for a start. Look at the way he goes on about what a perfect mother his own mother was…how she devoted her life to his father and himself…'

'I think it's rather touching that he's so devoted to her, so loyal and loving…' Lisa defended.

'Mmm… What's he like in bed?' Alison asked her curiously.

Even though Lisa was used to her friend's forthrightness, she was a little taken aback by her question, caught too off guard to do anything other than answer honestly.

'I…I don't know… We…we haven't… We don't…'

'You don't *know*. Are you crazy? You're planning to *marry* the man and you don't know yet what he's like in bed. How long have you two known one another?'

'Almost eight months,' Lisa replied slightly stiffly.

'Mmm… Hardly the type to be overwhelmed by passion, then, is he, our Henry?'

'Henry believes in old-fashioned courtship, that couples should get to know one another as…as people. He doesn't…he doesn't care for the modern approach to casual sex…'

'Very laudable,' Alison told her sardonically.

'Look, the fact that we haven't…that we don't…that

we haven't been to bed together yet isn't a problem for *me*,' Lisa told her vehemently.

'No? Then it should be,' Alison returned forthrightly. 'How on earth can you think of marrying a man when you don't even know if the two of you are sexually compatible yet?'

'Easily,' Lisa replied promptly. 'After all, our grandparents did.'

Alison rolled her eyes and mocked, 'And you claim that you aren't romantic.'

'It takes more to build a good marriage than just sex,' Lisa told her quietly. 'I'm tired of men who take you out for dinner and then expect you to take them to bed as a thank-you... I want stability in a relationship, Alison. Someone I can rely on, depend on. Someone who respects and values me as a *person*... Yes, all right, Henry might be slightly old-fashioned and...and...'

'Sexless?' her friend came back, but Lisa shook her head and continued determinedly.

'But he's very loyal...very faithful...very trustworthy...and...'

'If that's what you're looking for you'd be better off with a dog,' Alison suggested critically, but Lisa wasn't prepared to argue the matter any further.

'I'm just not the type for excitement and passion,' she told her friend. 'I like stability. Marriage isn't just for now, Alison; it's for the future too. Look, I'd better go,' she announced, glancing at her watch. 'Henry's taking me out for dinner this evening.' As she got up and headed for the door, she added gratefully, 'Thanks for recommending that shop to me.'

'Yes, I'm really envious. You've got some lovely things and at a knock-down price. All current season's stuff too... Lucky you.'

*   *   *

As she made her way home to her own flat Lisa was ruefully aware of how difficult her friends found it to understand her relationship with Henry, but then they had not had her upbringing and did not possess her desire— her craving in a sense—for emotional tranquillity, for roots and permanence.

Her parents were both by nature not just extremely artistic—and because of that at times wholly absorbed by their work—they were also gypsies, nomads, who enjoyed travelling and moving on. The thought of basing themselves somewhere permanently was anathema to them.

During her childhood Lisa couldn't remember having spent a whole year at any one school; she knew her parents loved her, and she certainly loved them dearly, but she had a different nature from theirs.

All right, so she knew that it would be difficult persuading Henry to accept that there was no reason why she should not still pursue her career as well as being a mother, but she was sure that she would be able to make him understand that her work was important to her. At the moment Henry worked for a prestigious firm of insurance brokers, but they had both agreed that once they were married they would move out of London and into the country.

She let herself into her small flat and carefully carried her new purchases into her bedroom.

After she had had a shower she intended to try them all on again, if she had time before Henry arrived. However, when she replayed her answering-machine tape there was a message on it from Henry, cancelling their date because he had an important business dinner that he had to attend and reminding her that they still had to shop for suitable Christmas presents to take for his family.

She had already made several suggestions based on

what Henry had told her about his family, and specifically his parents—a very pretty petit point antique footstool for his grandmother, some elegant tulip vases for his mother, who, he had told her, was a keen gardener. But Henry had pursed his lips and dismissed her ideas.

She had been tempted to suggest that it might be better if he chose their Christmas presents on his own, but she had warned herself that she was being unfair and even slightly petty. He, after all, knew their tastes far better than she did.

She had just put on her favourite of all the outfits she had bought—the cream wool crêpe trouser suit—when her doorbell rang.

Assuming that it must be Henry after all, she went automatically to open the door, and then stood staring in total shock as she realised that her visitor wasn't Henry but the man she had last seen striding past her and storming into the dress agency as she'd left it.

'Lisa Phillips?' he demanded curtly as he stepped past her and into her hall.

Dumbly Lisa nodded her head, too taken aback by the unexpectedness of his arrival to think to question his right to walk uninvited into her home.

'My name's Oliver Davenport,' he told her curtly, handing her a card, barely giving her time to glance at it before he continued, 'I believe you purchased several items of clothing from Second Time Around earlier today.'

'Er…yes,' Lisa agreed. 'But—'

'Good. This shouldn't take long then. Unfortunately the clothes that you bought should not have been put on sale. Technically, in fact, the shop sold them without the permission of their true owner, and in such circumstances, as

with the innocent purchase of a stolen car or indeed any
stolen goods, you have no legal right to—'

'Just a minute,' she interrupted him in disbelief. Completely taken aback by his unexpected arrival and his infuriatingly arrogant manner, Lisa could feel herself becoming thoroughly angry. 'Are you accusing the shop of
selling stolen clothes? Because if so it should be the police
you are informing and not me.'

'Not exactly. Look, I'm prepared to refund you the full
amount of what you spent plus an extra hundred pounds
for any inconvenience. So if you'll just—'

'That's very generous of you,' Lisa told him sarcastically. 'But I bought these clothes for a specific purpose
and I have no intention of selling them back to you. I
bought them in good faith and—'

'Look, I've just explained to you, those clothes should
never have been sold in the first place,' he cut across her
harshly, giving her an impatiently angry look.

Lisa didn't like the way he was filling her small hall,
looming almost menacingly over her, but there was no
way she was going to give in to him. Why should she?

'If that's true, then why hasn't the shop been in touch
with me?' Lisa challenged him.

She could see that he didn't like her question from the
way his mouth tightened and hardened before he replied
bitingly, 'Probably because the idiotic woman who runs
the place refuses to listen to reason.'

'Really?' Lisa asked him scathingly. 'You seem to have
a way with women. Has it ever occurred to you that a
little less aggression and a good deal more persuasion
might produce better results? Not that any amount of persuasion will change my mind,' she added firmly. 'I bought
those clothes in good faith, and since the shop hasn't seen

fit to get in touch with me concerning their supposedly wrongful sale I don't see why—'

'Oh, for God's sake.' She was interrupted furiously. 'Look, if you must know, the clothes belong to my cousin's girlfriend. They had a quarrel—it's a very volatile relationship. She walked out on him, vowing never to come back—they'd had an argument about her decision to go on holiday with a girlfriend, without him apparently—and in a fit of retaliatory anger he gave her clothes to the dress agency. It was an impulse…something he regretted virtually as soon as he'd done it, and when Emma rang him from Italy to make things up he asked me to help him get her things back before she comes home and discovers what he's done.'

'He asked *you* for help?'

There was very little doubt in Lisa's mind about whose girlfriend the absent Emma actually was, and it wasn't Oliver Davenport's fictitious cousin.

The look he gave her in response to her question wasn't very friendly, Lisa recognised; in fact it wasn't very friendly at all, but even though, concealed beneath the sensual elegance of her newly acquired trousers, her knees were knocking slightly, she refused to give in to her natural apprehension.

It wasn't like her to be so stubborn or so unsympathetic, but something about him just seemed to rub her up the wrong way and make her uncharacteristically antagonistic towards him.

It wasn't just the fact that he was demanding that she part with her newly acquired wardrobe that was making her combative, she admitted; it was something about the man himself, something about his arrogance, his…his maleness that was setting her nerves slightly on edge, challenging her into a mode of behaviour that was really quite foreign to her.

She knew that Henry would have been shocked to see her displaying so much stubbornness and anger—she was a little bit shocked herself.

'He was about to go away on business. Emma's due back at the end of the week. He didn't want her walking into the flat and discovering that half her clothes are missing...'

'No, I'm sure you...he...' Lisa corrected herself tauntingly '...doesn't...'

She saw from the dark burn of angry colour etching his cheekbones that he wasn't pleased by her deliberate 'mistake', nor the tone of voice she had delivered it in.

'You have no legal claim over those clothes,' he told her grimly. 'The shop sold them without the owner's permission.'

'If that's true, then it's up to the shop to get in touch with me,' Lisa pointed out. 'After all, for all I know, you could want them for yourself...' She paused. His temper was set on a hair-trigger already and although she doubted that he would actually physically harm her...

'Don't be ridiculous,' she heard him breathe softly, as though he had read her mind.

Inexplicably she realised that she was blushing slightly as, for no logical reason at all, she remembered exactly what she had been thinking about him—and his body— earlier in the day. Just as well he hadn't second guessed her private thoughts *then*!

'So you're not prepared to be reasonable about this?'

She be reasonable? Lisa could feel her own temper starting to rise.

'Doesn't it mean anything to you that you could be

putting someone's whole relationship at risk by your refusal?'

'*Me* putting a relationship at risk?' Lisa gasped at the
unfairness of it. 'If you ask me, I'm not the one who's
doing that. If your relationship is so important to you you
should have thought of that before you lost your temper
and decided to punish your girlfriend by selling her
clothes—'

'Emma is not *my* girlfriend,' he told her with ominous
calm. 'As I've already explained to you, I am simply acting as an intermediary in all of this for my cousin. But
then I suppose it's par for the course that you should think
otherwise. It goes with all the rest of your illogical behaviour,' he told her scathingly.

'If you ask me,' she told him, thoroughly incensed now,
'I think that Emma…whoever's girlfriend she is—yours
or your cousin's…is better off without you. What kind of
man does something like that…? Those clothes were virtually new and—'

'Exactly. New and expensive and paid for by my
cousin, who is a rather jealous young man who objects to
his girlfriend wearing the clothes he bought her to attract
the attentions of other men…'

'And because of that he stole them from her wardrobe
and sold them? It sounds to me as though she's better off
without you…without him,' Lisa corrected herself
fiercely, her eyes showing her contempt of a man—any
man—jealous or otherwise, who could behave in such a
petty and revengeful way.

'Well, I'm sorry,' she continued, patently anything but.
'But explaining to Emma just exactly what's happened to
her clothes is your problem and not mine. I bought them
in good faith—'

'And you'll be able to buy some more with the money

I'm willing to refund you for them, especially since… Oh, I get it,' he said softly, his eyes suddenly narrowing.

'You get what?' Lisa demanded suspiciously, not liking the cynicism she could see in his eyes. 'Those clothes were virtually brand-new, this season's stock, and I'd be very lucky indeed to pick up anything else like them at such a bargain price, especially at this time of year, and—'

'Oh, yes, I can see what you're after. All right then, I don't like blackmailers and I wouldn't normally give in to someone who plainly thinks she's onto a good thing, but I haven't got time to waste negotiating with you. What would you guess was the full, brand-new value of the clothes you bought today?'

'The full value?' A small frown puckered Lisa's forehead. She had no idea at all of what he was getting at. 'I have no idea. I don't normally buy exclusive designer-label clothes, especially not Armani…but I imagine it would have to be several thousand pounds…'

'Several thousand pounds.' A thin, dangerous smile curled his mouth, his eyes so coldly contemptuous that Lisa actually felt a small, icy shiver race down her spine.

'Why don't we settle for a round figure and make it five thousand pounds? I'll write you a cheque for five thousand here and now and you'll give me back Emma's clothes.'

Lisa stared at him in disbelief.

'But that's crazy,' she protested. 'Why on earth should you pay me five thousand pounds when you could go out and buy a whole new wardrobe for her for that amount…?' She shook her head in disbelief. 'I don't—'

'Oh, come on,' he interrupted her cuttingly. 'Don't give me that. You understand perfectly well. Even *I* understand how impossible and time-wasting an exercise it would be for me to go out and replace every single item with its exact replica…even if I knew what it was I was supposed to be buying. Don't overplay your hand,' he warned her. 'All that mock innocence doesn't suit you.'

Mock innocence!

As she suddenly recognised just what he was accusing her of, Lisa's face flushed a brilliant, furious scarlet.

'Get out… Get out of my flat right now,' she demanded shakily. 'Otherwise I'm going to call the police. How dare you accuse me of…of…?' She couldn't even say the word, she felt such a sense of outrage and disgust.

'I wouldn't give you those clothes now if you offered to pay me ten thousand…twenty thousand,' she told him passionately. 'You deserve to lose Emma… In fact, I think I'm probably doing her a favour by letting her see just what kind of a man you are. I suppose you thought that just because you bought her clothes for her you had a right to…to take them back… If I were her… If I were her…'

'Yes? If you were her, what?' he goaded her, just as furious as she was herself, Lisa recognised as she saw the small pulse beating fiercely in his jaw and the banked-down fury in his eyes.

'I wouldn't have let you buy them for me in the first place,' she threw emotionally at him, adding, 'I'd rather—'

'Rather what?' he challenged her, his voice dropping suddenly and becoming dangerously, sensually soft as he raked her from head to foot in such a sexually predatory and searching way that it left her virtually shaking, trembling, her body overreacting wildly to the male sexuality in the way he was looking at her, the sensual challenge in the way his eyes deliberately stripped her of her clothes, leaving her body vulnerable…exposed…naked.

'You'd rather what?' he repeated triumphantly. 'Go naked?'

Lisa couldn't speak; she was too shocked, too outraged,
too aware of her feminine vulnerability to the blazing heat
of his sexuality to risk saying anything.

'But then in actual fact, according to you—since you
refuse to believe the truth and accept that I am acting for
my cousin and not for myself—you are wearing clothes
that I have chosen…bought…' he added softly, his glance
slipping suggestively over her body for a second time, but
this time more slowly, more lingeringly…more…more seductively, Lisa recognised as she felt herself responding
helplessly to the sheer force of the magnetic spell he
seemed to have cast over her.

From somewhere she managed to find the strength to
break free. Stepping back from him, putting a safer distance between them, averting her eyes and her over-
flushed face from his powerful gaze, she demanded huskily, 'I want you to leave. Now. Otherwise…'

'You'll call the police. I know,' he agreed drily. 'Very
well, since it's obvious I can't make you see reason… I
won't forget how co-operative you've been,' he added,
sending a small shiver down her spine as she saw the look
in his eyes. 'Although I can understand why you're so
loath to part with your borrowed finery.

'The suit looks good on you,' he added unexpectedly
as he turned towards the door, pausing to look at her before lifting his hand and outrageously tracing a line with
the tip of his index finger all the way along the deep V
of the neckline of the waistcoat just where the upper
curves of her breasts, naked underneath it, pressed against
the creamy fabric.

'It's a bit tighter here on you than it was on Emma,
though,' he told her. 'She's probably only a 34B whereas

you must be a 34C. Nice—especially worn the way you're wearing it now, without anything underneath it...'

Lisa swallowed back all of the agitated, defensive remarks that sprang to her lips, knowing that none of them could do anything to wipe out what he had just said to her, or the effect his words had had on her.

Why, she wondered wretchedly as he opened her front door and left her flat far more calmly than he had entered it, did her body have to react so...so...idiotically and erotically to his touch? Even without looking down she knew how betrayingly her nipples were still pressing against the fine fabric of her waistcoat—as they certainly hadn't been doing when he'd first arrived. As they had, in fact, only humiliatingly done when he had reached out and touched her with that lazily mocking fingertip which had had such a devastating effect on her senses.

It was because she was so overwrought, that was all, she tried to comfort herself half an hour later, the front door securely bolted as she hugged a comforting mug of freshly made coffee.

She would have to ring the shop, of course, and find out exactly what was going on, and if they asked her to return the clothes then morally she would have no option other than to do so.

How dared he accuse her of trying to blackmail him...? *Her*. The coffee slopped out of the mug as her hands started to shake. As if she would ever...ever do any such thing. She felt desperately sorry for the unknown Emma. It was bad enough that he should have sold her clothes, but how would she feel, knowing that he had touched her, another woman, so...so...? No, in her view Emma was better off without him. Much better off.

How dared he touch her like that...as though...as though...? And he had known exactly what he was doing as well. She had seen it in those shockingly knowing steel-grey eyes as she'd read the message of male triumph and awareness that they'd been giving her. He had known that he was arousing her—had known it and had enjoyed knowing it.

Unlike her. She had hated it and she hated him. Emma was quite definitely better off without him and she certainly wasn't going to be the one to help him make up their quarrel by returning her clothes.

At least he was not likely to be able to carry out that subtle threat of future retribution against her—thank goodness.

CHAPTER TWO

LISA stood in front of the guest-bedroom window of Henry's parents' large Victorian house looking out across the wintry countryside.

They had arrived considerably later than expected the previous evening, due, in the main, to the fact that Henry's car had been so badly damaged whilst parked in a client's car park that their departure had been delayed and they had had to use her small—much smaller—model, much to Henry's disgust.

They had arrived shortly after eleven o'clock, and whilst Henry had been greeted with a good deal of maternal anxiety and concern Lisa had received a considerably more frosty reception, Henry's mother giving her a chilly smile and presenting a cool cheek for her to kiss before commenting, 'I'm afraid we couldn't put back supper any longer. You know what your father's like about meal times, Henry.'

'It was Lisa's fault,' Henry had grumbled untruthfully, adding to Lisa, 'You really should get a decent car, you know. Oh, and by the way, you need petrol.'

Lisa had gritted her teeth and smiled, reminding herself that she had already guessed from Henry's comments about his family that, as an only child and a son, he was the apple of his mother's eye.

Whilst Henry had been despatched to his father's study, Lisa had been quizzed by Henry's mother about her family and background. It had subtly been made plain to Lisa that so far as Henry's mother was concerned the jury was still out on the subject of her suitability as Henry's intended wife.

Normally she would have enjoyed the chance to visit the Yorkshire Dales, Lisa acknowledged—especially at this time of the year. Last night she had been enchanted to discover that snow was expected on the high ground.

Henry had been less impressed. In fact, he had been in an edgy, difficult mood throughout the entire journey—and not just, Lisa suspected, because of the damage to his precious car.

It had struck her, over the previous weekend, when they'd been doing the last of their Christmas shopping together, that he was obviously having doubts about her ability to make the right impression on his parents. There had been several small lectures and clumsy hints on what his family would expect, and one particularly embarrassing moment when Alison had called round to the flat just as Henry had been explaining that he wasn't sure that the Armani trouser suit was going to be quite the thing for his parents' annual pre-Christmas supper party.

'What century are Henry's parents living in?' Alison had exploded after Henry had left the room. 'Honestly, Lisa, I can't—'

She had stopped when Lisa had shaken her head, changing the subject to ask instead, 'Any more repercussions about the clothes you bought from Second Time Around, by the way?'

Lisa had told Alison all about her run-in with Oliver Davenport, asking her friend's advice as to what she ought to do.

'Ring the shop and find out what they've got to say,' had been Alison's prompt response.

'I've already done that,' Lisa had told her. 'And there was just a message on the answering machine saying that the owner has had to close the shop down indefinitely because her father has been taken seriously ill.'

'Well, if you want my opinion, you bought those clothes in all good faith, and I feel that their original owner deserves to know exactly what kind of miserable rat her boyfriend is… I mean…selling her clothes… It's… it's… Well, I'd certainly never forgive any man who tried to pull that one on me. I think you did exactly the right thing in refusing to give them back,' Alison had said comfortingly.

'No. No further repercussions,' Lisa had told her in response to her latest question. 'Which I find surprising. I suppose I did overreact a little bit, but when he virtually accused me of trying to blackmail him into paying almost more for them than they had originally cost…'

Her voice had quivered with remembered indignation as she recalled how shocked and insulted she had felt to be confronted with such a contemptuous assessment of her character.

'You overreacting—and to a man… Now that's something I *would* like to see,' Alison had told her.

'Who are you discussing?' Henry had asked, coming back into the room.

'Oh, no one special,' Lisa had told him, hastily and untruthfully, hoping that he wouldn't question the sudden surge of hot, guilty colour flooding her face as she remembered the shocking unexpectedness and intimacy of the way Oliver Davenport had reached out and touched her, and her even more shocking and intimate reaction to his touch.

The whole incident was something that was best forgotten she told herself firmly now as she craned her neck to watch a shepherd manoeuvring his flock on the distant hillside. She felt very sorry for Emma, of course, in the loss of her clothes, but hopefully it would teach Oliver Davenport not to behave so arrogantly in future. It was certainly a lesson he needed to learn.

Lisa glanced at her watch.

Henry's mother had announced last night that they sat down for breakfast at eight o'clock sharp, the implication being that she suspected that Lisa lived too decadent and lazy a lifestyle to manage to get up early enough to join them.

She couldn't have been more wrong, Lisa acknowledged. She was normally a very early riser.

The build-up to Christmas, and most especially the week before it, was normally one of her favourite times of the year. Her parents might live a rather unconventional lifestyle by Henry's parents' standards, but wherever they had lived when she'd been a child they had always made a point of following as many Christmas traditions as they could—buying and dressing a specially chosen Christmas tree, cooking certain favourite Christmas treats, shopping for presents and wrapping them. But Lisa had always yearned for the trappings of a real British Christmas. She had been looking forward to seeing such a traditional scenario of events taking place in Henry's childhood home, but it had become apparent to her the previous evening that Henry's parents, and more specifically Henry's mother, did not view Christmas in the same way she did herself.

'The whole thing has become so dreadfully commercialised that I simply don't see the point nowadays,' she had commented when Lisa had been describing the fun she had had shopping for gifts for the several small and *not* so small children who featured on her Christmas present list.

Her father in particular delighted in receiving anything

toy-like, and had a special weakness for magic tricks. Lisa had posted her gifts to her parents to Japan weeks ago, and had, in turn, received hers from them. She had brought the presents north with her, intending to add them to the pile she had assumed would accumulate beneath the Christmas tree, which in her imagination she had visualised as tall and wonderfully bushy, dominating the large hallway that Henry had described to her, warmed by the firelight of its open hearth and scenting the whole room with the delicious aroma of fresh pine needles.

Alas for her imaginings. Henry's mother did not, apparently, like real Christmas trees. They caused too much mess with their needles. And as for an open fire! They had had that boarded up years ago, she had informed Lisa, adding that it had caused far too much mess and nuisance.

So much for her hazy thoughts of establishing the beginnings of their own family traditions, her plans of one day telling her own children how she and their father had spent their first Christmas together, going out to choose the family Christmas tree.

'You're far too romantic and impractical,' Henry had criticised her. 'I agree with Mother. Real Christmas trees are nothing but a nuisance.'

As she turned away from the window Lisa was uncomfortably aware not only of Henry's mother's reluctance to accept her, but also of her own unexpectedly rebellious feeling that Henry was letting her down in not being more supportive of her.

She hadn't spent one full day with Henry's family yet, and already she was beginning to regret the extended length of their Christmas stay with them.

Reluctantly she walked towards the bedroom door. It was ten to eight, and the last thing she wanted to do now was arrive late for breakfast.

＊　　＊　　＊

'Off-white wool... Don't you think that's rather impractical?' Henry's mother asked Lisa critically.

Taking a deep breath and counting to ten, Lisa forced
herself to smile as she responded politely to Mary
Hanford's criticism.

'Perhaps a little, but then—'

'I never wear cream or white. I think they can be so
draining to the pale English complexion,' her prospective
mother-in-law continued. 'Navy is always so much more
serviceable, I think.'

Lisa had arrived downstairs half an hour ago, all her
offers to help with the preparation of the pre-Christmas
buffet supper having been firmly refused.

So much for creating the right impression on Henry's
parents with her new clothes, Lisa reflected wryly, wishing that Alison was with her to appreciate the ironic humour of the situation.

She could, of course, have shared the joke with Henry,
but somehow she doubted that he would have found it
funny... He had, no doubt, inherited his sense of humour,
or rather his lack of it, from his mother, she decided
sourly, and was immediately ashamed of her own mean-
spiritedness.

Of course, it was only natural that Henry's mother
should be slightly distant with her. Naturally she was protective of Henry—he was her only son, her only child...

He was also a man of thirty-one, a sharp inner voice
reminded Lisa, and surely capable of making his own
mind up about who he wanted to marry? Or was he?

It hadn't escaped Lisa's notice during the day how
Henry consistently and illuminatingly agreed with whatever opinion his mother chose to voice, but she dismissed
the tiny niggling doubts that were beginning to undermine
her confidence in her belief that she and Henry had a

future together as natural uncertainties raised by seeing him in an unfamiliar setting and with people, moreover, who knew him far better than she did.

In the hallway the grandfather clock chimed the hour. In a few minutes the Hanfords' supper guests would be arriving.

Henry had already explained to her that his family had lived in the area for several generations and that they had a large extended family, most of whom would be at the supper party, along with a handful of his parents' friends.

Lisa was slightly apprehensive aware that she would be very much on show, which was one of the reasons why she had chosen to wear the cream trouser suit.

Henry, however, hadn't been any more approving of her outfit than his mother, telling her severely that he thought that a skirt would have been more appropriate than trousers.

Lisa had no doubt that Oliver Davenport would have been both highly amused and contemptuous of her failure to achieve the desired effect with her acquired plumage.

Oliver Davenport. Now what on earth was she doing thinking about such a disagreeable subject, such a contentious person, when by rights she ought to be concentrating on the evening ahead of her?

'Ah, Lisa, there you are!' she heard Henry exclaiming. 'Everyone will be arriving soon, and Mother likes us all to be in the hall to welcome them when they do.

'I see you didn't change after all,' he added, frowning at her.

'An Armani suit is a perfectly acceptable outfit to wear for a supper party, Henry,' Lisa pointed out mildly, and couldn't help adding a touch more robustly, 'And, to be honest, I think I would have felt rather cold in a skirt. Your parents—'

'Mother doesn't think an overheated house is healthy,' Henry interrupted her quickly—so quickly that Lisa suspected that she wasn't the first person to comment on the chilliness of his parents' house.

'I expect I'm feeling the cold because we're so much further north here,' she offered diplomatically as she followed him into the hallway.

Cars could be heard pulling up outside, their doors opening and closing.

'That's good!' Henry exclaimed. 'Mother likes everyone to be on time.'

Mother would, Lisa thought rebelliously, but wisely she kept the words to herself.

Henry's aunt and her family were the first to arrive. A smaller, quieter edition of her elder sister, she was, nevertheless, far warmer in her manner towards Lisa than Henry's mother had been, and Lisa didn't miss the looks exchanged by her three teenage children as they were subjected to Mary Hanford's critical inspection.

Fifteen minutes later the hallway was virtually full, and Lisa was beginning to lose track of just who everyone was. The doorbell rang again and Henry went to answer it. As Lisa turned to look at the newcomers her heart suddenly stood still and then gave a single shocked bound followed by a flurry of too fast, disbelieving, nervous beats.

Oliver Davenport! What on earth was he doing here? He couldn't have followed her here to pursue his demand for her to return Emma's clothes, could he?

At the thought of what Henry's mother was likely to say if Oliver Davenport caused the same kind of scene here in public as he had staged in the privacy of her own flat, Lisa closed her eyes in helpless dismay, and then

heard Henry saying tensely to her, 'Lisa, I'd like to intro-
duce you to one of my parents' neighbours. Oliver—'

'Lisa and I already know one another.'

Lisa's eyes widened in bemused incomprehension.

Oliver Davenport was a neighbour of Henry's parents!
And what did he mean by implying that they knew one
another…by saying her name in that grossly deceptive,
softly sensual way, which seemed to imply that he…that
she…?

'You do? You never said anything about knowing
Oliver to me, Lisa,' Henry said almost hectoringly.

But before Lisa could make any attempt to defend herself or explain Oliver Davenport was doing it for her,
addressing Henry in a tone that left Lisa in no doubt as
to just what kind of opinion the other man had of her
husband-to-be, as he announced cuttingly, 'No doubt she
had more important things on her mind. Or perhaps she
simply didn't think it was important…'

'I…I…I didn't realise you two knew one another,' was
the only response Lisa could come up with, and she saw
from Henry's face that it was not really one that satisfied
him.

She nibbled worriedly at her bottom lip, cast Oliver
Davenport a bitter look and then was forced to listen helplessly whilst Oliver, who still quite obviously bore her a
grudge over the clothes, commented judiciously, 'I like
the outfit… It suits you… But then I thought so the first
time I saw you wearing it, didn't I?'

Lisa knew that she was blushing. Blushing…? She was
turning a vivid and unconcealable shade of deep scarlet,
she acknowledged miserably as she saw the suspicious
look that Henry was giving her and recognised from the
narrow, pursed-lip glare that Henry's mother must have
also overheard Oliver's comment.

'Oliver, let me get you a drink,' Henry's father offered, thankfully coming up to usher him away, but not before Oliver managed to murmur softly to Lisa,

'Saved by the cavalry…'

'How on earth do you come to know Oliver Davenport?' Henry demanded angrily as soon as Oliver was out of earshot.

'I don't *know* him,' Lisa admitted wearily. 'At least not—'

'What do you mean? Of course you *know* him…and well enough for him to be able to comment on your clothes…'

'He's… Henry…this isn't the time for me to explain…' Lisa told him quietly.

'So there *is* something to explain, then.' Henry was refusing to be appeased. 'Where did you meet him? In London, I suppose. His business might be based up here at the Hall, but he still spends quite a considerable amount of time in London… His cousin works for him down there—'

'His cousin…?' Lisa couldn't quite keep the note of nervous apprehension out of her voice.

'Yes, Piers Davenport, Oliver's cousin. He's several years younger than Oliver and he lives in London with his girlfriend—some model or other…Emily…or Emma…I can't remember which…'

'Emma,' Lisa supplied hollowly.

So Oliver hadn't been lying, after all, when he had told her that he was acting on behalf of his cousin. She glanced uneasily over her shoulder, remembering just exactly how scathingly she had denounced him, practically accusing him of being a liar and worse.

No wonder he had given her that look this evening which had said that he hadn't finished with her and that he fully intended to make her pay for her angry insults, to exact retribution on her.

Apprehensively she wondered exactly what form that silently promised retribution was going to take. What was he going to do? Reveal to Henry and his parents that she had bought her clothes second-hand? She could just imagine how Mary Hanford would react to that information. At the thought of her impending humiliation, Lisa felt her stomach muscles tighten defensively.

It wasn't all her fault. Hers had been a natural enough mistake to make, she reminded herself. Alison had agreed with her. And Oliver had to share some of the blame for her error himself. If he had only been a little more conciliatory in his manner towards her, a little less arrogant in demanding that she return the clothes back to him…

'I do wish you had told me that you knew Oliver,' Henry was continuing fussily. 'Especially in view of his position locally.'

'What position locally?' Lisa asked him warily, but she suspected she could guess the answer. To judge from Mary Hanford's deferential manner towards him, Oliver Davenport was quite obviously someone of importance in the area. Her heart started to sink even further as Henry explained in a hushed, almost awed voice.

'Oliver is an extremely wealthy man. He owns and runs one of the north of England's largest financial consultancy businesses and he recently took over another firm based in London, giving him a countrywide network. But why are you asking me? Surely if you know him you must—?'

'I don't know him,' Lisa protested tiredly. 'Henry, there's something I have to tell you.' She took a deep breath. There was nothing else for it; she was going to have to tell Henry the truth.

'But you evidently do know him,' Henry protested, ignoring her and cutting across what she was trying to say. 'And rather well by the sound of it… Lisa, what exactly's going on?'

Henry could look remarkably like his mother when he pursed his lips and narrowed his eyes like that, Lisa decided. She suddenly had a mental image of the children they might have together—little replicas of their grandmother. Quickly she banished the unwelcome vision.

'Henry, nothing is going on. If you would just let me explain—' Lisa began.

But once again she was interrupted, this time by Henry's mother, who bore down on them, placing a proprietorial hand on Henry's arm as she told him, 'Henry, dear, Aunt Elspeth wants to talk to you. She's over there by the French windows. She's brought her god-daughter with her. You remember Louise. You used to play together when you were children—such a sweet girl…'

To Lisa's chagrin, Henry was borne off by his mother, leaving her standing alone, nursing an unwanted glass of too sweet sherry.

What should have been the happiest Christmas Eve of her adult life was turning out to be anything but, she admitted gloomily as she watched a petite, doe-eyed brunette, presumably Aunt Elspeth's god-daughter, simpering up at a Henry who was quite plainly wallowing in her dewy-eyed, fascinated attention.

It was a good thirty minutes before Henry returned to her side, during which time she had had ample opportunity to watch Oliver's progress amongst the guests and to wonder why on earth he had accepted the Hanfords' invitation, since he was quite obviously both bored and irritated by the almost fawning attention of Henry's mother.

He really was the most arrogantly supercilious man she

had ever had the misfortune to meet, Lisa decided critically as he caught her watching him and lifted one derogatory, darkly interrogative eyebrow in her direction.

Flushing, she turned away, but not, she noticed, before Henry's mother had seen the brief, silent exchange between them.

'You still haven't explained to us just how you come to know… You really should have told us that you know Oliver,' she told Lisa, arriving at her side virtually at the same time as Henry, so that Lisa was once again prevented from explaining to him what had happened.

What was it about some people that made everything they said sound like either a reproach or a criticism? Lisa wondered grimly, but before she could answer she heard Mary Hanford adding, in an unfamiliar, almost arch and flattering voice, 'Ah, Oliver, we were just talking about you.'

'Really.'

He was looking at them contemptuously, as though they were creatures from another planet—some kind of subspecies provided for his entertainment, Lisa decided resentfully as he looked from Mary to Henry and then to her.

'Yes,' Mary continued, undeterred. 'I was just asking Lisa how she comes to know you…'

'Well, I think that's probably best left for Lisa herself to explain to you,' he responded smoothly. 'I should hate to embarrass her by making any unwelcome revelations…'

Lisa glared angrily at him.

'That suit looks good on you,' he added softly.

'So you've already said,' she reminded him through gritted teeth, all too aware of Henry and his mother's silently suspicious watchfulness at her side.

'Yes,' Oliver continued, as though she hadn't spoken. 'You can always tell when a woman's wearing an outfit bought by a man for his lover.' As he spoke he reached out and touched her jacket-clad arm—a brief touch, nothing more, but it made the hot colour burn in Lisa's face, and she was not at all surprised to hear Henry's mother's outraged indrawn breath or to see the fury in Henry's eyes.

This was retribution with a vengeance. This wasn't just victory, she acknowledged helplessly; it was total annihilation.

'Have you worn any of the other things yet?' he added casually.

'Lisa…' she heard Henry demanding ominously at her side, but she couldn't answer him. She was too mortified, too furiously angry to dare to risk saying anything whilst Oliver Davenport was still standing there listening.

To her relief, he didn't linger long. Aunt Elspeth's goddaughter, the same one who had so determinedly flirted with Henry half an hour earlier, came up and very professionally broke up their quartet, insisting that Oliver had promised to get her a fresh drink.

He was barely out of earshot before Henry was insisting, 'I want to know what's going on, Lisa… What was all that about your clothes…?'

'I think we know exactly what's going on, Henry,' Lisa heard his mother answering coolly for him as she gave Lisa a look of virulent hostility edged with triumph. So much for pretending to welcome her into the family, Lisa thought tiredly.

'I can see what you're *both* thinking,' she announced. 'But you are wrong.'

'Wrong? How can we be wrong when Oliver more or

less announced openly that the pair of you have been lov-ers?' Mary intoned.

'He did not announce that we had been lovers,' Lisa defended herself. 'And if you would just let me explain—'

'Henry, it's almost time for supper. You know how hopeless your father is at getting people organised. I'm going to need you to help me…'

'Henry, we need to talk.' Lisa tried to override his mother, but Henry was already turning away from her and going obediently to his mother's side.

If they married it would always be like this, Lisa sud-denly recognised on a wave of helpless anger. He would always place his mother's needs and wants above her own, and presumably above those of their children. They would always come a very poor second best to his loyalty to his mother. Was that really what she wanted for her-self…for her children?

Lisa knew it wasn't.

It was as though the scales had suddenly fallen from her eyes, as though she were looking at a picture of ex-actly how and what her life with Henry would be—and she didn't like it. She didn't like it one little bit.

In the handful of seconds it took her to recognise the fact, she knew irrevocably that she couldn't marry him, but she still owed him an explanation of what had hap-pened, and from her own point of view. For the sake of her pride and self-respect she wanted to make sure that he and his precious mother knew exactly how she had come to meet Oliver and exactly how he had manipulated them into believing his deliberately skewed view of the situation.

Still seething with anger against Oliver, she refused Henry's father's offer of another drink and some supper.

She would choke rather than eat any of Mary Hanford's food, she decided angrily.

Just the thought of the kind of life she would have had as Henry's wife made her shudder and acknowledge that she had had a lucky escape, but knowing that did not lessen her overwhelming fury at the man who had accidently brought it about.

How would she have been feeling right now had she been deeply in love with Henry and he with her? Instead of stalking angrily around the Hanfords' drawing room like an angry tigress, she would probably have been upstairs in her bedroom sobbing her heart out.

Some Christmas this was going to be.

She had been so looking forward to being here, to being part of the family, to sharing the simple, traditional pleasures of Christmas with the man she intended to marry, and now it was all spoiled, ruined… And why? Why? Because Oliver Davenport was too arrogant, too proud…too…too devious and hateful to allow someone whom he obviously saw as way, way beneath him to get the better of him.

Well, she didn't care. She didn't care what he did or what he said. He could tell the whole room, the whole house, the whole world that she had bought her clothes second-hand and that they had belonged to his cousin's girlfriend for all she cared now. In fact, she almost wished he would. That way at least she would be vindicated. That way she could walk away from here…from Henry and his precious mother…with her head held high.

'An outfit bought by a man for his lover…' How dared he…? Oh, how dared he…? She was, she suddenly realised, almost audibly grinding her teeth. Hastily she stopped. Dental fees were notoriously, hideously expensive.

She couldn't leave matters as they were, she decided fiercely. She would have to say something to Oliver Davenport—even if it was to challenge him over the implications he had made.

She got her chance ten minutes later, when she saw Oliver leaving the drawing room alone.

Quickly, before she could change her mind, she followed him. As he heard her footsteps crossing the hallway, he stopped and turned round.

'Ah, the blushing bride-to-be and her borrowed raiment,' he commented sardonically.

'I bought in good faith my second-hand raiment,' Lisa corrected him bitingly, adding, 'You do realise what impression you gave Henry and his mother back there, don't you?' she challenged him, adding scornfully before he could answer, 'Of course you knew. You knew perfectly well what you were doing, what you were implying...'

'Did I?' he responded calmly.

'Yes, you did,' Lisa responded, her anger intensifying. 'You knew they would assume that you meant that you and I had been lovers...that *you* had bought my clothes—'

'Surely Henry knows you far better than that?' Oliver interrupted her smoothly. 'After all, according to the local grapevine, the pair of you are intending to marry—'

'Of course Henry knows me...' Lisa began, and then stopped, her face flushing in angry mortification. But it was too late.

Swift as a hawk to the lure, her tormentor responded softly, 'Ah, I see. It's because he knows you so well that he made the unfortunate and mistaken assumption that—'

'No... He doesn't... I don't...' Lisa tried to fight back gamely, but it was still too late, and infuriatingly she knew it and, even worse, so did Oliver.

He wasn't smirking precisely—he was far too arrogant for that, Lisa decided bitterly—but there was certainly mockery in his eyes, and if she hadn't known better she could almost have sworn that his mouth was about to curl into a smile—but how could it? She was sure that he was incapable of doing anything so human. He was the kind of man who just didn't know what human emotions were, she decided savagely—who had no idea what it meant to suffer insecurity or…or any of the things that made people like herself feel so vulnerable.

'Have you any idea what you've done?' she challenged him, changing tack, her voice shaking under the weight of her suppressed emotion. 'I came here—'

'I know why you came here,' he interrupted her with unexpected sternness. 'You came to be looked over as a potential wife for Mary Hanford's precious son.

'Where's your pride?' he demanded scornfully. 'However, a potential bride is all you will ever be. Mary Hanford knows quite well who she wants Henry to marry, and I'm afraid it isn't going to be you…'

'Not now,' Lisa agreed shortly. 'Not—'

'Not ever,' Oliver told her. 'Mary won't allow Henry to marry any woman who she thinks might have the slightest chance of threatening her own superior position in Henry's life. His wife will not only have to take second place to her but to covertly acknowledge and accept that fact before she's allowed to marry him. And besides, the two of you are so obviously unsuited to one another that the whole thing's almost a farce. You're far too emotionally turbulent and uncontrolled for Henry… He wouldn't have a clue how to handle you…'

Lisa couldn't believe her ears.

'You, of course, would,' she challenged him with acid sweetness, too carried away by her anger and the heat of the moment to realise what she was doing, the challenge she was issuing him, the risks she was taking.

Then it was too late and he was cutting the ground from beneath her feet and making a shock as icy-cold as the snow melting on the tops of the Yorkshire hills that were his home run down her spine as he told her silkily, 'Certainly,' and then added before she could draw breath to speak, 'And, for openers, there are two things I most certainly would do that Henry obviously has not.'

'Oh, yes, and what exactly would they be?' Lisa demanded furiously.

'Well, I certainly wouldn't have the kind of relationship with you—or with any woman who I had the slightest degree of mild affection for, never mind being on the point of contemplating marrying—which would necessitate you feeling that you had to conceal anything about yourself from me, or that you needed to impress my family and friends with borrowed plumes, with the contents of another woman's wardrobe. And the second...' he continued, ignoring Lisa's quick, indrawn breath of mingled chagrin and rage.

He paused and looked at her whilst Lisa, driven well beyond the point of no return by the whole farce of her ruined Christmas in general and his part in it in particular, prompted wildly, 'Yes, the second is...?'

'This,' he told her softly, taking the breath from her lungs, the strength from her muscles and, along with them, the will-power from her brain as he stepped forward and took her in his arms and then bent his head and kissed her as Henry had never kissed her in all the eight months of their relationship—as no man had ever kissed her in the whole history of her admittedly modest sexual experience, she recognised dizzily as his mouth moved with unbelievable, unbeatable, unbearable sensual expertise on hers.

Ordinary mortal men did not kiss like this. Ordinary mortal men did not behave like this. Ordinary mortal men did not have the power, did not cup one's face with such tender mastery. They did not look deep into your eyes whilst they caressed your mouth with their own. They did not compel you, by some mastery you could not understand, to look back at them. They did not, by some unspoken command, cause you to open your mouth beneath theirs on a whispered ecstatic sigh of pure female pleasure. They did not lift their mouths from yours and look from your eyes to your half-parted lips and then back to your eyes again, their own warming in a smile of complicit understanding before starting to kiss you all over again.

Film stars in impossibly extravagant and highly acclaimed, Oscar-winning romantic movies might mimic such behaviour. Heroes in stomach-churning, body-aching, romantically sensual novels might sweep their heroines off their feet with similar embraces. God-like creatures from Greek mythology might come down to earth and wantonly seduce frolicking nymphs with such devastating experience and sensuality, but mere mortal men…? Never!

Lisa gave a small, blissful sigh and closed her eyes, only to open them again as she heard Henry exclaiming wrathfully, 'Lisa…what on earth do you think you're doing?'

Guiltily she watched him approaching as Oliver released her.

'Henry, I can explain,' she told him urgently, but he obviously didn't intend to let her speak.

Ignoring Oliver's quiet voice mocking, 'To Henry,

maybe, but to Mary, never,' she flushed defensively as his taunting comment was borne out by Henry's furious declaration.

'Mother was right about you all along. She warned me that you weren't—'

'Henry, you don't understand.' She managed to interrupt him, turning to appeal to Oliver, who was standing watching them in contemptuous amusement.

'Tell him what really happened… Tell him…'

'Do you really expect me to give you my help?' he goaded her softly. 'I don't recall you being similarly sympathetic when I asked you for yours.'

Whilst Lisa stood and stared at him in disbelief he started to walk towards the door, pausing only to tell Henry, 'Your mother is quite right, Henry. She wouldn't be the right wife for you at all… If I were you I should heed her advice—now, before it's too late.'

'Henry,' Lisa began to protest, but she could see from the way that he was refusing to meet her eyes that she had lost what little chance she might have had of persuading him to listen to her.

'It's too late now for us to change our plans for Christmas,' he told her stiffly, still avoiding looking directly at her. 'It is, after all, Christmas Eve, and we can hardly ask you to… However, once we return to London I feel that it would be as well if we didn't see one another any more…'

Lisa could scarcely believe her ears. Was this really the man she had thought she loved, or had at least liked and admired enough to be her husband…the man she had wanted as the father of her children? This pompous, stuffy creature who preferred to take his mother's advice on whom he should and should not marry than to listen to her, the woman he had proclaimed he loved?

Only he had not—not really, had he? Lisa made herself admit honestly. Neither of them had really truly been in love. Oh, they had liked one another well enough. But liking wasn't love, and if she was honest with herself there was a strong chord of relief mixed up in the turbulent anger and resentment churning her insides.

Stay here now, over Christmas, after what had happened…? No way.

Without trusting herself to speak to Henry, she turned on her heel and headed for the stairs and her bedroom, where she threw open the wardrobe doors and started to remove her clothes—her borrowed clothes, not her clothes, she acknowledged grimly as she opened her suitcase; they hadn't been hers when she had bought them and they certainly weren't hers now.

Eyeing them with loathing, her attention was momentarily distracted by the damp chilliness of her bedroom. Thank goodness they had driven north in her car. At least she wasn't going to have the added humiliation of depending on Henry to get her back to London.

The temperature seemed to have dropped since she had left the bedroom earlier, even taking into account Mary Hanford's parsimony.

There had been another warning of snow on high ground locally earlier in the evening, and Lisa had been enchanted by it, wondering out loud if they might actually have a white Christmas—a long-held childhood wish of hers which she had so far never had fulfilled. Mary Hanford had been scornful of her excitement.

As she gathered up her belongings Lisa suddenly paused; the clothes she had bought with such pleasure and which she had held onto with such determination lay on the bed in an untidy heap.

Beautiful though they were, she suddenly felt that she

knew now that she could never wear them. They were tainted. Some things were just not meant to be, she decided regretfully as she stroked the silk fabric of one of the shirts with tender fingers.

She might have paid for them, bought them in all good faith, but somehow she had never actually felt as though they were hers.

But it was her borrowed clothes, like the borrowed persona she had perhaps unwittingly tried to assume to impress Henry's family, which had proved her downfall, and she was, she decided firmly, better off without both of them.

Ten minutes later, wearing her own jeans, she lifted the carefully folded clothes into her suitcase. Once the Christmas holiday was over she would telephone the dress agency and explain that she no longer had any use for the clothes. Hopefully they would be prepared to take them back and refund most, if not all, of her money.

It was too late to regret now that she had not accepted Alison's suggestion that she join her and some other friends on a Christmas holiday and skiing trip to Colorado. Christmas was going to be very lonely for her alone in her flat with all her friends and her parents away. A sadly wistful smile curved the generous softness of her mouth as she contemplated how very different from her rosy daydreams the reality of her Christmas was going to be.

'You're going to the north of England—Yorkshire. I know it has a reputation for being much colder up there than it is here in London, but that doesn't mean you'll get snow,' Alison had warned her, adding more gently, 'Don't invest too much in this visit to Henry's family, Lisa. I know how important it is to you but things don't always work out the way you plan. The Yorkshire Dales are a beautiful part of the world, but people are still people and—well, let's face it, from what Henry has said about his family, especially his mother, it's obvious that she's inclined to be a little on the possessive side.'

'I know you don't really like Henry...' Lisa had begun defensively.

But Alison had shaken her head and told her firmly, 'It isn't that I don't care for Henry, rather that I *do* care about you. He isn't right for you, Lisa. Oh, I know what you're going to say: he's solid and dependable, and with him you can put down the roots that are so important to you. But, to be honest—well, if you want the truth, I see Henry more as a rather spoiled little boy than the kind of man a woman can rely on.'

It looked as if Alison was a much better judge of character than she, Lisa acknowledged as she zipped her case shut and picked it up.

CHAPTER THREE

LISA was halfway down the stairs when Henry walked into the hallway and saw her.

'Lisa, why are you dressed like that? Where are you going?' he demanded as he looked anxiously back over his shoulder, obviously not wanting anyone else to witness what was going on.

'I'm leaving,' she told him calmly. It was odd that she should be able to remain so calm with Henry who, after all, until this evening's debacle had been the man she had intended to marry, the man she had planned to spend the rest of her life with, and yet with Oliver, a complete stranger, a man she had seen only twice before and whom she expected…hoped…she would never see again, her emotions became inflamed into a rage of gargantuan proportions.

'Leaving? But you can't… What will people think?' Henry protested. 'Mother's got the whole family coming for Christmas dinner tomorrow and they'll all expect you to be there. We were, after all, planning to announce our engagement,' he reminded her seriously.

As she listened to him in disbelief Lisa was shocked to realise that she badly wanted to laugh—or cry.

'Henry, I can't stay here now,' she told him. 'Not after what's happened. You must see that. After all you were the one—'

'You're leaving to go to him, aren't you?' Henry accused her angrily. 'Well, don't expect Oliver to offer to marry you, Lisa. He might want to take you to bed but, as Mother says, Oliver isn't the kind of man to marry a woman who—'

That was it. Suddenly Lisa had had enough. Her face flushing with the full force of her emotions, she descended the last few stairs and confronted Henry.

'I don't care what your mother says, Henry,' she told him through gritted teeth. 'And if you were half the man I thought you were *you* wouldn't care either. Neither would you let her make up your mind or your decisions for you... And as for Oliver—'

'Yes, as for me...what?'

To her consternation Lisa realised that at some point Oliver had walked into the hall and was now standing watching them both, an infuriatingly superior, mocking contempt curling his mouth as he broke into her angry tirade.

'I've had enough of this... I've had enough of both of you,' Lisa announced. 'This is all your fault. All of it,' she added passionately to Oliver, ignoring Henry's attempts to silence her.

'And don't think I haven't guessed why you've done it,' she added furiously, her fingers tugging at the strap of her suitcase. She wrenched the case open and cried out angrily to him, 'You want your precious clothes back? Well, you can have them...all of them...'

Fiercely she wrenched the carefully packed clothes from her case and hurled them across the small space that lay between them, where they landed in an untidy heap at Oliver's feet.

She ignored Henry's anguished, shocked, 'Lisa...what on earth are you doing...? Lisa, please...stop; someone might see... Mother...'

'Oh, and we mustn't forget this, must we?' Lisa continued, ignoring Henry, an almost orgasmic feeling of release drowning out all her normal level-headedness and common sense. For the first time in her life she could understand why it was some people actually seemed to enjoy losing their temper, giving up their self-control.. causing a scene…all things that were normally completely foreign to her.

Triumphantly she threw the beautiful Armani suit which she had bought with such pleasure at Oliver's feet whilst he watched her impassively.

'There! I hope you're satisfied,' she told him as the last garment headed his way.

'Lisa,' Henry was still bleating protestingly, but she ignored him. Now that the sudden, unfamiliar surge of anger was retreating she felt oddly weak and shaky, almost vulnerably light-headed and dangerously close to tears.

In the distance she was aware that Henry was still protesting, but for some reason it was Oliver whom her attention was concentrated on, who filled her vision and her prickly, wary senses as she deliberately skirted around him, clutching her still half-open but now much lighter suitcase, and headed for the front door.

There had been a look in his eyes as she had flung that trouser suit at him which she had not totally understood— a gleam of an emotion which in another man she could almost have felt was humour mixed with a certain rueful respect, but of course she must have been imagining it.

As she tugged open the front door and stepped outside a shock of ice-cold air hit her. She hadn't realised how much the temperature had dropped, how overcast the sky had become.

Frost crunched beneath her feet as she hurried towards her car. Faithful and reliable as ever, it started at the second turn of the key.

As Lisa negotiated the other cars parked in the drive she told herself grimly that she had no need to try to work out whom that gleaming, shiny Aston Martin sports car belonged to. It just had to be Oliver Davenport's.

As she turned onto the main road she switched on her car radio, her heart giving a small forlorn thud of regret as she heard the announcer forecasting that the north of England was due to have snow.

Snow for Christmas and she was going to miss it.

It was half past eleven; another half an hour and it would be Christmas Day, and she would be spending it alone.

Stop snivelling, she told herself as she felt her throat start to ache with emotional tears. You've had a lucky escape.

She knew she had a fairly long drive ahead of her before she reached the motorway. As she and Henry had driven north she had remarked on how beautiful the countryside was as they drove through it. Now, however, as she drove along the empty, dark country road she was conscious of how remote the area was and how alone she felt.

She frowned as the car engine started to splutter and lose power, anxiety tensing her body as she wondered what on earth was wrong. Her small car had always been so reliable, and she was very careful about having it properly serviced and keeping the tank full of petrol.

Petrol. Lisa knew what had happened from the sharp sinking sensation in her stomach even before she looked fearfully at the petrol gauge.

Henry had not bothered to replace the petrol they had used on the journey north and now, it seemed, the tank was empty.

Lisa closed her eyes in mute despair. What on earth

was she going to do? She was stranded on an empty country road miles from anywhere in the dark on Christmas
Eve, with no idea where the nearest garage was, no means
of contacting anyone to ask, dressed in jeans and a thin
sweater on a freezing cold night.

And she knew exactly who she had to blame for her
sorry plight, she decided wrathfully ten minutes later as
the air inside her car turned colder and colder with ominous speed. Oliver Davenport. If it hadn't been for him
and his cynical and deliberate manipulation of the truth
to cast her in a bad light in front of Henry and his parents,
none of this would have happened.

Even now she still couldn't quite believe what she had
done in the full force of that final, unexpected burst of
temper, when she had thrown her clothes at him.

Lisa hugged her arms tightly around her body as she
started to shiver. It was too late to regret her hasty departure from Henry's parents' home now, or the fact that
she had brought nothing with her that she could use to
keep her warm.

Just how far was it to the nearest house? Her teeth were
chattering now and the windscreen had started to freeze
over.

Perhaps she ought to start walking back in the direction
she had come. At least then the physical activity might
help to keep her warm, but her heart sank at the thought.
So far as she could remember, she had been driving for
a good fifteen minutes after she had passed through the
last small hamlet, and she hadn't seen any houses since
then.

Reluctantly she opened the car door, and then closed it
again with a gasp of shock as the ice-cold wind knifed
into her unprotected body.

What on earth was she going to do? Her earlier frustration and irritation had started to give way to a far more ominous and much deeper sense of panicky fear.

One read about people being found dying from exposure and hypothermia, but it always seemed such an unreal fate somehow in a country like Britain. Now, though, it suddenly seemed horribly plausible.

Her panic intensified as she realised that unless she either managed to walk to the nearest inhabited building, wherever that might be, or was spotted by a passing motorist, it would be days before anyone realised that she was missing. There was, after all, no one waiting at home in London for her. Her parents had agreed not to telephone on Christmas Day because they knew she would be staying with Henry's family. Henry would assume—if indeed he gave her any thought at all—that she was back in London.

As she fought down the emotions threatening to overwhelm her Lisa happened to glance at her watch.

It was almost half past twelve…Christmas Day.

Now she couldn't stop the tears.

Christmas Day and she was stuck in a car miles from anywhere and probably about to freeze to death.

She gave a small, protesting moan as she sneezed and then sneezed again, blinking her eyes against the dazzling glare of headlights she could see in her driving mirror.

The dazzling glare of headlights… Another car…

Frantically Lisa pushed on her frozen car door, terrified that her unwitting rescuer might drive past her without realising her plight.

The approaching car was only yards behind her when she finally managed to shove open the door. As she half fell into the icy road in her haste to advertise her predicament any thoughts of the danger of flagging down a stranger were completely forgotten in the more overriding urgency of her plight.

The dazzle of the oncoming headlights was so powerful that she couldn't distinguish the shape of the car or see its driver, but she knew he or she had seen her because the car suddenly started to lose speed, swerving to a halt in front of her.

Now that the car was stationary Lisa recognised that there was something vaguely familiar about it, but her relief overrode that awareness as she ran towards it on legs which suddenly seemed as stiff and wobbly as those of a newborn colt.

However, before she could reach it, the driver's door was flung open and a pair of long male legs appeared, followed by an equally imposing and stomach-churningly recognisable male torso and face.

As she stared disbelievingly into the frowning, impatient face of Oliver Davenport, Lisa protested fatalistically, 'Oh, no, not you…'

'Who were you hoping it was—Henry?' he retorted sardonically. 'If this is your idea of staging a reconciliation scene, I have to tell you that you're wasting your time. When I left him you were the last thing on Henry's mind.'

'Of course I'm not staging a reconciliation scene,' Lisa snapped back at him. 'I'm not staging a scene of any kind… I—it isn't something I do…'

The effect of her cool speech was unfairly spoiled by the sudden fit of shivering that overtook her, but it was plain that Oliver Davenport wouldn't have been very impressed with it anyway because he drawled, 'Oh, no? Then what was all that highly theatrical piece of overacting in the Hanfords' hall all about?'

'That wasn't overacting,' Lisa gritted at him. 'That was…'

She shivered again, this time so violently that her teeth chattered audibly.

'For God's sake, put a coat on. Have you any idea what the temperature is tonight? I know you're from the south and a city, but surely common sense—?'

'I don't have a coat,' Lisa told him, adding bitterly, 'Because of you.'

The look he gave her was incredulously contemptuous.

'Are you crazy? You come north in the middle of December and you don't even bother to bring a coat—'

'Oh, I brought a coat all right,' Lisa corrected him between shivers. 'Only I don't have it now…'

She gritted her teeth and tried not to think about the warmth of the lovely, heavenly cream cashmere coat which had been amongst the things she had thrown at his feet so recklessly.

'You don't… Ah… I see… What are you doing, anyway? Why have you stopped?'

'Why do you think I've stopped? Not to admire the view,' Lisa told him bitterly. 'The car's run out of petrol.'

'The car's run out of petrol?'

Lisa felt herself flushing as she heard the disbelieving male scorn in his voice.

'It wasn't my fault,' she defended herself. 'We were supposed to be coming north in Henry's car, only it was involved in an accident and couldn't be driven so we had to use mine, and Henry was so anxious to get…not to be late that he didn't want to stop and refill the tank…'

Lisa hated the way he was just standing silently looking at her. He was determined to make things as hard for her as he could. She could see that… He was positively enjoying making her look small…humiliating her.

In any other circumstances but these she would have been tempted simply to turn her back on him, get back in her car and wait for the next driver to come by, but common sense warned her that she couldn't afford to take that kind of risk.

Her unprotected fingers had already turned white and were almost numb. She couldn't feel her toes, and the rest of her body felt so cold that the sensation was almost a physical pain.

Taking a deep breath and fixing her gaze on a point just beyond his left shoulder, she said shakily, 'I'd be very grateful if you could give me a lift to the nearest garage...'

Tensely she waited for his response, knowing that he was bound to make the most of the opportunity which she had given him to exercise his obvious dislike of her. But when it came the blow was one of such magnitude and such force that she physically winced beneath the cruelty of it, the breath escaping from her lungs in a soft, shocked gasp as he told her ruthlessly, 'No way.'

It must be the cold that was making her feel so dizzy and light-headed, Lisa thought despairingly—that and her panicky fear that he was going to walk away and simply leave her here to meet her fate.

Whatever the cause, it propelled her into instinctive action, making her dart forward and catch hold of the fabric of his jacket as she told him jerkily, 'It wasn't *my* fault that your cousin sold his girlfriend's clothes without her permission. All *I* did was buy them in good faith... He's the one you should be punishing, not me. If you leave me here—'

'*Leave* you here...?'

Somehow or other he had detached her hand from his jacket and was now holding it in his own. Dizzily Lisa marvelled at how warm and comforting, how strong and safe it felt to have that large male hand enclosing hers.

She could almost feel the warmth from his touch—his body—flooding up through her arm like an infusion of life-giving blood into a vein.

'Leave you *here* in this temperature?' he said, adding roughly, 'Are you crazy…?'

She couldn't see him properly any more, Lisa realised, and she thought it must be because the tears that had threatened her eyes had frozen in the intense cold. She had no idea that she had actually spoken her sentiments out loud until she heard him respond, 'Tears don't freeze; they're saline…salty.'

He had let go of her hand and as Lisa watched him he stripped off his jacket and then, to her shock, took hold of her and bundled her up in it like an adult wrapping up a small child.

'I can't walk,' she protested, her voice muffled by the thickness of the over-large wrapping.

'You're not going to,' she was told peremptorily, and then, before she knew what was happening, he was picking her up and carrying her the short distance to his car, opening the passenger door and depositing her on the seat.

The car smelled of leather and warmth and something much more intangible—something elusive and yet oddly familiar… Muzzily Lisa sniffed, trying to work out what it was and why it should inexplicably make her want to cry and yet at the same time feel oddly elated.

Oliver had gone over to her car, and as he returned Lisa saw that he was carrying her case and her handbag.

'I've locked it…your car,' he told her as he slid into the driver's seat alongside her. 'Not that anyone would be likely to take it.'

'Not unless they had some petrol with them,' Lisa agreed drowsily, opening her mouth to give a yawn which suddenly turned into a volley of bone-aching sneezes.

'Here.' Oliver handed her a wad of clean tissues from a pack in the glove compartment, telling her, 'It's just as well I happened to be passing when I did. If you're lucky the worst you'll suffer is a bad cold; another hour in these temperatures and it could have been a very different story. This road is never very heavily trafficked, and on Christmas Eve, with snow forecast, the locals who do use it have more sense than to…'

He went on talking but Lisa had heard enough. Did he think she had wanted to run out of petrol on a remote Yorkshire road? Had he forgotten whose fault it was that she had been there in the first place instead of warmly tucked up in bed at Henry's parents' home?

Tears of unfamiliar and unexpected self-pity suddenly filled her eyes. 'It isn't Christmas Eve,' she told him aggressively, fighting to hold them back. 'It's Christmas Day.'

It was the wrong thing to say, bringing back her earlier awareness of how very fragile were the brightly coloured, delicate daydreams that she had cherished of how this Christmas would be—as fragile and vulnerable as the glass baubles with which she had so foolishly imagined herself decorating that huge, freshly cut, pine-smelling Christmas tree with Henry.

It was too much. One tear fell and then another. She tried to stop them, dabbing surreptitiously at her eyes, and she averted her face from Oliver's as he started the engine and set the car in motion. But it was no use. He had obviously witnessed her distress.

'Now what's wrong?' he demanded grimly.

'It's Christmas Day,' Lisa wept.

'Christmas Day.' He repeated the words as though he had never heard them before. 'Where would you have been spending it if your car hadn't run out of petrol?' he asked her. 'Where were you going?'

'Home to London, to my flat,' Lisa told him wearily. Despite the fact that at some point, without her being aware of it, he had obviously noticed that she was shivering and had turned the heater on full, she still felt frighteningly cold.

'My parents are both working away in Japan so I can't go to them, and my friends have made other plans. I could have gone with them, but...'

'But you chose to subject yourself to Henry's mother's inspection instead,' he taunted her unkindly.

'Henry and I were planning to get engaged,' Lisa fought back angrily. 'Of course he wanted me to meet his parents, his family. There was no question of there being any "inspection".'

'No? Then why the urgent necessity for a new wardrobe?'

Lisa flushed defensively.

'I just wanted to make a good impression on them, that's all,' she muttered.

'Well, you certainly did that all right,' he mocked her wryly. 'Especially—'

'I would have done if it hadn't been for your interference,' she interrupted him hotly. 'You had no right to imply that you and I had been...that those clothes...' She paused, her voice trailing away into silence as she saw the way he lifted one eyebrow and glanced unkindly at her.

'I spoke nothing but the truth. Those clothes were bought by my cousin for his girlfriend—his lover...'

'It might have been the truth, but you twisted it so that it seemed...so that it sounded...so that...'

Lisa floundered, her face flushing betrayingly as he invited helpfully, 'So that what?'

'So that people would think that you and I…that you had bought those clothes for me and that you and I were lovers,' she told him fiercely.

'But surely anyone who really knows you…a prospective fiancé, an established lover, for instance…would automatically know that it was impossible for us to be lovers?' he pointed out to her.

'Henry and I are not lovers.'

Lisa bit her lip in vexation. Now what on earth had prompted her to tell him that? It was hardly the sort of thing she would normally discuss with someone who was virtually a stranger.

Again the dark eyebrows rose—both of them this time—his response to her admission almost brutally comprehensive as he asked her crisply, 'You're not? Then what on earth were you doing thinking of getting engaged to him?'

Lisa opened her mouth but the words she wanted to say simply wouldn't come. How could she say them now? How could she tell him, I loved him, when she knew irrevocably and blindingly that it simply wasn't true, that it had possibly and shamingly never been true and that, just as shamingly, she had somehow managed to delude herself that it might be and to convince herself that she and Henry had a future together?

In the end she had to settle for a stiff and totally unconvincing, 'It seemed a good idea at the time. We had a lot in common. We were both ready to settle down, to commit ourselves. To—' She stopped speaking as the sound of his laughter suddenly filled the car, drowning out the sound of her own voice.

He had a very full, deep, rich-bodied and very male

laugh, she acknowledged—a very…a very…a very sensual, sexy sort of laugh…if you cared for that sort of thing…and of course she didn't, she reminded herself firmly.

'Why are you laughing?' she demanded angrily, her cheeks flying hot banners of scorching colour as she turned in her seat to glare furiously at him. 'It isn't…there isn't anything to laugh at…'

'No, there isn't,' he agreed soberly. 'You're right… By rights I— How old are you? What century are you living in? "We had a lot in common. We were both ready to settle down…"' he mimicked her. 'Even if that was true, which it quite patently is not—in fact, I doubt I've ever seen a couple more obviously totally unsuited to one another—I have never heard of a less convincing reason for wanting to get married.

'Why haven't you been to bed with him?' he demanded, the unexpectedness of the question shocking her, taking her breath away.

'I don't think that's any of your business,' she told him primly.

'Which one of you was it who didn't want to—you or him?'

Lisa gasped, outraged. 'Not everyone has…has a high sex drive…or wants a…a relationship that's based on…on physical lust,' she told him angrily. 'And just because…'

Whilst they had been talking Oliver had been driving, and now unexpectedly he turned off the main road and in between two stone pillars into what was obviously the drive to a private house—a very long drive, Lisa noted, before turning towards him and demanding, 'What are you doing? Where are you taking me? This isn't a garage.'

'No, it isn't,' he agreed calmly. 'It's my home.'

'Your home? But—'

'Calm down,' Oliver advised her drily. 'Look, it's gone one in the morning, Christmas morning,' he emphasised. 'This isn't London; the nearest large petrol station is on the motorway, nearly thirty miles away, *if* it's open—and personally what I think you need right now more than anything else is a hot bath and a good night's sleep.'

'I want to go home,' Lisa insisted stubbornly.

'Why?' he challenged her brutally, and reminded her, 'You've already said yourself that there's no one there. Look,' he told her, 'since it is Christmas, why don't we declare a cease-fire in our…er…hostilities? Although by choice neither of us might have wanted to spend Christmas together, since we are both on our own and since it's patently obvious that you're in no physical state to go anywhere, never mind drive a car—'

'You're spending Christmas on your own?' Lisa interrupted him, too astonished to hold the question back.

'Yes,' he agreed, explaining, 'I was to have spent it entertaining my cousin and his girlfriend, but since they've made up their quarrel their plans have changed and they flew to the Caribbean yesterday morning. Like you, I'd left it too late to make alternative plans and so—'

'I can't stay with you,' Lisa protested. She was, she recognised, already starting to shiver as the now stationary car started to cool down, and she was also unpleasantly and weakly aware of how very unappealing the thought of driving all the way back to London actually was—and not just unappealing either, she admitted. She was uncomfortably conscious that Oliver had spoken the truth when he had claimed that she was not physically capable of making the journey at present.

'We're strangers…'

'You've already accepted a lift in my car,' he reminded her drily, adding pithily, 'And besides, where else can you go?'

All at once Lisa gave in. She really didn't have the energy to argue with him, she admitted—she was too cold, too tired, too muzzily aware of how dangerously light-headed and weak she was beginning to feel.

'Very well, then,' she said, adding warningly, 'But only until tomorrow…until I can get some petrol.'

'Only until tomorrow,' he agreed.

CHAPTER FOUR

'YOU live here all alone?' Lisa questioned Oliver, breaking into his conversation as she curled up in one corner of the vast, deep sofa where he had taken her and told her sternly she was to remain until he returned with a hot drink for her.

'Yes,' he said. 'I prefer it that way. A gardener comes twice a week and his wife does the cleaning for me, but other than that—'

'But it's such a big house. Don't you...?'

'Don't I what?' Oliver challenged her. 'Don't I feel lonely?' He shook his head. 'Not really. I was an only child. My mother died when I was in my teens and my father was away a lot on business. I'm used to being on my own. In fact I prefer it in many ways. Other people's company, their presence in one's life isn't always a pleasure—especially not when one has to become responsible for their emotional and financial welfare.'

Lisa guessed that he was referring obliquely to his cousin, and she sensed that he was, by nature, the kind of man who would always naturally assume responsibility for others, even if that responsibility was slightly irritably cynical rather than humanely compassionate. It also probably explained why he wasn't married. He was by nature a loner—a man, she suspected, who enjoyed women's company but who did not want to burden himself with a wife or children.

And yet a house like this cried out for children. It had that kind of ambience about it, that kind of warmth; it was a real family home for all its obviously priceless antiques. It had a lived-in, welcoming feel to it, Lisa acknowledged—a sense of having been well used and well loved, a slightly worn air which, to her, gave it a richness that far surpassed the sterile, elegant perfection of a house like Henry's parents'.

It didn't surprise Lisa to learn that the house had been in Oliver's family for several generations but what did surprise her was how at ease, how at home she actually felt here, how unexpectedly easy it was to talk to Oliver after he had returned from the kitchen with a huge mug of piping-hot chocolate which he insisted she drink, virtually standing over her until she had done so.

She had suspected from the taste of it that something very much more alcoholic than mere milk had been added to it, but by that stage she had been so grateful for the warmth of her comfortable niche in the deep sofa, so drowsily content and relaxed that there hadn't seemed to be any point in mentioning it, never mind protesting about it.

Now, as she yawned sleepily, blinking owlishly, her forehead pleating in a muzzy frown as she tried to focus on the fireplace and discovered that she couldn't, she was vaguely aware of Oliver getting up from his own chair and coming over to her, leaning down towards her as he firmly relieved her of the now empty mug.

'Bath for you, and then bed, I think,' he told her firmly, sounding so much as her father had when she had been a little girl that Lisa turned her head to look at him.

She hadn't realised that he was quite so close to her, nor that his grey eyes had a darker outer rim to them and were not flat, dead grey at all but rather a mystical mingling of so many silvers and pewters that she caught her breath a little at the male beauty of them.

'You've got beautiful eyes,' she heard herself telling him in a soft, slightly slurred…almost sexy voice that she barely recognised as her own.

She was unaware that her own eyes were registering the shock of what she had said as Oliver responded gravely, 'Thank you.'

She was, she recognised, still holding onto her mug, even though his own fingers were now wrapped securely around it—so securely in fact that they were actually touching her own.

Some of that molten silver heat from his eyes must have somehow entered his skin, his blood, she decided dizzily. There could be no other reason for those tiny, darting, fiery sensations of heat that she could feel where her own flesh rested against his.

'So are yours…'

'So are yours'? Uncomprehendingly, Lisa looked at him and watched as he smiled a slow, curling, sensual smile that made her heart soar and turn over and do a bellyflop that left her as shocked and winded as though her whole body had actually fielded a blow.

'Your eyes,' Oliver told her softly. 'Your eyes are beautiful too. Do you always keep them open when you kiss?'

'Why?' Lisa heard herself croak shakily. 'Do you?'

As she spoke her glance was already drifting down to his mouth, as though drawn there by some potent force that she couldn't control.

'That depends,' Oliver was drawling, 'on who I'm kissing…'

He was looking at her mouth now, and a panicky, unfamiliar feeling of mingled excitement and shock kicked into life inside her, bringing with it some much needed sobering sanity, bringing her back to reality.

Lisa gulped and turned her head away, quickly withdrawing her hand from the mug.

'I...I...'

As she fought to find the words to explain away her totally uncharacteristic behaviour and conversation, she was overcome by a sudden fit of sneezing.

Quickly reaching for the box of tissues that Oliver had brought her, she hoped that he would put her flushed complexion down to the fever or the cold that she had obviously caught rather than to her self-conscious embarrassment at what she had said.

What on earth had come over her? She had practically been flirting with him...asking him...inviting him...

Thankfully, Lisa buried her face in another tissue as she sneezed again.

When she had finished, determined to dispel any erroneous ideas that he might have gained from her unguarded and totally foolish comments, she said quickly, 'It must have been wonderful here at Christmas when you were young—your family...this house...'

'Yes, it was,' he agreed, before asking, far too perceptively for Lisa's peace of mind, 'Weren't your childhood Christmases good?'

'Yes, of course they were,' Lisa responded hastily.

'But?' he challenged her.

'My parents travelled a lot with their work. They still do. Whilst I dreamed of traditional Christmases in a house with log fires and a huge tree surrounded by aunts and uncles and cousins, going to church on Christmas morning and doing all the traditional British Christmas things, the reality was normally not roast turkey with all the trimmings but ice cream on an Australian beach or sunshine in Japan.

'My parents did their best, of course. There were always mounds of presents, and they always made sure that we spent Christmas and Boxing Days together, but somehow it just wasn't the same as it would have been if we'd been here… It's silly of me, really, but I suppose a part of me still is that little girl who—'

She stopped, embarrassed by how much of herself she had inadvertently revealed. It must be whatever it was he had obviously added to her hot chocolate that was making her so loquacious and communicative, she thought. She certainly wasn't normally so open or confiding with people she barely knew, although in some odd way it felt as though she had actually known Oliver for a very long time.

She was still frowning over this absurdity when he handed her a glass of amber liquid that he had just poured.

'Drink it,' he told her when she looked at it doubtfully. 'It's pure malt whisky and the best antidote for a heavy cold that I know.'

Reluctantly, Lisa took the glass he handed her. Her head was already swimming slightly, and she felt that the last thing she needed was any more alcohol, but her father was also a great believer in a hot toddy as a cure for colds and so hesitantly she began to sip the tawny golden liquid, closing her eyes as it slid smoothly down her throat, spreading the most delicious sense of beatific warmth throughout her body.

There was something so comforting, so safe, so…so pleasurable about being curled up cosily here in this house…with this man… With this man? What did that mean? Where had that thought come from?

Anxiously Lisa opened her eyes and started to sit up.

'Was that why you wanted to marry Henry, because you thought he could provide you with the traditional lifestyle you felt you'd missed out on?' she heard Oliver asking her.

'Yes…yes, I suppose it was,' she agreed huskily, caught too off guard to think of prevaricating or avoiding the question, and then flushing slightly as she saw the way Oliver was looking at her.

'It would have been a good marriage,' she defended herself. 'We both wanted the same things…' As she saw the way his eyebrows rose, she amended herself shakily, 'Well, I thought that we did.'

'I've heard of some odd reasons for getting married,' she heard Oliver telling her drily, 'but marrying someone because you think he'll provide you with a traditional Christmas has to be the oddest…'

'I wasn't marrying him for that—' Lisa began indignantly, stopping when another volley of sneezing mercifully prevented her from having to make any further response or explanation.

'Come on,' Oliver told her. 'I think it's time you were in bed.'

The whisky that she had drunk was even more potent than she had realised, Lisa acknowledged as Oliver led the way back into the warm, panelled entrance hall and up the stairs.

Just where the stairs started to return towards the galleried landing, Lisa paused to study two large oil paintings hung side by side.

'My grandparents,' Oliver explained, adding informatively, 'My grandfather commissioned the artist to paint them as a first wedding-anniversary present for my grandmother.'

'You look very like him,' Lisa told him. And it was the truth, only the man in the portrait somehow looked less acerbic and much happier than Oliver—much happier and obviously very much in love with his young wife. In the portrait his face was turned slightly towards her matching portrait, so that for a moment it seemed as though the two of them were actually looking at one another.

'It's this way,' Oliver told Lisa, touching her briefly on her arm as he directed her across the landing and towards one of the bedrooms.

'Since my cousin Piers and his girlfriend were supposed to be spending Christmas here a room had already been made up for them and you may as well sleep there.' As he spoke he pushed open one of the seven wooden doors leading off the landing. Lisa blinked dizzily as she stepped inside the room.

It seemed huge—almost as large, she was sure, as the entire floor space of her own small flat. It was so large, in fact, that in addition to the high, king-sized bed there was also a desk and chair and a small two-seater sofa drawn up close to the open fireplace.

'The bathroom's through that door,' Oliver told her, indicating one of a pair of doors set into the wall. 'The other door opens into a walk-in wardrobe.'

A walk-in wardrobe. Lisa blinked owlishly before reminding him, 'Well, that's something I shan't be needing.' When he frowned she explained, 'I don't have any other clothes with me. The others are the ones I—'

'Hurled at me in a fit of temper,' Oliver finished for her.

She had started to shiver again, Lisa noticed, hugging her arms around herself despite the warmth of the bedroom, with its soft fitted carpet and heavy damask curtains.

That whisky really had gone to her head, she acknowledged as a wave of dizziness swept over her, making her sway and reach out instinctively for the nearest solid object to cling onto—the nearest solid object being Oliver himself.

As he detached her hand from his arm she looked up at him muzzily, only to gasp in startled surprise as she was suddenly swung very firmly up into his arms.

'What…what are you doing?' she managed to stammer as he strode towards the bed, carrying her.

'Saving us both a lot of time,' he told her drily as he deposited her with unexpected gentleness on the mattress before asking her, 'Can you manage to get undressed or…?'

'Yes, of course I can,' Lisa responded in a flurry of mingled indignation and flushed self-consciousness, adding defensively, 'I…I just felt a little bit dizzy, that's all…I'm all right now…'

He didn't look totally convinced, and Lisa discovered that she was holding her breath as she watched him walk towards the bedroom door, unable to expel it until she was sure that he had walked through it and closed it behind him.

He really was the most extraordinary man, she decided ten minutes later as she lay in a huge bath of heavenly, deep hot water.

At Henry's parents' house both baths and hot water had been rationed and now it was sheer bliss to ease her aching limbs into the soothing heat, even if something about the steamy atmosphere of the bathroom did somehow seem to increase the dizzying effect that the whisky had had on her system. She felt, she recognised when she eventually reluctantly climbed out of the bath and wrapped herself in one of the huge, warm, fluffy towels on the heated rail, not just physically affected by the alcohol but mentally and emotionally affected by it as well, as though she was on some sort of slightly euphoric high, free of the burden of her normal, cautious, self-imposed restraints.

Shaking her head, she towelled herself dry, remembering only when she had finished that she had no nightclothes.

Shrugging fatalistically, she wrapped herself in another towel instead and padded towards the bed, discarding it as she climbed into the bed's welcoming warmth.

The bedlinen was cotton and deliciously soft against her skin. It smelled faintly of lavender. She breathed in the scent blissfully as she closed her eyes. After the austere regime of Henry's parents' home this was luxury indeed.

She was just on the point of falling asleep when she heard the bedroom door open. In the half-light from the landing she could see Oliver walking towards the bed carrying something.

As he reached the bed she struggled to sit up.

'I've brought you a hot-water bottle,' he told her. 'Just in case you get cold during the night.'

His thoughtfulness surprised her. He was the last person she would have expected to show such consideration, such concern.

Tears filled her eyes as she took it from him, and on some impulse, which when she later tried to rationalise it she could only put down to the effects of the whisky on her system, she reached out and lifted her face towards his, kissing him.

He must have moved, done something…turned his head, because she had never intended to kiss him so intimately, only to brush her lips against his cheek in a small gesture of gratitude for his care of her. She had certainly never planned to do anything so bold as kiss him on the lips, but oddly, even though her brain had registered her error, her body seemed to be having trouble responding to its frantic message to remove her mouth from the male one which confusingly, instead of withdrawing from her touch, seemed to be not merely accepting it but actually actively…

Lisa swallowed, panicked, swallowed again and jerked her head back, only to find that somehow or other Oliver's hand was resting on her nape, preventing her from doing anything other than lift her lips a mere breath away from his.

'If that's the way you kissed Henry, I'm not surprised the two of you never went to bed together,' she heard him telling her sardonically. 'If you want to kiss a man you should do it properly,' he added reprovingly, and then before she could explain or even object he had closed the small distance between them and his mouth was back on hers, only this time it wasn't merely resting there against her unintended caress but slowly moving on hers, slowly caressing hers, slowly and then not so slowly arousing her, so that…

It must be the drink, Lisa decided giddily. There could be no other reason why she was virtually clinging to Oliver with both her hands, straining towards him almost as though there was nothing she wanted more than the feel of his mouth against her own.

It *had* to be the drink. There could be no other explanation for the way her lips were parting, positively inviting the masterful male thrust of his tongue. And it had to be the drink as well that was causing her to make those small, keening, soft sounds of pleasure as their tongues meshed.

And then abruptly and shockingly erotically Oliver's mouth hardened on her own, so that it was no longer possible for her to deceive herself that what they were sharing was simply a kiss of polite gratitude. No longer possible at all, especially when the rest of her body was suddenly, urgently waking up to the fact that it actively liked what Oliver was doing and that in fact it would very much like to prolong the sensual, drugging pleasure of the way his mouth was moving on hers and, if at all possible, to feel it moving not just on her mouth but on her…

Shocked by her own reactions, Lisa sobered up enough to push Oliver away, her eyes over-bright and her mouth trembling—not, she admitted inwardly, because he had kissed her, but because he had stopped doing it.

'I never meant that to happen,' she told him huskily, anxious to make sure that he understood that even though she might have responded to him she had not deliberately set out to encourage such intimacy between them.

'I just wanted to say thank you for—'

'For making Henry think you're having an affair with me,' he mocked her as he sat back from her. 'Go to sleep,' he advised her, adding softly, 'unless you want me to take up the invitation these have been offering me…' As he spoke he reached out and very lightly touched one of her exposed breasts.

The bedclothes must have slipped down whilst he'd been kissing her, revealing her body to him, even though she herself hadn't realised it, Lisa recognised. And they hadn't just revealed her body, either, she admitted as her face flushed to a pink as deep as that of her tight, hard nipples.

Quickly she pulled the bedclothes up over herself, clutching them defensively in front of her, her face still flushed, and flushing even deeper as she saw the fleeting but very comprehensive and male glance that Oliver gave her now fully covered body.

'Forget about Henry,' he advised her as he turned to leave. 'You're better off without him.'

He had gone before Lisa could think of anything to say—which in the circumstances was probably just as well, she decided as she settled back into the warmth of the bed. After all, what was there she possibly could have said? Her body grew hot as she remembered the way he had kissed her, her toes curling protestingly as she fought down the memory of her own far from reluctant reaction.

No wonder there had been that male gleam of sensual triumph in his eyes as he'd looked at her body—a look which had told her quite plainly that he enjoyed the knowledge that he had been responsible for that unmistakable sexual arousal of her body—his touch…his kiss… *him*.

It had been an accident, that was all, Lisa reassured herself. A fluke, an unfortunate sequence of events which, of course, would never be repeated. Her toes had relaxed but there was a worrying sensual ache deep within her body—a sense of…of deprivation and yearning which she tried very firmly to ignore as she closed her eyes and told herself sternly to go to sleep.

CHAPTER FIVE

LISA opened her eyes, confused by her unfamiliar surroundings, until the events of the previous evening came
rushing back.

Some of those events were quite definitely ones that
she did not want to dwell on and which had to be pushed
very firmly back where they belonged—in a sealed box
marked 'very dangerous'. And some of those events, and
in particular the ones involving that unexpectedly passionate kiss she had shared with Oliver, were, quite simply, far too potentially explosive to be touched at all.

Instead she focused on her surroundings, her eyes widening in disbelief as she looked towards the fireplace. She
rubbed them and then studied it again. No, they were not
deceiving her; there was quite definitely a long woollen
stocking hanging from the fireplace—a long woollen
stocking bulging with all sorts of odd shapes, with a notice pinned to it reading, 'Open me.'

Her curiosity overcoming her natural caution, Lisa
hopped out of bed and hurried towards the fireplace, removed the stocking and then returned to the sanctuary of
her bed with it.

As she turned it upside down on the coverlet to dislodge
its contents, a huge smile curled her mouth, her eyes dancing with a mixture of almost childlike disbelief and a
rather more adult amusement.

Wrapped in coloured tissue-paper, a dozen or more
small objects lay on the bed around her. Some of them

76

she could recognise without unwrapping them: the two tangerines, the nuts, the apple...

There could, of course, only be one person who had done this; the identity of her unexpected Father Christmas could not be in doubt, but his motivation was.

Her fingers trembled slightly as she removed the wrapping from what turned out to be a tube of thick white paper. As she unrolled it she began to frown, her frown turning to a soft gasp as she read what had been written on it in impressive copperplate handwriting.

In this year of our Sovereign Queen Elizabeth it is hereby agreed that there shall be a formal truce and a cessation of hostilities between Mistress Lisa and Oliver Esquire in order that the two aforenamed may celebrate the Festival of Christmas in true Christian spirit.

Beneath the space that he had left for her to sign her own name Oliver had signed his.

Lisa couldn't help it. She started to laugh softly, her laugh turning into a husky cough and a fit of sneezes that told her that she had not, as she had first hoped, escaped the heavy cold Oliver had warned likely the previous evening.

At least, though, her head was clear this morning, she told herself severely as she scrabbled around amongst the other packages on the bed, guessing that somewhere amongst them there must be a pen for her to sign their truce.

It touched her to think of Oliver going to so much trouble on her behalf. If only Henry had been half as thoughtful... But Henry would never have done anything like this. Henry would never have kissed her the way Oliver had done last night. Henry would never...

Her fingers started to tremble as she finally found the parcel containing the pen.

It hurt to think that the future that she had believed she and Henry could have together had been nothing more than a chimera...as childish in its way as her daydreams of a perfect Christmas which she had revealed to Oliver last night, under the effects and influence of his malt whisky.

Her eyes misted slightly with fresh tears, but they were not, this time, caused by the knowledge that she had made a mistake in believing that she and Henry had a good relationship.

After she had signed the truce she noticed that her signature was slightly wobbly and off balance—a reflection of the way she herself had felt ever since Oliver had thrust his way into her life, demanding the return of his cousin's girlfriend's clothes.

Thinking of clothes reminded Lisa that she had nothing to wear other than the things she had discarded the previous evening. Hardly the kind of outfit she had planned to spend Christmas Day in, she acknowledged as she mourned the loss of the simply cut cream wool dress that she had flung at Oliver's feet before her departure from Henry's parents' house.

Still, clothes did not make Christmas, she told herself, and neither did Christmas stockings—but they certainly went a long way to help, she admitted, a rueful smile curling her mouth as she pictured Oliver painstakingly wrapping the small traditional gifts which for generations children had delighted to find waiting for them on Christmas morning.

It was a pity that after such an unexpected and plea-

surable start the rest of her Christmas looked so unap-
pealingly bleak. She wasn't looking forward to her return
to her empty flat. She glanced at her watch. She had slept
much later than usual and it was already nine o'clock—
time for her to get up and dressed if she was going to be
able to retrieve her car, fill it with petrol and make her
return journey to London before dark.

She had just put one foot on the floor when she heard
Oliver knocking on the bedroom door. Hastily she put her
foot back under the bedclothes and made sure that the
latter were secured firmly around her naked body as she
called out to Oliver to come in. She didn't want there to
be any repeat of last night's still blush-inducing *faux pas*
of not realising that her breasts were clearly on view.

The sight of him carrying a tea-tray complete with a
china teapot, two cups and a plate of wholemeal toast
made her eyes widen slightly.

'So you found it, then. How are you feeling?' he asked
her as he placed the tray on the empty half of her bed,
half smiling as he saw the clutter of small objects still
surrounding her and the evidence of her excitement as she
had unwrapped them in the small, shredded pieces of paper torn by her impatient fingers.

'Much better,' Lisa assured him. 'Just as soon as I can
get my car sorted out I should be off your hands and on
my way back to London. I still haven't thanked you properly for what you did,' she added, half-shyly. Last night
the intimacy between them had seemed so natural that she
hadn't even questioned it. This morning she was acutely
conscious of the fact that he was, after all, a man she
barely knew.

His soft, 'Oh, I wouldn't say that,' as he looked directly
at her mouth made her flush, but there was more amuse-

ment in his eyes than any kind of sexual threat, she acknowledged.

'I haven't thanked you for the stocking either,' she hurried on. 'That was... I... You must think me very childish to want... I'm not used to drinking, and your whisky... I've signed this, by the way.' She tried to excuse herself, diving amongst her spoils to produce the now rerolled truce.

As she did so she suddenly started to sneeze, and had to reach out for the box of tissues beside the bed.

'I thought you said you were feeling all right,' Oliver reminded her sardonically.

'I am,' Lisa defended herself, but now that she was fully awake she had to acknowledge that her throat felt uncomfortably raw and her head ached slightly, whilst yet another volley of sneezes threatened to disprove her claim to good health.

'You're full of a cold,' Oliver corrected her, 'and in no fit state to drive back to London—even if we could arrange for someone to collect your car.'

'But I have to... I must...' Lisa protested.

'Why...in case Henry calls?'

'No,' Lisa denied vehemently, her face flushing again as she suddenly realised how little thought she had actually given to Henry and the end of their romance.

But it was obvious that Oliver had mistaken the cause of her hot face because he gave her an ironic look and told her, 'It will never work. He'll always be tied to his mother's apron strings and you'll always have to take second place to her...

'It's half past nine now,' he told her, changing the subject. 'The village is only ten minutes away by car and we've got time to make it for morning service. I've put the turkey in the oven but it won't be ready until around three…'

Lisa gaped at him.

'But I can't stay here,' she protested.

'Why not?' he asked her calmly. 'What reason have you to go? You've already said that you'll be alone in your flat, and since I'll be alone up here—if you discount a fifteen-pound turkey and enough food to feed the pair of us several times over—it makes sense for you to stay…'

'You want me to stay?' Lisa asked him, astonished. 'But…'

'It will be a hell of a lot easier having you to stay than trying to find a reputable mechanic to sort out and make arrangements for a garage to collect your car, check it over and refuel it. And having one guest instead of two is hardly going to cause me any hardship…' He gave a small shrug.

It was a tempting prospect, Lisa knew. If she was honest with herself she hadn't been looking forward to returning to her empty flat, and even though she and Oliver were virtually strangers there was something about him that… Severely she gave herself a small mental shake.

All right, so maybe last night her body *had* reacted to him in a way that it had certainly never reacted to Henry… Maybe when he had kissed her she *had* felt a certain…need…a response…but that had only been the effect of the whisky…nothing more.

She opened her mouth to decline his invitation, to do the sensible thing and tell him firmly that she had to return home, and instead, to her chagrin, heard herself saying in a small voice, 'Could we really go to church…?' As she realised what she was saying she shook her head, telling him hastily, 'Oh, no, I can't... I haven't anything to wear. My clothes...your cousin's girlfriend's clothes...'

'Are hanging in the closet,' Oliver informed her wryly.

Lisa looked at him. 'What? But they can't be... I left them at Henry's parents'.'

'I didn't,' Oliver informed her succinctly.

'But...but you wanted to give them back to Emma.'

'Originally, yes, but only because Piers was so convinced that the moment she knew what he had done she'd walk out again. However, it transpires that she's off Armani and onto Versace so Piers was allowed to make his peace with her by taking her out and buying her a new wardrobe.'

'So you went to all that trouble for nothing,' Lisa sympathised, knowing how she would have felt in his shoes.

The look he gave her in response made her heart start to beat rather too fast, and for some reason she found it impossible to hold his gaze and had to look quickly away from him.

His slightly hoarse, 'You'd have been wasted on a man like Henry,' made her want to curl her toes in much the same way as his kiss had done last night, and the small shiver that touched her skin had nothing to do with any drop in temperature.

'I'll meet you downstairs in half an hour,' Oliver was saying to her as he moved away from the bed.

Silently, Lisa nodded her agreement. What had she done, committing herself to spend Christmas with him? She gave a small, fatalistic shrug. It was too late to worry about the wisdom of her impulsive decision now.

Thirty-five minutes later, having nervously studied her reflection in the bedroom mirror for a good two minutes, Lisa walked hesitantly onto the landing.

The cream wool dress looked every bit as good on as

she had remembered; the cashmere coat would keep her warm in church.

Her hair, freshly washed and dried, shone silkily, and as yet the only physical sign of her cold was a slight pinky tinge to her nose, easily disguised with foundation.

At the head of the stairs she paused, and then determinedly started to descend, coming to an abrupt halt as she reached the turn in the stairs that looked down on the hallway below.

In the middle of the large room, dominating it, stood the largest and most wondrous Christmas tree that Lisa had ever seen.

She gazed at it in rapt awe, unaware that the shine of pleasure in her eyes rivalled that of the myriad decorations fastened to the tree.

As excited as any child, she positively ran down the remaining stairs and into the hall.

'How on earth…?' she began as she stood and marvelled at the tree, shaking her head as she was unable to find the words to convey her feelings.

'I take it you approve,' she heard Oliver saying wryly beside her.

'Yes. Yes. It's wonderful,' she breathed, without taking her eyes off it to turn and look at him. 'But when… how…?'

'Well, I'm afraid I can't claim to have gone out last night and cut it down. It had actually been delivered yesterday. Piers and I were supposed to be putting it up… It's a bit of a family tradition. He and I both used to spend Christmas here as children with our grandparents, and it was our job to ''do the tree''. It's a tradition we've kept up ever since, although this year…

'I brought it in last night after you'd gone to bed. Mrs

Green had already brought the decorations down from the attic, so it was just a matter of hanging them up.'

'Just a matter...' Lisa's eyebrows rose slightly as she studied the rows and rows of tiny lights, the beautiful and, she was nearly sure, very valuable antique baubles combined with much newer but equally attractive modern ones.

'It must have taken you hours,' she objected.

Oliver shrugged.

'Not really.'

'It's beautiful,' she told him, her throat suddenly closing with emotion. He hadn't done it for her, of course. He had already told her that it was a family tradition, something he and his cousin did together. But, even so, to come down and find it there after confiding in him last night how much she longed for a traditional family Christmas...suddenly seemed a good omen for her decision to stay on with him.

'It hasn't got a fairy,' she told him, hoping he wouldn't notice the idiotic emotional thickening in her voice.

As he glanced towards the top of the tree Oliver shook his head and told her, 'Our fairy is a star, and it's normally the responsibility of the woman of the house to put it on the tree, so I left it—'

'You want me to do it?' Fresh emotion swept her. 'But I'm not... I don't belong here,' she reminded him.

'But you are a woman,' he told her softly, and there was something in the way he said the words, something in the way he looked at her that warned Lisa that the kiss they had shared last night wasn't something he had forgotten.

'We'll have to leave it for now, though,' he told her. 'Otherwise we'll be late for church.'

*   *   *

It had been a cold night, and a heavy frost still lay over the countryside, lending it a magical quality of silvered stillness that made Lisa catch her breath in pleasure.

The village, as Oliver had said, was ten minutes' drive away—a collection of small stone houses huddled together on one side of the river and reached by a narrow stone bridge.

The church was at the furthest end of the village and set slightly apart from it, small and weathered and so old that it looked almost as though it had grown out of the craggy landscape around it.

The bells were ringing as Oliver parked the car and then led her towards the narrow lych-gate and along the stone-flagged path through a graveyard so peaceful that there was no sense of pain or sorrow about it.

Just inside the church, the vicar was waiting.

The church was already almost full, but when Lisa would have slipped into one of the rear pews Oliver touched her arm and directed her to one at the front. A family pew, Lisa recognised, half in awe and half in envy.

The service was short and simple, the carols traditional, the crib quite obviously decorated by very young hands, and yet to Lisa the whole experience was more movingly intense than if they had been in one of the world's grandest cathedrals.

Afterwards the vicar was waiting to shake hands and exchange a few words with all his congregation, including them, and as they ambled back to where Oliver had parked the car the final magical seal of wonderment was put on the day when the first flakes of the forecast snow started to fall.

'I don't believe it,' Lisa whispered breathlessly as Oliver unlocked the car doors. 'I just don't believe it.'

As she whirled round, her whole face alight, Oliver

laughed. The sound, so spontaneous and warmly masculine, had the oddest effect on Lisa's body. Her heart seemed to flip helplessly, her breathing quickening, her gaze drawn unerringly to Oliver's mouth.

She shouldn't be feeling like this. It wasn't fair and it certainly wasn't sensible. They barely knew one another. Yesterday they had been enemies, and but for an odd quirk of fate they still would be today.

Shakily she walked towards the car, the still falling snowflakes forgotten as she tried to come to terms with what was happening to her.

What exactly *was* happening to her? Something she didn't want to give a name to... Not yet... Perhaps not ever. She shivered as she pulled on her seat belt.

'Cold?' Oliver questioned her, frowning slightly.

Lisa shook her head, refusing to give in to the temptation to look at him, to check and see whether, if she did, she would feel that heart-jolting surge of feminine awareness and arousal that she had just experienced in the car park for a second time.

'Stop thinking about him,' she heard Oliver say harshly to her as she turned away from him and stared out of the window. It took her several seconds to realise that he thought that Henry was the reason for her sudden silence. Perhaps it was just as well he did think that, she decided— for both their sakes.

Through the now drifting heavy snowflakes Lisa could see how quickly they had obscured the previously greeny-brown landscape, transforming it into a winter wonderland of breathtaking Christmas-card white.

Coming on top of the poignant simplicity of a church service which to Lisa, as an outsider, had somehow symbolised all she had always felt was missing from her own Christmases—a sense of community, of sharing...of involvement and belonging, of permanence going from one generation to the next—the sight of the falling snow brought an ache to her throat and the quick silvery shimmer of unexpected tears to her eyes.

Ashamed of her own emotionalism, she ducked her head, searching in her bag for a tissue, hoping to disguise her tears as a symptom of her cold. But Oliver was obviously too astute to be deceived by such a strategy and demanded brusquely, 'What is it? What's wrong?' adding curtly, 'You're wasting your tears on Henry; he isn't—'

'I'm not crying because of Henry,' Lisa denied. Did he really think that she was so lacking in self-esteem and self-preservation that she couldn't see for herself what a lucky escape she had had, if not from Henry then very definitely from Henry's mother?

'No? Then what are these?' Oliver demanded tauntingly, reaching out before she could stop him to rub the hard pad of his thumb beneath one eye and show her the dampness clinging to his skin. 'Scotch mist?'

'I didn't say I wasn't crying,' Lisa defended herself. 'Just that it wasn't because of... It's not because of Henry...'

'Then why?' Oliver challenged, obviously not believing her.

'Because of this,' Lisa told him simply, gesturing towards the scene outside the car window. 'And the church...'

She could see from the look he was giving her that he didn't really believe her, and because for some reason it had suddenly become very important that he did she took a deep breath and told him quickly, 'It's just so beautiful... The whole thing...the weather, the church service...'

As she felt him looking at her she turned her head to

meet his eyes. She shook her head, not wanting to go on, feeling that she had perhaps said too much already, been too openly emotional. Men, in her experience, found it rather discomforting when women expressed their emotions. Henry certainly had.

If Oliver was discomforted by what she had said, though, he certainly wasn't showing it; in fact he wasn't showing any kind of reaction that she could identify at all. He had dropped his eyelids slightly over his eyes and turned his face away from her, ostensibly to concentrate on his driving, making it impossible for her to read his expression at all, his only comment, as he brought the car to a halt outside the house, a cautionary, 'Be careful you don't slip when you get out.'

'Be careful you don't slip...!' Just how old did he think she was? Lisa wondered wryly as she got out of the car, tilting up her face towards the still falling snowflakes and breathing in the clean, sharp air, a blissful expression on her face as she studied her surroundings, happiness bubbling up inside her.

'I still can't believe this...that it's actually snowing... on Christmas Day... Do you realise that this is my very first white Christmas?' As she whispered the words in awed delight she closed her eyes, took a deep breath of snow-scented air and promptly did what Oliver had warned her not to do and lost her footing.

Her startled cry was arrested almost before it had begun as Oliver reached out and caught hold of her, his strong hands gripping her waist, holding her tightly, safely...

Holding her closely, she recognised as her heart started to pound with unfamiliar excitement and her breath caught in her throat. Not out of shock, Lisa acknowledged, her face flushing as she realised just what it was that was causing her heart and pulse-rate to go into overdrive, and she prayed that Oliver wouldn't be equally quick to recognise that her shallow breathing and sudden tension had nothing to do with the shock of her near fall and everything to do with his proximity.

Why was this happening to her? she wondered dizzily. She didn't even like the man and he certainly didn't like her—even if he *had* offered her a roof over her head for Christmas.

He was standing close enough for her to smell the clean man scent of his skin—or was it just that for some extraordinary reason she was acutely sensitive to the scent and heat of him?

Her legs started to tremble—in fact, her whole body was trembling.

'It's all right,' she heard Oliver saying calmly to her. 'I've got you…'

'Yes,' Lisa heard herself responding, her own voice unfamiliarly soft and husky, making the simple affirmation sound something much more sensual and inviting. Without having had the remotest intention of doing any such thing—it simply wasn't the kind of thing she did—ever— Lisa found that she was looking at Oliver's mouth, and that her gaze, having focused on it for far, far too long, was somehow drawn even more betrayingly to his eyes.

Her breath caught in her throat as she saw the way he was looking back at her, his head already lowering towards hers—as well it might do after the sensually open invitation that she had just given him.

But instead of avoiding what she knew was going to happen, instead of moving away from him, which she could quite easily have done, she simply stood there waiting, with her lips softly parted, her gaze fixed on the downward descent of his head and his mouth, her heart thudding frantically against her chest wall—not in case he kissed her, she acknowledged in semi-shock, but rather in case he didn't.

But of course he did. Slowly and deliberately at first, exploring the shape and feel of her mouth, shifting his weight slightly so that instead of that small but oh, so safe distance between them and the firm grip of his hands on her waist supporting her, it was the equally firm but oh, so much more sensual strength of his body that held her up as his arms closed round her, holding her in an embrace not as intimate as that of a lover but still intimate enough to make her powerfully aware of the fact that he was a man.

Lisa had forgotten that a man's kiss could be like this—slow, thorough and so sensually inventive and promising as he hinted at all the pleasures that there could be to come. And yet it wasn't a kiss of passion or demand—not yet—and Lisa was hazily aware that the slow stroke of his tongue against her lips was more sensually threatening to her self-control than to his, and that she was the one who was having to struggle to pull herself back from the verge of a far more dangerous kind of arousal when he finally lifted his mouth from hers.

'What was that for?' she asked stupidly as she tried to drag her gaze away from his eyes.

'No reason,' he told her in response. But as she started to turn her head away, expecting him to release her, he lifted one hand to her face, cupping the side of her jaw with warm, strong fingers, holding her captive as he told her softly, 'But this is.'

And he was kissing her again, but this time the passion that she had sensed was missing in his first kiss was clearly betrayed in the way his mouth hardened over hers, the way his body hardened against hers, his tongue probing the softness of her mouth as she totally abandoned her normal, cautious behaviour and responded to him with every single one of her aroused senses—every single one.

Her arms, without her knowing quite how it had happened, were wrapped tightly around him, holding him close, her fingertips absorbing the feel of his body, its warmth, its hardness, its sheer maleness; her eyes opened in dazed arousal as she looked up into his, her ears intensely attuned to the sound of his breathing and his heartbeat and their tell-tale quickened rate, the scent of him reaching her with every breath she took, and the taste of him. She closed her eyes and then opened them again as she heard him whispering against her mouth, 'Happy Christmas.'

'Happy Christmas'! Lisa came back to earth with a jolt. Of course. Hot colour flooded her face as she realised just how close she had been to making a complete fool of herself.

He hadn't kissed her because he had wanted her, because he had been overwhelmed by desire for her. He had kissed her because it was Christmas, and if that second kiss had been a good deal more intense than their extremely short-lived acquaintanceship really merited then that was probably her fault for... For what? For responding too intensely to him the first time?

'Happy Christmas!' she managed to respond as she hurriedly stepped back from him and turned towards the house.

As Oliver opened the door for her Lisa could smell the rich scent of the roasting turkey mingling with the fresh crispness of the tree.

'The turkey smells good,' she told him, shakily struggling to appear calm and unaffected by his kiss, sniffing the richly scented air. The kiss that they had so recently exchanged might never have been, judging from the way he was behaving towards her now, and she told herself firmly that it was probably best if she pretended that it hadn't too.

Oliver could never play a permanent role in her life, and this unfamiliar and dangerous intensity of physical desire that she had experienced was something she would be far better off without.

'Yes, I'd better go and check on it,' Oliver agreed.

'I'll come and give you a hand,' Lisa offered, adding as she glanced down at her clothes, 'I'd better go and get changed first, though.'

It didn't take her long to remove her coat and the dress she was wearing underneath it, but instead of re-dressing immediately she found that she was standing staring at her underwear-clad body in the mirror, trying to see it as a man might do... A man? Or Oliver?

Angry with herself, she reached into the wardrobe and pulled out the first thing that came to hand, only realising when she had started to put it on that it was the cream trouser suit which had caused so many problems already.

She paused, wondering whether or not to wear something else, and then heard Oliver rapping on the bedroom door and calling out, 'Lisa, are you all right...?'

'Yes, yes. I'm fine... I'm coming now,' she told him quickly, pulling on the jacket and fastening it. Hardly sensible apparel in which to help cook Christmas lunch, but with the sleeves of the jacket pushed back, she thought... And she could always remove the jacket if necessary. So what if the pretty little waistcoat that went underneath it was rather brief? Oliver was hardly likely to notice, was he?

He was waiting for her outside the bedroom door, and caught her off guard by catching hold of her arm and placing his hand on her forehead.

'Mmm…no temperature. Well, that's something, I suppose. Your pulse is very fast, though,' he observed as his hand circled her wrist and he measured her pulse-rate.

Quickly Lisa snatched her wrist away. 'I've just got a cold, that's all,' she told him huskily.

'Just a cold,' he reiterated. 'No broken heart…'

Lisa flashed him a doubtful look, half suspecting him of deliberately mocking her, but unable to make any response, knowing that she would be lying to him if she tried to pretend that she felt anything other than half-ashamed relief at breaking up with Henry.

'You might not want to accept it now, but you didn't really love him,' Oliver told her coolly. 'If you had—'

'You have no right to say that,' Lisa objected suddenly, angry with him—and, more tellingly, with herself, without wanting to analyse or really know why.

'What do you know about love?'

'I know enough about it to recognise it when I see it—and when I don't,' Oliver countered as she fell silent, but Lisa wasn't really listening; she was too caught up in the shock of realising that the pain spearing her, pinning her in helpless, emotional agony where she stood, was caused by the realisation that for all she knew there could have been, could still be a woman in Oliver's life whom he loved.

'Stop thinking about it,' she heard Oliver telling her grimly, her face flushing at the thought that he had so easily read her mind and guessed what she was feeling, until he added, 'You must have seen for yourself that it would never have worked. Henry's mother would never have allowed him to marry you.'

Relief made her expel her breath in a leaky sigh. It had been Henry whom he had warned her to stop thinking about and not him. He had not guessed what she had been thinking or feeling after all.

'I thought we'd agreed a truce,' she reminded him, adding softly, 'I still haven't thanked you properly for everything you've done. Helping—'

'Everything?'

For some reason the way he was looking at her made her feel closer to the shy teenager she had once been than the adult woman she now was.

'I meant…' she began, and then shook her head, knowing that she wouldn't be able to list all the reasons she had to thank him without at some point having to look at him, and knowing that once she did her gaze would be drawn irresistibly to his mouth, and once it was…

'I… That turkey smells wonderful.' She gave in cravenly. 'How long did you say it would be before we could eat?'

She could tell from the wry look he gave her as she glanced his way that he wasn't deceived, but to her relief he didn't push matters, leaving her to follow him instead as he turned back towards the stairs.

CHAPTER SIX

'I NEVER imagined you'd be so domesticated.'

They were both in the large, well-equipped, comfortable kitchen, Lisa mixing the ingredients for the bread sauce whilst Oliver deftly prepared the vegetables, and she knew almost as soon as she had voiced her surprise that it had been the wrong thing to say. But it was too late to recall her impulsive comment because Oliver had stopped what he was doing to look frowningly across at her.

'I'm sorry,' she apologised ruefully. 'I didn't mean to—'

'To sound patronising,' Oliver supplied for her.

Lisa glanced warily at him and then defended herself robustly, telling him, 'Well, when we first met you just didn't seem the type to—'

'The "type".' Oliver pulled her up a second time. 'And what "type" would that be, exactly?'

Oh, dear. He had every right to sound annoyed, Lisa acknowledged.

'I didn't mean it the way it sounded,' she confessed. 'It's just that Henry—'

'Doesn't so much as know how to boil an egg,' Oliver supplied contemptuously for her. 'And that's something to be admired in a man, is it?'

Lisa's face gave her away even before she had protested truthfully, 'No, of course it isn't.'

'The reason Henry chooses to see even the most basically necessary domestic chores such as cooking for himself as beneath his male dignity is because that's the way his mother has brought him up and that's the way she intends him to stay. And woe betide any woman who doesn't spoonfeed her little boy the way she's taught him to expect.'

There was no mistaking the disgust in Oliver's voice as he underlined the weakness of Henry's character and Lisa knew that there was no real argument that she could put forward in Henry's defence, even if she had wanted to do so.

'It might come as something of a surprise to you,' Oliver continued sardonically, obviously determined to drive home his point, 'but, quite frankly, the majority of the male sex—at least the more emotionally mature section of it—would not take too kindly at having Henry held up to them as a yardstick of what it means to be a man. And neither, for future reference, do most of us relish being classified as a ''type''.'

'I didn't mean it like that,' Lisa protested. 'It's just that when we first met you seemed so... I could never have imagined you...us...' She was floundering, and badly, she recognised, adding lamely, 'I wasn't comparing you to Henry at all.'

'No?' Oliver challenged her.

'No,' Lisa insisted, not entirely truthfully. She *had* been comparing them, of course, but not, as Oliver fortunately had incorrectly assumed, to his disadvantage. Far from it... She certainly didn't want to have to explain to him that there was something about *him* that was so very male that it made laughable the idea that he should in any way fail to measure up to Henry.

Measure up to him! When it came to exhibiting that certain quality that spelled quite essential maleness there was simply no contest between them. Oliver possessed it, and in abundance, or so it seemed to Lisa, and Henry did not have it at all. She was faintly shocked that she should so clearly recognise this—and not just recognise it, she admitted uneasily. She was quite definitely somehow or other very sensitively aware of it as a woman—too aware of it for her peace of mind.

'I happen to have an orderly mind,' Oliver was telling her, thankfully unaware of what she was thinking, 'and I loathe any unnecessary waste of time. To live in the midst of chaos and disorder seems to be totally counter-productive, and besides...' he gave a small shrug and drained the peeled and washed potatoes, turning away from her as he started to cut them, so that she could not see his expression '...after my mother died and my father and I were on our own, we both had to learn how to look after ourselves.'

Lisa discovered that there was a very large lump in her throat as she pictured the solemn, lonely little boy and his equally lonely father struggling together to master their chores as well as their loss.

'The behavioural habits one learns as a child have a tendency to become deeply ingrained, hence my advice to you that you are well rid of Henry. He will never cease being his mother's spoilt and emotionally immature little boy...' His tasks finished, he turned round and looked directly at her as he added drily, 'And I suspect that you will never cease thinking of Christmas as a specially magical time of year...'

'No, I don't expect I shall,' Lisa admitted, adding honestly, 'But then I don't really want to. I don't suppose I'll ever stop wanting, either, to put down roots, to marry and have children and to give them the stability and permanence I missed as a child,' she confessed, wanting to be as open and honest with him as he had been with her.

'I know a lot of my friends think that I'm rather odd

for putting more emphasis on stability and the kind of relationship that focuses more on that than on the romantic and sexual aspects of love—'

'Does there have to be a choice?' Oliver asked her.

Lisa frowned. 'What do you mean?'

'Isn't it possible for there to be romance and good sex between a couple, as well as stability and permanence? I thought the modern woman was determined to have it all. Emotional love, orgasmic sex, a passionately loyal mate, children, career...'

'In theory, yes,' Lisa agreed ruefully. 'But I suppose if I'm honest...I'm perhaps not very highly sexed. So—'

'Who told you that? Henry?'

'No,' she said, stung by the mocking amusement that she could see in his eyes, aware that she had allowed herself to be drawn onto potentially very treacherous ground and that sex was the very last topic she should be discussing with this particular man—especially when her body was suddenly and very dangerously reinforcing the lack of wisdom in her laying claim to a low libido when it was strongly refuting that. Too strongly for her peace of mind. Much, much too strongly.

'I...I've always known it,' she told him hastily, more to convince herself, she suspected, than him.

'Always...?' The way the dark eyebrows rose reminded her of the way he had looked when he had come round to see her and demand the return of Emma's clothes, and that same frisson of danger that she had felt then returned, but this time for a very, very different reason.

'Well, from when I was old enough... When I knew... After...' she began, compelled by the look he was giving her to make some kind of response.

'You mean you convinced yourself that you had a low sex drive because, presumably, that was what your first lover told you,' Oliver challenged her, cutting through her unsuccessful attempts to appear breezily nonchalant about the whole thing.

'It wasn't just because of that,' Lisa defended herself quickly and, she realised uneasily, very betrayingly.

'No?' Oliver's eyebrows rose again. 'I'll take a bet that there haven't been very many… Two, maybe three at the most, and that, of course, excludes Henry, who—'

'Three…?' Lisa was aghast. 'Certainly not,' she denied vehemently. 'I would never…' Too late she realised what she was doing…what she was saying.

It was one thing for her to feel that, despite the amusement of her peers, she had the sort of nature that would not allow her to feel comfortable about sharing the intimacy of her body with a variety of lovers and that her low sex drive made it feel right that there had only been that one not really too successful experience in her late teens, and it was one thing to feel that she could quite happily remain celibate and wait to re-explore her sexuality until she found a man she felt comfortable enough with to do so, but it was quite another to admit it to someone like Oliver, who, she was pretty sure, would think her views archaic and ridiculous.

'So, there has only been one.' He pounced, immediately and humiliatingly correct. 'Well, for your information, a man who tells a virgin that she's got a low sex drive tends to be doing so to protect his own inadequacy, not hers.'

Her inadequacy! Lisa drew in a sharp breath of panic at the fact that he should dare so accurately and acutely to put her deepest and most intimate secret fears into words, and promptly fought back.

'I'm twenty-four now, not eighteen, and I think I know myself well enough to be able to judge for myself what kind of sex drive I have…'

'You're certainly old enough and, I would suspect, strong-willed enough to tell yourself what kind of sex drive you think it safe to allow yourself to have,' Oliver agreed, staggering her with not just his forthrightness but his incisive astuteness as well.

Pride warred with caution as Lisa was torn between demanding to know exactly what he meant and, more cravenly, avoiding what she suspected could be a highly dangerous confrontation—highly dangerous to her, that was. Oliver, she thought, would thoroughly enjoy dissecting her emotional vulnerabilities and laying them out one by one in front of her.

In the end caution won and, keeping her back to him, she told him wildly, 'I think this bread sauce is just about ready... What else would you like me to do?'

She thought she heard him mutter under his breath, 'Don't tempt me,' before he said far more clearly, 'Since it's Christmas Day I suppose we should really eat in the dining room, although normally I prefer to eat in here. I'll show you where everything is, and if you could sort it all out—silver, crystal, china...'

'Yes...of course,' Lisa agreed hurriedly, finding a cloth to wipe her hands on as she followed him back into the hall.

The dining room was a well-proportioned, warm, panelled room at the rear of the house, comfortably large enough to take a table which, Oliver explained to her, could be extended to seat twelve people.

'It was a wedding present to my grandparents. In those days, of course, twelve was not a particularly large number. My grandmother was one of seven and my grandfather one of five.'

'Oh, it must be wonderful to be part of a large family,'

Lisa could not help commenting enviously. 'My parents were both onlys and they only had me.'

'Being an only child does have its advantages,' Oliver told her firmly. 'I'm an only myself, and—'

'But you had the family—aunts, uncles, cousins...'

'Yes,' Oliver agreed.

But he had also lost his mother at a very vulnerable age, Lisa recognised, and to lose someone so close must inevitably have a far more traumatic effect on one's life than the mere absence of a non-existent extended family.

'I can guess what you're thinking,' she told him wryly. 'I just sound pathetically self-absorbed and self-pitying. I know how much both my parents need their work, their art, how important it is to them. It's just that...'

'There have been times when you needed to know that you came first,' Oliver guessed shrewdly. 'There are times when we all feel like that,' he told her. 'When we all need to know that we come first, that we are the most important person in someone else's life... What's wrong?' he asked when he saw the rueful acknowledgement of his perception in Lisa's eyes.

'Nothing,' she said. 'It's just that I can't...that you don't...' She shook her head. 'You seem so self-contained,' was the only thing she could say.

'Do I?' He gave her a wry look. 'Maybe I am now. It wasn't always that way, though. The reason for the breakup of my first teenage romance was that my girl-friend found me too emotionally demanding. She was right as well.'

'You must have loved her an awful lot,' was all she could find to say as she tried to absorb and conceal the unwanted and betraying searing surge of envy that hit her as she listened to him.

'I certainly thought I did,' Oliver agreed drily, 'but the

reality was little more than a very intense teenage crush. Still, at least I learned something from the experience.'

What had she been like, the girl Oliver had loved as a teenager? Lisa wondered ten minutes later when he had returned to the kitchen and she was removing silverware and crystal from the cupboards he had shown her.

She found it hard to imagine anyone—*any* woman— rejecting a man like him.

Her hand trembled slightly as she placed one of the heavy crystal wineglasses on the table.

What was the matter with her? she scolded herself. Just because he had kissed her, that didn't mean... It didn't mean anything, and why should she want it to? If she was going to think about any member of the male sex right now she ought to be thinking about Henry. After all, less than twenty-four hours ago she had believed that she was going to marry him.

It unnerved her a little bit to realise how far she had travelled emotionally in such a short space of time. It was hard to imagine now how she could ever have thought that she and Henry were suited—in any way.

'I really don't think I should be drinking any more of this,' Lisa told Oliver solemnly as she raised the glass of rich red wine that he had just refilled to her lips.

They had finished eating fifteen minutes earlier, and at Oliver's insistence Lisa was now curled up cosily in one corner of the deep, comfortable sofa that he had drawn up close to the fire and where she had been ordered to remain whilst he stacked the dishwasher.

The meal had been as good as any Christmas dinner she could ever remember eating and better than most. It had amazed her how easily the conversation had flowed between them, and what had surprised her even more was to discover that he was a very witty raconteur who could make her laugh.

Henry had never made her laugh.

Hastily she took a quick gulp of her wine. It was warm and full-bodied and the perfect accompaniment for the meal they had just enjoyed.

When they had left the table to come and sit down in front of the fire to finish their wine, Oliver had closed the curtains, and now, possessed by a sudden urge to see if it was still snowing, Lisa abandoned her comfortable seat and walked rather unsteadily towards the curtained window.

The wine had been even stronger than she had believed, she admitted. She wasn't drunk—far from it—but she certainly felt rather light-headed and a little giddy.

As she tugged back the curtain she gave a small, soft sigh of delight as she stared through the window.

It was still snowing—thick, whirling-dervish-like, thick white flakes, like those in a child's glass snowstorm. As she looked up into the darkening sky she could see the early evening stars and the thin sickle shape of the moon.

It was her childhood dream of a white Christmas come true. And to think that if she had returned to London as she had originally planned to do she would have missed it! Emotion caught her by the throat.

She dropped the curtain, turning back into the room, stopping as she saw Oliver watching her. She hadn't heard him come back in and unaccountably she could feel herself starting to tremble slightly.

'What is it? What's wrong?' he asked her.

'Nothing,' she denied. 'It's just…' She gave a small shrug, closed her eyes and then opened them again as the darkness increased the heady effects of the wine. 'It's just that all of this…is so…so perfect,' she told him huskily, gesturing to the room and then towards the window and the view that lay beyond it. 'So...so magical... This house...the weather...the tree...church this morning...my stocking and...'

'And...?' Oliver prompted softly.

He was looking at her very intently—so intently, in fact, that she felt as though she could drown in the dark intensity of his eyes, as though she was being compelled to...

'And you,' she breathed, and as she said it she felt her heart slam fiercely against her chest wall, depriving her of breath, whilst the silence between them seemed to pulse and quicken and to take on a life of its own.

'I really shouldn't drink any more of this,' she heard herself whispering dizzily as she picked up her glass and took a nervous gulp, and then watched as Oliver walked softly towards her.

'No, you really shouldn't,' he agreed as he reached her and took the glass from her unresisting fingers, and then he took her equally unresisting body in his arms and her quiescent mouth into the warm captivity of his.

'We shouldn't be doing this,' she reproached him, mumbling the words against his mouth, her arms wrapped around him, her fingers burrowing into the thick darkness of his hair, her eyes luminous with the desire that was turning her whole body into molten liquid as she gazed up into his eyes.

'Oh, yes, we should,' was his sensuously whispered response. 'Oh, yes, we most definitely, assuredly should.' And then he was kissing her again. Not forcefully, but oh, so compellingly that it was impossible for her to resist him—impossible for her to want to resist him.

'You've already kissed me once for Christmas,' Lisa

reminded him unsteadily as he slowly lifted his mouth from hers and looked down at her.

'This isn't for Christmas,' he whispered back as his hand slid under her hair, tilting her head back up towards him, sliding his other hand down her back, urging her closer to his own body.

Lisa could feel her heart hammering against her ribs as sensations that she had never experienced before—not with Henry and certainly not with the man who had been her first and only lover—flooded her body.

'Then what is it for?' she forced herself to ask him huskily.

'What do you think?' Oliver responded rawly. 'I wanted you the first time I saw you—did you know that?'

'How could you have done?' Lisa argued. 'You were so furious with me, and—'

'And even more furious with myself…with my body for the way it was reacting to you,' Oliver told her, adding rawly, 'The same way it's reacting to you right now.'

Uncertainly Lisa searched his face. Everything was happening so quickly that she couldn't fully take it all in. If she had felt dizzy before, with the combination of the rich wine and the warm fire, that was nothing to the headiness affecting her now, clouding her ability to reason logically, making her heart thump dangerously, heavily as her body reacted to what was happening to her—to them.

'I'll stop if you want me to,' she heard Oliver telling her hoarsely as he bent his head and gently nuzzled the soft, warm flesh of her throat. As she stifled the small, betraying sound she made when her body shuddered in shocked pleasure Lisa shook her head.

'No. No. I don't want you to stop,' she admitted huskily.

'Good,' Oliver told her thickly. 'Because I don't want

to either. What I want is you, Lisa… God, how I want you.'

'I'm not used to this,' Lisa said shakily. 'I don't—'

'Do you think that I am…that I do?' he interrupted her almost roughly. 'For God's sake, Lisa, have you any idea how long it is since I was this intimate with a woman… since I wanted to be this intimate with a woman? I'm not a teenager,' he half growled at her when she shook her head. 'I don't normally… It's been a hell of a long time since anyone has affected me the way you do… One hell of a long time.'

Lisa was trembling as he took her back in his arms, but not because she was afraid. Oh, no, not because of anything like that.

At any other time the eagerness with which she met Oliver's kiss would have shocked her, caused her to deny what she was experiencing, but now, for some reason, things were different—*he* was different. This was Christmas, after all—a special, magical time when special, magical things could happen.

As she felt the probing thrust of Oliver's tongue she reached out towards him, wrapping her arms around him, opening her mouth to him.

Somewhere outside this magical, firelit, pine-scented world where it seemed the most natural thing of all for her and Oliver to come together like this there existed another, different world. Lisa knew that, but right now…right now…

As she heard the rough deep sound of pleasure that Oliver made in his throat when he tasted the honeyed interior of her mouth Lisa gave up trying to think and behave logically. There was no point and, even more important, there was no need.

Instead, as she slid her fingers through the thick softness of Oliver's hair, she let her tongue meet his—slowly, hesitantly at first, such intimacy unfamiliar to her. The memories of her much younger, uncertain teenage explorations recalled sensations which bore no resemblance whatsoever to the sensations she was experiencing now as Oliver's tongue caressed hers, the weight of his body erotically masculine against the more slender femininity of her own as his hands caressed her back, her waist, before sliding down over her hips to cup the soft swell of her buttocks as he lifted her against him.

Lisa knew already that he was aroused, but until she felt the taut fullness of his erection against her own body she hadn't realised how physically and emotionally vulnerable and responsive she was to him. A sensation, a need that was totally outside her previous experience overtook her as she felt the liquid heat filling her own body, her hips lifting automatically, blindly seeking the sensual intimacy that her flesh craved.

'So much for your low sex drive,' she heard Oliver muttering thickly against her ear, before he added throatily, 'You're one hell of a sexy lady, Lisa. Do you know that? Do you know what you're doing to me...? How you're making me feel...? How you've made me feel since you stood there in your flat in that damned suit, with your breasts...?'

Lisa heard him groan as his hand reached upwards towards her breast, sliding beneath the fabric that covered it to cup its soft, eager weight, his thumb-tip caressing the hard peak of her nipple.

'Let me take this off,' he urged her, his hands removing her jacket, and then starting on the buttons of the waistcoat underneath it, his eyes dark with arousal as he looked deeply into hers. And then, without waiting for her to respond, his mouth curled in a small, sensual half-smile and he bent his head and kissed her briefly but very hard on her half-parted mouth. 'I want to see you, Lisa—all of you. I want to touch you, hold you, taste you, and I want you to want to do the same as me.'

Lisa knew that he must have felt the racking, sensual shudder that convulsed her body even if he hadn't heard her immediate response to the mental image that his words had aroused, in the low groan she was not quite able to suppress.

'You want that,' he pressed huskily. 'You want me to undress for you. You want to see me…to touch me…' He was kissing her again now—slow, lingering kisses all over her face and throat—whilst his hands moved deftly, freeing her from her clothes. But it wasn't the thought of her own nakedness beneath his hands that was causing her breath to quicken and her heart to lurch frantically against her ribs, but rather the thought of his nakedness beneath hers.

What was happening to her? she wondered dazedly. Her, to whom the thought of a man's naked body was something which she normally found rather discomforting and not in the least erotic. What was happening that she should now be so filled with desire that her whole body ached and pulsed with it at the mere thought of seeing Oliver's? The mere thought… Heaven knew what she would be like when that thought became a reality, when she was free to reach out and touch and taste him too.

Helplessly she closed her eyes, and then opened them again to find Oliver watching her.

'*Is* that what you want, Lisa?' he asked her softly whilst his thumb-tip drew a sensual line of pleasure around her sensitised mouth. 'Is that what you want—to see me… touch me…feel me…?'

Dry-mouthed, Lisa nodded. Her top was unfastened

now, and she was vaguely aware of the half-exposed curves of her breasts gilded by the firelight, but her own semi-nudity seemed unimportant and irrelevant; her whole concentration was focused on Oliver, on the deft, steady movements of his hands as he unfastened the buttons on his shirt, his gaze never wavering from her as he started to remove it.

His chest was broad and sleekly muscled, tanned, with a dark arrowing of silky black hair down the centre, the sight of which made her muscles clench and her breath leak from her lungs in a rusty ache of sensory overload. His nipples, flat and dark, looked so different from her own.

As his hands reached for the fastening on his trousers, Lisa leaned forward, acting on impulse. The scent of him filled her nostrils, clouding her thought processes, drugging her…

As her lips closed around the small dark nub of flesh, she made a soft sound of feminine pleasure deep in her throat. Her tongue-tip circled his flesh, stroked it, explored the shape and texture of it before she finally returned to sucking gently on it.

'Lisa.'

The shock of being wrenched away from him was like having her whole body plunged in icy-cold water after it had been lapped in tropical warmth, the pain so great that it made her physically ache and cry out, her shocked gaze focusing in bewilderment on Oliver's, quick emotional tears filming her eyes as she wondered what it was she had done, why it was that he was being so cruelly brutal with her.

'It's too much, too soon,' she heard him telling her harshly. 'I can't… It's…'

Still half in shock she watched him as he shook his head.

'You're turning me on too much,' he told her more gently, 'and I can't...'

Lisa could feel the shock of it all the way through her body—the shock and an intensely feminine thrill that she could have such a powerful effect on him. As though he had guessed what she was feeling, she heard Oliver groan softly, and then he was reaching for her, holding her in his arms before she could evade them, kissing her now tightly closed eyelids, and then her mouth, and then he was telling her, 'Another few seconds of that and right now I'd be inside you and without—' He broke off and then added, 'That isn't how I want it to be for our first time together.'

Lisa moved instinctively against him, and then tensed as she felt the rough brush of his body hair against her naked breasts.

As she bent her head to look down at where her top had slid away from her Oliver's gaze followed hers, and then he bent his head, slowly easing her top completely away from her as he gradually kissed his way down her body, stopping only when he had reached the dark pink tautness of her nipple.

As he closed his mouth on it, repeating on her the caress she had given him, Lisa tensed in shock beneath the surge of pleasure that arced through her, arching her spine, locking her hands against his head, making her shudder as her body, beneath the weight of the flooding waves of pleasure that pulsed through her, was activated by the now urgent suckle of his mouth on her breast.

Was this how *he* had felt when she had caressed him in the same way? No, it couldn't have been, she denied. She could feel what he was doing to her, right deep down

within her body, her womb. She could feel... With a
small, shocked gasp she started to push him away.

'What is it?' she heard Oliver asking thickly as he released her nipple. He was breathing heavily and she could
feel the warmth against her skin resensitising it, making
her...

'I...' Nothing, she had been about to respond, but instead she heard herself saying helplessly in an unfamiliar
and huskily sensual voice, 'I want you, Oliver... I want
you.'

'Not one half as much as I want you,' he responded
tautly as she quickly removed the remainder of her clothes
and his own, and then, like a mystical, almost myth-like
personification of all that was male inspired by some
Greek legend, and filling her receptive senses with that
maleness, he knelt over her, his dark head bowed as he
gently eased her back against the soft fabric of the sofa
and made love to her with a sensuality that took her breath
away.

It didn't matter that no man had ever touched her, caressed her, kissed her so intimately before or that she had
never imagined wanting one to do so. Somehow, when it
was Oliver's hands, Oliver's mouth that caressed her...

So this was desire, need, physically wanting someone
with an intensity that could scarcely be borne.

Lisa gasped, caught her breath, held out her arms, her
body opening to him, wanting him, enfolding him as she
felt the first powerful thrust of him within her and then
felt it again and again until her whole world, her whole
being was concentrated on the powerful, rhythmic surge
of his body within her own and the sensation that lay
beyond it—the ache, the urgency...the release...

Lisa heard herself cry out, felt the quickening thrust of
Oliver's body, the hard, harsh sound of his breathing and

his thudding heartbeat as she clung to him, moved with him, against him, aching, urging and finally losing herself completely, drowning in the liquid pulse of pleasure that flooded through her.

Later, still drowsy, sated, relaxed as she lay within the protective curve of Oliver's body, she told him sleepily, 'I think this is the best Christmas I have ever had.'

She could feel as well as hear him laughing.

'You do wonders for my ego, do you know that?' he told her as he tilted her face up to his own and kissed her lingeringly on the mouth.

'It's the truth,' Lisa insisted, her eyes clouding slightly as she added more self-consciously, 'I…I never realised before that it could be so… That I could feel…'

'It?' Oliver teased her.

'Sex,' Lisa told him with dignity.

'Sex?' She heard the question in his voice. She looked uncertainly up at him. He looked slightly withdrawn, his expression stern, forbidding…more like the Oliver she had first met than the man who had just held her in his arms and made such wonderful, cataclysmic, orgasmic love to her.

'What's wrong?' she asked him hesitantly, her heart starting to thump nervously. Wasn't this what all the books warned you about—the man's withdrawal and coldness after the act of sex had been completed, his desire to separate himself from his partner whilst she wanted to maintain their intimacy and to share with him her emotional awe at the physical pleasure their bodies had given one another?

'What we just shared may have been sex to you,' he told her quietly, 'but for me it was more than that. For me it was making love in the true sense of those words.

Experimenting teenagers, shallow adults without maturity or sensitivity have sex, Lisa…'

'I don't understand,' she told him huskily, groping through the confusion of her thoughts and feelings to find the right words. 'I… You… We don't really know one another and…'

'And what?' Oliver challenged her. 'Because of that we can't have any feelings for one another?' He shook his head. 'I disagree.'

'But until today…until now…we didn't even like one another… We…'

'We what?' Oliver prompted her as she came to an uncertain stop. 'We were very physically aware of one another.'

Lisa opened her mouth to deny what he was saying and then closed it again.

'Not so very long ago you told me that you wanted me,' Oliver reminded her softly, 'and I certainly wanted you. I agree that the circumstances under which we met initially clouded our ability to judge one another clearly, but fate has given us an opportunity to start again…a second chance.'

'Twenty-four hours ago I was still planning to marry Henry,' Lisa protested helplessly.

'Twenty-four hours ago I still wanted to wring your pretty little neck,' Oliver offered with a smile.

'What's happening to us, Oliver?' she asked him uneasily. 'I don't understand.' She sat up and pushed the heavy weight of her hair off her face, her forehead creased in an anxious frown. 'I just don't do things like this. I've never… I thought it must be the wine at first… That…'

'That what? That the effect of three glasses of red wine was enough to make you want me?' He gave her a wry look. 'Well, I haven't even got that excuse. Not then, and certainly not now,' he added huskily as he reached towards her and took hold of her hand, guiding it towards his body whilst he bent his head and kissed her slowly.

To be aroused by him the first time might just possibly have been some kind of fluke, Lisa acknowledged, but there was no way she could blame her desire for him now on the wine. Not a second time, not now. And she did desire him, she acknowledged shakily as her fingers explored the hard strength of him. Oh, yes, she did want him.

It was gone midnight before they finally went upstairs, Lisa pausing to draw back the curtains and look out on the silent, snow-covered garden.

'It's still snowing,' she whispered to Oliver.

'Mmm…' he agreed, nuzzling the back of her neck. 'So it is… Lovely…'

But it wasn't the view through the window he was studying as he murmured his rich approval, and Lisa laughed softly as she saw the way he was studying her still naked breasts.

'No,' Oliver said to her, shaking his head as she paused outside the guest-bedroom door. 'Tonight I want you to sleep with me…in my bed…in my arms,' he told her, and as she listened to him Lisa felt her heart flood with emotion.

It was too soon yet to know just how she really felt about him, or so she told herself. And too dangerous, surely, when her body was still flooded with the pleasure he had given it? She was by nature cautious and careful; she always had been. It wasn't possible for her to fall in love over the space of a few hours with a man she barely knew.

But then less than twenty-four hours ago she would also

have vehemently denied that it was possible for her to want that same man so much and with such a degree of intensity that, as he drew her towards his bed and held out his arms to her, her body was already starting to go liquid with pleasure and yearning for him.

CHAPTER SEVEN

'OUCH. That's not fair. I was retying the snowman's scarf.'

Lisa laughed as Oliver removed from his collar the wet snow of the snowball she had just thrown at him, quickly darting out of the way as he bent down mock-threateningly to make a retaliatory snowball of his own.

She had been awoken two hours earlier by the soft thud of a snowball against the bedroom window, Oliver's half of the bed that they had shared all night being empty. Intrigued and amused, she had slid out of bed, wrapping the quilt around her naked body as she'd hurried across to the window. As she'd peered out she'd been able to see beneath the window Oliver standing in the garden next to a huge snowman, a pile of snowballs stacked at his feet.

'At last, sleepyhead, I thought you were never going to wake up,' he'd teased her as she had opened the window, laughing at her as she'd gasped a little at the cold shock of the frosty air.

'I'm not sleepy,' Lisa had corrected him indignantly. 'It's just that I'm…' she had begun, and then had stopped, flushing slightly as she'd acknowledged the real reason why her body was aching so deliciously, why her energy so depleted.

As Oliver had looked silently back at her she had known that he too was remembering just why it was that she had fallen into such a deep sleep in the early hours of the morning.

116

She was remembering the night, the *hours* they had spent together again now as she went to help him brush the snow from his collar, the scent of him, overlaid by the crisp, fresh smell of the snow, completely familiar to her now and yet at the same time still headily erotic.

When previously she had read of women being aroused by the body smell of their lover she had wrinkled her own nose just a little fastidiously, never imagining that there would ever come a time when she not only knew just how those women had felt but also actively wanted—no, *needed,* she corrected herself as her stomach muscles clenched on a weakening surge of emotion—to bury her face against her lover's body and breathe his scent, to trace the outline of his bones, his muscles, absorb the texture of his flesh and the whole living, breathing essence of him.

'It's too soon for this...for us...' she had whispered shakily last night in the aftermath of their second loving. 'We can't be...'

'Falling in love,' Oliver had supplied for her, and had challenged her softly between kisses. 'Why not? People do.

'What is it you're really afraid of, Lisa?' he had asked her later still, after his mouth had caressed every inch of her body, driven her to unimaginable heights of ecstasy and he had whispered to her that she was everything he had ever dreamed of finding in a woman...everything he'd begun to think he would never find, and she had tensed in his arms, suddenly afraid to let herself respond to him as her senses were urging her to do, to throw caution to the wind to tell him what she was feeling.

'I'm afraid of this,' she had whispered huskily back, 'of you...'

'Of me?' He held her slightly away from him, frowning

at her in the darkness. 'Look, I know the circumstances surrounding our initial meeting weren't exactly auspicious, and yes, I agree, I did rather come the heavy, but to be confronted with Piers within thirty minutes of my plane landing from New York after a delay of over five hours and to discover what he'd done—'

'No, it's not that,' Lisa assured him quickly. She was fully aware now that the arrogance that she had believed she had seen in him was simply part of a protective mask behind which he hid his real personality. 'It's us…us together,' she told him, searching for the right words to express her feelings. 'I'm afraid that…everything's happening so fast. And it's not…I'm not…

'This isn't how I ever thought it would be for me,' she told him simply in the end. 'I never imagined I could feel so…that I could…' She paused, fumbling for the words and blushed a little as she tried to tell him how bemused, how shocked, almost, she still was by the intensity not just of his desire for her but of her own for him. It was so out of character for her, she told him, so unexpected…

'So unwanted,' he guessed shrewdly.

'It isn't how I thought my life was going to be,' she persisted. 'None of it seems quite real, and I'm afraid. I don't know if I can sustain this level of emotional intensity, Oliver… I feel like a child who has been handed a Christmas gift so far outside its expectations that it daren't believe it's actually got it. I'm afraid of letting myself believe because I'm afraid of the pain I'll suffer if…if it proves not to be real after all.'

'Don't you think I feel exactly the same way?' Oliver challenged her.

'You've been in love before,' she told him quietly. 'You've experienced this kind of sexual intimacy…sexual ecstasy before, but I—'

'No.' He shook his head decisively. 'Yes, I'm more sexually experienced than you are, but *this*… Take my word for it, Lisa—this is something different…something special.

'Look,' he added when she said nothing. 'With all this snow, there's no way either of us can leave here now until it thaws; let's use the time to be together, to get to know one another, to give our feelings for one another a chance. Let's suspend reality, if you like, for a few days and just allow ourselves to feel instead of questioning, doubting…'

He had made it all sound so easy, and it was easy, Lisa acknowledged now as his arms closed around her. Too easy… That was the trouble.

Already after only a few short, fateful hours she was finding it hard to imagine how she had ever lived without him and even harder to imagine how she could ever live without him in the future. It would be so easy simply to close her eyes, close her mind to her thoughts and concentrate instead on her feelings. She could feel her heart starting to thump heavily with the intensity of her emotions.

'Stop worrying,' Oliver whispered against her mouth, correctly guessing what she was thinking. 'Everything's going to be fine. We're going to be fine.'

'This really is the best Christmas I have ever had,' she told him huskily ten minutes later as he lifted his mouth from hers.

'*You* are the best Christmas I have ever had,' Oliver responded. 'The best Christmas I ever will have.'

In the end they had four full days together, held for three of them in a captivity from which neither of them truly wanted to escape by the icy frost that kept the roads snowbound. And during those four days Lisa quickly discovered how wrong she had been in her original assessment of Oliver as being arrogantly uncaring.

He did care, and very deeply, about those who were closest to him but, as he freely admitted, the loss of his mother whilst he had still been so young had made him cautious about allowing others to get too close to him too quickly.

'But of course there are exceptions to every rule,' he had told her huskily, 'and *you* are my exception.'

She had given up protesting then that it was too soon for them to be in love. What was the point in denying what she knew she felt about him?

'I still can't believe that this...that we...that it's all really happening,' she whispered to Oliver on the fourth morning, when the thaw finally set in, her voice low and hushed, as though she was half-afraid of even putting her doubts into words.

'It *is* happening,' Oliver reassured her firmly, 'and it's going to go on happening for the rest of our lives.'

They were outside, Lisa watching as Oliver chopped logs to replace those they had used. Dressed in jeans and a black T-shirt, he had already discarded the checked woollen shirt that he had originally been wearing, the muscles and tendons on his upper arms revealed by the upward swing of the axe as he chopped the thick fir trunks into neatly quartered logs.

There was something about watching a man engaged in this kind of hard physical activity that created a feminine frisson of awareness of his masculinity, Lisa acknowledged as Oliver paused to wipe the sweat from his skin. She didn't want this special time that they were sharing to come to an end, she admitted. She was afraid of what might happen when it did. Everything had happened so fast—too fast?

'Nearly finished,' Oliver told her, mistaking the reason for her silence. 'I should be back from New York by the end of the week,' he added as Lisa bent down to retrieve the logs that he had already cut and carry them over to where the others were neatly stacked.

Lisa already knew that he was booked on a flight to New York to complete some protracted and difficult business talks he had begun before Christmas—the reason he had been so irritable and uncompromising the first time they had met, he had explained to her.

'I wish I didn't have to go,' he added, 'but at least we'll be able to spend New Year's Eve together and then... When are your parents due back from Japan?'

'Not until the end of February,' Lisa told him.

'That long.' He put down the axe and demanded hastily, 'Come here.'

Automatically Lisa walked towards him. The hand he extended to cup the side of her face and caress her skin smelled of freshly cut wood and felt slightly and very, very sensually abrasive, and the small shiver that ran through her body as he touched her had nothing to do with being cold.

'I could take some leave at the end of January and we could fly out to Japan together to see them then...'

Lisa knew what he was suggesting and her heart gave a fierce bound. So far they had not talked seriously about the future. Oliver had attempted to do so but on each occasion she had forestalled him, not wanting to do or say anything that might destroy the magic of what they were sharing, fearing that by allowing reality and practicality into their fragile, self-created world they might damage it. Their relationship, their love was so different from anything she had ever imagined experiencing or wanting to experience that part of her was still half-afraid to trust it…half of her?

And besides, she had already written to her parents to tell them that she and Henry would be getting engaged at Christmas and, whilst she suspected that they would never have been particularly keen on the idea of having Henry for a son-in-law, she felt acutely self-conscious about suddenly informing them that she had fallen head over heels in love with someone else.

It was so out of character for her, and the mere thought of having to confess her feelings for Oliver to anyone else made her feel defensive and vulnerable. She had always taken such a pride in being sensible and level-headed, in making carefully thought-out and structured decisions about her life. She wasn't sure how she herself really felt about this new aspect to her personality yet, never mind being ready to expose it to anyone else.

'What's wrong?' Oliver asked her as he felt her tensing against his touch. 'You don't seem very happy with the idea of me meeting your parents.'

'It's not that,' Lisa denied. There was, she had discovered, an unexpected corner of vulnerability in him which she suspected sprang from the loss of his mother—something that, if not exactly a fear of losing those close to him, certainly made him slightly more masculinely possessive than she would have expected in such an otherwise controlled and strongly emotionally grounded man. And it was, at least in part, because of this vulnerability that she had felt unable to tell him of her own fears and uncertainties.

'No? Then what exactly is it? Or is that yet another subject you don't want to discuss?' Oliver asked her sarcastically as he released her and picked up the axe, hefting it, raising it and then bringing it down on the log that he had just positioned with a force that betrayed his pent-up feelings.

Dismayed, Lisa watched him. What could she say? How could she explain without angering him still further? How could she explain to him what she felt when she truthfully didn't fully understand those feelings herself?

'It isn't that I don't want you to meet them,' she insisted. 'It's just…well, they don't even know yet that Henry and I aren't…' She knew immediately that she had said the wrong thing and winced as she witnessed the fury with which Oliver sliced into the unresisting wood, splitting it with one unbelievably powerful blow, the muscles in his arms cording and bunching as he tightened his grip on the axe.

'You're saying that they'd prefer you to be marrying Henry, is that it?' he suggested dangerously.

'No, of course they wouldn't,' Lisa denied impatiently. 'And besides, I'm old enough to be able to make up my own mind about who I want to commit myself to.'

'Now we're coming to it, aren't we?' Oliver told her, throwing down the axe and confronting her angrily, his hands on his hips, the faded fabric of his jeans stretching tautly against his thighs.

Just the sight of him made her body ache, Lisa acknowledged, but physical desire, sexual desire, could surely never be enough to build an enduring relationship on? And certainly it was not what she had envisaged building a lifetime's commitment on.

'It's not your parents who might reject me, is it, Lisa? It's you… Despite everything that has happened, all that we've shared.'

'No, that isn't true,' Lisa denied.

'Isn't it?' Oliver bit out grimly as he turned away from her to pick up another large chunk of wood.

Numbly Lisa watched him manhandling it onto the trestles that he was using to support the fir trunks whilst he chopped them into more easily manageable pieces. Above them the sky had started to cloud over, obliterating the bright promise of the morning's sunshine, making her feel shivery and inadequately protected from the nasty, raw little wind which had sprung up, even in the fine wool jacket she was wearing.

The weather, she recognised miserably, was very much only echoing what was happening to them—the bright promise of what they had shared was being threatened by the ominous thunderclouds furrowing Oliver's forehead and her own fear that what he had claimed he felt for her might prove too ephemeral to last.

After all, wasn't the classic advice always to treat falling in love too quickly and too passionately with caution and suspicion? Wasn't it an accepted rationale that good love—real love—needed time to grow and didn't just happen overnight?

As she watched Oliver silently releasing his anger on the wood, his jaw hardening a little bit more with each fierce blow of the axe, Lisa knew that she couldn't blame him for what he was feeling, but surely he could understand that it wasn't easy for her either? She was not programmed mentally for the kind of thing that had happened to her with him; she had not been prepared for it either, not...

'There's no need for you to stay.'

Lisa stared at Oliver as she heard the harsh words, the cutting edge to his voice reminding her more of the man she had first met than the lover she had become familiar with over the last few precious days.

'The wind's getting cold and you're shivering,' he added when she continued to stare mutely at him. 'You might as well go back inside; I've nearly finished anyway.'

He meant that there was no need for her to stay outside and wait for him, Lisa realised, and not that she might as well leave him and start her return journey home, as she had first imagined.

The relief that filled her was only temporary, though. Didn't the fact that she had so easily made such a mistake merely confirm what her sense of caution was already trying to make her understand—that she didn't really *know* Oliver, that no matter how compatible they might be in bed out of it there were still some very large and very important gaps in their knowledge of each other?

Quietly she turned away from him and started to walk back towards the house. Behind her she heard the sound of the axe hitting a fresh piece of wood. She had almost reached the house when she heard Oliver calling her name. Stopping, she turned to watch him warily as he came running towards her.

As he reached her he took hold of her, wrapping her in his arms, telling her fiercely, 'God, Lisa, I'm such a… I'm sorry…the last thing I want us to do is fight, especially when we've got so little time left… Lisa?'

As she looked up at him he cupped her face in his hands, his thumbs caressing her skin, his hair tousled from the wind, his eyes dark with emotion.

Standing close to him like this, feeling the fierce beat of his heart and the heat of his body, breathing in the scent of him, unable to resist the temptation to lift her hand and rub away the streak of dried earth on his cheek, to feel already the beginning of the growth of his beard on his jaw which he had shaved only that morning, Lisa acknowledged that she might just as well have downed a double helping of some fatally irresistible aphrodisiac.

'Lisa…'

His voice was lower now, huskier, more questioning, and she knew that the shudder she could feel going through him had nothing to do with the after-effects of the punishing force he had used to cut up the logs.

She was the one who was responsible for that weakness, for that look in his eyes, that hardness in his body, and she knew that she was responding to it, as unable to deny him as he was her, her body nestling closer to his, her head lifting, her lips parting as he started to kiss her, tenderly at first and then with increasing passion.

'I can't bear the thought of losing you,' he whispered to her minutes later, his voice husky and raw with emotion. 'But you don't seem so concerned. What is it, Lisa…? Why won't—?'

'It's too soon, Oliver, too early,' Lisa protested, interrupting him, knowing that if she didn't stand her ground now, if she allowed her brain to be swayed not just by his emotions but by her own as well, it would be oh, so fatally easy, standing with him like this now, held in his arms, to believe that nothing but this mattered—it would be too late, and there would be no one but herself to blame if at some future date she discovered…

'I could make you commit yourself to me,' Oliver warned her, his mood changing as his earlier impatience returned. 'I could take you to bed now and show you…'

'Yes, you could,' Lisa agreed painfully. 'But can't you see, Oliver…? Please try to understand,' she begged him. 'It isn't that I don't love you or want you; it's just that… this…this…us…isn't how I envisaged it would be for me. You're just not the kind of man I—'

'You mean that I'm not Henry,' Oliver supplied harshly for her, his arms dropping back to his sides as he stepped back from her.

Lisa closed her eyes. Here we go again, she thought tiredly. She had meant one thing and Oliver had taken the words to mean something completely different—just as she had misunderstood him earlier when she had thought he was telling her to leave. And if they could misunderstand one another so easily what real chance did they have of developing the harmonious, placid relationship that she had always believed she needed? Some people enjoyed quarrels, fights, emotional highs and lows, but she just was not one of them.

'I don't want to fight with you, Oliver,' she told him quietly now. 'You must know that you have no possible reason to feel…to think that I want you to be Henry…'

'Haven't I?' he demanded bitterly. 'Why not? After all, you were prepared to marry him. Wanted to marry him… Wanted to so much in fact that you were prepared to let his mother browbeat and bully you and—'

'That's not true,' Lisa interrupted him swiftly. 'Look, Oliver, please,' she protested, spreading her hands in a gesture of emotive pleading for his temperance and understanding. 'Please… I can't talk. I don't want us to argue…not now, when everything has been so…perfect, so special and—'

'So perfect and special in fact that you don't want to continue it,' Oliver cut across her bitterly.

'You've given me the most wonderful Christmas I've ever had,' she whispered huskily, 'in so many different ways, in all the best of ways. Please don't spoil that for me…for us…now. I need time, though, Oliver; we *both* need time. It's just…'

'Just what?' he demanded, his eyes still ominously watchful and hard. 'Just that you're still not quite sure…that a part of you still thinks that perhaps Henry—?'

'No. Never,' Lisa insisted fiercely, adding more emotionally, 'That's a horrible thing to say. Do you really think that if I had any doubts about…about wanting you, that I would have—?'

'I didn't say that you don't prefer me in bed,' Oliver told her curtly, correctly guessing what she had been about to say, 'but the implication was there none the less—in the very words you used to describe what you wanted from marriage the first time we discussed it, the fact that you've been so reluctant to accept what's happening between us…the fact that you don't seem to want me to meet your parents.'

'You've got it all wrong,' she protested. 'My feelings…my doubts,' she amended when he snorted derisively over her use of the word 'feelings', 'they…they don't have anything to do with you. It isn't because I don't…because I don't care; in fact—'

'Oh, no,' Oliver told her cynically, not allowing her to finish what she was saying.

'It's me…not you,' Lisa told him. 'I've always been so cautious, so…so sensible… This…this falling in love with you—well, it's just so out of character for me and I'm afraid.'

'You're afraid of what?' he demanded.

The wind had picked up and was flattening his T-shirt against his body, but, unlike her, he seemed impervious to the cold and Lisa had to resist the temptation to creep closer to him and beg him to wrap his arms protectively around her to hold her and warm her.

'I don't know,' she answered, lifting her eyes to meet his as she added, 'I'm just afraid.'

How could she tell him without adding to his anger that a good part of what she feared was that he might fall out of love with her as quickly as he had fallen in love with her? He was quite obviously in no mood to understand her vulnerability and fear and she knew that he would take her comment as an indication that she did not fully trust him, an excuse or a refusal to commit herself to him completely.

'Please don't let's quarrel,' she repeated, reaching out her hand to touch his arm. His skin felt warm, the muscles taut beneath her touch, and the sensation of his flesh beneath her own even in this lightest of touches overwhelmed her with such an intense wave of desire that she had to bite down hard on her bottom lip to prevent herself crying out her need to him.

They were still standing outside, and through the windows she could see the tree that he had decorated for her, the magic he had created for her.

'Oh, Oliver,' she whispered shakily.

'Let's go inside,' he responded gruffly. 'You're getting cold and I'm... You're right,' he added rawly. 'We shouldn't be spoiling what little time we've got left.'

'It is still Christmas, isn't it?' Lisa asked him semi-pleadingly as he turned to open the door for her.

'Yes, it's still Christmas,' he agreed, but there was a look in his eyes that made her heart ache and warned her that Christmas could not be made to last for ever—like their love?

Was *that* why she doubted it—him? Because it seemed too perfect, too wonderful...too precious to be real?

They said their private goodbyes very early in the morning in the bedroom they had shared for the last four nights, and for Lisa the desolation which swept over her at the thought that for the next two nights to come she would not be sleeping within the protection of his arms, next to the warmth and intimacy of his body, only confirmed what in her heart of hearts she already knew.

It was already too late for her to protest that it was too soon for them to fall in love, too late to cling to the sensible guidelines that she had laid down for herself to live her life by—the sensible, cautious, pain-free guidelines which in reality had been submerged and obliterated days ago—from the first time that Oliver had kissed her, if she was honest—and there were tears in her eyes as she clung to him and kissed him.

What was she doing? she asked herself helplessly. What did guidelines, common sense, caution or even potential future heartache matter when they had this, when they had one another; when by simply opening her mouth and speaking honestly and from her heart she could tell Oliver what she was feeling and that she had changed her mind, that the last thing she wanted was to be apart from him?

'Oliver...' she began huskily.

But he shook his head and placed his fingertips over her mouth and told her softly, 'It's all right—I know. And I do understand. You're quite right—we do need time apart to think things through clearly. I've been guilty of trying to bully you, to coerce you into committing yourself to me too soon. Love—real love—doesn't disappear or vanish when two people aren't physically together; if anything, it strengthens and grows.

'I didn't mean to put pressure on you, Lisa, to rush you. We both have lives, commitments, career responsibilities to deal with. The weather has given us a special opportunity to be together, to discover one another, but the snow, like Christmas, can't last for ever.

'If I'd managed to get you to come to New York with me as I wanted, I probably wouldn't have got a stroke of work done,' he told her wryly. 'And a successful conclusion to these negotiations is vitally important for the future of the business—not just for me personally but for everyone else who is involved in it as well. Oh, and by the way, don't worry about not taking your car now; I'll make arrangements to have it picked up and returned to you later. I don't want you driving with the roads like this.'

Oliver had already told her about a large American corporation's desire to buy out part of his business, leaving him free to concentrate on the aspects of it he preferred and giving him the option to work from home.

'If Piers goes ahead and marries Emma, as he's planning, he's going to need the security of knowing he has a good financial future ahead of him. Naturally the Americans want to get the business as cheaply as they can.' He had started to frown slightly, and Lisa guessed that his thoughts were not so much on her and their relationship but on the heavy responsibility that lay ahead of him.

Her throat ached with pain; she desperately wanted to reach out to him and be taken in his arms, to tell him that she had made a mistake, that she didn't want to let him go even for a few short days. But how could she now after what he had said?

Suddenly, illuminatingly, she realised that what she had feared was not loving him but losing him. The space that she had told herself she needed—they both needed—had simply been a trick her brain had played on her, a coping mechanism to help her deal with the pain of being without his love.

Quietly she bowed her head. 'Thank you,' Lisa whispered to him as tears blurred her eyes.

*   *   *

'Are you sure there's nothing else you want…a book or…?'

Lisa shook her head. 'You've already bought me all these magazines,' she reminded Oliver huskily, indicating the pile of glossies that he had insisted on buying for her when they'd reached the station and which he was still carrying for her, together with her case, as he walked her along the platform to where the train was waiting.

She had tried to protest when he had insisted on buying her a first-class ticket but he had refused to listen, shaking his head and telling her, 'That damned independence of yours. Can't you at least let me do something for you, even if it's only to ensure that you travel home in some degree of comfort?'

She had, of course, given in then. How could she not have done so? How could she have refused not just his generosity but, she sensed, from the expression in his eyes at least, his desire to protect and cherish her as well?

'Make sure you have something to eat,' he urged her as they reached the train. 'It will be a long journey and…'

And she wouldn't be spending it eating, Lisa thought as he went on talking. Nor would she be doing anything more than flipping through the expensive magazines he had bought her. No, what she would be doing would be trying to hold back the tears and wishing that she were with him, thinking about him, reliving every single moment they had spent together…

A family—mother, father, three small children—paused to turn round and hug the grandparents; the smallest of them, a fair-haired little boy, clung to his grandmother, telling her, 'I don't want to go, Nana… Why can't you come home with us…?'

'I have to stay here and look after Grandpa,' his grandmother told him, but Lisa could hear the emotion in her voice and see the tears she was trying not to let him see.

Why did loving someone always seem to have to cause so much pain?

'Oh, to be his age and young enough to show what you're feeling,' Oliver murmured under his breath.

'It wouldn't make any difference if I did beg you to come home with me,' Lisa pointed out, trying to sound light-hearted but horribly aware that he must be able to hear the emotion in her voice. 'You'd still have to go to New York. We'd still have to be apart...'

'Yes, but I... At least I'd know that you want me.'

It was too much. What was the point in being sensible and listening to the voice of caution when all she really wanted to do was to be with him, to be held in his arms, to tell him that she loved and wanted him and that all she wanted—all she would ever want or need—was to be loved by him?

He was looking at her...watching...waiting almost.

'Oliver...' She wanted so desperately to tell him how she felt, to hear him tell her that he understood her vulnerability and that he understood all the things she hadn't been able to bring herself to say, but the guard was already starting to close the carriage doors, advancing towards them, asking her frowningly, 'Are you travelling, miss, because if so...?'

'Yes... Yes...'

'You'd better get on,' Oliver advised her.

She didn't want to go. She didn't want to leave him. Lisa could feel herself starting to panic, wanting to cling to him, wanting him to hold her...reassure her, but he was already starting to move away from her, lifting her case onto the train for her, bending his head to kiss her fiercely but far, far too briefly.

She had no alternative. She had to go.

Numbly Lisa stepped up into the train. The guard slammed the door. She let down the window but the train was already starting to move.

'Oliver. Oliver, I love you...'

Had he heard her, or had the train already moved too far away? She could still see him...watching her...just.

Oliver waited until the train had completely disappeared before turning to leave, even though Lisa had long since gone from view. If only he didn't have these damned negotiations to conclude in New York. He wanted to be with Lisa, wanted to find a way to convince her.

Of what...? That she loved him?

Lisa pushed open the door of her flat and removed the pile of mail which had accumulated behind it. Despite the central heating, the flat felt cold and empty, but then that was perhaps because *she* felt cold and empty, Lisa recognised wryly—cold without Oliver's warmth beside her and empty without him...his love.

In her sitting room the invitation she had received from her friend Alison before Christmas to her annual New Year's Eve party was still propped up on the mantelpiece, reminding her that she would have to ring Alison and cancel her acceptance. The telephone started to ring, breaking into the silence. Her heart thumping, she picked up the receiver.

'You got home safely,then.'

'Oliver.'

Suddenly she was smiling. Suddenly the world was a warmer, brighter, happier place.

'Lisa, I've been thinking about what you said about us not rushing into things...about taking our time...'

Something about the sombreness in his voice checked the happiness bubbling up inside her, turning the warmth at hearing his voice to icy foreboding.

'Oliver…'

Lisa wanted to tell him how much she was missing him, how much she loved him, but suddenly she wasn't sure if that was what he wanted to hear.

'Look, Lisa, I've got to go. They've just made the last call for my flight…' The phone line went dead.

Silently she replaced the receiver. Had it really only been this morning that he had held her in his arms and told her how much he loved her? Suddenly, frighteningly, it was hard to believe that that was true. It seemed like another world, another lifetime, already in the past… over…as ephemeral as the fleeting magic of Christmas itself.

'No…it's not true,' she whispered painfully under her breath. 'He loves me; he said so.' But somehow her re-assurance lacked conviction.

Even though she had been the one to insist that it was too soon for them to make a public commitment to one another, that they both needed time, she wished passionately now that Oliver had overruled her, that he had confirmed the power and strength of his love for her. How? By refusing to let her leave him?

What was the matter with her? Lisa asked herself impatiently. Could she really be so illogical, saying one thing, wanting another, torn between her emotions and her intelligence, unable to harmonise the two, keeping them in separate compartments in much the same way as Oliver had accused her of doing with sex and marriage?

Had she after all any real right to feel chagrined at the sense of urgency, almost of impatience in his voice as he had ended his brief call? She had, she admitted, during the last few days grown accustomed to being the sole focus of his attention, and now, when it was plain that he had something else on his mind...

She frowned, aware that instead of feeling relief when he had told her that he agreed that they did need time to think things over she had actually felt—*still* felt—hurt and afraid, abandoned, vulnerably aware that he might be having second thoughts about his feelings for her.

How ironic if he had—especially since she had spent almost the entire journey home dwelling on the intensity of her own feelings and allowing herself to believe...

It would only be a few days before they were together again, she reminded herself firmly. Oliver had promised that he would be back for the New Year and that they would spend it together. There would be plenty of time for them to talk, for her to tell him how much she loved and missed him.

Even so... Sternly she made herself pick up her case and carry it through to her bedroom to unpack. A small, tender smile curled her mouth as she picked up the stocking that she had so carefully packed—the stocking that Oliver had left for her to find on Christmas morning.

There were other sentimental mementoes as well—a small box full of pine needles off the tree, still carrying its rich scent, the baubles that Oliver had removed from it and hung teasingly on her ears one night after dinner, a cracker that they had pulled together... She touched each and every one of them gently.

Through what he had done for her to make her Christmas so special Oliver had revealed a tender, compassionate, emotional side to his nature that made it impossible for her not to love him, not to respond to the love he had shown her. *Had* shown her?

Stop it, she warned herself. Stop creating problems that don't exist. Determinedly, she started to unpack the rest of her things.

CHAPTER EIGHT

IT WAS New Year's Eve and almost three o'clock in the afternoon, and still Oliver hadn't rung. Lisa glared at the silent telephone, mentally willing it to ring. She had been awake since six o'clock in the morning and gradually, as the hours had ticked by, her elation and excitement had changed to edgy apprehension.

Where *was* Oliver? *Why* hadn't he been in touch? Was he just going to arrive at her door without any warning so that he could surprise her, instead of telephoning beforehand as she had anticipated?

Nervously she smoothed down the skirt of her dress and just managed to restrain herself from checking her reflection in the mirror for the umpteenth time.

She had spent most of her free time the previous day cleaning the flat and shopping for tonight. The lilies she had bought with such excitement and pleasure were now beginning to overpower her slightly with their scent. The champagne waiting in the fridge was surely chilled to perfection; the special meal she had cooked last night now only required reheating. Oliver might be planning to take her out somewhere for dinner, but the last thing she wanted was to have to share him with anyone else.

And even if she had dressed elegantly enough to dine at the most exclusive restaurant in town and her hair was immaculately shiny, her make-up subtly enhancing her features, it was not to win the approval of the public at large that she had taken such pains with her appearance, or donned the sheer, silky stockings, or bought that outrageously expensive and far too frothily impractical new silk underwear. Oh, no!

Where *was* Oliver? Why hadn't he been in touch? The small dining table which was all her flat could accommodate was lovingly polished and set with her small collection of good silver and crystal—unlike Oliver's grandparents she did not possess a matching set of a dozen of anything, and her parents—peripatetic gypsy souls that they were—would have laughed at the very idea of burdening themselves with such possessions.

However, through her work Lisa had developed a very good eye for a bargain, and the small pieces that she had lovingly collected over the years betrayed, she knew, the side of her nature that secretly would have enjoyed nothing better than using her dormant housewifely talents to garner a good old-fashioned bridal bottom drawer.

To help pass the time she tried to imagine Oliver's eventual arrival, her heartbeat starting to pick up and then race as she visualised herself opening the door to him and seeing him standing there, reaching out for her, holding her, telling her how much he had missed her and loved her.

Oliver, where are you? Where are you…?

Almost on cue the telephone started to ring—so much on cue in fact that for several seconds Lisa could only stand and listen to the shrill sound of it, before realising that she wasn't merely imagining it and that it had actually rung, was actually ringing.

A little to her own disgust she realised as she picked up the receiver that her hand was actually trembling slightly.

'Lisa…'

Her heart sank.

'Oliver…where are you? When will you—?'

'Bad news, I'm afraid.' Oliver cut her off abruptly. 'I'm not going to be able to make it after all; I'm stuck in New York and—'

'What?'

There was no way Lisa could conceal her feelings—shock, disappointment, almost disbelief, and even anger was sharpening her voice as she tried to take in what he was telling her. A horrid feeling of sick misery and despair was beginning to fill her but Lisa's pride wouldn't let her give in to it, although her hand was clenched so tightly on the receiver that her skin was sharp white over her knuckles.

'I'm still in New York,' she heard Oliver telling her, his voice curt and almost—so her sensitive ears told her—hostile as he added brusquely, 'I know it's not what I'd planned but there's simply nothing I can do…'

Nothing he could do or nothing he *wanted* to do?

All the doubts, the fears, the insecurities and the regrets that Lisa had been holding at bay ever since they had had to part suddenly began to multiply overwhelming and virtually obliterating all her self-confidence, her belief in Oliver's love. She had been right to be mistrustful of his assurances, his promises; she had been right to be wary of a love that had sprung into being so easily and now, it seemed, could just as easily disappear.

'Lisa?' Oliver said sharply.

'Yes, I'm still here.'

It was an effort to keep her voice level, not to give in to the temptation to beg and plead for some words of reassurance and love, but somehow she managed to stop herself from doing so, even though the effort made her jaw ache and her muscles lock in painful tension.

'You do understand, don't you?' he was asking her.

Oh, yes, she understood. How she understood.

'Yes,' she agreed indistinctly, her voice chilly and distant as she tried to focus on salvaging her pride instead of giving in to her pain. 'I understand perfectly.'

She wasn't going to weaken and let herself ask when he would be coming home, or why he had changed his mind…so obviously changed his mind.

Before he could say any more and before, more importantly, she could break down and reveal how hurt and let down she was feeling, Lisa fibbed tersely, 'I must go; there's someone at the door.' And without waiting to hear any more she replaced the receiver. She must not cry, she *would* not cry, she warned herself fiercely.

In the mirror she caught sight of her reflection; her face was paper-white, her eyes huge, revealing all too clearly what she was feeling, the contrast between her carefully made-up face and the misery in her eyes somehow almost pathetically grotesque.

Her flat, her clothes, her whole person, she decided angrily, made her feel like some modern-day Miss Havisham, decked out all ready for the embrace of a man who had deserted her. The thought was unbearable. She couldn't stay here, not now…not when everything around her reminded her of just how stupid she had been. Why, even now she was still emotionally trying to find excuses for Oliver, to convince herself that she had overreacted and that he felt as bad as she did and that he wasn't having second thoughts.

Alison's invitation was still on her mantelpiece. She reached for the telephone.

'Of course you can still come, you didn't need to ask,' Alison reproved her when she'd explained briefly that there had been a change in her plans and that she was now free for the evening. 'What happened? Has Henry—?'

'It's all off with Henry,' Lisa interrupted her.

There hadn't been time to explain to Alison just what had happened when she had telephoned her to ask her how her skiing holiday had gone and cancel her acceptance to her party and now Lisa was grateful for this omission, even though it did give her a small twinge of guilt when Alison immediately and staunchly, like the good friend she was, declared, 'He's let you down, has he? Well, you know my feelings about him, Lisa. I never thought he was the right man for you. Look, why don't you come over now? Quite a few people are coming early to help but we can always use another pair of hands.'

'Oh, Alison…'

Ridiculously, after the way she had managed to control herself when she'd been speaking to Oliver, she could feel her eyes starting to fill with tears at her friend's sturdy kindness.

'Forget him.' Alison advised her. 'He's not worth it… he never was. You may not believe me now, but, I promise you, you are better off without him, Lisa. Now go and put your glad rags on and get yourself over here… Are we going to party!'

As she replaced the telephone receiver Lisa told herself that Alison's words applied just as much to Oliver as they did to Henry, although for very different reasons.

Forget him. Yes, that was what she must do.

Tonight, with the old year ending and the new one beginning, she must find a way of beginning it without Oliver at her side. Without him in her life.

On impulse she went into the kitchen and removed the champagne from the fridge, pouring herself a glass and quickly drinking it. It was just as well that Alison's flat was within reasonably easy walking distance, she decided as the fizzy alcohol hit her empty, emotionally tensed stomach.

There was no need for her to get changed; the little black dress she was wearing—had put on for Oliver—was very suitable for a New Year's Eve celebration. All she had to do was redo her make-up to remove those tell-tale signs of her tears.

She poured herself a second glass of champagne, re-alising too late that instead of filling the original glass, which still had some liquid in the bottom, she had actually filled the empty one—Oliver's glass. Grimacing slightly, she picked them both up and carried them through to her bedroom with her, drinking from one before placing them both on the table beside her bed and then quickly repairing her make-up.

In New York Piers frowned as he walked into his cousin's hotel suite and saw Oliver seated in a chair, staring at the telephone.

'Is something wrong?' he asked him. His curiosity had been alerted earlier by the fact that Oliver had been ex-tremely impatient to bring their discussions with the Americans to a conclusion, stating that he had to return to England without explaining why. Piers had happened to be looking at him when they had heard the news that the talks would have to continue. Oliver had been none too pleased.

'No,' Oliver responded shortly. Why had Lisa been so distant with him—so uninterested, so curt to the point of dismissal? She had every right to be angry and even upset about the fact that he had had to change their plans, but she had actually sounded as though she hadn't wanted to see him.

'Well, Jack Hywell is anxious to get on with the negotiations,' Piers told him. 'Apparently he's due to take his kids away the day after tomorrow, which is why he wants to take the discussion through the New Year period.

'Oh, by the way, Emma rang me this morning. She's been up to Yorkshire, and whilst she was up there she heard that Henry is getting married. Apparently, he's marrying someone he's known for a while. I must admit I'm surprised his mother finally sanctioned a marriage. Still, good luck to him, I say, and to her.

'What is it?' he asked Oliver. 'Hey, Oliver, watch it…' he warned his cousin as he watched the latter's hand clench tightly on the glass he was holding. 'Look, I know how much pressure these negotiations are putting you under,' he commiserated, 'but with any luck they'll be over soon now, and… Oliver, where are you going?'

'Home,' Oliver told him brusquely.

'Home? But you *can't*,' Piers protested. 'The negotiations.'

Oliver snarled at him, telling him in no uncertain terms what should be done with the negotiations and leaving the room.

Piers stared open-mouthed at his departing back. Oliver hardly ever swore, and he certainly never used the kind of language that Piers had just heard him use. He was normally so laid back… Something was obviously wrong, but what?

'Ugh?'

Reluctantly Lisa opened her eyes. What *was* that noise? Was someone really banging a hammer inside her head or was someone at the door?

Someone was at the door. Flinging back the duvet, she reached for her robe, wincing at both the pain in her aching head and the state of her bedroom—clothes scattered everywhere in mute evidence of the decidedly unsober state in which she had returned to her flat in the early hours of the morning. She had never had a strong head for alcohol, she admitted to herself, and Alison's punch had been lethal. She would have to ring her later and thank her for the party, and for everything else as well.

'Don't even think about it,' Alison had advised Lisa drolly the previous evening after she had determinedly rescued her from the very earnest young man who had buttonholed her.

'He's even worse than Henry,' she had warned Lisa, rolling her eyes. 'He still lives with his parents and his hobby is collecting beetles or something equally repulsive. I only invited him because it was the only way I could escape from his mother. I know how much you like a lame dog, but really, Lisa, there are limits. Has he invited you round to look at his beetle collection yet?' she asked wickedly, making Lisa laugh in spite of herself.

'That's better,' she had approved, adding more seriously, 'I hadn't realised that Henry meant quite so much to you, but—'

'It isn't Henry,' Lisa had started to say, but someone had come up and dragged Alison away before she could explain properly and after that, rather than cause her friend any more concern, she had forced herself to be more enthusiastic and convivial, the result of which was her aching head this morning. No, this afternoon, she acknowledged as she saw in horror what time it was.

The doorbell was still ringing. Whoever it was was very determined. What if Oliver had changed his mind and come back after all? What if…?

Her fingers were trembling so much that she could hardly tie the belt of her robe. Quickly she hurried into the hallway, leaving her bedroom door open, and went to open the door, her heart beating so fast that she could hardly breathe.

Only it wasn't Oliver, it was Henry.

Henry!

Dumbly Lisa stood to one side as he walked self-importantly into her flat without bothering to close the door. Henry—what on earth was he doing here? What did he want? He was the last person Lisa wanted to see.

She pressed her fingers to her throbbing head. How could she have been stupid enough to think it might be Oliver? So much for all her promises to herself last night, as they'd all waited for midnight to come and the new year to start, that she would put him completely out of her mind and her heart.

'Henry, what is it? What are you doing here? What do you want?' she demanded shortly.

As she watched him breathe in then puff out his cheeks disapprovingly when he looked at her, she wondered how on earth she could ever have contemplated marrying him, how she had ever been so blind to the true reality of his character, his small-mindedness and fussiness, his lack of humour and generosity. Disapproval was written all over him as he looked at her.

'Surely you weren't still in bed?' he criticised her.

'No, I always dress like this. Of course I was still in bed,' Lisa snapped, losing her patience with him. She could hear him clearing his throat, the sound grating on her over-stretched nerves. If she had known it was only Henry at the door she would have stayed where she was.

'Mother thought I should come and see you,' he told her.

Lisa stared at him in angry disbelief.

'Your mother wanted you to come and see *me*... What on earth for? I would have thought I was the last person she would want you anywhere near. In fact, if I remember correctly, she said—'

'Er—yes, well…' Henry was flushing slightly as he cut her off. Why had she never noticed that slightly fishy bulge to his eyes when he was under pressure? Lisa wondered distastefully. Why had she never noticed, either, how very like his mother's his features were? She shuddered.

'The thing is, Lisa, that Mother thought I should make the situation absolutely clear to you, and—'

'What situation?' she demanded.

'Well…' Henry tugged at his collar. 'The thing is that I'm getting married to…to someone I've known for some time. She and I… Well, anyway, the wedding will be in June and we're having our official engagement party in February and…'

'And what?' Lisa pressed, irritated, wondering what on earth Henry's engagement and intended marriage had to do with her and why his mother should think she might want to hear about them.

He coughed and told her. 'Well, Mother didn't want there to be any misunderstandings…or embarrassment… She felt that it was best that you knew what was happening just in case you tried…'

Lisa couldn't believe what she was hearing.

'Just in case I tried what?' she demanded with ominous calm. 'Just in case I tried to resuscitate our relationship—is *that* what you're trying to say?' she asked him sharply. 'Is that what your mother is afraid of?'

Did either of them really think…after what had been said, after the accusations which had been made, that she wanted anything…*anything* to do with Henry? Heavens, she wouldn't so much as cross the street to say hello to him now, never mind try to resuscitate a relationship which Oliver had been quite right to tell her she was better off without, and she opened her mouth to tell Henry as much and then closed it again.

There was no point in losing her temper with Henry; rather, she ought to be pitying him.

'Who is the lucky bride-to-be?' she asked him with acid sweetness instead. 'Or can I guess...? Your aunt's god-daughter...?'

She saw from his expression that her guess had been right. Poor girl—Lisa hoped she knew what she was taking on.

'It's all right, Henry,' she reassured him calmly. 'I *do* understand and you are quite safe. In fact I wish you and your wife-to-be every happiness.'

And as she spoke she pulled open her front door and firmly pushed Henry backwards towards it whilst at the same time raising herself on her tiptoes to place her hands on his shoulders and deposit a dismissive and cold con-temptuous kiss on his cheek—just as Oliver crossed the foyer outside her flat and to all intents and purposes saw her with her arms around Henry and kissing him.

There was a second's tense silence as Lisa saw Oliver over Henry's shoulder, his face set in a mask of furious anger, and then Henry was backing away from her and almost scurrying past Oliver as he headed for the stairs, whilst Oliver strode towards her, ignoring him.

'Oliver!' Lisa exclaimed weakly. 'What are *you* doing here? I wasn't expecting you. I thought you were in New York.'

'Very evidently,' Oliver agreed tautly as he slammed the front door behind him, enclosing them both in the suddenly far too small space of her hallway.

'It's just as well your fiancé has decided to leave. I want to have a few words with you... Not very brave of him, though. Some husband he's going to make… When I heard that your engagement was back on I couldn't believe it. I thought there must have been some mistake.'

'There has,' Lisa agreed. If only her head would stop aching, she thought.

'I tried to ring you from the airport,' she heard Oliver tell her.

'I was out at a party,' she responded.

'A party—to celebrate your engagement, no doubt,' he accused her grittily, adding savagely as he suddenly stiffened and looked past her and through her open bedroom door to where the clothes she had discarded the previous evening lay scattered all over the floor, 'Or did you save *that* until you were back here alone with him? My God, and to think I believed you when you told me that sexually he had never meant anything to you, that there had never been anything between you. What else did you lie to me about, Lisa? Not that it matters now…'

'I haven't lied to you,' Lisa protested, reminding him, 'And if anyone should be making any accusations surely it should be me? After all, I'm not the one who promised to be back for New Year's Eve and then broke that promise.'

Furious with herself, she closed her eyes. What on earth had prompted her to say that, to betray to him how much his broken promise had hurt her…how much *he* had hurt her?

'I had no choice,' she heard Oliver telling her angrily, 'but you did, Lisa, and you chose—'

'I chose nothing,' she interrupted him, as angry with him now as he patently was with her.

What right, after all, did he have to come back and make such ridiculous accusations—accusations he must surely know couldn't possibly be true? And how come he could manage to get back *now* when he hadn't been able to do so before?

'No?' Oliver strode past her and walked into her bedroom, demanding dangerously, 'No? Then would you mind explaining to me what the hell has been going on here?' He picked up the half-empty champagne glass that she had abandoned the previous evening and gestured to its now flat contents contemptuously as he · snarled, 'Couldn't he even wait to let you finish this? *His* glass is empty I note…'

His glass?

Indignantly Lisa opened her mouth to put him right, but before she could say anything Oliver demanded savagely, 'It must have been quite some celebration the two of you had. What the hell did he do—tear the clothes off your back? You should have told me that that was what you liked,' he advised her, his voice suddenly dropping dangerously, his eyes glittering as his glance raked her from head to toe. 'I'd no idea your sexual tastes ran to such things. If I had—'

'Oliver, no…' she protested as he reached for her, catching hold of her arm and dragging her towards him as he ignored her angry denial.

'You don't understand,' she said, but he was beyond listening to reason or to any of her explanations, she realised, her heart lurching against her chest wall as she saw the way his gaze raked her, his look a mingling of loathing and desire.

'I think it's you who doesn't understand,' Oliver was correcting her softly, but there was nothing remotely soft about the way he was holding onto her or the way he was watching her. Her body trembled, her toes curling protestingly into the carpet. 'I thought we had something special, you and I… I thought I could believe in you, trust you... Like a fool I thought, when you told me you needed me, that you...

'What is it, what's wrong?' he asked her as he felt her body shiver and his apparent concern almost caught her off guard, until she saw the steely, almost cruel look in his eyes.

'Nothing's wrong,' Lisa denied. 'I just want you to let me go.'

'You're trembling,' Oliver pointed out, still in that same nerve-wrenchingly soft voice. 'And as for letting you go... I will let you go, Lisa, but not until I've reminded you of exactly why you shouldn't be marrying Henry...'

I'm not marrying Henry, Lisa wanted to say, but she only got as far as, 'I'm not—' before Oliver silenced her mouth, coming down hard on hers in a kiss of angry possession.

She tried to resist him and even physically to repel him, her own anger rising to meet his as she alternately tried to push him away and twist herself out of his grasp, but the more she fought to escape, the more her body came into contact with his, and as though something about her furious struggles only added extra fuel to the flames of his anger Oliver responded by propelling her back against the bedroom wall and holding her there with the hard strength of his body whilst he lifted her arms above her head and kept them pinioned there as he continued to brutalise her mouth with the savagery of his punishing kiss.

Lisa could feel his heart thudding heavily against her body, her own racing in frantic counterpoint, her breathing fast and uneven as her anger rose even higher. How dared he treat her like this? All thoughts of trying to explain and pacify him fled as she concentrated all her energy on trying to break free of him.

She could feel the heat coming off his body, the rough abrasion of the fabric of his clothes on her bare skin where her robe had come unfastened. Her mouth felt swollen and bruised from the savagery of his kisses, but there was no fear or panic in her; she recognised only an unfamiliar and fierce desire to match Oliver's fury with her own.

'You want me... Me...' she heard Oliver telling her thickly between plundering kisses.

'No,' she denied, but the sound was smothered by the soft moan that rose up in her throat as her body responded to its physical contact with his. Somehow, against all logic, against everything she herself had always thought she believed in, she was becoming aroused by him and by the furious force of their mutual anger, Lisa recognised. And so was he.

On a wave of shocked despair she closed her eyes, but that only made things worse; the feel of him, the scent of him, the weight of him against her—these were all so familiar to her aching, yearning body that they immediately fed her roaring, feral need, turning her furious attempt to wrench herself free from him into something that even to her came closer to a deliberately sensual indication of her body's need to be possessed by his than a genuine attempt to break free.

Her anger now wasn't just directed at him, it was directed at herself as well, but with it now she could feel a surge of sensual, languid weakness, a heat which seemed to spread irresistibly throughout her body, so that under the hard pressure of Oliver's searing kiss, instead of resisting him, her body turning cold and lifeless in rejection of him, she was actually moving, melting, yielding, moaning softly beneath her breath.

'Lisa, Lisa...' She could hear the responsive urgency in Oliver's voice, feel it in his hands as he released her pinioned arms to push aside her robe and caress her body.

Her anger was still there, Lisa saw as she watched him studying her semi-naked body, and so was his, but somehow it had been transmuted into a form of such intense physical desire that she could barely recognise either herself or him in the two human beings who had suddenly become possessed of such a rage of physical passion.

She had never dreamed that she could feel like this, want like this, react like this, she acknowledged dazedly several minutes later as she cried out beneath Oliver's savage suckling of her breast, clawing at his back in a response born not of anger or pain or fear but rather of a corresponding degree of intensity and compulsion.

And she made the shocking acknowledgement that there was something—some hitherto secret and sensually dark part of her—that actually found pleasure...that actually wanted savagery, a sensation that was only seconds away from actual pain, that a part of her needed this release of her pent-up emotions and desires, that this dark self-created floodtide of their mutual fury and arousal possessed a dangerously addictive alchemy that made her go back for more, made her cling dizzily to him as he wrenched off his clothes and lifted her, still semi-imprisoning her, against the wall.

He entered her with an urgency that could have been demeaning and unwanted and even painful but which was, in fact, so intensely craved and needed by her body that even she was caught off guard by the intensity of her almost instantaneous orgasm and by her inner knowledge that this was how she had wanted him, that part of her had needed that kind of appeasement, as Oliver allowed her to slide slowly down towards the floor.

Shocked, not just at what had happened but by Oliver's behaviour and even more so by her own, Lisa discovered that she was trembling so much that she had to lean against the wall for support. Ignoring the hand that Oliver put out to steady her, she turned away from him. She couldn't bear to look at him, to see the triumph and the contempt she knew would be in his eyes.

'Lisa…'

Whatever it was he was going to say she couldn't bear to listen to it.

'Just go,' she told him woodenly. 'Now… I never want to see you again… Never…'

She could hear her voice starting to rise, feel herself starting to tremble as shock set in. Her face burned scarlet with mortification as she reached for her abandoned robe and pulled it around her body to shield her nakedness as Oliver got dressed in grim-faced silence. Now that it was over she felt sick with disbelief and shock, unable to comprehend how she could have behaved in the way that she had, how she could have been so…so…depraved, how she could have wanted…

'Lisa…'

Oliver was dressed now and standing by the door. A part of her could sense that he too had behaved in a way that was out of character but she didn't want to listen to him. What was the point? He had shown her with damning clarity just what he thought of her.

'No…don't touch me…'

For the first time panic hit her as she saw him turn and start to walk towards her. She couldn't bear him to touch her now, not after…

She could sense him, feel him willing her to look at him but she refused to do so, keeping her face averted from him.

'So that's it, then,' she heard him saying hoarsely. 'It's over…'

'Yes,' she agreed. 'It's over.'

It wasn't until well over an hour after he had gone, after she had cleaned the bedroom from top to bottom, changed the bed, polished every piece of furniture, thrown every item of discarded clothing into the washing machine and worked herself into a furore that she realised that she had never actually told Oliver that she and Henry were not getting married. She gave a small, fatalistic shrug. What did it matter? What did *anything* matter any more after the way the pair of them had destroyed and abused their love?

Their *love*… There had never been any love—at least not on Oliver's side. Only lust; that was all.

Lisa shuddered. How had it happened? How could anger—not just his but, even worse, her own—become so quickly and so fatally transmuted into such an intensity of arousal and desire? Even now she could hardly believe it had happened, that *she* had behaved like that, that she had felt like that.

Later she would mourn the loss of her love; right now all she wanted to do was to forget that the last few hours had ever happened.

CHAPTER NINE

LISA woke up with a start, brought out of her deep, exhausted sleep, which she had fallen into just after the winter dawn had started to lighten the sky, by the shrill bleep of her alarm.

Tiredly she reached out to switch it off. She had spent most of the night lying in bed trying not to think about what had happened—and failing appallingly. Round and round her thoughts had gone until she'd been dizzy with the effort of trying to control them.

Shock, anger—against herself, against Oliver—grief, pain, despair and then anger again had followed in a relentless, going-nowhere circle, her final thought before she had eventually fallen asleep being that she must somehow stop dwelling on what was now past and get on with her life.

Her head ached and her throat felt sore—a sure sign, she suspected, that she was about to go down with a heavy cold. The faint ache in her muscles and her lethargy were due to another cause entirely, of course.

Quickly she averted her gaze from the space on the bedroom wall—the place where Oliver had held her as he…as they… The heat enveloping her body had nothing to do with her head cold, Lisa acknowledged grimly, and nor had the hot colour flooding her face.

It was bad enough that she had actually behaved in such an…an abandoned, yes, almost sexually aggressive way in the first place, but did her memory *have* to keep reminding her of what she had done, torturing her with it?

155

she wondered wretchedly. She doubted that Oliver was tormented by any such feelings of shame and guilt, but then, of course, it was different for a man. A man was allowed to be sexually driven, to express anger and hurt.

But it hadn't been Oliver's behaviour—hurtful though it had been—that had kept her awake most of the night, she acknowledged; it had been her own, and she knew that she would never be able to feel comfortable about what she had done, about the intensity of her passion, her lack of control, her sexuality, unchecked as it had been by the softening gentleness of love and modesty.

Women like her did not behave like that—they did *not* scratch and bite and moan like wild animals, they did *not* urge and demand and incite...they did *not* take pleasure in meeting...in matching a man's sexual anger, they did *not*... Lisa gave a low moan and scrambled out of bed.

There was no point in going over and over what had happened. It wouldn't change anything; *she* couldn't change anything. How on earth *could* Oliver have possibly thought that she could want *any* other man, never mind a sorry specimen like Henry...? How could he have misinterpreted...accused her...?

Angrily she stepped into the shower and switched it on.

That was the difference between men and women, she decided bitterly. Whereas she as a woman had given herself totally, emotionally, physically, mentally to Oliver, committing herself to him and to her love in the act of love—an act which she naïvely had believed had been a special and a wonderful form of bonding between them—to Oliver, as a man, they had simply had sex.

Sex. She started to shudder, remembering. Stop thinking about it, she warned herself grimly.

As she dried her hair and stared into the mirror at her heavy-eyed, pale-faced reflection she marvelled that such a short space of time could have brought so many changes to her life, set in motion events which had brought consequences that she would never be able to forget or escape.

Such a few short days, and yet they had changed her life for ever—changed *her* for ever. And the most ironic thing of all was that even if Henry or another man like him were to offer her marriage now she could not accept it. Thanks to Oliver she now knew that she could never be content with the kind of marriage and future which had seemed so perfect to her before.

Fergus her boss gave her an uneasy look as he heard her sneezing. He had a thing about germs and was a notorious hypochondriac.

'You don't sound very well,' he told Lisa accusingly as she started to open the mail which had accumulated over the Christmas break. 'You've probably caught this virus that's going round. There was something on last night's TV news about it. They're advising anyone who thinks they've got it to stay at home and keep warm…'

'Fergus, I've got a cold, that's all,' Lisa told him patiently. 'And besides, aren't we due to go down to Southampton on Thursday to start cataloguing the contents of Welton House?'

Welton House had been the property of one of Fergus's clients, and following her death her family had asked Fergus to catalogue its contents with a view to organising a sale. Normally it was the kind of job that Lisa loved, and she thought that it would do her good to get away from London.

'That's next week,' Fergus told her, his voice quickening with alarm as Lisa burst into another volley of sneezes. 'Look, my dear, you aren't well. I really think you should go home,' he said. 'In fact, I insist on it. I'll ring for a taxi for you...'

There was no point in continuing to protest, Lisa recognised wearily; Fergus had quite obviously got it into his head that she was dangerously infectious, and, if she was honest, she didn't feel very well. Nothing to do with her slight head cold, though. The pain that was exhausting her, draining every bit of her energy as she fought to keep it at bay had its source not in her head but in her emotions.

Her telephone was ringing as she unlocked her door; she stared at it for a few seconds, body stiffening. What if it was Oliver, ringing to apologise, to tell her that he had made a mistake, that he...?

Tensely she picked up the receiver, unsure of whether to be relieved or not when she heard her mother's voice on the other end of the line.

'Darling, I'm glad I caught you. I'm just ringing to wish you a Happy New Year. We tried to get through yesterday but we couldn't. How are you? Tell me all about your Christmas with Henry...'

Lisa couldn't help herself; to her own consternation and disbelief she burst into tears, managing to tell her mother between gulped sobs that she had not, after all, spent Christmas with Henry.

'What on earth has happened?' she heard her mother enquiring solicitously. 'I thought you and Henry—'

'It's not Henry,' Lisa gulped. 'He's getting married to someone else anyway. It's Oliver...'

'Oliver. Who's Oliver?' her mother asked anxiously, but the mere effort of saying Oliver's name had caused her so much pain that Lisa couldn't answer her questions.

'I've got to go, Mum,' Lisa fibbed, unable to bear any more. 'Thanks for ringing.'

'Lisa,' she could hear her mother protesting, but she was already replacing the receiver.

There was nothing she wanted to do more than fling herself on her bed and cry until there were no more tears left, until she had cried all her pain away, but what was the point of such emotional self-indulgence?

What she needed, she acknowledged firmly, was something to keep her thoughts away from Oliver not focused on him. It was a pity that the panacea that work would have provided had been taken away from her, she fretted as she stared round her sitting room, the small space no longer a warm, safe haven but a trap imprisoning her with her thoughts, her memories of Oliver.

Impulsively she pulled on her coat. She needed to get away, go somewhere, anywhere, just so long as it was somewhere that wasn't tainted with any memories of Oliver.

Oliver was in a foul mood. He had flown straight back to New York after his confrontation with Lisa, ostensibly to conclude the negotiations he had left hanging fire in his furious determination to find out what was going on. Well, he had found out all right. He doubted if he would ever forget that stomach-sickening, heart-destroying, split second of time when he had seen Lisa—*his* Lisa—in Henry's arms.

And as for what had happened… His mouth hardened firmly as he fought to suppress the memory of how easily—how very and humiliatingly easily—with Lisa in his arms he had been on the point of begging her to change her mind, of pleading with her at least to give him a chance to show her how good it could be for them.

He had known, of course, how reluctant, how wary she had been about committing herself fully to him, how afraid she had been of her own suppressed, deeply passionate nature. Then it had seemed a vulnerability in her which had only added to his love for her. Then he had not realised… How could he have been so blind—he of all people? How could *she* have been so blind? Couldn't she see what they had had…what they *could* have had?

The American negotiations were concluded now and he and Piers were on their way back north. They had flown back into London four hours ago to cold grey skies and thin rain.

'Oliver, is something wrong?'

He frowned, concentrating on the steely-grey ribbon of the motorway as he pulled out to overtake a large lorry.

'No, why should there be?' he denied, without looking at his cousin.

'No reason. Only you never explained why you had to fly back home like that and since you flew back to the States…well, it's obvious that something is bothering you. You're not having second thoughts about selling off part of the business, are you?' Piers asked him.

Oliver relaxed slightly, and without taking his eyes off the road responded, 'No, it was the right decision, but the timing could, perhaps, have been better. When is Emma due back?' he asked, changing the subject.

His cousin's girlfriend had been away visiting her family, and to his relief Piers, not realising that he was being deliberately sidetracked, started to talk enthusiastically about the reunion with her.

'It's official, by the way,' he informed Oliver. 'We're definitely going to get married this summer. In Harrowby if that's OK with you. We thought…well, I thought with Emma's family being so scattered… We…we're not sure how many of them will want to come up for the wedding yet, but the house is big enough to house twenty or so and...' He paused and gave Oliver a sidelong glance.

'I...I'd like you to be my best man, Oliver. Funny things, women,' he added ruminatively. 'Up until we actually started talking properly about it Emma had always insisted she didn't want a traditional wedding, that they were out of date and unnecessary, and yet now...she wants the whole works—bridesmaids, page-boys... She says it's to please her mother but I know different.

'That will mean two big weddings for Harrowby this summer. I still can't get over old Henry getting married—or rather his mother allowing him to... Hell, Oliver... watch out!' he protested sharply as his cousin suddenly had to brake quickly to avoid getting too close to the car in front.

'You're sure you're OK?' he asked in concern. 'Perhaps we should have stayed in London overnight instead of driving north straight from the flight. If you're tired, I can take over for a while...'

Oliver made no reply but his mouth had compressed into a hard line and there was a bleak, cold look in his eyes that reminded Piers very much of a younger Oliver just after he'd lost his mother. Something was bothering his cousin, but Piers knew him well enough to know that Oliver wasn't likely to tell him or anyone else exactly what it was.

'What the hell is that still doing here?'

Piers frowned as Oliver glared at the Christmas tree in the hallway. There was nothing about it so far as he could see to merit that tone of icy, almost bitter hatred in his cousin's voice. In fact, he decided judiciously, it was a rather nice tree—wilting now slightly, but still...

'It's not Twelfth Night until tomorrow,' he pointed out

to Oliver. 'I'll give you a hand dismantling it then, if you like, and—'

'No,' Oliver told him curtly. 'I'll give Mrs Green a ring and ask her to arrange for Tom to come in and do it. We're going to be too busy catching up with everything that's been going on whilst we've been in New York.'

Thoughtfully Piers followed Oliver into the kitchen. It wasn't like his cousin to be so snappy and edgy, and, in point of fact, he had planned to drive across to York to see his parents whilst they were in the north, but now it seemed as though Oliver had other plans for him.

'Well, if we're going to work I'd better go and unpack and have a shower, freshen up a bit,' he told Oliver.

Upstairs he pushed open the door of the room which traditionally was his whenever he visited. The bed was neatly made up with crisp, clean bedlinen, the room spotless apart from...

Piers' eyes widened slightly as he saw the small, intimate item of women's clothing which Mrs Green had obviously laundered and left neatly folded on the bed, no doubt thinking that the small pair of white briefs belonged to Emma.

Only Piers was pretty sure that they didn't. So who did they belong to and where was their owner now?

Piers knew enough about his cousin to be quite sure that Oliver would not indulge in any kind of brief, meaningless sexual fling. Piers had endured enough lectures from his elder cousin on that subject himself to know that much.

So what exactly was going on? Oliver had made no mention to him of having any visitors recently, either male or female. He could always, of course, show him the briefs and ask him who they belonged to, but, judging from his current mood, such an enquiry was not likely to be very well received.

Another thought occurred to Piers. Was there any connection between the owner of the briefs and his cousin's present uncharacteristic bad mood?

When Piers returned downstairs Oliver was in his study opening the mail that had accumulated in his absence.

'Mmm…isn't it amazing how much junk gets sent through the post?' Piers commented as he started to help him. 'Oh, this one looks interesting, Oliver—an invite to Henry's betrothal party. Well, they certainly are doing things the traditional way, aren't they?'

'Give that to me,' Oliver instructed, his tone of voice so curt that Piers started to frown. He knew that Oliver had never particularly liked either Henry or his parents, especially his mother, but, so far as he knew, the anger he was exhibiting now was completely different from his normal attitude of relaxed indifference towards them.

Silently Piers handed him the invitation and saw the way Oliver's hands trembled slightly as he started to tear the invitation in two, and then he abruptly stopped, his concentration fixed on the black script which he had previously merely been glancing at furiously, his whole body so still and tense that Piers automatically moved round the desk to stand beside him, wondering what on earth it was that was written on the invitation that was causing such a reaction.

It had seemed unremarkable enough to him.

'"The betrothal is announced of Miss Louise Saunders, daughter of Colonel and Lady Anne Saunders, to—" Henry is marrying Louise Saunders,' Oliver intoned in a flat and totally unfamiliar voice.

'That's what it says,' Piers agreed, watching him in concern. 'It makes sense. They've known one another for ever and, of course, there's money in the family. Louise stands to inherit quite a considerable sum from her grandparents.

'Oliver, what is it, what's wrong?' he demanded as he saw the colour draining out of his cousin's face, leaving it grey and haggard, the skin stretched tightly over his facial bones as he lifted his head and stared unseeingly across the room.

'Nothing,' he told Piers tonelessly. 'Nothing.' And then he added in a sharper more incisive voice, 'Piers, there's something I have to do. I need to get back to London. I'll leave you here...'

'London...? You can't drive back there now,' Piers protested. 'It's too late. You haven't had any sleep in the last twenty-four hours that I know of, and not much in the three days before that. Oliver, what's going on? I—'

'Nothing's going on,' Oliver denied harshly.

'Look, if you must go back to London, at least wait until the morning when you've had some sleep,' said Piers. 'Surely whatever it is can wait that long?'

'Maybe it can,' Oliver agreed savagely, 'but *I* can't.'

In London Lisa's cold had turned into the full-blown virus, just as Fergus had predicted. Common sense told her that she ought to see a doctor but she felt too full of self-pity, too weak, too weighed down with misery to care how ill she was. And so instead she remained in her flat curled up in her bed, alternately sweating and shivering and being sick, wishing that she could just close her eyes and never have to open them again.

At first when she heard the sound of someone knocking urgently on her door after ten o'clock at night she thought she was imagining things, and then when the knocking continued and she realised that it was, in fact, real her heart started to bang so fiercely against her chest wall that it made her feel even more physically weak.

It was Oliver! It had to be. But it didn't matter what he had to say because she wasn't going to listen. She had always known that sooner or later he would discover his mistake. But nothing—no amount of apologising on his part—could take away the pain he had caused her.

If he had really loved her he would never have doubted her in the first place. *If* he had really loved her he would never…

The knocking had stopped, and Lisa discovered that she was almost running in her sudden urgency to open the door.

When she did so, flinging it wide, Oliver's name already on her lips, it wasn't Oliver who was standing there at all…

It was…

She blinked and then blinked again, and then to her own consternation she burst into tears and flung herself into the arms that had opened to hold her, weepingly demanding, 'Mother, what are you doing here?'

'You sounded so unhappy when I rang that I was worried about you,' her mother told her.

'You came all the way home from Japan because you were worried about me?'

Lisa stared at her mother in disbelief, remembering all the times when, as a child, she had refused to give in to her need to plead for her parents to return from whatever far-flung part of the world they were working in, telling herself stoically that she didn't mind that they weren't there, that she didn't mind that they didn't love her enough to be with her all the time.

'Don't sound so surprised,' her mother chided her gently. 'You may be an adult, Lisa, but to us, your father and me, you are still our child... Your father wanted to come with me, but unfortunately...' She spread her hands.

'Now,' she instructed as she smoothed Lisa's damp hair back from her forehead and studied her face with maternal intuition, 'tell me what's really wrong... All of it... Starting with this Oliver...'

'Oliver...'

Lisa shook her head, her mouth compressing against her emotions.

'I can't,' she whispered, and then added, 'Oh, Mum, I've been such a fool. I thought he loved me... I thought...'

'Oh, my poor darling girl. Come on, let me put the kettle on and make us both a drink and something to eat. You need it, by the looks of you. You're so thin... Oh, Lisa, what have you been doing to yourself?'

Half an hour later, having been bullied into having a hot bath by her mother, Lisa was ensconced on her small sofa, wrapped in her quilt, dutifully eating the deliciously creamy scrambled eggs that her mother had cooked for her whilst the latter sat on a chair opposite, waiting for her to finish eating before exclaiming as she removed the empty plate, 'Right, now! First things first—*who* is this Oliver?'

'He's... He's...' Lisa shook her head. 'I hate him,' she told her mother emotionally, 'and it hurts so much. He said he loved me but he couldn't have done—not and said what he did...'

Slowly, under her mother's patient and gentle questioning, the whole story came out. Although Lisa would not have said that she was particularly close to her parents, she had always felt able to talk to them. But, even so, she was slightly shocked to discover how easy it was to confide in her mother and how much she wanted to talk to her. Of course, there were bits she missed out—things so personal that she could not have discussed them with anyone. But she sensed from her mother's expression that she guessed when Lisa was withholding things from her and why.

Only when it came to outlining what had happened the night that Oliver had discovered her kissing Henry did her voice falter slightly.

'It must have been a shock for him to find Henry here,' her mother suggested when Lisa had fallen silent.

'He seemed to think that I was going to marry Henry. I...'

'And you told him, of course, that you weren't?' her mother offered.

Lisa shook her head. 'I tried to but...' She bit her lip, turning away, her face flushing slightly. 'He was so...

'I had been honest with him right from the start, told him why I was marrying Henry, told him that I hadn't... that I didn't think that sex...' She bit her lip again and stopped.

'After what had happened between us I don't understand how he could possibly have thought that I'd go back to Henry and to use what we had...all that we'd shared, to abuse it and destroy... To make me feel... How could he do that?' she whispered, more to herself than her mother.

'Perhaps because he's a man and because he felt jealous and insecure, because a part of him feared that what he had to offer you wasn't enough...that *he* wasn't enough.'

'But how could he possibly think that?' Lisa demanded, looking at her mother, her eyes dark and shadowed with pain. 'He knew how I felt about him, how I... He knew...'

'When you were in bed together, yes,' her mother agreed, softening the directness of her words with a small smile. 'But it isn't only our sex who fear that the emotions aroused when two people are sexually intimate may not be there once that intimacy is over.

'Your Oliver obviously knew he could arouse you, make you want him physically, but you had already told him that he was not what you wanted, what you had planned for. He already knew that a part of you feared the intensity of the emotions he had for you and aroused in you. You said yourself that he was anxious for you to make a commitment to him.'

'Initially, yes. But later…when I tried to tell him how I felt just before he left for New York, he didn't seem to want to listen.'

'Perhaps because he was afraid of what you might say,' her mother suggested gently, adding, 'He had no way of knowing you were going to tell him that you had changed your mind, that you were ready to make the commitment you had previously told him he must wait for. For all he knew, you might have wanted to say something very different—to tell him in fact that you had changed your mind and didn't want him at all.'

'But he couldn't possibly have thought that,' Lisa gasped, 'could he? It isn't important now anyway,' she said tiredly. 'I can never forgive him for—'

'Is it really *Oliver* you can't forgive, or yourself?' her mother interposed quietly, watching as Lisa stared at her and then frowned.

'You said that he was angry…that he made love to you,' she reminded Lisa. 'That he used your feelings to punish and humiliate you. But you never said that you didn't want him, or that he hurt or abused you. Anger against the person we love when he is our lover can result in some very passionate sex.

'For a woman, the first time she discovers that fact, it

can be very traumatic and painful because it goes against everything that society has told us we should want from sexual intimacy. It can seem very frightening, very alien, very wrong to admit that we found pleasure in expressing our sexuality and desire in anger and, of course, that it was the only way we could express it…'

'He was so angry with me,' Lisa told her mother, not making any response to what she had said but mentally digesting it, acknowledging that her mother had a point, allowing herself for the first time since it had happened to see her own uninhibited and passionate response to Oliver as a natural expression of her own emotions.

'Oliver was probably as shocked and caught off guard by what happened as you were,' her mother told her wryly.

'You're not the only one something like this has happened to, you know,' she added comfortingly. 'I can still remember the first time your father and I had a major row… I was working on a piece for a gallery showing and I'd forgotten that your father was picking me up to take me out to dinner… He came storming into my work room demanding to know what was more important to me—my work or him… I had just finished working on the final piece for the exhibition. He picked it up and threw it against the wall.'

Lisa stared at her mother in shock.

'Dad did that? But he always seems so laid back… so…'

'Well, most of the time he is, but this particular incident was the culmination of a series of small misunderstandings. He didn't take second place to my work at all, of course, but…'

'Go on—what happened, after he had broken the piece?' Lisa demanded, intrigued.

'Well, I'm ashamed to say that I was so angry that I actually tried to hit him. He caught hold of me, we struggled for a while and then…'

As her mother flushed and laughed, Lisa guessed what the outcome of their fight had been.

'Afterwards your father stormed off and left me there on my own… I vowed I wasn't going to have anything more to do with him, but then—well, I started to miss him and to realise that what had happened hadn't been entirely his fault.'

'So what did you do?' Lisa asked.

Her mother laughed. 'Well, I made a small ceramic heart which I then deliberately broke in two and I sent him one half of it.'

'What did he do?' Lisa demanded breathlessly.

'Well, not what I had expected,' her mother admitted. 'When I sent him the heart I had been trying to tell him that my heart was broken. I kept the other half hoping he would come for it and that we could mend the break, but when several days went by and he didn't I began to think that he had changed his mind and that he didn't want me any more.

'I was in despair,' she told Lisa quietly. 'Exactly the same kind of despair you are facing now, but then, just when I had given up hope, your father turned up one night.'

'With the broken heart,' Lisa guessed.

'With the mended heart,' her mother told her, smiling. 'The reason he had delayed so long before coming to see me had been because he had been having a matching piece to the broken one I had sent him made, and where the two pieces were bonded together he had used a special bond to, as he put it, ''make the mended heart stronger than it had been before and unbreakable''.'

'I never dreamed Dad could be so romantic!' Lisa exclaimed.

'Oh, he can,' her mother told her. 'You should have seen him the night you were born. He had desperately wanted you to be a little girl. He was overjoyed when you were born—we both were—and he swore that no matter where our work might take us, as long as it was physically possible, we would take you with us...'

Lisa could feel fresh tears starting to sting her eyes. All these years and she had misunderstood the motivation behind her parents' constant uprooting of her, had never known how much she was actually loved.

As they looked at one another her mother reached out and took Lisa's hand, telling her firmly, 'When Oliver comes to see you—and he will—listen to what he has to say, Lisa—'

'When,' Lisa interrupted her. 'Don't you mean if...?'

'No, I mean when.'

'But how could he believe I could go behind his back and return to Henry?'

'He's a man and he's vulnerable, as I've already told you, and sometimes, when we feel vulnerable and afraid, we do things which are out of character. You said yourself that losing his mother when he did made him feel wary of loving someone in case he lost them too. Such emotions, even when they're only felt subconsciously, can have a very dramatic effect on our actions.'

'He won't come back,' Lisa protested dully. 'I told him I never wanted to see him again. We both agreed it was over.'

'Well, in that case, why don't you come back to Japan with me?' her mother suggested prosaically.

'I can't... My job... Fergus—'

'Fergus would give you some extended leave if you

asked him,' her mother told her. 'He adores you, you know that…'

'Not when he thinks I'm full of germs,' Lisa told her ruefully. 'I'd like to come back with you,' she added hesitantly, 'but…'

'But not yet,' her mother finished for her, getting up to kiss her gently on the forehead and tell her, 'Well, I'm going to be here for a few days so you've got time to change your mind. But right now you're going to bed and I'm going to ring your father. I promised him I would. He'll be worrying himself to death wondering if you're all right. Now, bed…'

'Yes, Mum.' Lisa yawned obediently.

It felt so good to have her mother here with her, to know that she was cared for and loved, but no amount of parental love, no matter how valued, could erase the pain of losing Oliver.

He'll be back, her mother had promised her. But would he? Had they perhaps between them destroyed the tender, vulnerable plant of their love?

CHAPTER TEN

PIERS had been right to caution him against driving back to London tonight, Oliver admitted as his concentration wavered and he found himself having to blink away the grittiness of his aching eyes as he tried to focus on the road. With all that adrenalin and anxiety pumping through his veins it should have been impossible to start drifting off to sleep, but the compulsion to yawn and close his eyes kept on returning.

Up ahead of him he could see the lights of a motorway service station. Perhaps it would be wiser for him to stop, even if it was only for a hot, reviving cup of coffee. He knew there was no point in his trying to sleep; how could he when all he could think of was Lisa and the injustice he had done her?

The motorway services were closer than he had thought; he had started to pull into the lane taking him off the motorway, when the metal barrier at the edge of the road loomed up in front of him. The shrill squeal of brakes was followed by the harsh sound of metal against metal and his head jolted forward, pain exploding all around him.

'If it's that bad why don't you go out for a walk? It will be cheaper than wearing the carpet out.'

Lisa frowned as she looked at her mother.

'You've been pacing up and down the sitting room for the last half-hour,' her mother pointed out. 'And besides, it will do you good to get some fresh air.'

'Yes, perhaps you're right,' Lisa agreed. 'A walk might do me good.'

'Put your jacket on and some gloves,' her mother instructed her as Lisa headed for the hallway. 'I know the sun is out but we had frost last night.'

'Yes, Mother,' Lisa agreed dutifully, amusement briefly lightening her eyes and touching her mouth.

It had been three days since her mother's unexpected arrival now; in another two she would be returning to Japan. She was still pressing Lisa to return with her, and Lisa knew that she had spoken the truth when she had said that Fergus would give her the extra leave. There had been plenty of occasions in the past when she had put in extra hours at work, given up weekends and been cheerfully flexible about how long she worked. No, it wasn't the thought of Fergus that was stopping her.

'Why don't you come with me?' she suggested to her mother as she pulled on her jacket and found her gloves. The virus she had picked up had been thankfully short-lived, but Fergus had insisted that she did not return to work for at least a full week, and although she was enjoying her mother's company there were times when she was filled with restless energy that nothing seem to dissipate—a sense of urgency and anxiety.

Both of them knew what was causing it, of course, but since the night she had confided in her mother neither of them had ever referred to Oliver—Lisa because she couldn't bear to, couldn't trust herself to so much as think, never mind say his name, without losing control and being swamped by her emotions, and her mother, she suspected, because despite her initial conviction that Oliver would discover the truth and want to make amends she too was now beginning to share Lisa's belief that it was over between them.

'I won't be too long,' she told her mother as she opened the front door.

'No…there's an exhibition on at the Tate that I thought we might go to this afternoon, and then I thought we might have dinner at that Italian place in Covent Garden that your father likes so much.'

Her mother was doing her best to keep her occupied and busy, Lisa knew, and she was doing all she could to respond, but both of them also knew that she was losing weight and that she didn't sleep very well at night, and that sometimes when she did she woke up crying Oliver's name.

Her head down against the sharp January wind, she set off in the direction of the park.

Once she had gone Lisa's mother picked up the receiver and dialled her husband's number in Japan.

'I still haven't managed to persuade Lisa to come back with me,' she told him after they had exchanged hellos. 'I'm worried about her, David. She looks so pale and thin… I wish there was some way we could get in touch with this Oliver. No, I know we mustn't interfere,' she agreed, 'but if you could see her. She looks so… I must go,' she told him. 'There's someone at the door.' Quickly she replaced the receiver and went to open the front door.

The tall, dark-haired man wearing one arm in a sling with a huge, purpling bruise on his cheekbone and a black eye and a nasty-looking cut on his forehead was completely unfamiliar to her and yet she knew who he was immediately.

'You must be Oliver,' she told him simply, extending her hand to shake his. 'I'm so glad you're here. I'd just about begun to give up on you. Silly of me really, especially when… You look rather the worse for wear; have you been in an accident…? I'm Lisa's mother, by the way;

she's out at the moment but she'll be back soon. Do come in…'

'I had a bump in my car a few days ago,' Oliver told her as he followed her into the flat. 'Fortunately nothing too serious. I say fortunately because it was my own fault; I virtually fell asleep at the wheel…' He caught the frowning look that Lisa's mother gave him and explained tersely, 'I was on my way back to London to see Lisa. Where did you say she was…?'

'She's gone out for a walk; she shouldn't be too long. She's been ill and I thought some fresh—'

'How ill?' Oliver pounced sharply.

Hiding her small, satisfied smile, Lisa's mother responded airily, 'Well, as a matter of fact, the doctor seemed quite concerned, but I'm a great believer in the efficacy of plenty of fresh air myself. She did say she felt a bit weak but—'

'A bit weak… Should she be out on her own?'

Poor man, he really had got it badly, Lisa's mother decided. As she witnessed his obvious concern Lisa's mother relented a little; this was no uncaring sexual predator, this was quite definitely a man very, very deeply in love.

'She's a lot better than she was,' she told him more gently.

Her half-hour in the park might have brought a pink flush to her skin and made her fingertips and toes tingle, Lisa acknowledged, but it had done nothing to alleviate the pain of loving Oliver. Only one person could do that, and with every day that passed her common sense told her that there was less and less chance of Oliver doing what her mother had claimed he was bound to do and coming in search of her, to tell her that he had discovered his mistake and to beg her to forgive him.

Grimly, Lisa retraced her steps towards her flat. Part of her wished desperately that she had never met Oliver, that she had never been exposed to the agony of loving him and then losing him, and yet another part of her clung passionately to the memory of their brief time together.

As her mother opened the door to her knock she told Lisa, 'I'm just going out. Oh, and by the way, you've got a visitor.'

'Oliver?'

Hope, disbelief, the desire to push open the door and run to him and the equally strong desire to turn on her heels and run from him were all there in Lisa's eyes.

'Treat him gently,' her mother advised her as she took hold of her and gave her a supportive hug.

'Treat him gently', after what he had done to her? In a daze Lisa walked past her mother and into the flat, closing the door behind her. Oliver was actually here…here. The angry relief that flooded her was that same emotion so familiar to parents when a child had emerged unscathed from a forbidden risk—relief at its safety and anger that it should have taken such a risk with itself, with something so precious and irreplaceable.

In fact she was so angry that she was actually shaking as she pushed open the sitting-room door, Lisa discovered, her mouth compressing, and without even waiting to look directly at Oliver, without daring to take the risk of allowing her hungry heart, her starved senses to feast on the reality of him, she demanded tersely, 'What are you doing here?'

He was standing with his back to her, facing the window, apparently absorbed in the view outside. He must have seen her walking back to the flat, Lisa recognised, her heart giving a small, shaky bound. He turned round and every single thought, every single word she had been about to voice vanished as Lisa saw his cut and bruised face, his arm in a sling.

'Oliver...' Her voice cracked suddenly, becoming thready and weak, her eyes mirroring her shock and anxiety as she whispered, 'What's happened? Why...?'

'It's nothing...just a minor bump in my car,' Oliver assured her quickly. 'In fact I got off far more easily than I deserved.'

'You've been in an accident. But how?' she demanded, ignoring his attempts to make light of his injuries and instinctively hurrying towards him, realising only when it was too late and she was standing within easy distance of the free arm he stretched forward to her just how physically close to him she actually was.

Immediately she raised her hand in an automatic gesture of rejection, but Oliver had already stepped forward and the hand she had lifted in the body-language sign that meant 'No, keep away from me' was somehow resting against his shirt-covered chest with a very different meaning indeed.

'Oliver,' she protested weakly, but it wasn't any use; it wasn't just her legs and her body that were trembling now, her mouth was trembling as well, tears spilling over from her eyes as she said his name, causing Oliver to groan and reach for her, cradling her against his body with his good arm as he said, 'Lisa, darling, please don't...please don't cry. I can't bear to see you unhappy. I'll never forgive myself for what I've done—*never*. My only excuse is that I was half-crazed with jealousy over Henry.'

'Jealous?' Lisa questioned. 'You actually believed...? You were jealous of Henry?' She couldn't quite keep the disbelief out of her voice.

'Yes,' Oliver admitted ruefully. 'It all seemed to slot so neatly into place—your reluctance to commit yourself to me, the news that Henry was marrying an old flame, the sight of the two of you together. I know I overreacted. I was jealous, vulnerable,' he told her simply. 'You'd already made it plain that I wasn't the kind of man you wanted for a husband. I knew how reluctant you'd been to commit yourself to me, to our love.

'I knew, as well, how much I was rushing you, pressurising you, using the intensity of what we both felt for one another to win you over. I suppose a part of me will always be the child who felt that in dying my mother deliberately abandoned me. Logically I know that isn't what happened, but there's always that small worm of fear there—fear of losing the one you love—and the more you love someone, the greater the fear is. And I love you more than I can possibly tell you. I'm not trying to look for excuses for myself, Lisa; there aren't really any. What I did was...' He paused and shook his head as she touched his hand gently with understanding for what he was trying to say. 'At the time it seemed logical that you should have changed your mind, decided you preferred the safe life you had already mapped out for yourself.'

'Oh, Oliver.' Lisa shook her head.

'I was wrong, I know, and what I did was... unforgivable...'

The bleakness in his eyes and voice made Lisa want to reach out and hold him, but she restrained herself. She was already in his arms, and once she touched him...

'I...I didn't know that loving someone could be like that,' she told him in a husky voice. 'That anger could... That physically... I felt so ashamed after you had gone,' she admitted shakily.

'To have wanted you the way I did, to have responded

to you, said the things I did, when I knew that you weren't touching me out of love. I felt so…' She shook her head, unable to find the words to express her own sense of horror at what, at the time, had seemed to her to be her own totally unacceptable and almost abnormal behaviour.

'Being angry with someone doesn't stop you loving them,' Oliver told her quietly. 'I was angry, bitter—furiously, destructively so; I can't deny that. I wanted to hurt you in the same way that I felt you had hurt me, but those feelings, strong as they were, destructive as they were, did not stop me loving you. In fact…'

He paused and looked down into her upturned face, searching her eyes before telling her roughly, 'I tried to tell myself that I was punishing you…that I *wanted* to punish you…but almost from the moment I held you in my arms…' He stopped and shook his head. 'No matter what I might have *said*, my *body* was loving you, Lisa—loving you and wanting you and hating me for what I was trying to do.'

'What made you think I was marrying Henry in the first place?' Lisa questioned him.

'My cousin,' he informed her briefly. 'Emma had phoned from Yorkshire and she'd heard that Henry was getting married to someone he had already known for some time.'

'And you assumed it was me…'

'I assumed it was you,' Oliver agreed.

A little uncertainly Lisa looked up at him. The sadness she could see in his eyes made her heart jolt against her ribs.

'Have I completely ruined everything between us?' he asked her huskily. 'Tell me I haven't Lisa. I can't… Being without you these last few days has been hell, but if you…'

He paused and Lisa told him shakily, 'I've missed you as well…'

Missed him!

'I should have rung you from New York and talked to you instead of flying back like that, but it looked like those damned negotiations were going to go on for ever and I'd already missed being with you on New Year's Eve. And then when I reached your flat and saw you there with Henry…'

'He came to tell me that he was getting married. His mother had sent him,' Lisa explained drily. 'She was concerned that I might get in touch with him and try to patch up our differences… I had just finished telling Henry that there was absolutely no chance whatsoever of that happening when you appeared. I thought when you didn't make New Year's Eve that you were having second thoughts…about us,' she confessed.

'*Me* having second thoughts… There's no way I could ever have second thoughts about the way I feel about you…about what I want with you…'

Lisa took a deep breath. There was something she had to tell him now, whilst they were both being so open and honest with one another.

'I did,' she confessed. '*I* had second thoughts…the day we parted…' She looked anxiously up at him; his face was unreadable, grave, craven almost, as he watched her in silence.

'I tried to tell you then,' she hurried on. 'I tried to say that I had changed my mind, but you didn't seem to want to listen and I thought that perhaps you had changed yours and that—'

'Changed your mind about what?' Oliver demanded hoarsely, cutting across her.

'About…about wanting to make a commitment,' Lisa

admitted, stammering slightly as she searched his face anxiously, looking for some indication as to how he felt about what she was saying, but she could see none. Her heart started to hammer nervously against her ribs. Had she said too much? Had she…? Determinedly she pushed her uncertainty away.

'I knew then that it was just fear that had stopped me from telling you what I already knew… That I *did* love you and that I did want to be with you… I was even going to suggest that I went to New York with you.' She paused, laughing shakily. 'When it came to it I just couldn't bear the thought of not being with you, but you seemed so preoccupied and distant that I thought—'

'You were going to tell me that…?' Oliver interrupted her. 'Oh, my God, Lisa… Lisa…'

Any response she might have made was muffled by the hard pressure of his mouth against hers as, ignoring her protests that he might hurt his injured arm, he gathered her up, held her against his body and kissed her with all the hungry passion she had dreamed of in the time they had been apart.

'Lisa, Lisa, *why* didn't you say something to me?' Oliver groaned when he had finally finished kissing her. 'Why…?'

'Because I didn't think you wanted to hear,' Lisa told him simply. 'You were so distant and—'

'I was trying to stop myself from pleading with you to change your mind and come with me,' Oliver told her grimly. '*That* was why I was quiet.'

'Oh, Oliver…'

'Oh, Lisa,' he mimicked. 'How long do you suppose your mother will be gone?' he asked her as he bent his head to kiss her a second time.

'I don't know, but she did say something about going

to see an exhibition at the Tate,' Lisa mumbled through his kiss.

'Mmm...' He was looking, Lisa noticed, towards the half-open bedroom door, and her own body started to react to the message she could read in his eyes as she followed his gaze.

'We can't,' she protested without conviction. 'What about your arm? And you still haven't told me about the accident,' she reminded him.

'I will,' he promised her, and added wickedly, 'They said at the hospital that I should get plenty of rest and that I shouldn't stand up for too long. They said that the best cure for me would be...' And he bent his head and whispered in Lisa's ear exactly what he had in mind for the two of them for the rest of the afternoon.

'Tell me about the accident first,' Lisa insisted, blushing a little as she saw the look he gave her when he caught that betraying 'first'.

'Very well,' he agreed, adding ruefully, 'Although, it doesn't make very good hearing.

'I didn't find out until we were back in Yorkshire that you weren't marrying Henry, but once I did and I realised what I'd done I broke all the rules and drove straight back here despite the fact that I hadn't had any sleep for going on three days and that I was jet-lagged into the bargain. Hardly a sensible or safety-conscious decision but...' He gave a small, self-deprecatory grimace. 'I was hardly feeling either sensible or safety-conscious; after all, what else had I got left to lose? I'd already destroyed the most precious thing I had in my life.

'Anyway... I must have started to doze off at the wheel; fortunately I'd already decided to stop at a motorway service station and I'd slowed down and pulled onto the approach road, and even more fortunately there was no other vehicle, no other person around to be involved in my self-imposed accident. The authorities told me that I was lucky my car was fitted with so many safety features... otherwise...'

'No, don't,' Lisa begged him, shuddering as her imagination painted an all too vivid picture of just how differently things could have turned out.

'Lisa, I know there is nothing I can say or do that can take away the memory of what I did; all I can do is promise you that it will never happen again and ask if you can forgive me.'

'It did hurt that you could think such a thing of me,' Lisa admitted quietly, 'and that you could...could treat me in such a way, but I *do* understand. In a way both of us were responsible for what happened; both of us should have trusted the other and our love more. If we had had more mutual trust, more mutual faith in our love then... Oh, Oliver,' she finished, torn between laughter and tears as she clung onto him. 'How could you possibly think I could even contemplate the idea of marrying anyone else, never mind Henry, after you...after the way you and I...?'

'Even when mentally I was trying to hate you I was still loving you physically and emotionally,' Oliver told her huskily. 'The moment I touched you... I never intended things to go so far; I'd just meant to kiss you one last time, that was all, but once I had...'

'Once you had what?' Lisa encouraged him, raising herself up on tiptoe to feather her lips teasingly against his.

'Once I had...this,' Oliver responded, smothering a groan deep in his throat as he pulled her against him with his good arm and held her there, letting her feel the immediate and passionate response of his body to her as he kissed her.

* * *

'We really ought to get up,' Lisa murmured sleepily, her words belying her actions as she snuggled closer to Oliver's side. 'The day's almost gone and...'

'Soon it will be bedtime. I know,' Oliver finished mock-wickedly for her. 'It was very thoughtful of your mother to telephone and say that she'd decided to go and visit some friends this evening and to stay overnight with them...'

'Mmm...very,' Lisa agreed, sighing leisurely as Oliver's hand cupped her breast.

'Mmm...that feels nice,' she told him.

'It certainly does,' Oliver agreed, and asked her softly, 'And does this?' as he bent his head and started to kiss the soft curve of her throat.

'I'm not sure... Perhaps if you did it for a bit longer,' Lisa suggested helpfully. 'A lot longer,' she amended more huskily as his mouth started to drift with delicious intent towards her breast... 'A lot, *lot* longer.'

EPILOGUE

'How does that look?'

Lisa put her head to one side judiciously as she studied the huge Christmas tree that Oliver had just finished erecting in the hallway.

'I think it needs moving a little to the left; it's leaning slightly,' she told him, and then laughed as she saw his pained expression.

'No, darling, it's perfect,' she added with a happy sigh. They had been married for eight months, their wedding having preceded both Henry's and Piers'. Lisa's parents had both flown home for the wedding and Lisa and Oliver had flown out to Japan to spend three weeks with them in October.

Fergus had been disappointed when Lisa had handed in her notice but she and Oliver were talking about the possibility of her setting up her own business in the north in partnership with Fergus. It seemed almost impossible to Lisa that it was almost twelve months since that fateful night when Oliver had found her stranded on the road and brought her home with him. Her smile deepened as she glanced down at the Armani suit she was wearing—a surprise gift from Oliver to mark the anniversary of the day they had initially met.

'Happy?' Oliver asked her, bending his head to kiss her.

'Mmm...how could I not be?' Lisa answered, snuggling closer to him. 'Oh, Oliver, last Christmas was wonderful, special, something I'll never forget, but this

Christmas is going to be special too; I'm so glad that everyone's been able to come—your family and my parents.'

'We're certainly going to have a houseful,' Oliver agreed, laughing.

He had raised his eyebrows slightly at first when Lisa had suggested to him that they invite all his own relatives and her parents to spend their Christmas with them, but Lisa's enthusiasm for the idea had soon won him over.

'You really do love all this, don't you?' he commented now, indicating the large hallway festooned now for Christmas with the garlands and decorations that Lisa had spent hours making.

'Yes, I do,' Lisa agreed, 'but not anything like as much as I love you. Oh, Oliver,' she told him, her voice suddenly husky with emotion, 'you've made me so happy. It's hard to imagine that twelve months ago we barely knew one another and that—I love you so much.'

'Not half as much as I love you,' Oliver whispered back, his mouth feathering against hers and then hardening as he felt her happy response.

'We still haven't put the star on the tree,' Lisa reminded Oliver through their kiss.

'*You* are my star,' he told her tenderly, 'and without you I'd be lost in the darkness of unhappiness. You light up my life, Lisa, and I never, ever want to be without you.'

'You never, ever will,' Lisa promised him.

'Hey, come on, you two, break it up,' Piers demanded, coming into the hallway carrying a basket of logs for the fire. 'You're married now—remember?'

'Yes, we're married,' Oliver agreed, giving Lisa a look that made her laugh and blush slightly at the same time, as he picked up the star waiting to be placed at the top of the tree—the final touch to a Christmas that would be all the things that Christmas should be, that Christmas and every day *would* be for her from now on.

Oliver *was* her Christmas, all her special times, her life, her love.

Anne McAllister was born in California. She spent long lazy summers daydreaming on local beaches and studying surfers, swimmers and volleyball players in an effort to find the perfect hero. She finally did, not on the beach, but in a university library where she was working. She, her husband and their four children have since moved to the Midwest. She taught, copy-edited, capped deodorant bottles, and ghost-wrote sermons before turning to her first love, writing romance fiction.

Anne has now been writing for Mills & Boon® for nearly fifteen years and has published fifteen books, which have been distributed all over the world.

A BABY FOR CHRISTMAS

by

ANNE MCALLISTER

CHAPTER ONE

IT DIDN'T even begin to look a lot like Christmas.

In fact as far as Carly could see, when the outboard power boat which served as Conch Cay's only ferry approached the boat dock, Christmas might as well not exist on the tiny palm-studded island with its haphazard rows of pastel-colored houses climbing the hills that made up the one small town on it.

There were no Christmas trees for sale on every corner as there were back in New York City. There was no tinsel garland strung along the eaves of the custom house the way there was in the Korean grocery where Carly stopped every night to buy food for supper. There wasn't even any Salvation Army bell-ringer calling out, 'Mer-r-r-y Christmas,' the way he did every morning right outside the publishing house where she worked so that she felt like Scrooge whenever she passed him. It might as easily have been June.

And thank heavens for that, Carly thought. Actually it was exactly what she'd hoped for, the one—the only—good thing that coming to Conch Cay was going to accomplish in her life: helping her forget Christmas this year.

Most years she started December with fervent hopes for the holiday season. Most years she was a great believer in the seasonal joys espoused by popular songs, even if she'd rarely experienced them in her lifetime.

But this year she didn't want to think about them. Only three months after her mother's death, she didn't want to face Christmas with her stepfather and stepsisters out in

5

Colorado, even though they'd invited her. She didn't want visual reminders of how wonderful last year had been.

Maybe in time she would be able to look back on that year without the bittersweet knowledge that her mother's recent marriage to Roland had made her happy again, but that her happiness had been so shortlived. Maybe in time she could go see Roland and the girls without thinking about what might have been.

Not now.

'Come home with me,' John, her sort-of-boyfriend, had suggested when she'd tried to explain her feelings to him.

But she hadn't wanted to do that either.

John was far more serious about their relationship than she was. He wanted marriage.

Carly had nothing against marriage. She wanted it too, someday. But she wanted love first. She didn't love John yet. She wasn't sure she ever would. And she certainly didn't want to increase his expectations about her feelings for him by letting him take her home to Buffalo for Christmas.

She didn't want to be in Conch Cay either.

But at the moment it seemed like the least of several evils. And, if her boss was to be believed, the one that would at least help her keep food on the table when the holidays were over.

All she had to do, Diana had said simply, was 'help Piran St Just finish his book'.

The notion still had the power to stun her.

She hadn't believed it last week when Piran's younger brother Desmond had showed up in the office. He hadn't believed it when he'd found out that his ex-stepsister had turned out to be the assistant editor who'd done the line-editing on their last book.

But it had taken him barely two minutes to turn the circumstances to his advantage.

'Fate,' Des had proclaimed, looping an arm around her shoulders and giving her a hug. Then he'd turned to Diana, the editorial director. 'Don't you think so? After all, who better than Carly to go to Conch Cay and work with Piran in my place? Our sister—'

'Stepsister,' Carly had corrected him quickly. 'Ex-stepsister,' she'd added.

'Not really,' Des said. 'They didn't get divorced. Dad died.'

'That doesn't make us related,' Carly argued, not wanting Diana to misunderstand her relationship to the St Just brothers.

But Diana hadn't been listening to her. She'd been listening to Desmond. He, after all, was part of Bixby Grissom's bestselling duo; Carly was merely an assistant editor.

'She'll do a lot better job than I would,' Des had said. 'And you know how much you'd like a book set in Fiji next.'

Diana had let herself be convinced.

Carly hadn't. Not at first. She didn't want to go to Conch Cay. She didn't want to presume on her past relationship with the St Just brothers. Though she and Des had been quite happy with their sort-of-sibling relationship while their parents had been married, after his father's death, she hadn't seen Des. And she would happily have gone to her own grave without ever having to face his older brother again!

Once, when she was barely more than a girl and her mother had been married to his father, Carly's starry-eyed fantasies had caused her to believe that Piran St Just was her one true love. The mere mention of his name had sent shivers of anticipation right down her spine.

Now the shivers were of an entirely different kind.

'Come on, Carly, be a sport,' Des had cajoled.

But ultimately it wasn't Des she did it for. It was because she loved her job and wanted to keep it.

'You do like working here, don't you?' Diana had said casually, but there was nothing casual about what she'd meant.

'I'll go,' Carly had said at last.

And here she was. About to come face to face with Piran after nine long years. She wondered what he'd thought when Des had told him. He couldn't be looking forward to it any more than she was.

But they would manage because they were adults now. That thought was the only one that gave her solace. In fact it gave her a small amount of perverse pleasure. She wanted Piran to know that she was no longer the foolish, innocent child she'd been at eighteen.

'You sure he expectin' you?' Sam, the ferryman, asked her now as he cut the engine and the boat snugged neatly against the rubber tires edging the sides of the dock. No one was there waiting, except two men sitting in the shade thwacking dominoes on to a table with considerable vigor.

'Absolutely,' Carly said. Of course he was expecting her. Hadn't Des arranged it? 'I'm sure Mr St Just phoned.'

'Mr St Just don't got a phone,' Sam said.

'Not that Mr St Just,' Carly said. 'Desmond.'

'Ah.' Sam's dark head bobbed and he grinned widely. 'Mr Desmond. What a rascal that man is. Where he be?'

'In Fiji by now, I should think,' Carly said. She shifted her duffel bag from one hand to the other. 'But he said he'd call and tell you. To tell his brother, that is.'

Sam clambered out of the boat, took the duffel from her,

then held out a hand and hauled her up on to the dock beside him before turning to the two men. 'You, Ben. Mr Desmond, he call you?'

The man called Ben looked up and shook his head, a sympathetic smile on his face. 'Nope. Didn' phone me. He phone you, Walter?'

The other man shook his head too. 'Nope. Ain't never talked to Mr Desmond. But it don' matter,' he said to Carly. 'You here to see Mr St Just—no problem. We drive you out to the house.'

'Yes, but—'

It wasn't a matter of being driven. It was a matter of arriving unannounced. Carly hadn't expected Piran to pick her up. That bit of courtesy would certainly be beyond him. But she had at least expected him to know she was coming!

If no one else did, chances were he didn't either.

Carly felt an increasing sense of unease. She hadn't been unassailed by second thoughts ever since she'd knuckled under to Desmond's pleas and her boss's not so subtle blackmail.

But now those thoughts were multiplying like bunnies.

She licked her lips. 'No one told you I was coming?'

'No, missy, not a soul. We been 'spectin' Mr Desmond all right. Mr St Just, he been yellin' where he is for a week now.' Ben chuckled and shook his head.

'He be in Fiji,' Sam said. 'Imagine that. Don't that beat all? Ain't Mr St Just gonna be surprised?'

Wasn't he just? Carly thought grimly. Which was exactly what she was afraid of.

But there was nothing else to do—except go home. And even if Des weren't half a world away, and even if her job didn't depend on her bringing back the book, she couldn't go home. She had nowhere to go home to.

She'd told Lenny, her downstairs neighbor, that he could put his divorced sister from Cleveland and her three children up in her apartment over the holidays. And since Lenny's family celebrated both Hanukkah and Christmas she was going to be homeless for quite some time.

Carly shut her eyes and wondered if maybe Christmas in Buffalo or in Colorado might not have been a better alternative after all.

'So, you want to go now?' Ben asked her, getting up and moving slowly toward a psychedelic van with the word 'TAXI' painted on it.

Did she? No, she didn't. Did she have a choice? No, again. Though what Piran was going to say when he saw her was not something she wanted to contemplate.

'Let's go,' she said to Ben with more enthusiasm than she felt.

As little as she had been looking forward to the trip and seeing Piran again, she had been looking forward to seeing Conch Cay. And now, as Ben drove her up the hill through the narrow bumpy streets, she looked around, enchanted, taking it all in. It was every bit as lovely as she remembered it. When Arthur had first brought them here she'd thought it the closest thing to an island Garden of Eden she'd ever seen. Nine years later she had no reason to change her mind.

In a few minutes they left the small town where most of the islanders lived and drove up into the lush tropical vegetation that banked the narrow asphalt road that wound back up the hill toward the windward side. Every so often Carly caught a glimpse of a house through the trees and shrubs. In the distance, as they approached the ocean side of the island, she could hear the sound of the surf crashing against the sand.

She watched with a mixture of eagerness and trepidation

for the turn-off on to the gravel that would bring them at last to Blue Moon Cottage, the St Justs' home.

'Mr St Just goin' to be that surprised,' Ben said as he finally turned into the rutted gravel track leading up to the house. 'Course I don' 'spect he'll be too mad. You a sight prettier than Mr Desmond.'

Which might have been a recommendation for another woman, but had never been for her, Carly thought.

She still winced inwardly every time she recalled her last painful encounter with Piran St Just. But now, as she got her first glimpse of the ice-blue house among the trees, she turned her back on that memory and drew herself together, mustering her strength, her determination, her maturity.

Good thing, too, for at the sound of the van the back door to the cottage opened and a man appeared on the broad screened-in veranda.

Carly hadn't seen Piran except on television and in photographs for nine years. It didn't matter; she would have known him anywhere.

He was tall, dark and unshaven. His hair was as black as night and wanted cutting, just as it always had. His jaw was hard and firm, and she saw it tighten when he noticed that the person Ben was bringing wasn't Desmond. His scowl deepened, but he didn't look angry. Yet.

Carly took a deep breath and pasted on what she hoped would pass for a cool, professional smile. Then she stepped out of the van, lifted her gaze to meet his eyes, and was chagrined to realize she was glad she was wearing sunglasses so that he couldn't see how much the mere sight of him still affected her after all these years.

'Piran,' she said, grateful that her voice didn't betray her agitation. 'Long time, no see.'

His eyes widened momentarily, then narrowed. The hard jaw got even harder. '*Carlota*?'

Carlota. No one ever called her Carlota. Not even her mother whose fault it was that she was named that!

Her only consolation was that he sounded as if he'd had the air knocked out of him. He braced a hand against one of the pillars of the veranda and she noticed that his knuckles were white.

'You remember me, I see.'

He snorted. 'What in the hell are you doing here?'

'I gather Des didn't tell you?'

'Des?' He frowned. 'What about Des?'

'He sent me. Got my boss to insist, as a matter of fact.'

'What? What are you talking about? Why the hell would he send you? Where'd he find you?' The questions came fast and furious, but no more furious, obviously, than Piran himself. 'What are you talking about? Where is Des?'

'On his way to Fiji?' She meant it to sound like a statement and was mortified when it came out tentative enough to be a question.

'*What*!' There was no question in that exclamation, just pure disbelief. And even more fury.

Carly would have quailed before it nine years ago. Now she drew herself up to her full five feet six, determined not to let him intimidate her. 'Jim Taylor—you remember, your father's old cap—'

'I know who Jim Taylor is,' Piran snapped.

'Well, he bought a new boat and—'

'I don't give a damn about Jim Taylor's boat. Where's Des?'

'I'm trying to tell you,' Carly snapped back, 'if you'll kindly shut up and let me finish!'

Piran's mouth opened, then snapped shut again. He glowered at her, then finally he shrugged and stuffed his fists into the pockets of his shorts. 'By all means enlighten me, Carlota,' he drawled.

Carly took a careful breath, ran her tongue over parched lips and began again. 'Jim bought a new boat. He's sailing it out of Fiji, and he invited Des to go along and—'

'He *went*?' The drawl was gone. The fury was back.

'He said you'd understand that it was too good an opportunity to miss.'

'The hell I would! We have a commitment! A contract! Does he think the book is going to write itself?' Piran stalked from one side of the veranda to the other.

'No, actually he thinks I'm going to help you write it.'

He spun around and looked at her, poleaxed. 'You? *You* help me write it?'

Carly heard a soft chuckle and was suddenly aware that Ben was still there listening. No doubt the whole island would be hearing about this before nightfall.

'Let's not discuss this out here,' she said in a low tone. 'Let me get my bag and we can discuss it in the house.'

'You're not coming in the house.'

'Piran—'

'You're not! I don't know what kind of stunt Des is pulling, but you're getting in the van and going right back where you came from.'

Carly heard Ben choke on his laughter.

Her cheeks burned. 'Don't be ridiculous,' she said fiercely to Piran. 'I didn't come all this way to have you send me back.' She turned and reached back into the van and grabbed her duffel bag. 'How much do I owe you?' she asked Ben.

'Eight dollar.' He was still grinning all over his face.

Carly ignored the grin. She took a ten out of her wallet and handed it to him. He tucked it in his shirt pocket. 'Thank you, missy.' He slid back into the driver's seat.

'What are you doing?' Piran demanded. 'Stay where you are.'

'Mr St Just gettin' pretty mad,' Ben said as he leaned out the window. 'You sure 'bout this?'

Carly wasn't sure at all, but she didn't see that she had any option. Diana had made herself perfectly clear: when Carly next appeared in the office, she was going to be carrying Piran and Desmond St Just's next bestselling true-life archaeological adventure. Or else.

But she wasn't going to be doing that unless she helped Piran finish it. There was certainly no way she could find Des now and make him take her place.

Besides, she thought irritably, how dared Piran make her seem like some sort of unwanted interloper?

'I'm sure,' she said.

Ben shrugged. 'It be your neck, missy.'

Undoubtedly it would. Carly took a deep breath. 'I'll be fine.'

Ben gave a quick salute and put the van in reverse.

Piran started down the steps. 'Ben! Where the hell are you going? Get back here! Ben! *Ben*!'

But Ben apparently knew that absence was the better part of valor—at the moment at least. The van putted away down the gravel and disappeared around the bend.

It was a full minute before Piran turned from staring after it to fix his gaze on Carly.

'Well, some things never change, do they, Carlota?' he drawled at last, looking her up and down.

Carly met his gaze levelly. 'What does that mean?'

'You're still a conniving little bitch.'

So the battle lines were drawn. It certainly hadn't taken long. If he'd slapped her face with a glove, he could not have challenged her more clearly. Nor could he have found a better means of making Carly dig her heels in.

For a single instant, before he called her that…that—she couldn't even let herself think about what he'd called her!—she'd almost felt sorry for Piran St Just. She'd almost regretted that his brother had deserted him, regretted that he'd have to make do with her help, not Des's.

But when he threw those words at her she thought, Serves him right, damned judgmental jerk.

She supposed she was a bit of a jerk, too, for having thought even for one moment that they could manage this without problems, that he might have changed his opinion of her.

Once—in the very beginning—he'd defended her. It had been the first time they met and she hadn't even known who he was.

It had happened a month after Carly's mother had married Piran's father in Santa Barbara. She'd met Des at the wedding, but she'd never met Arthur's much heralded elder son. Piran hadn't come to the ceremony, Arthur had said, because he went to university in the east.

But he was coming for spring vacation. Carly was going to meet him that very night. In fact, if she didn't hurry, she was going to be late.

She'd waited to leave the beach until the last possible moment, hoping that the small group of inebriated college students standing by the steps up the cliff would disperse. They hadn't. Instead they'd stood watching her approach, whistling and making lewd suggestions that made her cheeks burn.

She'd tried to ignore them, then she'd tried brushing past them and going up the steps quickly. But she'd stumbled and one of them had grabbed her and hauled her hard against him.

'Please,' she babbled. 'Let me go.'

He rubbed against her. 'Let's go together, baby,' he rasped in her ear.

Carly struggled. 'Stop it! Leave me alone!'

He shook his head. 'You want it. You know you do,' he said as she tried to pull away.

A couple of the other men hooted and whistled. 'I like 'em feisty,' one of them called.

'Please!' Carly tried twisting away from him, but he held her fast until all at once, out of nowhere, a savior appeared.

The most handsome young man she'd ever seen jerked the drunken man away from her. 'Can't you hear?' he snarled. 'The lady said she wants to be left alone.'

'Lady? Who says she's a lady?'

Carly's black-haired savior stepped between her and the drunken student. 'I say so,' he said, his voice low and deadly.

The student gave a nervous, half-belligerent laugh. 'An' who are you? The Lone Ranger?' He shoved Piran hard, so hard that he wobbled himself.

The next thing Carly knew the man was flat on his rear in the sand with her savior standing over him, rubbing his right fist.

'It doesn't matter who I am,' he said. 'Apologize to the lady. Now.'

The man's jaw worked. He spat blood on to the sand and glanced around at his friends. They fidgeted and muttered, but they apparently didn't see much point in fighting over Carly. Some of them backed up the steps. A few moved away down the beach. At last it was just Carly and the two of them left.

Finally the student struggled to his feet and glowered at the lean, tanned man still standing there, his fists clenched.

He didn't move an inch. 'Say it.'

The drunken student's gaze flicked briefly to Carly. He scowled. 'Sorry,' he muttered in a surly tone. Then he fled.

Carly stared after him, shaking, still feeling the disgusting feel of his sweaty, sandy body pressed against hers.

'Hey, you OK?' The young man tilted his head to look into her eyes. He gave her a gentle smile. He had the most beautiful blue eyes and the most wonderful smile she'd ever seen.

'F-fine,' she'd mumbled.

'It's over,' he said, and put his arm around her, drawing her close, holding her gently until she'd stopped shaking.

It should have frightened her. He was as much a stranger as the drunken student. But she wasn't frightened. She felt safe. Cared for.

She remembered looking up into his face right at that moment and thinking she'd found the man she wanted to spend the rest of her life with—the man her mother had always told her was out there waiting.

She stammered, 'Th—thanks.'

He smiled at her and ran his knuckles lightly down her cheek. 'My pleasure. Always ready to help out a damsel in distress.' He gave her a wink, then asked if he could see her home.

And that was when he found out whose daughter she was.

'You live where?' he asked her when she pointed out the house on the hillside.

'The pink house. The great big one. Isn't it lovely? We just moved in, my mother and I. She married a professor—'

'Arthur St Just.' His voice was suddenly clipped and short.

'Yes. You know him?'

'I thought I did,' her savior said gruffly. 'He's my father. I'm Piran St Just.'

Her new stepbrother. The one she'd never met. The one, she quickly learned, who hadn't come to the wedding not simply because he went to school in the east but because he objected so strongly to his father's remarriage.

He thought Carly's unsophisticated dancer mother far beneath Arthur St Just's touch and he made no bones about it. In Piran's eyes, she was no more than the gold-digging hussy who had trapped his unsuspecting father into matrimony.

While Des accepted his stepmother with equanimity, at the same time acknowledging that she wasn't quite what one would have expected Arthur St Just to pick for a wife, the same was not true of Piran.

And once he found out that Carly was the gold-digging hussy's daughter his solicitous behavior and gentle concern vanished at once.

Sue, always optimistic, encouraged her daughter to be patient.

'He doesn't understand,' she said softly to Carly more than once. 'Piran is young, idealistic, and his parents' divorce hurt him. He hasn't known love himself. He doesn't understand how it can happen. Give him time.'

Over the months to come Carly gave him that—and more. Even though, once he knew who she was, he treated her with cool indifference, she couldn't help remembering the first Piran—the gentle, caring Piran who was really there inside.

She told herself that Sue was right. She saw his dislike as a blind spot, one that time and proximity—and her love—would cure.

Until the night of her eighteenth birthday…when she

understood finally just how determinedly blind Piran St Just really was...

She lifted her chin now and faced him once more. 'Think what you like, Piran. I'm sure you will anyway. I'm not going to argue with you.'

'Because you haven't got a leg to stand on.'

'Try not to insult me too much,' she suggested mildly, 'or you'll be doing this book on your own.'

'That's another thing. What's all this nonsense about you helping with the book?'

'I'm Sloan Bascombe's assistant editor.'

'The hell you say!' He didn't seem to believe for a minute that she did in fact work for his editor.

They glared at each other for a full minute. Impasse. There were a myriad emotions crossing Piran's face. Acceptance wasn't one of them. Finally Carly nodded once and picked up her duffel.

'Suit yourself,' she said, and turned to head back down the road toward town.

She'd gone perhaps twenty yards when Piran called after her. 'Tell me what Des said.'

She stopped and turned, but she didn't go back.

Piran stood where she'd left him. They stared at each other now down the length of the narrow rutted lane. His hands were still in his pockets, his jaw was thrust out, but there was a hint of concern—of doubt?—in his expression.

'I told you what Des said. Am I supposed to assume you believe me now?'

He shrugged irritably. 'For whatever difference it makes.'

'None to me,' Carly said with all the indifference she could manage. 'Rather a lot to Des, I gather. He was there trying to get an extension so he could go on the trip to

Fiji when Diana told him I'd been the one to do the line-editing on your last book.'

'Sloan did it.'

'Sloan signed it. I wrote it. He has forty writers. He can't do everything for everyone. And I know more about archaeology than he does.' She took considerable satisfaction in telling him that and, at first, she thought he was going to object about that too. But finally he gave a negligent lift of his shoulders.

'Go on.'

'You know the rest. As soon as Des found that out, he asked if I'd come and work with you.'

'And you jumped at the chance?'

'Hardly.'

'You're here,' Piran pointed out.

'Not by choice. Diana made it abundantly clear that my job depended on it. Nothing, believe me,' she added after a moment, 'to do with you.'

'Got over your infatuation, did you, Carlota?' His mouth curved, but his smile was hard, not pleasant. 'Or maybe it's like I thought: you weren't ever really infatuated at all, just money-grubbing like your mother.'

It was all Carly could do not to slap him. Abruptly she turned her back and started walking again. She had reached the main road before she heard footsteps coming after her.

'Carlota!'

She walked faster. She knew she could let him insult her. It would be good for her, cleanse her, wash away all her childish hopes and dreams. But she wasn't going to stand there and listen to him insult her mother!

Heaven knew Sue had had her share of faults. But she hadn't been a bad person. She'd been as idealistic as she'd considered Piran to be. She'd just been far more confused. And foolish. And unlucky—until the last.

Carly was willing to admit all those things. What else could you call a woman who had married seven times in search of the perfect love?

But her mother hadn't been evil. She hadn't been conniving.

Never.

But there was no point in telling that to Piran. She had no intention of defending her mother to the likes of Piran St Just! He could go to hell as far as she was concerned. And he could take his book with him.

'Carlota, damn it! Get back here!'

Carly hurried on. The day was hot and sticky for December. And while she hadn't felt the heat much in the van, now her shirt stuck to her back. Rivulets of sweat ran down her spine and between her breasts into the waistband of her chambray trousers. She shifted the duffel from one hand to the the other and continued on.

Heavy footsteps pounded after her. She ignored them.

'Carlota!'

She didn't turn around. She didn't falter.

'Carly, you stubborn witch, stop!'

A hand came out and snagged her arm, hauling her abruptly to a halt. Fingers bit into her skin, holding her fast.

She tried to jerk her arm away, but Piran wouldn't let go. The pull on her arm was so strong he almost dragged her to the ground. She looked at him closely. He seemed winded. His dark hair clung damply to his forehead. His lean cheeks were flushed, but he was white around the mouth, and he was breathing heavily.

'Let me go,' she said again, trying to pry his fingers loose.

His chest heaved. 'Only if you don't start walking again.'

She just looked at him, making no promises.

His fingers tightened. She winced. He looked at his hand still biting into her flesh and frowned, but he didn't let go. 'We need to talk.'

'I'm not talking—or listening—to anyone who insults my mother.'

A muscle ticked in his jaw. She could almost see the thoughts flashing across his brain, angry thoughts, disparaging thoughts. But finally Carly felt his fingers loosen reluctantly. His hand dropped and he shoved it once more into the pocket of his canvas trousers. He shrugged almost negligently. 'Whatever.'

Carly pressed her lips together. She wanted to rub her arm, but she wouldn't give him the satisfaction.

'So talk,' she said frostily.

Piran drew a deep breath, as if trying to decide where to start. Finally he lifted his gaze and met hers.

'Let me get this straight,' he said after a long moment, and she could still hear his disbelief. 'You just happen to work at Bixby Grissom and you just happened to edit our book?'

'More or less. As I said, Sloan has a lot on his plate, and since I know more about archaeology than he does he asked me if I would do your last revision letter for him and the last line-editing.'

'Which he signed.'

'He's your editor. I'm not. And Des came to see him, but he was out with the flu.'

'So Des just jumped at the chance to suggest you come in his place.'

'I'm sure Des was just there to ask for an extension. But when he saw me a light bulb went off in his head. You know Des and his ideas.'

Piran grimaced. 'Yeah, I know Des and his ideas. What I don't know is why you agreed.'

'I told you—because I like my job. And because I wasn't sure how much longer I'd have it if I didn't. It certainly wasn't because I was ecstatic about seeing you.'

Was that a flush making his cheeks darker? 'I'm glad to hear it,' he said gruffly after a moment.

She waited, the sun beating down on her back, but he didn't say anything else. He just shut his eyes. His jaw tightened.

'So,' Carly said finally, 'do I stay or leave?'

He sighed, then opened his eyes. 'Like you I have no choice. What else can I do if we're going to turn the book in on time?'

'Des said you had a draft.'

'Des is ever an optimist.' His tone was dry. 'I have a very rough draft—the operative word being "rough". I was counting on Des to shape it up. He's supposed to be here,' he muttered again.

'Yes, well, he's not. I'm it. Unless you want to plead with Diana for an extension.'

Piran shook his head. 'It's in the schedule. Promo's being done. You know that as well as I do.' All at once he muttered, 'God, it's hot. I need to sit down.'

And he did, right there at the side of the road, pulling his knees up and dropping his head between them.

Carly stared at him, astonished. Then she bent down to look at him more closely. 'Are you all right? Piran?'

He didn't answer. She could only see the shallow rise and fall of his back.

'Piran, for God's sake, what's wrong?'

He lifted his head. His face was white. 'Nothing.'

'Nothing?' she mocked. 'You're just resting?'

'Just resting,' he agreed, his voice hollow. Carly could see sweat beading on his forehead and upper lip.

'You're sick.'

He shook his head. 'I had a diving accident a while ago. No big deal.'

As far as Carly could recall from the days when she'd been a part of the St Just family, there was no such thing as a diving accident that was 'no big deal'.

'What kind of diving accident?' And why hadn't Des told her? Trust Des to stick her with Piran who was ill as well as harsh, fierce and moody.

Piran gave a quick shake of his head and straightened, putting his hands behind him and leaning back, dropping his head back so that now her eyes were drawn to the long column of his throat, the strong jut of his chin and the quick rise and fall of his chest.

'What kind of accident?' Carly repeated.

'Had to come up too fast.' He sighed. 'Damn, I hate this.'

'Then don't run after people,' Carly said, taking refuge in gruffness. She wasn't about to let him think she was concerned.

Piran's mouth quirked. 'I'll try not to.'

'Why'd you do a stupid thing like that? Come up too fast, I mean.'

'Cut myself. Lost a lot of blood.'

'Blood?' Carly looked at him, aghast.

'Gashed my leg on some coral. Not a bad wound, but there're sharks out there sometimes...'

His voice trailed off. He didn't have to finish; Carly knew exactly what could have happened. She felt sick.

'There were two of us,' Piran went on. 'The other guy wasn't cut, but he couldn't stay down either without me.

And they only had one decompression unit. He showed more effects, so they put him in.'

'You could have died!' The words were wrung from Carly in spite of herself. She couldn't have stopped them if she'd tried.

He slanted her a glance. 'Wishful thinking, Carlota?'

She glared at him. 'Sometimes you're such an ass, Piran.'

He looked at her quizzically. 'Am I?'

'Yes,' she said tersely. 'Come on.' She held out a hand to him.

He scowled. 'I don't need your help.'

'Fine. Sit there forever. I don't care.' She turned away.

'Carly!'

When she looked back he was glowering at her. He reached out a grudging hand. She hesitated, then grasped it. And there it was—the jolt she always felt when she touched Piran St Just.

She pulled him to his feet and let go at once.

'Thanks,' he muttered.

'Don't mention it.' She turned away again, but she didn't start toward the house until he did. Then she fell into step beside him, watching him worriedly out of the corner of her eye, half expecting him to topple over any moment.

'I'm all right now,' he said as they reached the veranda. 'I'm not going to croak on you.'

'What a relief.' She waited until he'd climbed the short flight of steps, then she picked up her duffel bag and started into the house.

Piran stopped at the door and turned back to face her. 'I'll work with you, but that's it. You're not staying here.'

'I beg your pardon?'

'You can stay in town.'

'Des said—'

'The hell with Des!'

'Well, fine. You want me to stay in town? I'd be delighted. But you're paying for it. Diana certainly isn't going to give me my expenses for something that's above and beyond my duties. And I'm not about to pay for them!' She was so angry that she didn't give a damn if he still thought she was money-grubbing!

Piran dug in his pocket and pulled out his wallet. He peeled off several large-denomination notes and handed them to her.

'You can take the bicycle. There's one along the side of the house. Leave your bag here. When you find something, send Ben back out to get your bag.' He turned away and he probably would have gone right in and shut the door in her face if she hadn't spoken up.

'No. Not now.'

'Wha—?'

'I'm hot, and I've been traveling since dawn. I seem to remember your father once saying that the St Justs were famous for their hospitality. I would like a moment to catch my breath and have a glass of water.'

At the remark about his father Piran turned sharply and shot her a hard glance. Then he grimaced and rubbed his hand against the back of his neck. 'Oh, hell, all right. Come on.'

CHAPTER TWO

GRACIOUS he was not, but Carly was every bit as tired and hot by that time as she'd said she was, and she was too annoyed to care what Piran's tone of voice conveyed.

She followed him in.

Nothing inside Blue Moon Cottage had changed at all in the intervening years. The walls were still white and cool. The terrazzo floors gleamed. The white wicker sofa and chairs with their bright blue and green patterned cushions still encouraged her to come and sit a while. The mini-blinds were open to let in the air, but slanted to cut down on the afternoon sun, and the outside vegetation filtered away most of the heat. Overhead a five-blade fan circled lazily.

It was the only place where Carly had spent any time while she was growing up that she remembered missing after they'd left.

In spite of having to see Piran again, she'd been looking forward to coming back just to see if the charm remained. It did. Though whether that was a good thing or not she wasn't sure.

'I know where the kitchen is,' she said to him. 'I'll just get a drink. You can go rest.' He still looked pale.

He ignored her. 'I'll rest when you're gone.' He headed for the kitchen. 'I've got iced tea if you'd rather,' he said over his shoulder, and Carly wondered if he only said it because of her comment about the St Just hospitality.

'Thank you. That would be lovely.'

He nodded, went to the refrigerator, poured her a glass,

then poured another for himself. Then he nodded toward the deck on the ocean side of the house. 'You can drink it here or we can go out there.'

'My, you are being hospitable,' she mocked.

Piran's jaw tightened, but he didn't rise to the bait and Carly felt faintly guilty for riding him.

She took her glass of tea and went out on to the deck. The view above the trees was of more than a mile of deserted pink sand beach. The first time Carly had seen it, she hadn't believed it was real. She'd thought Arthur St Just must have had the sand specially dyed and trucked in.

Des had laughed, but Arthur had patiently explained to her about the local corals, about how much time it took for the coral to grind down into the fine, powdery sand, how this sand was pink because that was the color of the coral.

Later that day he'd taken them down to the beach and had even built a sand castle with her and Des and her mother. Piran had come by and looked down his nose at them.

Carly remembered that Arthur had invited his elder son to join them, but Piran hadn't bothered to answer. He'd walked right past them and never said a word.

He wasn't saying anything now either. He stood leaning against the railing of the deck, holding his glass of iced tea, not looking at her, staring instead at the expanse of sand and water.

Carly took the opportunity to study him. He'd been twenty-five the last time she'd seen him in person, lean and gloriously handsome, in the prime of young manhood. Full of charm and charisma and promise.

He'd been working on his Ph.D. in archaeology at Harvard during the year, diving with his famous father during the holidays. And when he hadn't been diving he'd been squiring some of the world's loveliest women to trendy nightclubs and fast-lane parties.

As far as Carly could see, he'd fulfilled all those promises. He'd got his Ph.D. He was now, at age thirty-four, an internationally acclaimed expert in the field of underwater exploration and recovery of artifacts. He and Des had written three books to date about the family's escapades.

Or perhaps, Carly amended, Des had written the books. But it was Piran whom one saw on the televised documentaries. And it was Piran who still had all the charm, all the charisma, and all the ladies hanging on his arm.

She knew she wasn't the first woman to succumb to Piran St Just's incredible charm. And she hadn't been the last, either. She'd kept track of the number of beauties who'd been seen with him throughout the years. It hadn't been difficult.

Piran St Just attracted notice wherever he went. And, as she looked at him now, it wasn't hard to tell why.

He might be older now, but his thirty-four years sat well on him. The smooth, tanned skin of youth had weathered beautifully. The paleness of his complexion at the moment was simply a result of his illness, nothing to do with the man himself. There was a network of fine lines around his eyes, but they only called attention to their piercing blue. Just as the strong bones of his cheeks and jaw and the grooves that bracketed his mouth gave his face a sort of cragginess that spoke of battles fought and won.

Pity he didn't have a potbelly or slumping shoulders, Carly thought. He would be easier to ignore if he weren't so obviously gorgeous.

But from what she could tell the belly beneath the thin cotton T-shirt was rock-hard. And if his shoulders were slumped it was only because of the way he leaned with his forearms resting on the railing as he stared out to sea.

Yes, he'd aged well. Damn the man.

She took another sip of her iced tea.

Piran turned his head to glance at her. 'Finished?'

Carly looked at him across her barely touched glass. 'Not quite. Don't feel you have to entertain me, Piran. Go do whatever it is you were doing before I came. I'll drink my tea and I'll go.'

He hesitated, as if he was afraid to leave her alone for fear she might dig in or something. But finally he straightened up. 'Fine,' he said shortly. 'I'll see you tomorrow morning at nine and we can go over what I've got.'

So saying, he drained his glass, carried it back into the house and disappeared into one of the bedrooms. The door shut with a firm click after him.

Carly breathed far more easily when he was gone. She rubbed her fingers along the soft weathered wood of the railing and rued the dreams she'd once had about making Blue Moon her home—about making Piran St Just love her.

It was hard to imagine she'd been such a naïve little fool.

Well, she was a fool no longer. And it was probably just as well she wasn't going to be living here, given that he still seemed to be able to make her respond to him. She certainly didn't want him to know it.

The only thing she regretted was not getting to spend the time at Blue Moon. It was every bit as lovely as it had ever been. It might be easy enough to give up her dreams about Piran, but it would be harder to relinquish the ones about Blue Moon.

She finished her tea and put the glass back in the kitchen. Then she let herself out and found the bicycle, wheeled it back to the road and climbed on, avoiding the ruts as she pedaled slowly toward town.

Piran listened until he was sure she was gone. He lay on his bed, cursing his weakened condition and the twist of fate that had brought Carly O'Reilly into his life once more.

Only when he heard the rattle of the bicycle disappear into the distance did he allow his body to sag into the mattress and breathe deeply.

But still, he couldn't believe it.

God, what could Des have been thinking of?

Well, there was no point in even asking that question.

When had Des ever thought at all? Smart, clever, witty Des somehow never saw what was right under his nose— which was how much Piran hated Carly O'Reilly. And how much he'd once desired her.

It had nothing to do with liking. Never had. Never would. No, that wasn't true.

In the beginning, the first time he'd seen her, he'd liked her on sight. He'd left his father's house after the first of several fights he and Arthur had had. He'd been fuming at the way his father seemed like a besotted teenager around his new wife, a wife that Piran thought was far beneath him. And nothing had taken his mind off it until he'd spied a lovely smiling water nymph with waist-length dark hair and long, coltish legs.

He'd watched her swim, then he'd watched her come back up the beach and stretch out on her towel in the sand. She'd lain on her stomach looking up at the cliff and the bench where he sat. She'd fidgeted, looked up, looked away, looked up again.

Piran had watched her, intrigued, running over various lines, trying to decide on the best one to use for meeting her, when she'd got up and started up the beach toward the steps that would bring her up to where he was.

And that was when she'd met the students at the bottom of the steps. He'd watched her smile at them. He'd heard them speak, but he couldn't hear what they were saying. She'd smiled again. Then, as they'd closed around her, he'd momentarily lost sight of her. He'd got to his feet quickly and started down.

He'd been furious to reach them and discover a shy, innocent girl being preyed upon by hooligans. He hadn't hesitated to step in.

He remembered as if it were yesterday—the drunken shove, the satisfying smack when his fist had connected with the drunk's jaw, the adoring gray eyes that had looked up into his.

His hands, clenching now, remembered too. They could still feel the petal-softness of her skin as he'd held her briefly in his arms. The same softness they'd felt when she'd reached out her hand to help him up less than an hour ago.

In scant moments he'd become her hero. And he'd wanted to be her hero.

Until he'd found out whose daughter she was.

Then he'd felt as if he too had been duped. Her innocence hadn't seemed so innocent any longer. Her shyness had seemed calculated.

It had made him furious then because he'd seen it for what it was.

Pure animal magnetism. Sexual chemistry. Hormones. Exactly the same things that had drawn his poor foolish father to Carly's gorgeous shallow mother.

Piran was damned if he was going to let it happen to him!

And so he'd stayed away as much as he could.

Probably he'd only seen her half a dozen times over the not quite two years of his father's marriage to Sue. But every time he had Carly had changed. She'd grown more desirable than ever.

Her curves developed. Her eyes sparkled with tantalizing laughter and heady promise. Her lips grew full and tempting, just made to be kissed.

But Piran had refused to kiss them. He wasn't weak like his father. He knew there was more to a woman than a pretty face.

Ever since he was a tiny child, he'd idolized Arthur St Just, had grown up wanting to be just like him. He'd even taken his father's side in his parents' divorce.

In his eyes, Arthur St Just could do no wrong—until he'd met and married, in the space of a few short weeks, the blowsy, beautiful dancer Sue O'Reilly Delgado Gower Tremaine.

God, Piran thought, his fist clenching at his side and pounding on the mattress, even now he could remember the litany of her names!

Carly had told them to him once—recited them, actually, her wide gray eyes watching for his reaction. He'd gritted his teeth then. He gritted them now.

He couldn't believe his father had fallen for a tramp like Sue—a dancer, for heaven's sake! A woman with no education, no background, nothing—except a daughter.

Carly.

Carly, whose laughter and smiles and serious silvery eyes had tempted him increasingly each time he'd seen her, until at last, on her eighteenth birthday, he hadn't been able to resist what she was offering.

Or what he thought she'd been offering.

To his everlasting shame he could still remember how

ready he'd been for her. God, yes, he'd been ready! More than ready, he recalled with chagrin even now.

In another few moments he would have fallen completely under her spell. But then she'd opened her mouth and he'd found out that she hadn't really been offering at all. She'd been trading—just like her mother.

Sex for marriage.

Piran might be one kind of fool, but he was never going to be the fool that his father had been. Marriage to Carlota O'Reilly had never been on the cards.

'Marry you? You must be kidding!' he'd said, incredulous. And he'd turned away from her stricken look.

He'd never seen her again after that night. Not even at his father's funeral. He'd missed it, made up an excuse, hating her because he felt he had to, because he knew she would be there.

After that he'd put her—and her mother—out of his mind. He hadn't thought of her in years. And yet the moment he'd seen her this afternoon he'd recognized her at once.

And wanted her just as much as ever, God help him.

'What do you mean, there's no room at the inn?' Piran glowered at her from the doorway. The passage of four hours hadn't improved his mood any, that was certain.

'I was speaking metaphorically,' Carly said. She drooped on to one of the wicker chairs on the veranda, feeling as if she'd been dragged backwards through the mangrove swamp. 'There are no rooms available in Conch Cay.'

'Don't be ridiculous. Of course there are.' Piran shoved a hand through sleep-tousled hair.

To say that he'd been unhappy to see her come back would be something of an understatement.

He'd said, '*You*!' in a horrid voice and fumbled to fasten the top button of his trousers.

Carly had watched with undisguised interest. 'Perhaps you were expecting someone else?' she'd suggested, and fluttered her lashes at him, irritated that he would disbelieve her about a thing like this.

'I was taking a nap,' he'd retorted stiffly.

'Oh. Right. Sorry to disturb you.'

'You're not,' he'd said, which was the absolute truth.

He said now, 'What about Maisie Cash's house?'

'The Potters are there from Phoenix for the holidays,' Carly recited from memory.

'It's not the holidays yet.'

'Tell that to the Potters.'

'Well, what about the Kellys?' he said impatiently. 'They take in visitors.'

'Lots of people take in visitors, Piran. Tourism is the prime industry on the island.'

'I know that. So—'

'So Conch Cay has a bumper crop. It might not look like Christmas out here, but everyone is here to celebrate it. I stopped at the grocery. Old Bill gave me a list.'

'And?'

'And they were all full.'

'You can't have looked everywhere!'

Carly unfolded the list and shoved it at him. 'Then you look. I've looked until I'm ready to drop.' She lay back on the floor of the veranda and closed her eyes.

Piran muttered under his breath. He prowled up and down the veranda, then stood glowering down at her.

Carly opened one eye. 'And don't tell me to go over to Eleuthera and take the launch back every day, because I won't.'

He muttered again and paced the length of the veranda once more. 'I suppose that means you expect to stay here?'

'Unless you have a better idea, I don't see any other option.'

'Go home.'

'We've been through that already.'

Piran made a furious sound deep in his throat.

'What's the matter really, Piran? Are you afraid I'll take advantage of your virtue?'

He let out an explosive breath. 'Maybe I'm afraid I'll take advantage of yours?'

'I didn't think you thought I had any virtue.'

His teeth came together with a snap. 'Don't bait me, Carlota. If you want to stay here, don't bait me.'

'I have no intention of baiting you,' Carly said hastily.

'Good. Remember that. This is work. That's all.'

'You're damn right it is,' Carly said, incensed, sitting up and glaring at him. 'And you're a jerk if you think I want it to be any more than that!'

He met her gaze. 'Just so we understand each other.'

'We do.'

The look went on…and on. Finally he nodded curtly. 'Use your old bedroom. But leave me alone. We can start work in the morning.'

She was surprised Piran remembered which bedroom had been hers.

Or maybe he didn't, she thought when she finally got up and made her way toward the small bedroom next to the kitchen. Maybe he just assumed that she would re-member and didn't care as long as it wasn't anywhere near his.

It wasn't. It faced away from the ocean, bordering the narrow drive up which she'd come. The room Piran was using had been her mother's and his father's the last time they'd come here. It was on the other side of the house with access to the deck and the stairs to the path leading to the beach.

Bigger and airier than hers, it also had a lovely view across the treetops toward the ocean. But the small back bedroom with the narrow wicker bed and freestanding cupboard in which to hang her clothes suited Carly just fine.

She opened the windows and got a cross-breeze almost at once. But to aid its movement she turned on the overhead fan. Then she put her things away, slipped off her sandals and lay down on the bed.

She only intended to rest her eyes for a moment. Then she would go out and walk on the beach in the waning summer light. She would dig her toes in the sand and wade in the warm Caribbean water. She would savor the moment and appreciate the parts of Conch Cay she had no trouble enjoying. In just a few minutes she would do that...

It was pitch-dark when she woke up.

It took her a moment to remember where she was. Then it came back in a rush.

Des. Diana. The book. Piran. Christmas. The long trip by taxi, plane, taxi, and boat to Conch Cay. Piran's less than enthusiastic welcome. Her fruitless search for a room. Her return to Blue Moon Cottage. Piran's reluctant agreement to her staying with him. Piran. Always Piran.

Carly rolled over and tried to forget him, tried to go back to sleep because it was obviously quite late now. But she wasn't tired enough to go back to sleep, and trying not to think about Piran only insured that she would.

Finally, after she'd tossed and turned for half an hour, she got up and put her sandals on, then padded through the silent house.

The lights were all shut off and the door to Piran's room

was closed. She didn't know the time, but figured that it must be sometime after midnight.

Quietly she slid open the door to the veranda and padded out. A swath of silvery moonlight spilled across the ocean, lighting her way as she went down the steps. At the bottom she found the narrow path that led through the trees down the hill to the beach.

Before she was more than twenty yards along the path, she heard a rustling sound in the brush and saw a dark, slithering shape. Swallowing a scream, she stopped dead right where she was.

There were snakes on Conch Cay. She remembered Des showing her the marks they made in the sand which had looked to Carly like the imprints from bicycle tires. But she didn't know what kind they were and she didn't know if any of them were poisonous.

It wouldn't do to get herself bitten by a snake the first night she was here. Piran wouldn't be in the least bit understanding.

The rustling noise stopped and eventually Carly went on. She moved on carefully now, watching her every step, doing her best to make sure she didn't step on anything alive and capable of objecting.

She didn't notice when the path curved and the beach came into view. She didn't see the lean masculine form that slowly rose out of the water and made its way across the narrow sand beach toward the trail.

She didn't see Piran at all until it was too late, until she ran right into his bare wet chest.

'Ooof!'

'Bloody hell!' Hard fingers came out and grabbed her arms.

'P-Piran?'

'Who'd you think it was? The Loch Ness monster?' His fingers were still biting into her flesh as he snarled at her.

Carly looked up into hard eyes, then down at a shadowed but all too evident masculine nakedness, and finally, desperately, away into the jungle brush.

Snakes seemed suddenly far preferable.

'What the hell are you doing out here?' he demanded.

'G-going for a walk.'

'In the middle of the night?'

'I couldn't sleep.' She tried twisting away from him. 'Let me go.' Finally she managed to pry his fingers off her arms. Then she wrapped her arms against her chest, keeping her eyes firmly averted the whole time. 'I certainly wasn't looking for you, if that's what you think!'

Piran made a sound that could have been a snort of disgust or disbelief. 'You shouldn't be out walking now. It's almost two. It's dangerous.'

'You're out,' she said. Of course maybe that was why it was dangerous, she thought a little wildly.

'It's not dangerous for me.'

'How's that for the double standard?' Carly said bitterly.

'I don't make the rules, Carlota. But I can tell you what they are.'

'I'm sure you can,' she said. 'It's not fair,' she complained after a moment.

'Tell me about it,' Piran muttered under his breath. Then he said, 'No one ever promised that life would be fair.'

'Save me the time-worn platitudes.'

He reached for her arm. 'Come on, Carly. Let's go.'

She tried to shake him off. 'I said, I'm going for a walk.'

'No, you're not.'

'Yes, I am.' It was sheer stubbornness on her part and she knew it. But she was determined not to let him have the last word, not to allow him to tell her what to do.

She wrenched away from him and started down the path toward the beach at a run.

She'd got perhaps five steps when he caught her. With one hand he spun her round, then grasped her around the waist with both hands and flung her over his shoulder.

'Piran!' she shrieked as she pitched head-first, then stopped abruptly as her midriff lodged against his shoulder and she hung flailing upside down. 'Piran! Damn you! Put me down!'

But Piran only turned and strode back up the path with Carly slung over his shoulder like some bag of old clothes.

'Piran!'

She twisted and smacked him, her fists coming into contact with hard wet flesh. She opened her eyes and found herself staring down at a pair of lean, hair-roughened thighs and bare, muscular buttocks. She hit them. Hard.

'Damn!' He twisted and tried to catch her hands.

Carly kicked her feet, kneed him in the chest, then slapped him again, hoping the blows stung his wet skin.

'Stop it! Damn it, Carly!' He made it to the veranda, but he stumbled on the steps, and they both went down, a tangle of arms and legs, cool droplets of water and heated flesh. Carly landed face down between the backs of his thighs. It took only an instant's exposure to the hard warmth of his body to have her scrambling to her feet.

'I can't believe you did that!' she railed at him. 'Talk about cavemen!'

He was slower getting up. He winced as he pulled himself up and Carly noticed for the first time the angry scar on his leg. 'Are you all right?' she asked him.

'What do you care?' He snapped a towel off one of the lounges and knotted it around his waist, but not before she'd had a chance to glimpse definite signs of masculine arousal.

She swallowed and averted her eyes. 'I—I don't, actually.'

'I'm not surprised.'

They stared at each other. Piran's gaze was hard and angry, and any arousal that he might feel, Carly knew all too well, was unwanted.

So what else was new? He'd wanted her nine years ago, and he'd hated himself for it.

She glanced back at him and saw a muscle in his jaw tick in the moonlight. She thought he looked very pale. She felt a fleeting stab of guilt, then squelched it immediately. He hadn't had to carry her! He hadn't had to interfere at all.

She said as much.

'Just my chivalric nature, I guess,' he said through his teeth.

Carly remembered when he really had been chivalrous. That memory, sweet as it was, somehow hurt more than all the other painful memories did.

'Don't bother,' she said shortly.

Their eyes met and clashed once more. Piran ran his tongue over his lips.

'Fine,' he said harshly after a long moment. 'Go for a bloody walk if you want. Drown yourself if you want. I don't care what you do. I don't know why I bothered.'

CHAPTER THREE

To SAY that she slept badly was no exaggeration. It was close to dawn before Carly did more than toss and turn fitfully in her bed, her mind still playing with the image of Piran's naked body and the press of his flesh against hers. When at last she did sleep, her dreams were no less alluring and no more restful.

She was reminded all too much of the night of her eighteenth birthday—the last time she'd been held in Piran St Just's arms—the time she'd found out what he really thought of her.

For years she'd turned away from that memory every time it surfaced. She'd blotted it out as soon as she could because it had hurt so much.

But now she forced herself to remember. She had no choice. She needed to remember if only to protect herself from being drawn once more into the fanciful dreams that once upon a time had brought her down.

She'd certainly had her share of dreams about Piran in the days just before her birthday. She'd been living with her mother and Arthur in his home in the hills above Santa Barbara—the low, Spanish-style house she'd pointed out to Piran the day she'd first met him.

It was indeed a lovely house, built to blend in with the surrounding hillside, its gardens half wild. The latter weren't as wonderful as the wild areas surrounding Blue Moon on Conch Cay, but Carly had loved to ramble through them just the same. She'd loved to sit on the bench beside the bougainvillaea and look out over the city lights and the boats in the harbor at night.

Every night she would go there and sit, dreaming of Piran sitting next to her, of Piran touching her, holding her, kissing her.

She'd never really stopped dreaming of him after their first meeting. Perhaps she'd been foolish—no, there was no *perhaps* about it. She had been foolish. But in those days Carly had been as big an optimist, as big a dreamer as her mother.

And Piran, even though he clearly disapproved of his father's marriage, still fascinated her.

She knew there was more to him than his silent, brooding disapproval. She remembered his gentleness. She remembered his touch. And, even though he was silent and stern whenever he was around her afterwards, she wasn't unaware of the way he watched her.

Carly might not have been sophisticated in those days, but even she knew when a man was interested. And Piran's smoldering gaze was a sure sign that he was. Whenever he came home, or whenever he joined them at Blue Moon or in New York, he watched her with an intensity that tantalized her at the same time as it unnerved her.

Carly watched him too, avidly trying to understand him, to attract him. Even at eighteen and hopelessly naïve in the ways of love, she sensed a connection between them. It was tenuous, but it was very real. It had been from the first moment.

At least it was to Carly. She wanted Piran to see that, too.

When Piran came home for Thanksgiving he watched her. At dinner she caught him studying her out of the corner of his eye. On Friday, when Arthur took them to the botanical gardens, Carly noticed Piran keeping an eye on her.

And Sunday morning, before his plane left for Boston, he even went for a walk on the beach with her. He didn't say anything. They just walked. Every now and then Carly ventured a comment, which was met with a monosyllabic response, as if he was as tongue-tied as she was.

He loves me, she thought, and tucked the words away in the depths of her heart to take out and savor again and again.

They tided her over until Christmas, when she and Sue and Arthur and Des flew down to the Bahamas and met Piran at Conch Cay.

She watched Piran closely to see if he was still interested in her. It didn't take long to decide that he was.

There were more discreet glances. More tense, tongue-tied encounters. Another walk on a different beach.

She wanted to know about the cannons on the headland, and Arthur said, 'Piran knows. He'll tell you. Take her down there and explain to her, Piran.'

So Piran did. He didn't say much all the way down the beach. It was a cool, blustery day and he jammed his hands in his pockets and walked steadily, barely glancing her way. But he was as aware of her as she was of him. She knew it because when the sleeve of his jacket brushed her arm he sucked in his breath and flinched away.

As they walked, she picked up shells, asking if he knew what they were. He did, and Carly saved them. She asked him everything she could think of about the cannons, making their excursion last as long as possible. And finally she got him talking about his courses and his field work in archaeology.

She was fascinated, hanging on every word, wishing that someday she might get to go on a dig or underwater expedition with him. She didn't dare say so. Not yet. But she began to dream.

On the way back he stopped and picked up a piece of something shiny and red. She'd never seen anything like it before. He told her it was sea glass, smoothed now by years of being tossed about in the waves.

'Can I hold it?' she asked.

'You can have it if you want.'

Carly wanted. She put it in her pocket with the shells, rubbing it between her thumb and her forefinger all the way home. She knew that whenever she looked at it she would remember this day with Piran.

She must have daydreamed more than a hundred happy scenarios between them after he went back to school. In every one of them Piran came back and saw at last that she had become a woman. He cast aside the cool indifference or faintly disdainful tolerance with which he'd habitually treated her. He started treating her as the woman he loved.

Carly wanted it to happen so badly that she came to believe in it. It would happen, she decided, on her eighteenth birthday.

And when Arthur got a letter from Piran in March saying that, yes, he would be coming for the Easter vacation, she was certain it was true.

He came. She went with Des to meet him at the airport and for a moment she thought his eyes lit with pleasure when he spotted her there. But if they had the fires were banked by the time he was close enough to shake his brother's hand.

He didn't shake hers. He did, however, look at her mouth with a hungry, almost desperate gaze.

He loves me, she thought again. And she hugged the knowledge to herself, happy beyond belief.

From the moment they met at the airport, he didn't take his eyes off her. Everywhere she went, he watched her. Every time she looked up, he was there.

On the night of her birthday she barely ate her dinner, so aware was she of the dark, brooding young man directly sitting across the table from her. Arthur and her mother spoke to her frequently, encouraging her to talk about her plans for the summer, about the classes she would take at university in the fall. But Carly could barely form words.

Des teased her about the boys who were starting to hang around her, about one in particular whose name she couldn't even remember now. And Carly felt her face burn and dismissed all of them quickly, shooting Piran a quick glance and a small, encouraging smile, not wanting him to think she was fickle. He had to know she had eyes and ears only for him!

She didn't know what he thought. Through the entire meal he never said a word. Still, it seemed to Carly that he smoldered just sitting there. Every time she lifted her eyes, she saw him watching her from beneath hooded lids. And every glance was hotter than the last, inflaming the feelings growing between them.

She excused herself early, shortly after she'd opened her gifts, pleading the tiredness that came from an exciting day.

'Rest,' Sue encouraged her.

'Oh, yes,' Carly agreed.

But she didn't sleep. Instead she sat by the sliding door of her bedroom, waiting until she saw Piran leave the house, as she'd known he would, to stroll the grounds.

He paused on the path for a moment. He stood with his back to her, his legs outlined in faded denim, his strong shoulders flexing under the thin cotton of the pale gray polo shirt he wore. He stared out at the winking lights of the city. Then he turned and raked his hands through his hair. Slowly his gaze went from the lights of the city below to the darkened house where Carly stood unseen.

For a long moment he just stared at her room.

Carly stared back, her heart hammering. She knew he couldn't see her, and yet…

Come to me! her heart cried.

He took one step in her direction, then his fists clenched at his sides. His jaw tightened and he turned quickly away to hurry down the path.

Carly swallowed her disappointment, but she understood.

He didn't want to come to her at the house. Not at first. Not until he was sure she returned his feelings. As if there could be any doubt!

She waited until he disappeared. Then, hammering heart wedged in her throat, she slipped out the door and followed him.

There was a small bridge over a ravine partway up the hill behind the house. After the winter rains, a small stream ran down it. But this year there hadn't been a lot of rain and by mid-April the stream had dried up.

Still, when Carly came upon it, the first thing she saw was Piran standing on the bridge, arms braced against the railing, staring down into the ravine as if there were something there worth looking at.

She hesitated, then mustered her courage. What, after all, was she afraid of?

She loved him. She knew he loved her. Hadn't she, less than half an hour ago, seen the hunger in his eyes? Hadn't she seen him take that one small step toward her room?

He spun round, his eyes wide. 'Carly?'

She gave him a tremulous smile, wishing he'd hold out

his arms to her. In her fantasies, he had. She started toward him.

'What are you doing out here?' he demanded. His voice was ragged. He turned and braced himself against the railing.

'I came after you.' Wasn't it obvious?

'Why?'

'You know why,' she whispered.

She covered the few yards that remained between them until she was looking almost directly into his eyes. He was only three or four inches taller than she was so her eyes were almost on a level with his mouth.

His lips parted. She saw him run his tongue over them before he clamped them shut in a thin line. He shifted against the railing.

'I missed you while you were gone,' she told him softly.

'Did you?' He stuffed his hands into the pockets of his jeans. 'I can't imagine why.'

'Can't you?'

A harsh breath whistled out between his lips. 'Damn it, Carly, what the hell are you trying to do?'

She probably wouldn't have said it if it hadn't been her birthday, if she hadn't dreamed it so many times that she didn't see how it couldn't be true, if she hadn't trusted him to love her with the same fervor with which she loved him.

But she did, and so she said quite sincerely, 'Trying to get you to give me my birthday kiss, of course.' And she looked up into his eyes and parted her lips expectantly.

'For God's sake, Carly!'

She blinked at his explosive reaction. 'Well, your father did,' she said defensively after a moment. 'Even Des did. But not you.'

He muttered something indistinct under his breath. 'You know what you're asking for?' he said harshly.

She nodded slowly, but deliberately. Of course she knew. She'd dreamed of it—of him—for months.

He stared at her for a long moment, then he jerked his hands out of his pockets and reached for her, hauling her hard against him and taking her mouth with his.

It wasn't that Carly was a total innocent. Well, perhaps she was. She'd been kissed before. By Des. By that boy he'd been teasing her about. By another one or two sweaty-palmed, pimply-faced adolescents who'd pecked her lips like roosters pecking corn.

She'd never in her life been kissed like this.

She didn't feel kissed so much as plundered. Piran seemed more angry than desperate as he locked his mouth over hers. His tongue invaded the sweet recesses of her mouth, seeking, delving, tasting.

And Carly, both shocked and aroused by the force of his possession, hesitated a second, then responded in kind, even more desperate than he was, touching her tongue to his, dueling with him, challenging him.

And while their tongues fought and tangled their bodies did the same. One of Piran's legs slipped between hers, and she felt the soft denim of his jeans rub against the bare skin of her thighs below the hem of her shorts.

He drew her closer still and his knee rode higher, pressing against the juncture of her legs, inciting her further, making her moan and writhe against him.

His hands slipped inside the waistband of her shorts, skimming right down to cup her buttocks as he lifted her into his embrace. It was further than any boy had ever gone with her before.

But Piran wasn't just any boy, she reminded herself. In fact he wasn't a boy at all—he was a man. With a man's hunger and a man's needs.

And as his mouth and hands and knee learned her body

Carly was finding a woman's needs inside herself that night. She wanted Piran every bit as badly as he seemed to want her. Untutored though she was, somehow, instinctively, she knew what to do.

She knew how to tug his shirt out of his jeans, how to spread her hands against the heated flesh of his back. She knew how to nip and taste his lips in the same way that he nipped and tasted hers. She knew how to slide her hands round and press them against his chest, how to rub tiny circles against the sensitive nipples she found there, how to make him groan and drag his hands out of her shorts long enough to tug her T-shirt over her head.

'God! Carly!'

'Yes,' she murmured. 'Oh, yes.' It felt so good, touching him, feeling the contrast between his hot skin and the cool night air that caressed her flushed body.

It wasn't cool enough to calm her fevered blood. In fact the sudden touch of fresh air only made her ease closer to Piran, pressing her breasts against his chest, snuggling in as tight as she could.

She heard the quick intake of his breath. His hands sought the waistband of her shorts again, opening the fastener, easing down the zipper. Carly swallowed hard at the feel of his rough fingertips against her smooth skin. His touch was so possessive, so intimate.

And then it became more intimate still. One hand slipped between her legs, parted her tender flesh and touched her growing moistness, making her quiver with a need and desperation she'd never felt in all her seventeen years. She whimpered and pressed herself against his questing fingers.

Piran uttered a low sound deep in his throat, and thrust his hips against her, so that Carly could feel the taut bulge beneath his jeans. She'd never felt a man's erection before.

She'd taken the requisite sex-education classes, had tittered and snickered with her girlfriends about boys, had tried to imagine the changes that arousal would make in a man. But she'd never experienced the evidence of that arousal, had never felt the urgent press of masculine power until now.

Sometimes she'd wondered how she'd react. With wonder? With fear?

Now she knew. She felt nothing of fear, only a desire to know it—to know Piran—even more fully.

She wanted to touch him as intimately as he was touching her. Her hands went to the buttons of his jeans, fumbled, then succeeded in undoing them.

He tried to pull her hand away but she persisted, needing to touch him, wanting to caress the silken heat of his flesh.

'God, Carly!' he murmured again, his voice ragged as she did so.

'Am I hurting you?'

'No! Yes! You're killing me! God, I need—I can't—I don't want—! Stop!' He pressed against her, shuddering, his face buried against her shoulder, his hips thrusting against her.

'Piran? Are you all right?'

He groaned. 'No.' He took another shuddering breath. His whole body was trembling against hers. 'God! I'm… sorry. I… Oh, hell,' he muttered.

'Oh,' Carly said faintly. 'Oh, dear.' She felt her cheeks burn as she realized what had happened. And yet she felt an overwhelming tenderness for him and the need to let him know that she loved him all the more.

She smiled at him. 'I can wait,' she told him softly.

'You'll have to,' he said raggedly. 'I can't believe this. I've never—'

'It's OK,' Carly assured him resting her head against his chest. 'I don't mind. Truly. I'm really sort of glad.'

He pulled back and stared at her. 'Glad?'

She lifted her face and met his gaze, nodding. 'To wait till we're married.'

Hard hands came up and gripped her shoulders. 'What do you mean, *married*?'

'Isn't that what you meant? Waiting until we get married?' she repeated, looking into his eyes, which suddenly seemed large and even darker than normal.

'*Married*?' He almost choked on the word.

For the first time Carly felt a faint shiver run through her. 'Don't you want...?' she ventured finally. But she didn't even have to finish the sentence because the look on his face answered her question even before she asked it.

But just in case she couldn't tell he spelled it out for her. 'I never said anything about marriage. Did I? *Did I*?'

'No, but—'

'Marry you? You must be kidding!'

Carly stared at him, pulling away, hastily doing up her shorts, still never taking her eyes from his face. It was as if he was turning into a monster right before her eyes. 'But you—I—we—'

'We're hot for each other. That's all.'

'But—'

'I'm no sucker, Carlota,' he said. 'Just because my father was dumb enough to get trapped by a brazen hussy, it doesn't mean I'm fair game too.'

It took Carly a moment to realize what he meant. 'You think I—' She couldn't even say the words. She gaped at him. 'My mother never—!'

'Tell me your mother didn't set out to snare my old man! Go on, tell me. Better yet, prove it!'

Carly opened her mouth, but no words came out. Piran stood looking at her coldly, daring her.

And she couldn't answer him. As much as she would have loved to deny Piran's accusation, she couldn't.

Sue had in fact pursued Arthur. She'd taken one look at the tall, bespectacled archaeology professor and had fallen in love—at least she thought she had. And she'd made no bones about it. Carly knew it. Even Arthur knew it.

Arthur had been equally smitten. They might have seemed the oddest of couples, but their marriage worked. And, regardless of what Piran thought of her motives, Sue had never been after Arthur's money. She'd been after him.

But Piran wouldn't understand that.

Piran, Carly was beginning to realize, didn't know the first thing about love.

She looked at him as though she was seeing him for the first time. She still didn't speak.

'That's what I thought,' Piran said roughly. 'You can't.'

He zipped up his jeans and tucked in his shirt. Then he reached down and snagged Carly's T-shirt from the ground where it had fallen. He flipped it to her. She grabbed it and held it in front of her breasts.

They looked at each other, and Carly saw her dreams crumble right before her eyes.

'You don't understand,' she said sadly at last and then she turned and walked away.

The sun was high in the sky when Carly awoke. She groaned, knowing that the minute she walked into the living room Piran would be complaining that she was late for work. Well, too bad.

She'd lain awake half the night remembering in detail all the pain of her youthful encounter with Piran. She was glad she had, no matter however painful it had been to relive it.

Now she just needed to keep that memory at the forefront of her thoughts for the next month. Then there would be no chance of her finding herself giving in to her attraction to him again.

She hauled herself out of bed, washed, dressed and padded out into the living room. As she'd predicted, Piran was already there, seated at the computer.

'Nice of you to join me,' he said.

'Sorry,' Carly muttered, shoving a hand through her hair. 'Must be jet lag.'

'There was no time change,' he said without looking up from the keyboard.

'Then perhaps being tossed around after midnight doesn't agree with me.'

'I'd have thought you'd be used to it.'

She gasped at the rudeness of the remark, and at the look on her face he appeared momentarily discomfitted.

But it didn't last. He cleared his throat and said abruptly, 'In any case, if you're really here to work, Carlota, get yourself a cup of coffee and let's get at this.'

He turned back to the keyboard and started pecking at it with two fingers.

Irritated, Carly got herself a cup of coffee. She took a banana too, which she nibbled at while she tried to muster a sufficient amount of indifference to work side by side with Piran for the rest of the day.

But once he'd dished out the morning's ration of nastiness he seemed no more interested in rehashing last night's events than she was. He handed her the material he'd finished with, pointed out the parts he'd particularly wanted Des to clean up, said that she could prove her mettle by doing it in his stead, and then went back to work.

Carly went to work as well. She picked up a stack of paper labeled CHAPTER ONE and started to read. It was fascinating. It read like an adventure story—the tale of his father's belief in the elusive caravel, the older man's determination to find it despite the obstacles that nature, big business and several governments had thrown in his way, and his eventual triumph.

Carly found herself cheering Arthur—and his two sons. And then she looked up and found herself contemplating one of them as he sat with his back to her, frowning at the screen and pecking at the keyboard.

It helped, she reminded herself, that he was ignoring her.

She just wished it all helped more.

For, in spite of all her good sense and all the bad memories she'd dredged up during the night, she couldn't deny that Piran St Just was still a very attractive man.

Nor could she deny that, even against her better judgment, she still felt some perverse elemental pull between them.

Damn.

She watched him now, his head bent over the keyboard as he typed. He was wearing glasses, which gave him a scholarly air at odds with his generally roguish demeanor. Carly had never seen him in glasses before. Another man would have looked owlish and nerdy. Piran merely looked like a rogue intellectual. A very masculine attractive rogue intellectual.

Damn again.

'Here. What are you reading? Don't mess with that. I've finished adding some material I wanted to get in. There's lots to work with. Hurry up,' he said now, turning and shooting her an impatient look. 'I doubt Bixby Grissom is paying you to sleep till noon then dawdle the afternoon away.'

It was a good thing he talked, Carly thought crossly. Otherwise she might accidentally find herself in danger of liking him again. 'Give it to me.'

He did. Carly carried it across the room and settled into the chair across the room. She started to read, stopped, flipped through the small sheaf of papers, then looked over at Piran.

'This? This isn't anything like what I've just read.'

'You were reading the finished stuff. That's the part Des did in August. What you've got to work on is what I've just given you now.'

Carly stared at the typescript in her hands. She tried reading it again. It boggled her mind. 'You expect me to help you put together an entire book from this—this junk in less than a month?'

So it wasn't tactful; she wasn't wearing her editor's hat at the moment, and frankly she was appalled.

'I expected Des to,' he replied stonily, 'if you recall.'

Des would have had to perform a flaming miracle, Carly thought. Granted, it looked as if the facts were there, but nothing much else was.

Obviously the 'you were there' quality she'd enjoyed so much in their earlier books and in the first chapter of this one had been entirely Des's doing.

She wanted to wring Des's neck. 'I can't believe he did this to me,' she muttered.

'Neither can I,' Piran said tightly.

Their gazes met and held, a combination of distrust, dislike and dismay—and a faint, fleeting hint of camaraderie.

Immediately Piran's slid away and he scowled out the window. Carly scowled at him. Eventually he stretched his arms over his head and his shirt pulled up so that Carly caught a glimpse of several inches of hard, tanned midriff. Less than she'd seen of him last night, to be sure, but—

Quickly she averted her gaze, not wanting even a glimmer of attractive male to distract her dislike of the present situation.

'We can't do it, can we?' he said after a moment. He dropped his hands into his lap and shifted moodily in his chair. 'It's too much.' He turned his gaze on her. 'Go home and tell Diana you can't do it. We'll return the advance and that'll be that.'

Carly considered the possibility seriously. 'I'd love to,' she said finally. 'Unfortunately I can't.'

'Your job? If money's a problem, Carlota—'

'Money is not a problem, Piran,' Carly said flatly. And she took great pleasure in telling him so. Even though she wasn't making anywhere near the money he was, she was surviving and paying the bills. 'I'm speaking professionally. I take pride in my work. I agreed to do this—' she flicked the manuscript a distasteful glance '—and I keep my word.'

Piran frowned and raked a hand through his hair. 'Yeah, but how? Obviously you're not thrilled.'

'No, I'm not thrilled,' Carly confirmed. 'I'm appalled. But I can't do anything else. And I do have Des's first chapter to work with. I can match his style.'

'You can?'

She met his gaze. 'I can.' She dared him to challenge her, but he didn't.

'So what do I do?'

'Just keep spewing out the facts, I guess,' she said grimly. 'And I'll make a book out of them.'

Piran looked doubtful, but he didn't contradict her. Carly felt doubtful, but she didn't see what else she could do.

'Is this the whole thing? Do you have an outline? A

workable one, I mean. Not the one you sent to Diana when you sold her the book.'

Piran shuffled through the files on his desk and thrust a handful of dog-eared pages at her. 'This. Des and I put this much together in August when he came by the site. The *last* time he deigned to show his face as a matter of fact.'

Carly took it and slumped into the chair again. 'Get back to work,' she said.

They settled into a routine. Using the outline, Piran's rough draft and Des's first chapter, Carly did get a notion of where the book intended to go. She already knew from what Sloan had told her that once the adventure part was done this book would discuss life aboard a Spanish ship, a caravel, that had capsized in a storm off one of the smaller Bahamian islands over three hundred and fifty years before.

It was the ship that Arthur St Just had discovered shortly before he died.

Most experts in the field had doubted that Arthur would find it, but Carly, with the faith of the young, had believed in him. She'd desperately wanted to be a part of the search, and she'd always regretted that after Arthur's death she hadn't felt welcome. She'd never expected for a moment to be a part of writing the book about it.

Now, as she pored over the outline and Piran's draft, she felt some of that old excitement returning.

Maybe, just maybe, if they worked flat out they could get it done. And she could prove to Piran that she wasn't just a money-hungry parasite in the process. She would so love to make him choke on his words. She worked all afternoon, sorting pages and scribbling notes, making stacks of paper here and there on the living-room floor, muttering to herself as she did so.

'Well?' Piran said finally, breaking into her reverie.

Carly glanced over at him, startled, to find him looking at her. 'I think we can make it work.'

'You do?'

She nodded. 'As long as you're not going to jump down my throat if I change some things.'

A brow lifted. 'Me?'

The innocence of his tone made Carly roll her eyes. 'Don't tell me. You got an award for sweetness and light that I haven't heard about?'

Suddenly Piran grinned. It transformed his whole face, lightening the usual grim cast of his features, brightening the world, making Carly's heart kick over in her chest. Oh, help, she thought. Quickly she bent down to grab one of the stacks of paper.

'What about—?' Piran began, but she cut him off.

'Shut up and get to work. If I'm going to do my part, I don't need interruptions.'

Piran stared at her a moment without speaking. Then he shrugged and turned back to the computer.

Carly forced herself to concentrate on the manuscript for the rest of the afternoon, reading to herself, muttering under her breath, scribbling changes, scratching them out, scribbling in more and then reading it again. Once or twice she heard Piran clear his throat as if he might say something. She glared at him. He went back to typing.

The only time she stopped was when she heard the sound of a car, then a thump on the porch.

She expected a knock to follow, but nothing happened. She glanced over at Piran, but he didn't even look up. In a few moments the car drove away again.

'What was that?'

'The mail. Ben brings it by whenever the boat docks.

Saves me the trip into town.' He didn't even seem to want to make a trip to the porch.

To stretch her legs and get a few minutes' respite, Carly went to fetch it. She found a pile in a small wicker basket by the steps. She carried it back inside. There was some material from the Spanish government, background material which Piran pounced on at once, two journals which he set aside for later, last Sunday's *New York Times*, and one pale pink envelope exuding a fairly potent perfume on which Piran's name was written in loopy feminine script.

He tossed it aside.

Carly was curious in spite of herself. Who was hankering after him now? Was he really that cavalier about the letter or was he just being discreet?

And why should she care anyway? Carly asked herself. Piran's girlfriends were no concern of hers. She took her pencil and started slashing at the second chapter again.

'That bad?'

Carly's head jerked up and she glanced at Piran self-consciously, wondering if he had guessed her reaction to the envelope. His face was unreadable.

'You promised you wouldn't complain.'

'I'm not. But—' he grimaced '—you're going at it with a vengeance.'

'Just making a few notes.'

'You can use the computer if you want.'

'I will at the end of the chapter. I'll put them all in, smooth them out, then you can read over my corrections and make your own. All right?'

Piran hesitated, then he nodded and went back to work.

Imagine that, a civil exchange, Carly thought, heartened. Perhaps they would survive after all.

She glanced his way again, but her gaze landed on the

pink envelope near Piran's arm. Who—? No, it wasn't any of her business.

But, whether it was or not, the letter tantalized Carly for the rest of the afternoon. Only when they cleared up for the dinner that Ben's wife, Ruth, delivered that evening did Carly notice that the letter was gone.

Piran never mentioned it. In fact he barely spoke to her through the meal, preferring instead the company of an article from one of the journals that had come in the mail.

'You don't mind, do you?' he asked her.

'Not a bit,' Carly assured him. It was better this way, she told herself. She ate her grouper and salad in silence and tried not to even notice the man sitting across the table from her.

'I'll do up the dishes tonight,' she said when she'd finished. 'Then I'm going for a walk.'

'We're never going to get finished if you're always leaving.'

'I've worked all day!' And she'd fully intended to come back and work for the rest of the evening, but not if he thought he was pushing the buttons.

'So've I. I didn't even rest the way the doctor told me to.'

'So rest, then.'

Now that she took a good look at him, she thought he did look rather peaked, slumped in his chair, poking at his salad. He hadn't eaten a lot, either.

'You won't be any good to Bixby Grissom if you collapse,' she told him sharply.

'The only thing you care about is Bixby Grissom?'

'That's why I'm here!'

Piran grunted.

Carly's gaze narrowed. 'What's that supposed to mean?'

'Nothing.' He turned back to his article.

Carly looked at him a long moment, but he ignored her. Finally she stalked over to the sink, flicked on the faucet and scrubbed her dishes furiously, banging them into the drainer. Then she wiped her hands on the sides of her shorts and headed for the door.

'Be back before dark,' he said as she pushed it open.

'I'll be back when I want!'

'As long as it's before dark,' he said mildly.

She whirled around and glared at him. 'What'll you do—come after me and drag me back by the hair if I'm not?'

He smiled. 'Why don't you try it, Carlota, and find out?'

CHAPTER FOUR

HE SHOULD have rested. He wasn't kidding about the doctor having said he needed to. But Piran hadn't wanted to get up from working in the middle of the day and take a nap.

It was clear enough that Carly thought he'd done a lousy job on the book. He didn't want her to think he was weak as a kitten as well. Even if he was.

All he'd been able to do was ride her about sleeping in, make her look worse than he did. But she'd certainly worked all afternoon.

If he'd even faintly hoped that she was lying about her role in shaping up their last book, he knew now that the hope was in vain. He also knew that Carly O'Reilly was once more going to complicate his life.

He raked a hand through his hair now as he watched until her curvy little rear end had disappeared beyond the bend. Only then did he move away.

And did he go lie down and forget her the way he ought to?

No, damn it, he did not.

He stuffed his feet into a pair of thongs and followed her down to the beach.

Only because she was such a stubborn little witch that she'd probably drown just to spite him, he told himself as he made his way down the narrow path that wound through the trees. There certainly wasn't any other reason.

By the time he reached the spot where the brush ended and the coral sand beach began, Carly was more than a quarter of a mile down the beach, almost to the point that jutted into the sea.

Piran stopped at the edge of the trees, staying in their shadow, keeping out of sight as he kept an eye on her, not wanting her to look back and notice him.

He was damned if he'd let her think she mattered. As long as she stayed in sight, he didn't have to move.

If she rounded the point, he'd have to follow, of course. But when she got there she climbed up on to the exposed coral shelf and followed it out into the water.

There she sat down and wrapped her arms around her knees. Piran leaned against the trunk of a coconut palm and watched her.

Her hair fluttered out behind her in the early evening breeze and he remembered the way it had done just that the day he'd first seen her.

He shut his eyes, trying not to remember the quickening interest he'd felt in her back then. It was as if she'd been put on earth to haunt him, to mock him, to tease him with the simple love and innocence he'd once believed in and which he'd learned when his parents divorced was really a lie.

Don't think about it, he counseled himself.

And he tried not to. But putting out of his mind the Carly he'd first met didn't mean he could forget her altogether. Instead he found himself remembering her the Christmas they'd come to Conch Cay.

He'd tried to avoid her, but it hadn't been easy. Especially when his father had shanghaied him into taking her to see the cannons and giving her a history lecture. There had been no easy way to get out of it, so he'd gone.

Up until that afternoon, he'd managed to stay pretty well away from her, doing his best to ignore her even though his hormones objected mightily. He couldn't ignore her that afternoon, though God knew he'd tried.

She'd asked a ton of questions and most of them had been good, solid, intelligent ones. She was every bit as bright and inquisitive as he'd imagined her being. And he couldn't help it. Under her questions he'd found himself talking about all sorts of things—archaeology, history, shells. At first he'd managed to answer in monosyllables. But it hadn't lasted and pretty soon he couldn't seem to shut up.

Hell, he'd even shown her a piece of sea glass and given it to her to keep!

He could still remember the warmth of her fingers as they'd brushed his, closing around the glass orb. He still remembered her eager smile, her blowing hair. He'd wanted to run his fingers through it. He'd stuffed his hands into his pockets and stridden on, successfully fighting the temptation.

Then.

He hadn't been so lucky the following spring. His hands clenched into fists at his sides, remembering that night, remembering her touch. He'd never in his life lost control so completely. He leaned his head back against the tree trunk and deliberately shut his eyes.

How in hell was he going to get through the entire month living in the same house with Carly O'Reilly?

Unless…

It would be easy enough, he decided, if she wanted what he wanted—a roll between the sheets.

And maybe she did. She was grown-up now. Maybe she'd wised up and realized that holding out for marriage was pointless. Maybe he wouldn't have to keep his hands off her at all.

The notion made him open his eyes again and consider

her speculatively. She'd been no more than a child almost ten years ago—albeit a conniving one. But now?

What if he put the moves on her now? What if he suggested that they might do a little more during their month together than simply writing and editing?

And if she agreed, if they actually had sex, maybe this ridiculous fascination would cease and he could walk away at the end of the month with his curiosity about her assuaged.

And if she didn't?

Or if she did and it wasn't?

Piran didn't want to think about that.

Well, he certainly hadn't taken a nap while she was gone. As Carly came up the path, she saw Piran standing on the deck, leaning against the railing with a glass in his hand, looking for all the world like a jungle cat in wait for his prey.

Well, it wasn't going to be her, Carly thought. And it wasn't even close to dark so he could have nothing to say to her about that. She lifted her chin and didn't even speak to him as she mounted the steps.

He let her pass without comment, then followed her into the house. 'Have a nice walk?'

'Yes.'

'Where'd you go?'

She gave him a narrow, speculative look. 'Down the beach. What is this? Practice in conversational English?' She sat down on the sofa and set the manuscript in her lap, wishing she had a more substantial shield.

'Don't be testy, Carlota. I'm merely making conversation.'

'Why?'

'Why not? We have to live together. We ought to get along.'

'I thought you didn't want to get along. I thought you simply wanted to work.'

'Maybe I've changed my mind.'

She looked at him sharply. 'What's that mean?'

'You used to follow me down the beach.'

Carly's face flamed and her fingers tightened on the pages in her lap. 'There's a non sequitur if ever I heard one,' she said irritably.

Piran shrugged, but he was watching her intently. 'But true none the less,' he said.

Carly shrugged. 'I was young and stupid.'

'Young,' Piran allowed. He came over to the sofa and sat down beside her. Carly cursed herself for not having chosen one of the chairs. She edged away, but he laid his arm along the back of the sofa and his fingers nearly touched her shoulder. She moved as far as she could, hoping he wouldn't notice, but the faint smile that crept into his eyes told her that he had. Her teeth came together tightly.

'Go away, Piran,' she said through them.

'In a bit. Tell me, Carly, how come you never married?'

'How do you know I haven't?'

He looked momentarily taken aback. 'I guess I just assumed…' He stopped, frowning at her.

'I haven't,' she said. 'But it's typical of you, making assumptions like that.'

He frowned, then cleared his throat. 'So, why haven't you?' he persisted. 'You were pretty hot on it once, if I recall.'

'Like I said, I was stupid.' Was it just her imagination, or was he really moving closer?

'I suppose your mother wasn't much of an argument for marriage ultimately.'

Carly's jaw tightened and her fingers clenched. She didn't answer him. She wasn't going to justify her mother to Piran. She knew better than to even try.

'How is Sue?' he asked after a moment.

'My mother died in September.'

He opened his mouth to say something, then abruptly closed it again. He looked startled.

Carly brushed a lock of hair away from her face. 'Thank you for not saying you're sorry,' she said tightly.

Piran sighed and rubbed his hand against the back of his neck. One corner of his mouth lifted in a sort of wry grimace and he shrugged rather awkwardly. 'Because I'd be a hypocrite if I did?'

'Yes.'

'Yeah, well, I'm sure your mother was a fine person...' he began awkwardly.

'Oh, don't!' She didn't want to hear that from him. Maybe when her mother had been alive. But not now.

'I can't even talk about them?'

'Not unless you have something new to say. And you don't, do you?' She met his gaze with a challenge in her eyes.

'It doesn't matter now, does it?' Piran said. 'It's finished. He's dead. So's she.'

'But it's still going on now. Between us. You don't like me because of what you think my mother did.'

He shifted uncomfortably. 'I liked you all right,' he muttered after a moment. 'And you know it.'

'For sex,' Carly said flatly, a tiny part of her wanting desperately for him to deny it.

He didn't. 'You were an attractive girl. You're an attractive woman.'

'Thank you,' Carly said sarcastically.

'What's the matter with that?'

'I'd like to be valued for more than my physical attributes.'

'You're bright and intelligent, too,' Piran said.

She gave him a wary look.

'You're probably going to make a success of Des's and my disastrous book,' he went on.

'I'm going to try.'

'Good. I'll appreciate that.' He smiled at her. There was a speculative light in his eyes that Carly didn't understand fully.

'What?' she said, still feeling nervous.

He reached a hand out and brushed a strand of hair off her cheek. She trembled under this lightest of touches and he smiled again. 'I thought so,' he murmured.

'Thought what?'

'That you still want me.'

'I don't—'

'Don't you be the hypocrite, Carly. You know you do. Just the way I still want you.'

Carly's jaw dropped.

A small, humorless smile played on his lips. 'You're surprised? I doubt it somehow.'

'That's not what I'm here for!' she said quickly.

'Maybe not. But we'd be damn fools not to take advantage of what fate and Des have wrought. Don't you agree?'

And, without giving her a chance to agree or not, Piran leaned forward suddenly, closed the small space remaining between them, and touched his mouth to hers.

It had been over nine years since she'd felt Piran's lips, nine years since her mouth had opened beneath his, nine years since his tongue had tasted her, teased her, tantalized her. Nine long years!

But it might as well have been yesterday. She'd never forgotten.

She'd sought in vain to find that same need, those same feelings with other men. With one of her college boyfriends, with an engineer she'd dated last year, most recently with John. She'd never even come close.

She'd told herself it was just the night, the moon, young love that had caused her fervent response.

Yes, maybe she was a hypocrite, because one touch was all it took to tell her that it hadn't been the night or the moon or young love at all.

It had been then what it was now: Piran.

His kiss was firm and sweet and hungry. And it took her so much by surprise that she responded to it—to him. Her mouth melded with his, her tongue tangled with his, her breath mingled with his. And her heart—oh, dear heavens, what he did to her heart!

She wanted to pull away. No, that wasn't true. She didn't *want*—she *needed*—to pull away. But she was caught, like a fish on a line. And if finally Piran hadn't broken the contact she didn't know when she would have.

'Tell me you didn't like that,' he said unsteadily, his lips still only millimeters from her own. 'Tell me, Carly.'

Carly gave herself a shake, pulled back, licked her lips, tried to still her hammering heart. Oh, God, oh, God, she thought.

'You can't, can you?' he said, and his breath touched her heated skin. 'I didn't think so,' he whispered.

And then he was kissing her again, this time more hungrily than the last. If that kiss had been a test of her responsiveness, this proved that he'd got the answer he wanted.

His arms went around her and drew her to him, and

Carly's fingers tightened on the sheaf of paper in her hands, crumpling it.

'D-don't!' she tried vainly, desperately.

But he did. The kiss went on, teasing, tempting, persuading. Piran's hands slid up under her shirt; one flicked open the fastener to her bra with practiced ease, the other moved the thin scrap of lace aside and found the aching fullness of her breast. His fingers stroked and teased, stimulating her, maddening her.

She tried to wriggle away, but the wriggling only made his touch inflame her more. She seemed frozen right where she was. She could only manage words. 'Piran, stop.'

'Why? You want it. Tell me you don't want it, Carlota. Tell me and I'll stop.'

Even as he spoke, his other hand moved to cup her other breast, then to stroke it, arousing it as well.

Carly squirmed against the sofa, feeling the heat of desire curl open deep inside her even as she tried to fight it down. A tiny moan escaped her.

Piran made a satisfied sound deep in his throat. 'I thought so.' His voice was ragged and the color was high in his cheeks. He looked very much the way he had nine years ago—the aroused male, hungry for her.

No, not for her, Carly corrected herself. For a woman. Any woman. There was nothing to do with love in his response to her. It was biology.

And so, damn it, was her reaction to him. She didn't love him! Not the way she once had. Her body wanted him. *She* didn't.

And, realizing that, at last she found the strength to shove him away. 'Get off!'

She wriggled desperately until she fell right off the sofa on to the floor. Then she scrambled to her feet and put the width of the room between herself and Piran.

He shoved himself up and stood looking at her, still clearly aroused and a bit dazed. 'For God's sake, Carlota, you don't have to act like some frightened virgin!'

What if I told you I am one? Carly wondered, and suppressed an almost hysterical laugh.

She reached behind her, under her blouse, fumbling with the clasp of her bra, trying desperately to hook it again. Piran took a step toward her. 'Stay away from me,' she warned him.

'It's a little late for the outrage, sweetheart. You were panting for me.'

Maybe so, but, 'I'm not panting now, and I'm telling you, I don't want you coming anywhere near me,' she asserted.

'That's not what your body was saying.'

'It's what I'm saying, and I mean it, Piran. You touch me again—'

'Kiss you again,' he corrected her mockingly.

'Touch me, kiss me, anything, and I will be gone on the next boat. And I'll tell Diana exactly why I left.'

She saw his jaw tighten and a muscle tick in his cheek. 'You liked it,' he told her flatly.

Carly didn't answer him, just met his gaze levelly, trying to mask the hurt with outrage, determined not to let him destroy her again.

Finally he gave a sound that was close to a snort. 'I suppose you're still holding out for marriage, Carlota?'

Carly lifted her chin and stared him straight in the eye. 'You're damned right I am.'

Marriage.

God, what did it have to recommend it?

Not a damned thing Piran could think of as he wandered along the beach that night after dark.

His own parents' version had certainly been a sham. What a naïve fool he'd been to believe in it all those years. He'd just thought his parents liked going their separate ways.

How was he supposed to know that for years his mother had had a lover? How was he supposed to know that his father had known it, but hadn't challenged it, preferring instead to bury himself in his work?

It was only when Des was eighteen—'old enough to know what life is all about', his mother had said—that she and Arthur had let their sons in on the truth—and his mother had left to marry her long-time lover.

Good riddance, Piran had thought savagely, feeling betrayed to the depths of his soul. He'd turned his back on her too, determined to align himself with his serious, devoted, beloved father.

And then Arthur had let him down as well.

He couldn't believe it when, just six months after the divorce, his father had called to invite him to his wedding.

'You're getting married?' He'd been appalled.

'I am. I'm in love,' Arthur had said. And even over the phone he'd sounded brighter, younger, happier.

'Who is it?' Piran had asked.

'Her name's Sue,' Arthur had told him. 'She's a dancer.'

'A dancer?' Even now Piran could remember the astonishment he'd felt. He couldn't believe his father—Arthur St Just, BA, MA, Ph.D., D. Litt., Oxon, for heaven's sake—was about to take a nightclub dancer for a bride.

'Don't be a snob,' Arthur had told him.

'Don't be a fool,' Piran had snapped back at him.

He had heard his mild-mannered father's sharp intake of breath, but Arthur had only said quietly, 'I'm going to forget you ever said that. And you will keep a civil tongue in your head whenever you're around your stepmother, or you won't come around her.'

'Fine,' Piran had retorted. And he hadn't gone to the wedding. But he hadn't been able to stay away. He'd gone to visit them a few times—just out of morbid fascination, he told himself. He'd wanted to see Sue and his father together.

Or had he wanted to see Carly?

He raked his hands through his hair. Then he stripped off his shirt and plunged into the surf. Maybe working off his frustration would help him figure things out.

Well, they had certainly determined the boundaries of their relationship, though to Carly it seemed a pretty drastic way to do it.

She could still taste him on her lips hours later, but, if that was what it was going to take to get things out in the open, maybe it was all for the good.

At least afterwards he'd walked out and left her alone with her answer: marriage was apparently still not on the cards for Piran St Just.

Did she really mean that she wanted to marry him?

Heaven knew she hadn't come down here with any desire of the sort.

And now?

Well, she certainly hadn't proved to anyone's satisfaction that she was over him. On the contrary, he could still make her blood boil and her heart sing.

But marry?

Oh, lord, why did the thought still tempt her? It shouldn't. And it didn't make any difference that it did, she told herself sharply. He didn't want to marry her.

The following day they worked steadily, albeit in silence. The day after that brought with it a thundering rainstorm and Piran kept the computer turned off, afraid to risk having the system damaged by lightning.

It didn't keep Carly from working, but it did mean that every time she slashed through a paragraph or red-penciled a line he demanded to know what she thought she was doing.

'My job,' she answered shortly.

'You're tearing it apart as fast as I write it,' he grumbled.

'Then write better.'

'I'm doing the best I can.' Outside the lightning flashed and the thunder rumbled. 'I'm no writer.'

'Tell me about it,' Carly muttered under her breath. 'Now go away. I need to concentrate to make sense out of this.'

Piran looked affronted. 'It already makes sense.'

'To you. And perhaps to the three or four other people in the world who have your level of expertise,' Carly allowed. 'But Bixby Grissom is not an academic publisher, Piran. We're aiming this book at the mass market.'

'And that makes them stupid?'

'No,' she said patiently. 'It makes them generalists. Your other books weren't this difficult to understand.'

'Thank Des.'

At the moment thanking Des was not high on Carly's list of priorities. The thunder rumbled again as the storm moved closer, and, closer still, she heard the car and the thump of the mail in the basket on the veranda.

'I'll get it,' she said, glad of the excuse to escape even for a moment.

She brought back in several more journals, some business correspondence and two more lightly scented pastel envelopes. She flipped them on to the table closest to

Piran. 'She's an eager little soul, isn't she? Maybe you'll marry her.'

The moment the words were out of her mouth she regretted them. The last thing she wanted was for him to think she was pining for him.

But he seemed not to notice. He grunted, but left the letters where they were.

Carly scowled at him, then at the letters. Then, heaving a sigh, she forced herself to focus once more on the manuscript in her hands.

The sun came out and set the jungle-like growth steaming. Carly opened all the windows and turned on all the fans but still the sweat ran down her neck and between her breasts. It soaked the waistband of her shorts. The heat was bad enough. Piran prowling around the room made things worse.

'The rain's stopped, so you can type,' she told him.

'I'm composing in my head.'

It looked more like prowling to her. She tossed the manuscript down on the sofa and headed for her room.

'Where are you going?'

'To change. I need a swim.'

'Not alone.'

'Well, not with you.' That was more than she could bear. 'And I'm not refraining from swimming the whole time I'm here just because there's no one to come along,' she told him before he could suggest it.

She went into her room and changed into her swimsuit. It was a very respectable royal blue maillot, its only eye-catching attribute the high cut of the leg openings. She wrapped a towel around her waist and went back out and down the steps.

Piran followed her down.

'What the hell do you think you're doing?'

'Coming with you, obviously.'

'I told you I don't want—'

'And I don't give a damn what you want. It's a matter of safety.'

'I don't need you.'

'I thought you wanted to marry me,' Piran said mockingly.

'Go to hell, Piran.'

But he didn't. He went with her.

Carly did her best to ignore him, practically running down the path, then dropping her towel and plunging straight into the crystalline water, swimming out toward the reef. Only when she neared it did she turn and tread water as she squinted back in Piran's direction.

He was standing on the beach, hands on his hips, watching her. She thanked God that he didn't come in after her. Instead, once he was apparently satisfied that she wasn't going to require rescuing from her own folly, he stripped off his shirt and lay down on his towel.

Carly hoped he'd forgotten to bring his sunscreen. Maybe he'd broil like a lobster.

She swam for half an hour, letting him swelter. But finally she got tired and knew she couldn't outlast him. He would stay as long as she did, and she knew it. So she came out, grabbed her towel, and, without a word to him, began to walk back up the beach to the house.

Piran followed.

She felt naked, walking up the path with Piran's eyes on her the whole time. But she didn't stop and wrap her hips in the towel. He'd only laugh at her if she did.

'If you think wriggling your rear at me when you walk up the beach is going to get me to marry you, you've got another think coming,' he said when they got there.

'You didn't have to come along.'

'Whenever you go for a swim, I'm coming with you,' he replied in a tone that brooked no argument.

'Don't strain yourself,' Carly said. 'Maybe you can find some other watchdog to do it for you.'

Over the next few days she even tried to find someone herself. But no one could. Everyone was busy working and preparing for Christmas.

Christmas.

Well, at least that part of her trip was working. Days had gone by and she hadn't even thought about it.

Until Ruth came and, along with dinner, brought a sprig of mistletoe.

'You don' got a tree,' she chastised them. 'I bring you this. Got it at the grocery store. This be better for you young single people anyway,' she added, giggling.

Carly and Piran both looked at the mistletoe as if it were poison ivy.

'You got to hang it here, see?' Ruth said when neither of them made a move to take it from her. She pointed to the opening between the kitchen and the living room. 'Lotsa chances for kissin', see?'

Carly saw. Piran did too. 'We've got work to do, Ruth,' he complained.

'Too much work not good for you,' Ruth said. 'Here. You come hang it now.' And she wouldn't serve dinner until he had.

'Good. Now the kiss.' She stood back and looked at them expectantly.

Carly looked at her toes. She didn't know what Piran was looking at until all of a sudden Ruth squealed.

'Not me, you dumb boy! You s'posed to kiss Miss Carly.'

'She doesn't want to kiss me,' Piran said.

'Course she does. All us women like to kiss handsome men. Don'tcha, honey?' she asked Carly.

Carly, seeing that sinking through the floor wouldn't be an option, shrugged.

'She says yes,' Ruth translated. 'You kiss her now.'

Piran kissed her.

It was supposed to be a duty peck and Carly knew it. They both knew it. But something happened. Something fierce, something elemental, something between the two of them that no amount of common sense ever seemed to be able to control. One second it was a brief touch of his lips, and the next it was a hungry, desperate kiss that asked for things that Carly hadn't even dreamed of.

'Yeah, mon, that's a kiss all right!' Ruth cheered when at last Piran let her go and Carly stumbled back, shaken. 'Come along now. I done fixed a box fish for dinner.'

They barely spoke after that. There seemed nothing to say that wouldn't make things worse.

Then on Friday, while Carly was still working over the morning's writing, she heard a car and the thump of the mail on the porch. Glancing at her watch, she frowned. It wasn't even quite noon.

'Mail's early today,' she said. 'You get it. I'm in the midst.'

Piran glanced up from the article he was reading, looked about to protest, then shrugged. He walked out on to the veranda. Carly muttered the sentences in her head, trying to hear the way they sounded. She scribbled some more, then muttered what she'd written.

Piran came back in empty-handed.

'No mail? But I heard the car.'

Piran just looked at her. He was very pale.

'What's wrong?' she asked him.

'It wasn't the mail.'

Carly set down the manuscript and stood up. 'What was it?'

'A baby.'

CHAPTER FIVE

'WHAT do you mean, is it mine?' Piran said. No, he didn't actually say it; he shouted it. How dared she ask him something like that?

He paced to the far end of the veranda, then whirled round to glare at Carly. 'I think I'd know if I had a child!'

'Not necessarily,' Carly said so casually that he itched to smack her. 'If you were a woman, yes, of course, you'd know. But—'

'You think I just go around getting women pregnant?'

She didn't answer at once, which made it all too clear exactly what she thought. He scowled at her, then at the baby.

Cripes, a *baby*! He still couldn't believe it.

'Stop pacing, for heaven's sake,' Carly snapped at him. 'You're scaring it.'

Not half as much as it scared him, he thought grimly. But he stopped pacing and watched as Carly crouched next to the wicker basket and peered in at it.

The baby looked back with something akin to worried curiosity.

Piran came to loom over her shoulder and stare down at the infant, too. 'Where do you suppose it came from?'

Carly looked over her shoulder at him. 'Is this a request for a discussion on the birds and the bees?'

Damned if he didn't feel his face begin to burn. 'You know damned well what I mean.'

'Yes, and you know where it came from. The car that drove up.'

81

'Yes, but who—?' He stopped and shook his head, still dazed. He felt light-headed and this time it had nothing to do with his rapid decompression.

'I should think you'd know that better than I would,' Carly said. 'If you're the father—'

'I am bloody well *not* the father!'

'Then why would someone leave it here?' she asked with maddening logic.

'How should I know? And stop looking at me that way!'

Carly didn't say anything, but she didn't stop looking at him. Piran glared back at her. He could still feel the heat creeping up his neck and he hoped to God she didn't see it. She'd probably take it as a physical manifestation of paternity.

'Just because, once upon a time, you and I got carried away…' he muttered, raking his fingers through his hair.

'Once upon a time? What about when you wanted to go to bed with me just the other day?'

'Yes, well, we didn't, did we?'

'No thanks to you. And don't tell me you've been celibate for the entire past nine years. What about the pastel-envelope lady?'

Piran scowled. 'What about her?'

'Well, she's certainly been trying to communicate with you about something.'

Piran said something very rude under his breath. He didn't want to talk about the girl Carly called 'the pastel-envelope lady'. She was from a time he just wanted to forget. He hunched his shoulders.

'What about her?' Carly persisted.

Piran gritted his teeth. She—Wendy Jeffries was her name—had been pursuing him with single-minded determination ever since he'd met her at a party in Washington a little over a year ago.

He should have known better than to get involved with her, but it had been a hard time for him. His best friend and diving partner, Gordon Andrews, had just died in a car accident. Piran had been driving.

'It wasn't your fault,' Des had told him over and over. Everyone said the same thing. Even Gord's wife—his *pregnant* wife—had said so when Piran had gone to her to break the news.

But being told that he was blameless hadn't helped. Even though the other vehicle had run the red light, he kept questioning himself. What if…? If only… But what had happened had happened. And all the what ifs and if onlys in the world wouldn't bring Gord back.

Piran knew it, but it was hard to accept. He'd done some mind-bending drinking right after it happened.

And he'd met Wendy Jeffries.

He should never have gone to that damned party Des had insisted on dragging him to. And he certainly should never have drunk as much as he did there—or left with Wendy halfway through. He couldn't even remember what had happened after he'd left with her. The next thing he'd known was waking up in her bed the next morning.

His eyes widened and he looked at the baby more closely. Had *that* happened? Was this child Wendy's? Was that what she'd been writing about in all those letters he'd been pitching unopened into the trash?

Had he…? Was he…? God, no, he couldn't have slept with her, could he?

He couldn't remember having slept with her. But then, he couldn't remember *not* having slept with her either.

He felt sick.

He shook his head and frowned down fiercely at the child. *His* child?

The baby's face screwed up and it started to cry.

'Now look what you've done,' Carly admonished him.

'Me? What *I've* done?'

'Oh, poor thing,' Carly crooned, bending closer.

'It's not poor—'

'Damn it, Piran, shut up. Shh, now, baby, Daddy didn't mean to frighten you.'

'I'm not its daddy!' He hoped.

'Piran!' Carly shot him a furious glance. She patted the baby ineffectually. It screeched on.

Piran dragged both his hands through his hair. 'For God's sake, Carly, make it stop.'

'You made it cry.'

'So you can hardly expect I'd be able to make it stop,' he said as reasonably as he could. 'Do something.'

She looked at him helplessly. 'What?'

'You don't know?'

'Why should I? I don't have kids. And I never had any baby brothers or sisters…as you might recall.'

'You might've…after…' But he didn't want to get into anything about her mother. Not now.

'I didn't,' she said flatly.

'OK, you didn't,' he said desperately. 'But hell, you're a woman—'

'Hardly a qualification.'

'Better than I've got. Just shut it up,' he pleaded.

And he breathed a sigh of relief when finally Carly reached into the basket, scooped the baby up into her arms and cradled it awkwardly against her. It wailed, then hiccuped, then sniffled and stopped crying, looking at her with wide, curious blue eyes.

'Thank God,' Piran muttered.

'Try thanking me,' Carly said drily.

'Thank you.' He would have kissed her feet right then—

anything just so she made it stop. Why was the crying affecting him so much?

Maybe, he thought, because he wanted to cry himself!

He couldn't be a father! Could he?

Carly pointed to the cardboard box of baby clothes, bottles and canned formula sitting next to the basket. 'There's a note in there.'

Piran snatched it up. His lips drew into a thin line.

'What's it say?' Carly asked.

'Not much.'

'What?'

'His name.' His fingers crumpled the note.

'Which is…?' Carly prompted.

Piran let out a harsh breath. 'Arthur.'

'Arthur,' Carly said brightly. 'Imagine that.'

Piran gritted her teeth, knowing full well what she was thinking.

'Hello there, Arthur,' Carly crooned. At that the child blinked and looked at Carly with more interest.

'He knows his name,' she told Piran happily.

He jammed his hands into the pockets of his shorts. 'Swell.'

'And he has your nose.'

'He does not! My nose isn't beaky.'

'Neither's Arthur's. It's just—um—strong and determined.'

'Well, it doesn't look like mine. And *he's* not mine. No matter what that note implies.'

'Don't you think you're perhaps protesting a bit much, Piran? He's called Arthur, after all. Your father's name. And—'

'I know it's my father's name!'

'And he's got your nose, regardless of what you think.'

She said this quickly, before he could object. 'And his eyes are exactly the color of yours.'

'His eyes are blue.'

'The same blue as yours.'

'And hundreds of thousands of other people's…'

'But he's on *your* veranda.'

'Well, he can leave any time.'

Carly stared at him, then looked down at the baby. She made a tiny sound of dismay. 'He can't, can he?' she said after a moment as if the realization had just dawned. 'Oh, dear. What if whoever left him doesn't come back?'

'They'd damned well better. I'm not keeping him!'

'But he's—'

'No, he's not!' Piran insisted, as if, by repeating it often enough, he could convince himself beyond a doubt that it was true. 'I don't care if the note said his name was Piran St Just the second—he's not staying here!'

'How's he going to leave?'

'Whoever left him can come and get him.' He looked around suspiciously, as if whoever had left this baby might still be hiding in the bushes, thinking this was all a great joke. No such luck.

'I think,' Carly said after a moment, gesturing at the large box full of clothes sitting beside the basket, 'that whoever left him doesn't mean to come back.'

Piran had just been thinking the same thing, but he didn't like saying it. With his bare toe he traced the line between the bleached boards of the veranda.

'Of course they will,' he said with far more optimism than he felt.

If they didn't, he couldn't imagine what was going to happen.

What in God's name was he going to do with a baby?

*　*　*

By nightfall Carly was astonished to discover that she had a surprising, heretofore hidden instinct for motherhood. She wasn't sure how far it extended, but for the moment at least Arthur seemed to think she filled the bill.

But if she had a natural flair for mothering, Piran seemed to have no instinct for fatherhood whatsoever—beyond contributing the requisite sperm, at least.

He'd watched her and Arthur with a combination of irritation and nervousness from clear across the room while she'd fixed lunch. When she'd put Arthur down, and he'd cried, and she'd suggested that Piran might like to hold the baby, he'd looked at her askance.

'Not on your life,' he'd said.

When at last she'd set the meal on the table and settled down to eat with Arthur in her lap, Piran had picked up his plate and eaten his sandwich at the computer with his back to them both.

'He's not contagious, Piran,' Carly said.

'And thank God for that.'

He buried himself in his work for the rest of the day. At least, he called it work. As far as Carly could see it was a means of avoiding Arthur.

He didn't seem to get much done, either. Mostly he muttered and glanced at the baby and Carly over his shoulder, as if he was hoping they'd vanished in a puff of smoke. Finally he shut off the computer. 'I'm going to town. Someone must know who the devil he is.'

But when he returned at suppertime he was moving much more slowly and he had no clues as to Arthur's identity. There had been a sightseeing boat that brought forty or so tourists to the island that morning, according to Ben, including several family groups. No one had noticed a woman with a baby.

Piran reported all this tersely as he stood glumly at the

water's edge while Carly bounced in the waves with a gurgling Arthur in her arms.

'So it was a waste of time,' he finished heavily.

'Now what?'

'I don't know. And you aren't supposed to swim alone, if you recall,' he added irritably.

'I'm not alone, I'm with Arthur. Besides, I'm hardly going to drown in eighteen inches of water.'

Piran muttered something under his breath.

Carly looked at him closely. 'Are you all right?' she asked him. His face was red from the sun and the exertion of walking into town, but beneath his heightened color she thought she detected a pale tightness bracketing his mouth.

'Why wouldn't I be? Getting some kid dumped on my doorstep, walking all the way to town and back in the middle of the afternoon, finding out no one knows anything about who he is!'

Carly forbore reminding him that they knew who Arthur was, they just didn't know who'd left him there.

'I know,' she said quietly. 'And you've done all you can right now. So why don't you go take a rest? It might make you feel better.'

'I'll feel better when he's gone,' Piran snapped. Then he sighed and rubbed his hands down his face. 'Sorry. This has just got me—' He stopped and shook his head.

He looked so miserable that Carly felt almost compelled to go to him and put her arms around him. Only knowing that if she did he'd probably only get angrier kept her where she was.

'It'll work out,' she assured him.

He gave her a bleak look, but he did turn and walk back up the beach. He didn't go clear up to the house, though. He stopped instead where Carly had dropped her towel.

He spread it out and sat down on it, then turned to stare at her watchdog-fashion the way he always did.

'He'll come around,' Carly said to Arthur. 'I hope.'

Arthur grinned at her and waved his arms.

They played in the water for only another fifteen minutes because, though she'd put sunscreen on Arthur, it wasn't a very strong variety and she didn't want the sun to burn his baby-soft skin.

She stopped beside Piran on her way back to the house. 'May I have my towel, please?' She hoped he would offer to take the baby from her while she dried off.

He didn't. Though he did get off the towel and hand it to her. 'Would you?' She held Arthur out to him.

He backed away, shaking his head.

'Come on, Piran.'

'I can't.'

Carly rolled her eyes. 'He's only a baby.'

'That's precisely the problem.'

'Pretend he's a football. Here.' She stuffed Arthur into his arms before he could stop her, wedging the baby against his chest. 'There. Like that. Hug him close. See? Couldn't you run fifty yards with him?'

Piran looked at her in dismay, his body almost rigid as he held the baby. 'I'd rather run fifty yards from him.'

Carly grinned. 'You're doing fine.'

'You do better,' he said, an edge of panic in his voice. 'Hurry up and dry off.'

Not willing to push her luck, she did just that, then took Arthur back from him. Piran almost sagged with relief.

'That wasn't so bad, was it?' she asked him.

Piran just looked at her.

She hoped he would volunteer to help with Arthur while she took a shower. He didn't. So she took one with Arthur lying on a towel in the middle of the bathroom floor. She dressed with Arthur lying in the middle of her bed. Then she changed him and carried him out into the living room where Piran sat staring at the computer.

'Do you suppose your father was an ostrich in a former life?' she said to Arthur.

'Don't try laying guilt on me,' Piran said without looking at her.

'I wouldn't dream of it,' Carly said lightly. The look he gave her made her smile.

When Ruth came, bringing dinner, she also brought a rattle that her last child had long outgrown, and some bananas for Piran to mash, and lots of suggestions for dealing with a surprise baby.

'I bet you was that amazed,' she said to Piran, smiling all over her face.

'Oh, yes,' Piran agreed in the only case of understatement Carly had heard from him all day.

'Well, he sure be a handsome boy,' Ruth said, looking at the child in Carly's arms. She winked. 'Just like his daddy.'

'I'm not—' Piran began, but before he could say it Ruth grinned and tickled Arthur's bare belly.

'Sure can see that baby done got the St Just nose!'

'Does she think I *want* to claim paternity?' Piran groused at Carly after Ruth left.

'Maybe she just thinks you ought to.' Carly yawned mightily. 'I wouldn't mind if you'd show a little responsibility, either. I'm tired.'

'So'm I.'

'Unfortunately Arthur's not.' In fact he was staring at her wide-eyed and batting at the bottle she was trying to give him. 'Why don't you take him for a while?'

He shook his head. 'You're doing fine.'

'Thank you for the vote of confidence, but I'm tired of

doing fine. Come on, Piran. Just for a few minutes.' She got to her feet, walked over to him and plunked Arthur down in his lap.

'Carly!'

'Relax, Piran. You're fine. He won't hurt you.'

'But I might hurt him!'

'You won't. If I haven't so far today, you won't. Believe me. Just give him the bottle.' She handed him that too.

Piran fumbled with the bottle, finally succeeding in getting it into Arthur's mouth. Arthur took two sucks, then batted it away. Piran looked up at Carly, dismayed.

'Keep trying.'

'But—' But Piran poked it back in to his mouth. This time Arthur glommed on and began to suck. He snuggled down into Piran's arms and sighed.

Piran stared at him, an expression of amazement on his face. 'I'm feeding a baby.' He sounded thunderstruck.

'Will wonders never cease?' Carly said drily. But he really did look astonished, and she had to ask, 'You really haven't ever held one before? Or fed one?'

Piran shook his head. 'I tried once,' he said after a moment. 'When Des was born. I was six. Once I heard him crying and nobody came to get him, so I did.' He hesitated, then went on. 'I'd just got him out of the crib. He was maybe about as big as Arthur—and probably wigglier. My mother came into the room, saw me and shrieked, ''Be careful!'' and I dropped him.' Even now she could hear an echo of remembered anguish in his voice.

'Oh, Piran!' Carly's heart went out to the little boy he had been. 'You were only trying to help.'

'Yeah. But I wasn't much, was I?'

'She shouldn't have yelled at you.'

Piran shrugged. 'She was afraid I might hurt him. She was right.'

'Was he hurt?'

Piran thought for a moment, then shook his head. 'I don't think he was. He yelled a lot, though. And so did my mother. She told me never to touch him again.'

'It's amazing the two of you are friends now.'

Piran smiled wryly. 'He's taller than I am now. He can stick up for himself. And I need him. He writes better.'

'But you do the hard work,' Carly said. 'The day-to-day stuff. The painstaking stuff.'

'I do what I like,' Piran said simply. 'We work well together because we like different things.'

As he talked he relaxed into the chair and adjusted Arthur's weight in his arms almost unconsciously. Carly, watching him, smiled.

'What?' Piran asked her when he saw the smile.

'I was just thinking that fatherhood becomes you.'

He stiffened. 'Don't start that again.'

Carly perched on the arm of the sofa. 'You really don't think he's yours?' she asked, not wanting to admit how much she really wanted to believe that.

Piran shifted uncomfortably and ran his tongue over his lower lip. 'I don't know,' he said at last.

'How can you not know? Have there been so many women?'

'No, damn it, there haven't. It's just...' He hesitated, leaning his head back against the chair and shutting his eyes for a long moment; then he opened them again and looked at Arthur. 'How old do you figure he is? Like six months maybe?'

'I guess,' Carly said slowly. 'I mean, I'm not really good at babies' ages. I'd guess he was born in the summer— June or July. So if you count back nine months he would've been conceived in autumn sometime. September or October.'

Piran nodded grimly. 'That's what I thought.'

'So, the question appears to be who was the flavor of the month last October?'

'There wasn't any "flavor of the month".'

'Well, then you must have some idea. If there weren't hundreds of them. Just think and I'm sure—'

'I told you, damn it, I can't think! I don't know!'

He almost got up, realized he was holding the baby, and slumped back in the chair, a defeated look on his face. Carly watched him, mystified.

He stared at the fan whirling lazily in the ceiling. He didn't look at her. She saw his Adam's apple work in his throat. 'Remember Gordon Andrews?' he said finally.

'Gordon? You mean the boy you went to university with? Tall and thin? Fair-haired?'

'That's the one.'

'Of course I remember him. I met him in New York with you. He was nice to me. A lot nicer than you were. I liked him.'

'You and everyone else,' Piran said, his voice so soft that Carly could hardly hear him. 'Gordon was the best.'

'Was?'

'He died a year ago last August. In a car accident coming back to the airport. We'd been in Washington consulting with a couple of museum staffers, trying to put together an exhibit, and we were almost at the airport and…and a truck…ran a red light.' He stopped and swallowed. 'Hit us broadside. Behind the driver's seat. I came out with only scratches. Des had a broken arm. Gordon was in the back seat. He was killed.'

'Dear God.' Carly felt her own throat working.

'I was driving,' Piran said after a moment. 'I didn't even see the truck coming. I would have stopped if I'd seen him. I should've seen him!' His anguish made his voice ragged. He blinked rapidly, running his tongue over his lips and swallowing again as he stared up at the ceiling.

Carly didn't say anything. She reached out and took the baby and the bottle from him. Then the hand that wasn't holding the bottle reached for his fingers and clenched them.

She didn't say it wasn't his fault. She was sure he knew that—in his mind if not in his heart—just as sure as she was that he still wasn't reconciled to Gordon's death, that he berated himself constantly for not having been able to prevent it.

Piran raised his head slowly and their gazes met. His blue eyes were bright with unshed tears. Then his gaze dropped and he focused for a moment on their laced fingers, then at the child in her arms. A spasm of pain crossed his face and he shut his eyes once more. He pulled away and pressed his fists against his eyes.

'And that's why you don't remember?' Carly said faintly. 'After…after Gordon died…'

'I didn't cope real well. I got through telling Gordon's wife. I got through the wake and the funeral. And then I just took off. I didn't work for a month. I couldn't. I drank and I threw up and I drank some more. I asked God why the hell it wasn't me. *I* didn't have a wife. *I* didn't have a two-year-old kid and another on the way!' He sighed. 'Des tried to make me shape up, come out of it. He found some girl to get him through it, I guess. He got real involved with her. It seemed to help so I guess he thought I needed one too. He dragged me to parties, introduced me to a ton of them. One of them was your pastel-envelope lady.' He gave her a twisted smile.

And you slept with her? The words stuck in her throat.

'I got drunk the night I met her, wallowing in self-pity, mumbling in my beer. I guess she felt sorry for me. She took me home with her…and I…and I woke up the next morning in her bed.'

His eyes met Carly's only for a moment, then slid away.

Outside Carly heard the distant sound of waves against the shore and the croaking of frogs near by.

'So…' she began, but her voice wavered. She cleared her throat and began again, 'So you're saying…she could be Arthur's mother?'

'I don't know! I don't remember making love with her! But God, I don't remember *not* doing it either! I don't remember anything after we got to her apartment.'

'What about…? Were there…were there others be-sides…besides her?'

He rubbed his palms down his face, then rested his el-bows on his knees, knotted his fingers and propped his chin on them, looking at the baby in Carly's arms. 'I'm not sure,' he said at last, the words echoing with a hollow, aching tone.

Carly could hear his pain, could see it, could understand the circumstances that had driven him after Gordon's death. Piran always cared—he'd cared about her when he hadn't even known her. He'd cared about his father, even when he hadn't understood his father's marriage. He cared too much. And too often he acted before he thought things through.

They sat in silence for a good five minutes. Arthur's eyes closed and his lips stopped moving on the nipple. They parted slightly and a faint smile tipped the corners of his mouth.

'Is he my son?' Piran whispered. Then he looked at Carly, his eyes dark and desperate. 'What am I going to do with a son?'

CHAPTER SIX

THE sound seemed to come from a long way off—miles and years away. A high-pitched wail, rising and falling. Tentative at first, then stronger and more insistent. Finally a fierce, angry demand.

Crying.

A baby crying.

Piran didn't know how long he'd been hearing it. Forever, it seemed. First it was Des, the red-faced infant of his past and of his dreams. And then, as he awakened, he remembered who it really was.

This child called Arthur.

His son?

The very notion sent a shaft a panic right through him. He'd barely slept at all, trying to think, trying desperately to remember. Could he have had sex with Wendy? Was she the only woman he might have done it with? God, this was so unlike him! Indiscriminate sex had never, ever been his style. It was just that Gordon's death had hit him so hard.

A fine excuse that was, he thought grimly. God help him, it was no excuse at all. If Arthur really was his son, of course he'd support him; he'd raise him if he had to. But—Piran rolled on to his back and stared at the ceiling, willing the crying to stop—he just didn't want to have to pick him up and hold him!

He felt so helpless, so inadequate. Even last night when he'd given the baby the bottle he'd felt as if any moment he'd do something wrong.

The crying grew louder. Piran's fists clenched in the sheet. Come on, Carly, he begged silently. You get him.

But Carly didn't come.

Piran dragged the pillow over his head. No good. He pressed his palms against his ears. Didn't work.

Finally he could bear it no longer. He stumbled out of bed and made his way into the small bedroom next to his own. He opened the door and went to lean over the make-shift cot Carly had devised.

'Hey, kid, come on, calm down,' he whispered urgently. 'It's OK.'

But his words had no effect at all. If anything the yelling got louder.

'Shh. Hush now.' Piran bent closer. He rubbed his fingers against the baby's warm back, trying to soothe him the way he'd seen Carly doing earlier.

But apparently he didn't have a mother's—or a father's—touch. In any case, Arthur was too wound up to notice. He yelled on.

Finally, desperate, hoping to God he wouldn't drop this child, Piran scooped the baby awkwardly into his arms.

'Hey! Hey, kid. Quiet. It's all right.' He nestled the baby against his chest, holding him snugly as he bounced lightly on the balls of his feet. 'Shh. Really. C'mon, please. Stuff a sock in it!'

Arthur gummed his bare shoulder, his warm little body pressing against Piran's chest, rocking, and Piran began to walk with him. And that at last did the trick. Arthur gulped, then sobbed, then hiccuped and gulped again.

And at last silence filled the room.

'All right.' Piran breathed the words, a smile lighting his face. 'You hungry? Is that what this is all about? We'll get you something to eat. How 'bout that?'

He started toward the kitchen and ran right into Carly.

She jumped back at once. She was wearing only a thin cotton gown that ended halfway down her thighs. Her wild hair was even wilder in the night. She looked gorgeous and desirable as hell. Piran sucked in air.

Then the writhing bundle in his arms kicked his ribs and howled once more, and he had no time to concentrate on Carly or on the immediate stab of lust that he'd felt at the sight of her.

Desperate, Piran thrust the baby at her. 'Here. Do something for him, for God's sake.'

But Carly kept her hands at her sides and shook her head. 'You're doing fine.'

'I'm not doing fine. I've lucked out for the moment. You want the kid to scream all night?'

'He won't if you feed him. You should probably change him, too. He must be wet.'

'Change him?' Piran goggled at her.

She pointed him toward the bedroom. 'You change him. I'll fix a bottle.'

'How about you change him, I'll fix the bottle?'

But Carly shook her head. 'Just be glad I'm doing anything.'

'You're cruel, you know that?' he grumbled.

'A witch, I know. You've told me,' Carly said. She patted his cheek and vanished into the kitchen, leaving him standing there with Arthur still in his arms.

Piran touched one hand briefly to his cheek where he could still feel Carly's touch. Then he looked at Arthur warily. 'I'm supposed to change you,' he told the baby. 'Are you going to yell?'

The answer was yes.

Piran felt like yelling a bit too before he managed to get Arthur out of his tiny yellow stretchsuit, out of his plastic pants and out of his sopping wet diaper, then into another diaper, into another pair of plastic pants and finally into the tiny yellow stretchsuit once more. He felt as if he'd expended enough energy to have salvaged an entire Spanish caravel by the time he was done and Carly reappeared with the bottle.

'Good job,' she said cheerfully.

Piran grunted. 'He peed on me.'

'Occupational hazard. Here.' She held out the bottle to him.

'Nope. Your turn. I did my bit.'

'But—'

'Come on, Carly. Have mercy on me. I've just gone ten rounds with the little devil. You can't expect me to go another five.'

'You're only going to feed him.'

'And give him more strength to battle us tomorrow.'

Carly laughed. 'That's about it.' But then she shrugged. 'All right,' she said, climbing on to the bed. 'Give him here.'

He handed Arthur over to her and she nestled him easily into the curve of her arm then slipped the nipple into his mouth. Arthur didn't hesitate this time. He glommed on to it eagerly and began to suck. His gaze flickered up to meet Carly's and he seemed to say, About time.

Carly smiled down at him. 'That's what you wanted, isn't it?' she said softly. She snuggled him closer and dropped a light kiss on his forehead. Arthur sucked contentedly. She stroked his hair.

And Piran, watching the two of them, felt an odd tight aching sensation in his throat that he'd never experienced before. He didn't understand it, wasn't sure he wanted to. He backed away.

'I'll leave you to it, then,' he said gruffly.

Carly glanced up. 'All right. See you in the morning. Sleep well.'

Piran went back to bed. He lay there and thought about the solid warmth of Arthur's body snug against his chest. He thought about the way the baby had yelled, but then had stopped yelling. He thought about the way Arthur had looked in Carly's arms.

He thought about Carly. About her beauty and her gentleness. About the way she'd looked all those years ago. About the way she'd looked tonight holding the child.

Every time he thought about her he got confused. If she was what she seemed to be, how could she be her mother's daughter?

And yet…she'd make a good mother, he thought.

He didn't sleep at all.

Carly had been up with Arthur for over two hours when Piran emerged the next morning shortly after nine. He didn't look very cheerful. Nor did he look especially rested. His cheeks were stubbled with a day's growth of dark whiskers, his eyes were bleary and bloodshot, his hair spiky and uncombed.

Carly wasn't sure that that was all bad. In fact, she thought that if it meant he had lain awake considering the implications of fatherhood and resolving to face them it might be all to the good.

She watched him warily, waiting to take her cue from some sign from him.

He gave her a bleak look and then walked right past where she sat with the baby on the sofa, without even a 'good morning' to her or a glance at Arthur, straight to the coffee maker, and added enough water and coffee for a full ten-cup pot.

He stood with his back to her, bracing his hands on the

counter and staring down at the pot while he waited for it to heat.

So much for becoming resolved to fatherhood.

Carly regarded him with increasing irritation. She stuck out her tongue at his back, then turned her gaze once more to the chapter she was trying to read with Arthur's help.

She noted but didn't look up when Piran left the coffee maker, walked over to the door and stood brooding, staring out into the jungle-like surroundings. She saw but didn't comment when he rubbed his hands through his already mussed hair then stalked back to the coffee maker to scowl down at it and drum his fingers on the counter. She kept her eyes focused on either the chapter or the baby.

When the coffee was ready at last, Piran poured himself a cup without offering her one.

Surprise, surprise, she thought, and nailed him with a glare, then turned back to the baby before he looked up.

He turned, but didn't move to take a chair. Instead he leaned against the counter, staring morosely into the mug that he held against his chest. He sipped once, sighed, then sipped again.

'I don't know what I'm going to do.'

His words dropped like stones into the silence of the room.

Carly looked up to see a desolate look on his face that made her want to go to him and comfort him, reassure him, tell him that everything would be all right.

She didn't do it. After everything that had passed between them she knew exactly how he'd interpret any move toward him on her part. He wouldn't call it reassurance.

Besides, even if it had been in her best interests to reassure him, she couldn't.

She didn't know if everything would be all right.

Looking at the situation honestly meant admitting that

there was very little chance that it would be—at least, not in the near future.

Not for him—and not for Arthur.

And for the missing mother, Miss Pastel Envelopes?

Carly didn't want to think about her. She shook her head and looked down at the chapter she'd been reading. Yesterday morning just getting the book into shape had seemed an all-consuming task. Now it hardly signified.

Arthur reached up with the hand that wasn't clutching the bottle and patted her hand, and even though he was the cause of their present difficulties she couldn't help smiling at him.

'All finished?' she asked. But when she started to take the bottle away from him his face screwed up as if he might cry. Quickly she put the nipple back in his mouth and he began to suck eagerly once more.

'Faker,' she chided him.

Out of the corner of her eye she saw Piran's bare feet come a step closer, then stop. She glanced up. His gaze was still bleak, but he was looking interested in what was happening.

'I think,' she said carefully, 'that if you just take things one day at a time it will sort itself out.'

'Who gave you the ability to forecast the future?'

His sarcasm stung and she looked away sharply, pressing her lips together in a tight line.

'Ah, hell, I'm sorry,' he muttered after a moment. 'It's not your fault. I shouldn't take it out on you.' He looked at her, abashed. Then he shut his eyes and shook his head. 'Maybe you're right. But God…a baby!'

'Don't think of him as a baby. Think of him as a person, as Arthur.'

'Stupid name for a kid.'

'What would you have named him?'

Piran shoved his hands into his pockets. 'I've never thought about it. Having kids was never high on my list of priorities,' he said after a moment.

Obviously not, since marriage wasn't high on it either. Still, Carly felt compelled to say, 'Priorities have a way of shifting.'

'Don't they just?' Piran took another swallow of coffee and stared out the window once more.

'I was…wondering,' Carly ventured after a moment, not quite sure how to phrase this without bringing his wrath down on her again.

'About what?' he said when she couldn't figure out how to continue.

'Um, those letters?' He didn't look pleased, so she hurried on. 'I mean, if she's been writing you all the time, surely she must've said something, or hinted at least?'

'I didn't read them.'

Carly goggled at him.

'There was nothing Wendy—that's her name—had to say that I wanted to read.' He rubbed his palms down his face. 'At least, I didn't think there was,' he added ruefully.

Carly considered that, actually finding that his admission made her feel better. She didn't want to think about why. 'Where are they?'

'I threw them out. And don't tell me to go get 'em 'cause Ruth took the trash with her when she went home last night. Believe me, I already looked.'

'But—' But clearly there was no recovering the letters. Carly sighed. 'Well, maybe when you get a letter today…'

'Maybe,' Piran said, a hint of hope in his tone.

But, perversely enough, when the mail arrived there was no pastel-colored envelope. There was no letter from Wendy at all, pastel or otherwise.

Nor was there a letter the day after or the day after that.

Piran practically pounced on the mail each afternoon, but, though he blustered and fumed when it arrived, an entire week went by and he never managed to conjure up a pastel envelope.

Carly supposed it was the result of sheer panic and desperation, but they got a lot of work done, even with Arthur there. Maybe it was because they took advantage of every possible moment, or maybe it was simply that Arthur was an easy enough baby to become a part of the routine quickly; whatever, the book was certainly moving along.

And Carly, who'd had virtually no experience with babies before, seemed truly to have a natural instinct for motherhood. Either that or her job had prepared her.

'I think it's the editing,' she told Piran one afternoon.

He gaped at her. '*Editing* prepared you for motherhood? How?'

'The ability to do seven things at once, I think.' Carly grinned. 'There was always more to do than Sloan could handle, so he'd give me one job and before I got ten minutes into that he'd have another one for me. I learned to juggle. Besides that, I learned to placate fractious, temperamental authors. There's not a lot of difference between some of them and Arthur at his worst.'

She said this while balancing Arthur on one hip and stirring the spaghetti sauce that was left over from last night's supper. On the counter next to the stove was the current bit of Piran's writing that she was polishing up. Periodically she glanced over at it, read a bit, set down the spoon, shifted Arthur, and made notes in the margin.

'I never noticed you going out of your way to placate me,' Piran said gruffly.

'Perhaps not,' Carly allowed. 'But in the circumstances I'm sure you can understand why.'

'Maybe,' he muttered. But his tone wasn't quite as sarcastic as it usually was. In fact he'd been fairly silent on all fronts the last few days.

Carly supposed that finding out he had a son was a bit of a jolt—something he still hadn't completely assimilated. They'd had Arthur almost a week and Piran still wasn't really comfortable with him. He gave the baby a bottle every day because Carly said she needed a break. And he changed him, grumbling as he did so, when Carly claimed to be right in the middle of a very important piece of work.

But he wouldn't let her leave Arthur with him alone.

'I'm not ready for that,' he told her whenever she suggested taking a walk by herself or going into town.

And, sucker that she was, Carly caved in.

She was no expert at child care certainly, but she didn't worry about being perfect at it the way Piran did. She'd always learned by doing anyway, and Arthur was a good teacher. If she didn't fulfill his needs, he let her know. If he was wet, he fussed. If he was hungry, he cried. If he wanted attention, he found ways of getting it.

And in one way he'd made her life easier.

Seeing her with Arthur had apparently put a damper on Piran's sexual appetite. Or if it hadn't it had clearly switched away from her for, now that Arthur had arrived, Piran didn't say another word about getting her into bed.

Holding Arthur, she decided, was as effective as holding a can of Mace.

She held him now and studied the back of Piran's head as he sat at the computer trying to work. He didn't seem to be getting very far, if the amount of muttering and blocking and deleting he was doing was any indication.

She had to give him credit—he'd been working like fury since Arthur had arrived—as much to avoid the baby as to get the book done, she suspected. But he looked like hell. He needed a break—an afternoon off. However, Carly had had no luck at all in getting him to take one.

'You want the book done, don't you?' he snapped whenever she suggested it.

And of course she did. But not at the expense of his health. Besides, the book would be done. Of that she was certain.

'But he needs a break,' she told Arthur in a soft voice so that Piran didn't hear her. 'And you're going to have to see that he takes one.'

Arthur looked at her wide-eyed and waved his arms.

'I'll help you.' She carried him into the kitchen, peered into the fridge, spied the milk bottle with only a cup or so in it, considered her options and poured it down the drain.

Then, shifting the baby to her other hip, she went back into the living room.

'We're out of milk,' she said.

Piran frowned. 'None?'

'Nope. And I don't know if Ruth will be bringing any so I'll go into town and get some.'

'I'll go.'

'No. I will.'

'Fine, if you take Arthur.'

'I'm not taking Arthur.'

'But—'

'Piran, it's almost a hundred degrees in the shade. And the humidity is awful. I'm not going to lug him all the way to town.'

'Then let me go.'

'No. I need a break. You'll be fine, both of you.' And, so saying, she plopped Arthur into his lap.

'Carly! I'm working!'

'He can help you.' She stuffed her feet into her sandals and fled toward the door.

'Wait!'

'See you by suppertime,' she called over her shoulder, and vanished down the trail before he could stop her.

It was beginning to look a lot more like Christmas.

Even on tiny Conch Cay.

Sutters' fruit store had a dusting of artificial snow in the corners of each pane of window glass. Cash's hardware and video store had a small sleigh crafted out of spare auto parts perched precariously on the tin roof. There were half a dozen strings of colored lights winking brightly all along the eaves of the government building even in broad daylight. There was even a wreath made of coconut palm fronds and bougainvillaea flowers hanging on the jailhouse door.

In the yard of the church she saw a life-size manger scene, complete with a shepherd, three magi, a couple of cracked plastic sheep which had clearly seen better days and a real-live donkey who lifted his head a moment as Carly stopped outside the gate, then went back to cropping the grass. Several chickens clucked around him, and a mongrel dog slept in the shade cast by Mary and Joseph.

There was no baby. It didn't even look as if one was expected.

Rather like Arthur, she thought.

And then she thought, This will be Arthur's first Christmas. And suddenly she wanted to celebrate the holiday after all.

She knew Arthur wouldn't remember it, so in that sense it wouldn't really matter. But at the same time she was sure it mattered a great deal.

Whether he remembered or not, Carly felt it was important to mark the occasion for him, to welcome him into the world, into the family—even as unexpected as he was, perhaps *because* he was as unexpected as he was.

It wasn't her place to do so, she supposed. But maybe, as an ex-stepsister of his probable father, she could argue that she had the right.

She smiled ruefully when she realized how much she wanted the right. She might only have known Arthur a week or so, but he mattered to her. She was going to have trouble letting him go. The thought of losing him so quickly gave her heart a twist that she wasn't expecting.

It should be no big surprise, she reminded herself. Her entire life had been spent in short-term relationships. This would just be another one.

But maybe a few more bittersweet Christmas memories would help both of them.

Maybe they would help Piran, too.

Piran had never felt so responsible in his life. Nor so inadequate. Not when he couldn't hold his parents' marriage together, not when he couldn't talk his father out of marrying Carly's mother. Not even when Gordon had died.

He knew, intellectually if not emotionally, that he wasn't responsible for his parents' divorce or his father's remarriage or even for Gordon's death.

He was responsible for Arthur. Now and forever. Past, present and future.

He was the reason that Arthur existed at all.

He hadn't wanted to believe it. Heaven knew he hadn't wanted a child—not now and certainly not like this—unplanned and unexpected.

But, oddly enough, now that he had Arthur, he found stirrings inside that he'd never felt before.

They weren't merely signs of academic interest as he'd told himself at first. They were something more. Something basic, elemental. They were so foreign, they scared him. Arthur scared him.

And yet Arthur fascinated him too.

He was so resilient, so cheerful. His whole world had been turned upside down by whoever was his mother—Wendy, Piran guessed. And yet he smiled and cooed and snuggled up to Carly just as if she'd given birth to him.

And Carly snuggled up to him.

Piran liked watching them together. He liked seeing Carly cuddle the child in her arms while she gave him his bottle. He liked watching her bend over the baby while she changed him and dressed him. He liked the silly noises she made and the nonsense she talked, and he was amazed at the noises Arthur made in return. It was as if they were really communicating.

He looked down at the baby in his arms, then got up and carried him over to the sofa and set him in the corner, banked on either side by blue and green pillows.

Arthur regarded the pillows and Piran with equal curiosity.

'Are you going to yell?' Piran asked him nervously.

'Ba,' Arthur said. He patted a pillow.

Piran's eyes lit up. 'That's right,' he said. 'It's blue. And that one's green. Can you say green?'

'Ba ga,' said Arthur. He grabbed a pillow and stuffed the corner of it in his mouth, gumming it furiously.

'You're a genius,' Piran told him. 'You can say blue and green. My God! Carly!' he shouted. Then he remembered that Carly wasn't here.

He was alone. With a genius.

He gulped. He picked Arthur up again. 'Come on,' he said. 'Let's see what else you can say.'

He carried the baby all around the house, pointing out lamps and sofas, books and chairs. He took him outside and showed him palm trees and frangipani trees, breadfruit trees and bougainvillaeas.

'You might want to consider botany as a career,' he told Arthur. 'If you don't go into archaeology. I won't mind if you don't,' he assured the baby.

'Ga,' said Arthur. 'Da.'

Piran's eyes bugged. He held Arthur out at arm's length. 'Say that again,' he demanded. 'By George, kiddo, I think you just said Daddy!'

Carly started listening as soon as she came around the bend in the path, keeping her ears open for sounds of babies yelling. One particular baby at least.

She heard only the surf and the birds and a frog next to the mangrove tree.

She shifted the grocery bag from one arm to the other and climbed the steps to the deck. The vertical blinds were slanted to keep the afternoon sun out. The doors were open, but the screens were shut. Carly slid one open and looked around.

No Arthur. No Piran.

'Piran?' she said softly.

She got no response.

She frowned. If Arthur had gone to sleep, surely Piran would be working? If he had taken Arthur to the beach, she certainly would have seen them. She'd come back along the water and they weren't down there.

She carried the milk into the kitchen and put it in the fridge, then went in search of them.

They weren't on the veranda. They weren't in the small garden that faced the narrow drive. They weren't in Arthur's room either.

But they had been there. Carly saw a wet diaper on the floor. The romper she'd put Arthur in this morning was on the dresser. Several other T-shirts and rompers had been tossed aside.

Carly winced, wondering if Piran had taken Arthur and gone in search of someone who could help take care of him. She crossed the living room and pushed open the half-closed door to Piran's room.

And she smiled.

Piran, wearing only a pair of cut-off jeans, was sprawled flat on his back sound asleep on the bed. Arthur, clad in a diaper and a T-shirt, his knees drawn up under him and his thumb in his mouth, slept equally soundly on Piran's bare chest, one of his father's big hands cupped protectively around his back.

CHAPTER SEVEN

'WHAT on earth is that?' Piran demanded as she came up the path. He had apparently awakened after she'd left to go back for the rest of her bounty, and now he was standing on the veranda staring down at her muzzily.

'It's a tree,' Carly panted.

'What are you dragging a tree around for?'

'Christmas.'

Piran blinked. '*What*?'

''Tis the season to be jolly. I'd forgotten.' She didn't say she'd been trying to forget. 'But when I went into town it became obvious and, well, I thought we ought to celebrate so I brought us a Christmas tree.' The explanation took every available bit of breath she had. She stopped and sagged against the railing at the bottom of the steps, fanning herself.

Piran looked at her as if she'd lost her mind. 'It looks like something you'd throw on a brush heap.'

'Well, there wasn't a lot of choice,' Carly said. 'Most of the pines I saw that looked sort of traditionally Christmassy were far too big. I thought about a banana tree because it came equipped with built-in ornaments—' she grinned '—but I didn't want to be the cause of the destruction of lots of little unripened bananas.'

He shook his head. 'What are you talking about?'

'Ben says that everyone who wants to just cuts a tree from the ones that grow near the beach. He told me where, so I walked back that way. Fortunately I found this one not far from the path up to the house.'

'And you just…cut it down?'

'Ben lent me a machete and—'

'What happened to the milk?' Piran demanded. 'You went to town to get milk.'

'I did, and I put it in the fridge. I bought some other things, too. Christmas presents. For Arthur.'

'You went Christmas shopping?' Piran gaped at her. 'You left me all morning and went Christmas shopping?'

'Yes, I did,' Carly said firmly. 'There's only eight more shopping days, you know. Besides, you did fine without me. You were both sleeping when I came in with the milk.'

He looked momentarily discomfitted. 'Luck,' he muttered. 'Anyway, don't you think we have enough to do with Arthur and the book without worrying about Christmas?'

'No, I don't. I think it's the most important thing we can do.'

'More important than the book?' he challenged her.

'Yes. Look,' she said with all the earnestness she could muster. 'I know it's due in barely more than two weeks. I know we've got a long way to go. And I know you're going to tell me Arthur won't remember.'

He opened his mouth to comment, but Carly went right on without letting him say a word.

'You're right, of course. He won't remember actual presents, actual events. But he'll sense it, I know he will. And it will matter, Piran. And later, when he's big enough to know and to ask, he will ask. He'll want to know about what happened when you first got him. He'll ask about *when* it happened. And you'll have to tell him it was near Christmas. And he'll want to know about his first Christmas. He'll want to know how you celebrated it. And you'll have to tell him that, too.

'So what are you going to tell him, Piran? That you

were too busy writing your book to bother about it? That his first Christmas didn't matter? That it came and went and was no more than an annoyance? I don't think you want to do that. I think you want to be able to talk to him about the joy of the day, the joy of celebration. It was, after all, because of the arrival of a baby that we're celebrating Christmas at all!' Carly stopped, out of breath at last, and looked at him beseechingly.

Piran just stared at her. Then slowly he shook his head. 'My God, you're wasted on editing. Have you ever considered a career in law? You'd make a dynamite prosecuting attorney. Such incredible rhetorical talent going to waste...'

Carly felt her cheeks warm. 'Don't be obnoxious.'

'I'm not. I'm in awe.'

'You're laughing at me.'

He shook his head. 'I'm not laughing. There's damned little to laugh at right now, and you know it.'

She wasn't sure how broadly to interpret that comment so she steered away from it altogether. Their whole relationship was so complex that there had been little to laugh at since the beginning. Arthur only complicated it.

Or maybe, Carly thought, he simplified it. Maybe he made what was really important clear at last.

'I want Christmas,' Carly said, looking straight into Piran's deep blue eyes.

'And whatever Carly wants Carly gets?'

She was glad her gaze didn't falter. 'I think you already know the answer to that.'

He had the grace to wince a little.

'Never mind. It's all in the past,' Carly said. 'It's not important now.' She changed the subject briskly. 'Did Arthur give you a hard time?' She remembered the clothing scattered around the bedroom, remembered the sight of Piran on the bed with the baby asleep on his chest.

'He made his wishes known,' Piran said drily after a moment. 'And I wasn't always good at deciphering them.'

'I saw the clothes.' She slanted him a glance. 'Don't tell me he already has preferences in what to wear.'

A faint smile touched Piran's face. 'No. It turned out I did. Half of them I couldn't seem to get on him before he wiggled away from me. Finally I opted for the easiest route.'

'But you survived.'

'We survived. Did you know he can talk?'

'Piran, he's six months old!'

'Yeah, but he can say blue and green and good. At least I think he said good, and once he even said Daddy.'

'Daddy?'

He shrugged, embarrassed. 'Well, he doesn't enunciate very well yet, but what else could it have been?'

Carly shook her head. 'I can't imagine. Does this mean you're accepting the fact that you are his daddy?'

'Yeah, I guess I am,' he said. 'At least until another daddy comes along.'

It was a step. A small one, but still a step. They were bonding, Piran and Arthur. They had plenty more steps to take, of course, but they were finally on their way to becoming a family. Carly smiled. But it was a bittersweet smile because, heaven help her, she wanted to be part of the bond as well.

So she was a fool. So what else was new?

She was as incurable a romantic as her mother, as determined a believer in happy endings or at least in wonderful memories as the woman who'd given her life.

'Better to live and to love than to regret,' Sue had said to her daughter time and time again.

And while Carly could never see herself like Sue, trying to live and love seven different men, apparently she couldn't seem to stop trying to live and love with one—even if he didn't love her. Even if living with him meant only for the next two weeks and loving him meant only helping him learn to become a father and then walking away because that was the way he wanted it—just him and his child alone.

And for herself?

For herself Carly would take memories. They hurt sometimes—thinking about that joyous last Christmas which she'd spent with her mother and Roland and his daughters in Colorado still hurt. But hurting, Carly began to realize, was better than an empty life; it was better by far than feeling nothing at all.

So she dug in to make this Christmas a Christmas to remember.

She started with the tree.

Granted it wasn't beautiful, and Piran didn't seem to see its potential as he took it out of her hands and dragged it up the stairs for her. But maybe he would when they got it set up and began to decorate it. Carly dared to hope.

'Where do you want it?' he asked her when he'd lugged it up on to the deck.

'Er, perhaps in the living room in front of the window? I don't know. I mean, it's your house.'

'Nice of you to realize that,' he said drily. He carried the tree in and hoisted it upright and held it there. 'I don't suppose you bought a stand?'

'Oh, dear,' Carly said. She ran a nervous tongue over her lips and gave him a smile that was at least half sheepish grimace. 'I hadn't thought. Just—er—prop it in the corner. I'll walk back to town and see if I can find a tree stand at the hardware store.'

'Not on your life. We've got a book to do.'

'But the tree! I'm not going to abandon it, Piran!' she said stubbornly.

'Obviously.'

'Well, then…'

He raked a hand through his hair. 'Don't worry. I'll think of something.'

'You will?' She looked at him hopefully.

'I will. I promise,' he added when she gave him a look that said she wasn't entirely convinced. 'Now, for the ten thousandth time, we have to get going on the book. I didn't get a single thing done this morning—'

'And you look far better for it. More rested. And you probably feel better too, don't you, having spent some time with Arthur?'

He scowled. 'What is this? Dr O'Reilly's shrink shop?'

Carly smiled slightly. 'Yes. And now Dr O'Reilly says we need to decorate the Christmas tree.'

'Yeah? Well, first Dr St Just says you'd better work on chapter seven.'

'But—'

'I mean it.'

Carly knew better than to push him further. She let him think about it. But she wasn't above putting on a tape of holiday music that she'd bought in town on the stereo.

'Subliminal persuasion?' Piran arched a brow at her when the first notes of 'Joy to the World' reached his ears.

Carly smiled.

Piran studied her silently. 'It really means a lot to you?'

'Yes,' she said simply. 'It does.'

When Arthur woke up, Piran still hadn't done anything about the tree, but she thought he'd got the message. He was busy typing furiously so Carly went and got the baby. She brought him back out into the living room after she'd changed him. He looked happy and well-rested and none the worse for spending the morning with Piran.

He giggled as she danced him around the room to the tune of 'Frosty the Snowman'. Piran turned around to watch them. Carly waved Arthur's hand at him, then held it out in invitation.

'Want to dance with him?' she offered.

'I'll dance with you.'

'I already have a partner, thank you.'

'Frosty' ended and there was a moment's pause before the soft sound of 'What Child Is This?' began. Carly began to move with Arthur once more as Piran stood up and came toward them.

He took her hand, his grip firm and warm around her fingers. Then he wrapped his other arm around her back and, holding Arthur between them, he danced with her.

They moved slowly but smoothly with the music, looking into each other's eyes over the top of Arthur's head. The expression in Piran's gaze was warm and hungry and something more. Carly thought she saw a sort of puzzlement in them, as if he wasn't quite sure he had all the answers for a change.

They danced, and only when the last notes had long since died away did they stop at last.

Under the mistletoe.

Keeping his eyes on Carly's, Piran bent his head and kissed Arthur lightly on the top of his. Then he ran his tongue over still slightly parted lips.

'Kissing's not enough, Carlota,' he said, his voice ragged.

No, it's not, Carly wanted to say. But, fighting her own inclination as much as his because there was a limit to the amount of hurt she knew she could stand, she told him simply, 'It has to be.'

'For now,' he said.

The mail came very late that day, and Carly found herself holding her breath while Piran went to fetch it, though whether she hoped there was or wasn't a letter from Wendy she couldn't have said.

Only after Piran came back and all he had were two letters from colleagues, a postcard of a bathing beauty from Des in Fiji and a journal on Greek archaeology did she breathe again.

He tossed Carly the postcard as she sat giving Arthur a bottle and humming along to 'Silver Bells'. It was written in Des's almost illegible scrawl.

> Great so far. Meeting up with Jim and crew *mañana* for our sail into the great unknown. Be out of touch for a couple of weeks. Don't kill each other in the meantime—or me when I get back! Have a merry, merry one with lots of jolly surprises. Love, Des.

'Jolly surprise, huh?' Carly said, smiling and looking down at the baby in her arms. 'Wouldn't Des be shocked?'

Arthur gazed up at her solemnly.

'You're a very nice surprise,' Carly told him softly, and bent her head to drop a kiss on his nose. His eyelids began to droop. In minutes he was sound asleep. But Carly made no move to go put him down in his bed. Instead she listened as the music softly wove its holiday spell and looked at the child in her arms, marveling at the beauty of new life.

There was an ache in her throat as she envied Piran this wonderful child and the future they would share. And the ache got even worse when she started envying Arthur his future with Piran.

A sudden sound made her look up and she saw Piran standing in the doorway to the kitchen, watching her. The look on his face was intense, brooding and disturbingly sensual. If the embers had been banked when they'd held Arthur between them after the dance, they burst into flame now.

'Is he asleep?' Piran asked.

Carly nodded.

'Then put him down.'

And come to me. She didn't have to hear him say the words. She could see them in his eyes, in his slightly parted lips, in the heightened color that ran along his cheekbones.

And if she did go to him, if she did make love with him, what would she have then?

Memories, she told herself. You'd have memories.

And it was almost enough. But not enough to cancel out what she would have as well—a broken heart.

'Not now,' she said.

The look he gave her was long and fierce and aching. And then he turned away.

She wanted him. He *knew* she wanted him—probably as badly as he wanted her.

And yet she said no. And no again.

Why?

For *marriage*? What did marriage matter so much? When she'd been eighteen and using it to barter, he'd seen her as simply following in her mother's footsteps. But now…?

He was supposed to be working. He couldn't keep his mind on the caravel. He was supposed to be writing. He couldn't even spell words.

Except one. Carly. He typed it on to the screen. He erased it. His fingers typed it again.

He was as obsessed with her as he had been nine years ago. Only now he didn't have the folly of youth on which to blame it. He was old enough to know better—and he didn't.

He wanted Carly O'Reilly.

But even more, he discovered, he wanted to *understand* Carly O'Reilly.

With the folly of youth, he was sure he had.

Now he was far less certain.

She didn't need a man for support the way her mother had. She had a job and he'd be the first to admit she was good at it. She didn't need a man for self-esteem. She had plenty on her own. Yet she seemed very willing to share herself—except in bed, that was.

She positively doted on Arthur.

A part of Piran had assumed that watching her play mother to Arthur would quell his interest. But he'd been wrong about that, too. If anything, that interest was heightened.

Heightened, hell! It was driving him up the wall.

He finally heard her put Arthur down to bed. He expected her to leave, go for a walk, avoid him. But instead she came back through the living room and went into the kitchen and started doing something with pots and pans. He could hear her in there, humming along with that Christmas tape she'd bought. He deleted her name again and tried once more to make sense out of his notes.

It wasn't long until the sweet smell of Christmas baking drifted out of the kitchen and filled every corner of the house. His mouth watered. His stomach growled. He tried to ignore them. It wasn't any easier than ignoring her.

He got up and followed his nose into the kitchen. Carly

was bent over taking a sheet of cookies out of the oven. He shut his eyes and braced his hand against the doorjamb.

'More subliminal suggestion?' he asked when he opened them again.

She smiled faintly. 'I wasn't going to,' she confessed. 'I didn't think I wanted to be reminded…' Her voice trailed off.

'Reminded?'

'These are my mother's recipes. She made the same kind of cookies every Christmas no matter where we were. And some of the places, to be honest, were pretty crummy. But she believed in keeping Christmas, in "keeping hope", she called it.' Carly smiled, a wistful, tender smile that tugged at something deep inside Piran.

'Last Christmas when she was with Roland and his daughters,' Carly went on, 'it was definitely the Christmas she'd always been hoping for—a celebration of family and love and joy. I didn't think I wanted to be reminded this year. I didn't think I wanted to remember what I'd lost.' She stopped and rubbed at the corner of her eye, then smiled again. 'I was wrong. I still hope, I guess. And I wanted to share it with Arthur. Maybe he'll have some memory of these smells and remember the happiness of his first Christmas.' She cleared her throat. 'Sorry. I'm getting sappy. It's the season, I guess.'

Piran just looked at her. She shifted uncomfortably under his gaze. 'Forget it. You can have one when they're cool. You might not have liked my mother, Piran, but she did make good cookies.'

'She did,' he said quietly. Then he said, 'I'm going for a walk.'

'It's hot out there. You'll die,' Carly warned.

Possibly. But he would definitely die in here if he didn't give in to the urge to go to her, to take her in his arms and hold her, to kiss her gently, to love her tenderly, and then to start all over again, replacing tenderness with passion, until both of them were sated with these feelings that had been growing between them for years.

He walked the length of the pink sand beach. He tried to cool his ardor, to get his perspective, to remind himself that the last thing he needed right now was a roll in a bed or on the sand or anyplace else with Carly O'Reilly. It would only complicate his already far too complicated life.

It worked only until he came around the point and saw her paddling in the shallows with Arthur in her arms. Then all his perspective vanished, all his ardor returned, and his preoccupation with Carly O'Reilly grew greater.

Carly saw him and waved Arthur's hand and her own.

Piran lifted a hand in reply. He didn't say anything, even as he came closer, and she gave him another smile.

'The cookies are cool now.'

'I'm not,' he said gruffly.

Her cheeks turned red. 'Piran, I—'

'Not your fault,' he muttered, and plunged past her into the surf. And the moment his head broke the surface he started stroking out to sea.

'Where are you going?' Carly called after him.

He didn't answer, just swam on.

Not until he reached the outer reef did Piran stop swimming and turn around, treading water and looking back at the woman and child on the shore. Carly was watching him. She was too far away for him to see the expression on her face, but the intensity of her gaze told him she was worried.

About him?

Did she think he was going to drown? Get eaten by a barracuda?

Did she care?

Yes, she probably did.

He'd seen enough of Carly over the past few weeks to know that she wasn't quite the manipulator he'd thought she was. No matter what he thought of her mother's marriage to his father, Carly clearly believed it had been for love. She'd been there for them both during his father's last illness. He hadn't. Stubborn and righteous to the last, he hadn't come even come to the old man's funeral.

God, what a bull-headed, moralistic prig he'd been.

He'd done his share of moralizing at Des, too, for all the good it had ever done, trying to get him to take their explorations seriously, to spend his time working and writing instead of sailing and partying.

Probably, he thought grimly, that was why Des had taken off for Fiji and left him alone with the book.

But Des hadn't left him totally alone; he'd sent him Carly.

Everything ultimately came back to Carly.

He looked at her now, never taking her eyes off him, as if he might vanish if she did. As if it were her responsibility to keep him safe. She held Arthur. His responsibility. She'd worked on the book for weeks. His book. She'd given up her holiday and taken over for Des who had left her to do his work.

When, Piran wondered, had anyone ever done anything for her?

Arthur squirmed in her arms when he saw Piran approach and Carly almost dropped him, so slick was he from having sunscreen rubbed all over his small body.

'Careful there,' Carly warned him. 'Hold still.'

'Give him to me.'

She looked round, startled to see Piran standing barely five feet from her. He held out his arms for Arthur.

She hesitated. 'You're volunteering?'

Taking the baby bodily out of her embrace seemed to be all the answer he was going to give her. But since Carly had no desire to get into a tug-of-war over the baby she let go and stepped back, feeling almost naked to his gaze as she did so.

But Piran's gaze didn't travel seductively down her body the way it often did. 'You go for a swim,' he suggested. 'Arthur and I will watch.'

Carly stared at him, uncertain how to take this turn of events. 'Fatherhood taking hold, is it?' she joked.

'Maybe.'

'Well, good. I really shouldn't swim, though. If you're going to take him, I'll just go back and get some work done.' She turned and started toward the beach.

'No, don't!'

At the urgency of his tone, Carly turned and looked at him again.

'Stay,' he entreated her.

It was a command, and yet it wasn't—quite. Carly looked back over her shoulder at him.

One corner of his mouth lifted in a wry smile. 'Arthur will think you're abandoning him if you go. He'll want to watch you.'

'Or you will?' she challenged him.

His lips pressed together for a moment. 'I can't help it,' he said eventually. He seemed almost unhappy about it. Probably he was, Carly thought. He'd never wanted to want her the way he did.

'I'll go for a quick swim,' she said. 'But then I really have to go back and finish what I was working on before Arthur woke up. I finished the cookies,' she said awkwardly. 'I didn't take all afternoon on them.'

'It doesn't matter. You deserve the break.'

'Well, it was nice. I'm glad I took it. But now I'm working on the part about the discovery and dating of the artifacts. It's going really fast. You're getting better,' she told him.

Piran grunted.

'Really,' Carly said, seeing the doubt on his face. 'Once you got into that it became almost like reading a detective novel.'

He nodded. 'It was almost like living a detective novel when we were doing it. When Des and I brought up that old gun like the ones they were making in Holland at the time, we had to try to figure out what circumstances existed that made the owners of a Spanish caravel buy Dutch guns...' He grinned self-consciously. 'Sorry. I'm babbling.'

Carly shook her head. 'No, you're not. I'm interested. Truly. I wish...' she began, then stopped abruptly.

'You wish what?'

'Nothing.' She turned away and started out into the water. 'Never mind. I'll swim.' She headed out toward the breakers.

Piran came with her.

'Piran! Arthur will be scared!'

'No, he won't. Will you?' he asked the baby, keeping pace with her. The water was almost to her breasts now. Bigger waves were coming in. Arthur's eyes were like dishpans, they were so huge. He gripped Piran's shoulders, but he didn't make a sound.

'You wish what, Carly?' Piran persisted.

Carly shrugged, letting her body rise with the lift of the wave. 'It's...not important. Just silliness.' She started to turn away. Piran's hand reached out and caught her arm.

'Tell me.'

She shrugged irritably. 'I was only going to say that I

wish I had been able to go on a dive like that. There. See? No big deal.'

'An archaeological dive, you mean?'

'Any dive. I never have—except in the pool in New York. I—' she hesitated, then figured she might as well admit it '—took a course in scuba while I was helping Sloan with your last book. I thought it would give some insight into the process, the feeling, you know?'

'I'll take you.'

'Don't be ridiculous. The caravel is miles from here! Besides, we don't have any time. We don't have—'

'Not the caravel. Just out near the point at the top of the island in the narrows.' He pointed north. 'There's a wreck there—a Revolutionary War ship. Not a major discovery. Everyone has always known it was there, and it's been salvaged. But if it's your first time…just to give you a taste. You are certified?'

'Yes, but—'

'Fine. How about it?'

'We don't have time, remember?'

'We'll make time.'

'Arthur—'

'We can get an Arthur-sitter from somewhere. I'll ask Ruth and see if she knows someone.'

'It's silly.'

'No, it isn't. It's something you want to do.'

'And since when has that mattered to you?'

He winced. 'It matters,' he said. 'Besides, you're right. It might make you a better editor.'

'I doubt—'

'Come on, Carly. One lousy morning. We can go tomorrow.'

'I don't—'

'Chicken?'

'I am not chicken!' Her face flamed.

He grinned. 'Prove it. You must have wanted to pretty bad to get certified. Look me in the eye and say you don't want to do it, Carlota.' Deep blue eyes fastened on hers, challenging her, daring her to lie.

Carly sighed and positioned herself to try to catch the next wave. 'If you can get a sitter,' she muttered finally, secure in the knowledge that with the holiday coming he wouldn't be able to.

He did.

'Ruth's cousin, Mirabelle,' he told her that night after Ruth brought them supper. 'She'll keep Arthur while we're gone. We can drop him off first thing in the morning.'

'Drop him off?'

'Why not? He'll be fine,' Piran assured her. 'If he can cope with being dropped off on us, he'll be able to handle a morning at Mirabelle's.'

Carly was sure that he was right, but it still made her nervous. She was feeling more and more as if Arthur was her responsibility and less and less as if she wanted to entrust him to anyone else.

'She is qualified, isn't she?' she asked Piran.

'If having six of your own qualifies you,' he answered with a grin.

So Carly had to be satisfied with that.

If she could have, she'd have said she'd changed her mind. It was crazy going diving with Piran. It wouldn't serve any purpose at all—except to make her more aware than ever of what life would have been like if he'd loved her and married her years ago.

She didn't want to know, damn it!

And yet she did.

Heaven help her, she wanted to spend the morning diving with Piran. She would have nothing else. She wouldn't make love with him. She didn't want those memories. They'd hurt too much.

But memories of diving, of sharing their experience underwater, of fulfilling one of her dreams—yes, those she could handle. At least, she would try to.

She was in such a turmoil thinking about that and trying instead to think about the chapter she was supposed to be editing once Arthur went to sleep that she wasn't really paying much attention to what Piran was up to.

It was a shock, therefore, to hear a thud on the deck and to look out to see him wrestling a good sized bucket up the steps.

'What are you doing?'

'Putting up your Christmas tree.' He hoisted the bucket again and carried it into the house. He set it in front of the window, fetched the tree and planted it in the bucket which was, she saw, filled a third of the way up with sand. 'Come here and hold this while I finish shoring it up.'

Bemused, Carly did as she was told, holding the tree, marveling not simply at Piran's resourcefulness, but at the fact that he'd actually bothered.

Now he came back to kneel next to the tree and put rocks around it inside the bucket, wedging it tightly, then filling the rest of the bucket with sand.

As he worked, Carly watched the ripple of the muscles in his back. He was so close that his dark hair brushed against her bare legs. She stepped away. But she couldn't go far without letting go of the tree and she didn't dare do that. Piran finished with the rocks and the sand.

He straightened and said, 'Hold out your hand.'

Carly looked at him warily, but he didn't say anything, just waited, and she finally did what he said.

He reached in his pocket and placed two pieces of sea glass—one red, one blue—into her palm. 'I found them when I was picking up rocks,' he told her. A corner of his mouth twisted. 'I—uh—remembered you liked the one we found a long time ago. I...thought you might like these.'

Carly blinked, then swallowed. 'Thank you.' Her fingers closed on them. They looked at each other for a long moment—there were so many messages in that look. So many confusing feelings.

'Now water,' Piran decreed abruptly, and got to his feet once more to go and fetch some.

Carly watched him go, her fingers tight around the smooth pieces of glass. She had told herself for years that all her fascination with Piran had been one-sided, that she had built everything up in her head, that no one else would remember all the details she remembered.

How had Piran remembered about the sea glass?

He came back with a bucket full of water, then added more sand as the water packed it more densely. 'There,' he said at last, nodding his approval. 'That ought to hold it. What do you think?'

'It's wonderful,' she said, then looked away, still feeling dazed. Her eyes flickered back to him briefly. 'Thanks.'

'Did you buy lights?'

'What? Oh—er—yes. Of course.' She managed to get her brain functioning again, went to where she had left the bag on the counter in the kitchen and take out the three strings of colored lights.

She held them out to Piran. He shook his head. 'I did my part. You can decorate.' He paused for a split second after he said it, making her wonder if she could have argued with him. But, before she could make up her mind, abruptly he turned away and went back to the keyboard.

For a long moment Carly stood with the lights in her hands, looking at the back of Piran's dark head and the hunch of his broad shoulders. She felt such a crazy mix of emotions that she didn't think she would ever sort them out.

He felt only lust for her, she told herself. Lust and passion. He wanted sex. And a good editing job. And someone to care for Arthur.

But he had remembered the sea glass.

And he had offered to take her diving in the morning. He had taken the time to find a way to put the tree up tonight.

God, she had to stop thinking like this! It was useless. Worse than useless.

But where Piran was concerned she was like a moth with a flame, attracted, mesmerized. Yet she knew full well what would befall her if she gave in to her fascination with him and dared too much, ventured too close.

She put the lights on the tree alone. She went to bed without saying goodnight. She tossed and turned for hours.

Piran went to bed shortly after midnight. She heard him get up an hour or so later, prowl around the house, then let himself out to go down to the beach.

She was still awake at past two when he came back and came to stand just outside her door. She lay unmoving, every nerve alert and aware.

Wanting. Hoping? Fearing.

Then she heard his footsteps as he walked into his own room and the sound of the springs as he fell into his bed once more.

She should be glad, she told herself. She should be rejoicing that he respected her boundaries.

She did. Of course she did.

It was perverse, then, that, having got what she wanted, she felt even worse.

CHAPTER EIGHT

MIRABELLE thought Arthur was the most beautiful child she had ever seen. She clucked and fussed over him, bouncing him on her hip and tickling his tummy. She got belly laughs out of him that Carly had never thought were in there. And then she shooed Piran and Carly on their way.

'You don't be worryin' about him now. He be fine. Won't you, mon?' she asked a still giggling Arthur. He grinned and waved his arms.

'I think he likes her,' Carly grumbled to Piran as they left and walked down to the dock.

'That's bad?' He slanted her a sidelong glance.

'I suppose not,' she said, but she still felt unaccountably irritated.

Piran grinned. 'Just a little jealous, maybe?'

Carly scowled at him.

His grin widened. 'Relax. He'll be fine, just like she said. Come on.' He grabbed her hand and hauled her with him down the hill. 'Stop thinking about Arthur and think about what a good time you're going to have fulfilling your heart's desire.'

How could he have known? Carly wondered an hour later as she swam lazily alongside him, heading down to the wreck of the old ship that she could see in the crystalline depths.

Maybe he didn't, she conceded. But he was right.

Ever since she'd known the St Justs, ever since she had been so briefly and disastrously a part of their lives, she'd dreamed about a day like this one—a day when she would dive with Piran, swim with him, share with him the joy of his profession.

She turned her head to see him swimming half a length ahead of her. His dark hair was streaming back except where it was pressed against his head by the rubber strap of the mask he wore. He was pointing at something and she looked where he was indicating to see a school of shimmering, almost iridescent blue fish.

Everywhere she looked, life abounded. When you were in a boat or even simply wading, you never saw all the things that lived around you just below the surface. Not only the fish, but the corals, the sponges, the huge array of kelps and anemones. At least, that was what she thought they were. When she got back to the city, she would have to take a class, have to learn what all these amazing things were that she was seeing now firsthand.

Piran beckoned to her, then swam down closer to the wreck. It was encrusted with years and years of coral, and of course all the significant archaeological artifacts had long since been removed. There wasn't the thrill of discovery that Carly knew must come from the excavation and careful salvage of a newly discovered wreck. But still there was excitement.

There was the wonder she felt at seeing the boat right where it had gone down, still a part of the natural world, not merely an exhibit in a museum. There was a flicker of astonishment that the boat was so small. When she thought of ships, she thought of the *QE II* or the *Queen Mary*. It was probably an optical illusion, but she thought the lifeboats on the *QE II* were probably as big as this entire ship was.

And most of all there was Piran.

She was sure that a dive to show her a wreck like this

one must be tedious to a man like him. But if it was he gave no sign. On the contrary, he seemed almost eager. He moved ahead, pointing to things, explaining by hand signals as best he could what they had once been.

Twice he caught her hand and tugged her close so that he could point out something small that she might have missed otherwise. If she could have, with the breathing apparatus in her mouth, Carly would have been smiling all over her face. As it was, she simply followed him eagerly, taking it all in, relishing every moment. She didn't want to leave, even when Piran indicated that their tanks were running low on air.

It wasn't until they were back in the boat that she actually thought again about Arthur. Even then she only thought of him fleetingly, long enough to hope that he was still enjoying his morning at Mirabelle's, before her attention was captured once more by the man she had been diving with.

Piran was taking off his gear while Ben helped her with hers. She stumbled as the boat rocked and it was Piran who caught her before she fell. He righted her, but didn't let go.

'You OK?'

'F-fine,' Carly assured him. She turned, her eyes sparkling. 'Wonderful.' She had to say it, had to let him know how much the dive had meant to her. 'It was fantastic.'

He grinned. 'Yes. It was.'

'You was down there long enough,' Ben grumbled. 'Didn't catch nothing up here.'

'Sorry,' Piran said lightly as he tugged her down and sat beside her.

But Carly didn't think he sounded as if he regretted it. He looked as if he'd enjoyed it as much as she had, though of course that was impossible. Still, it made her feel almost light-headedly happy as Ben piloted them back toward the harbor.

'Tell me all about what we were seeing down there,' she said to him. 'You were pointing out some stuff, but I didn't know what it was.'

He began to explain. Carly listened intently, absorbing it all. When she didn't understand, she asked more. Perhaps she was making a fool of herself, betraying her ignorance. But she really wanted to know. She wanted to know everything he did.

And as she listened she lifted her face into the balmy tropical breeze, letting it caress her damp skin. The December sun warmed her gently. Piran's hard, hair-roughened thigh pressed against her own with a heat far more intense. She knew she should move away.

But this was fantasy. Make-believe. The stuff of which dreams and memories were made. As long as she knew it wasn't real, wasn't going anywhere, she could enjoy it.

Couldn't she?

Their diving expedition had started as a way to do something for her. It had become more than that almost at once and he'd been doing it for himself as much as for her. She bewitched him.

Of course, he reminded himself as they walked back to pick up Arthur from Mirabelle's, she always had.

Her long legs and lithe figure and saucy smile had intrigued him since the moment he'd laid eyes on her. But other things about her attracted him as well.

The way she handled Arthur, of course. And the way she'd dug in and helped him make something of the book Des had left him with. And her desire to make this Christmas special. But now, this morning, it was her fascination with diving that bewitched him.

He'd taken plenty of starry-eyed women diving. He'd known what to expect. To a woman, they'd shown cursory interest in the wreck and a whole lot more interest in the tangling of limbs with him underwater.

Not Carly. Carly had been all business. She'd followed him intently, but unless he'd touched her to point something out she'd kept her distance.

Still, her interest in what he'd shown her had been genuine. After they'd come up, she'd plied him with questions that she'd really seemed to want to know the answers to. Piran never liked talking about diving or archaeology when he felt he could be boring his listeners. He didn't feel he bored Carly.

'There's a train underwater near here,' he told her as they turned the corner on to Mirabelle's street. 'You should see it. You'd like it.'

'I'd like anything,' Carly agreed, her eyes shining.

I'll take you, Piran almost said. We'll make a day of it. You and me.

But he didn't say it. Because they didn't have time. There was no way they could go to see the train. Carly had been right when she'd said they really hadn't had time for this dive. But he wanted to.

He wanted to share it with her, to show her, to see her eyes light up the way they'd lit up today.

So they'd lost a morning on the book. He was glad. It had been good for both of them.

And after the book was done? he asked himself.

After the book was done, well, she'd go back to New York, and he'd take off for Greece to his next project.

Chances were he'd never see Carly O'Reilly again.

The thought gave him a curiously hollow feeling.

They were almost at Mirabelle's gate when Piran knew

he had to say the one thing he'd never thought he would
say.

'Remember...your birthday nine years ago?'

Carly's head jerked round and she stared at him, the
expression in her eyes like that of a doe caught in a
hunter's sight. He saw her swallow.

'What about it?'

Now that he'd brought it up, he wasn't sure where to
start. He ducked his head briefly, then lifted it again to
meet her gaze. 'I was a jerk. What I said...what I thought.'
He paused, then continued grimly, 'I was a jerk when you
got here, thinking the same thing.'

Carly didn't say anything. Her eyes were as round as
old Spanish doubloons.

'I don't know what excuse I can give you,' he said
gruffly, aware of the hot blood in his cheeks. 'That I was
young and stupid and full of myself? That I didn't trust
women? Any women? Even young naïve ones? Hell, I
don't know. Take your pick.'

He saw Carly wince when he said the bit about young
naïve ones.

She licked her lips before she spoke. 'Yes, well, I'm
sure that my mother marrying your father must have been
a terrible shock,' she began slowly.

He nodded. 'It's just that she was just so bloody different from him—from us! I know my folks didn't get along,
I know my mother left my father for another man. But I
never figured my dad would go for...for...'

'Someone like my mother?' Carly suggested drily, with
only the faintest hint of hurt in her voice.

Piran shifted uncomfortably. 'Someone so different,' he
said. 'My mother was so quiet and remote and...and elegant, despite what she did.' He grimaced. 'I guess I

thought that was what my father liked. But then he met yours and she was…she was…'

'Flamboyant?' Carly suggested wryly. 'Jolly? Devil-may-care?'

'I wasn't used to it. It made me suspicious. I…think she made my dad happy, though,' he admitted after a moment, rubbing a hand through his salt-stiffened hair. 'She must have.' He stared off into the distance, remembering, then he swallowed against the suddenly tight feeling in his throat. 'He chose her.'

'Over you, you mean?' Carly said.

Piran pressed his lips together. It sounded so rotten put that way, but she was right. 'I shouldn't have pushed him to forget her,' he said. 'I shouldn't have walked out when he wouldn't.'

'You did what you thought was right,' Carly said. 'But you should have come back…at the end.'

He bowed his head. 'I know.' He lifted his gaze and met hers. 'I'm sorry I didn't.'

'He knew you loved him,' Carly said. 'And he loved you. He told me so.'

Piran ran his tongue across dry lips. 'I'm glad.'

'My mother loved him, you know,' Carly said, and he heard a catch in her throat. 'She really did.'

Yes, she probably had, Piran realized now. He looked at the ground between his feet. He didn't know what he expected. Absolution, maybe? A blessing from the young woman he'd disbelieved all those years ago, from the woman he'd been rude to just days before?

Fat chance. Whatever words he was waiting for never came. Carly didn't move to go through the gate, but she didn't speak either. She simply stood there, and finally Piran flicked a sidelong glance in her direction.

'He deserved being loved,' Piran said softly. 'He was a

good man.' A better man than I'll ever be, he added silently.

'Everyone deserves to be loved,' Carly said softly.

Their eyes met. Hers were wide and caring and seemed to offer him her heart. The same way she'd offered it to him nine years ago.

He shut his eyes against the memory of the innocent child she had been.

'Well,' she said more briskly after a moment, 'thank you for taking me diving today. I enjoyed it.'

Once more he thought about offering to take her to see the train.

And then he knew he'd better leave well enough alone.

The next afternoon there was a pastel envelope in the post. Carly picked it out of the basket with a quiver of apprehension, studied it for a moment, then carried it in and dropped it on the keyboard on top of Piran's fingers.

They closed around it. His knuckles went almost white.

'It's postmarked over two weeks ago,' Carly said.

Piran reached for the letter-opener and slit it open and began to read.

Carly bit her lip, resisting the temptation to step round behind him and read it over his shoulder.

It wasn't long. In mere seconds she saw his teeth come together. He leaned his head back against the chair and shut his eyes. He swallowed. Then he opened his eyes, folded the letter carefully once more and stuck it back in the envelope.

'Well, I guess that's it,' he said flatly.

'What'd she say?'

'That she has a surprise for me. She says she's sure I'll be thrilled. At least—' he lifted his gaze and met Carly's again '—she hopes I will be.'

'A surprise,' Carly echoed hollowly, and felt sick.

She didn't know what she'd expected the letter to say. She supposed maybe she'd been hoping it would say, In case you find a baby on your veranda someday, it isn't mine.

Piran's lips pressed together in a flat line. 'Must've got lost in the mail for a while. It should've got here before Arthur came.'

'So I suppose that makes Wendy Arthur's mother,' Carly said in a voice as toneless as his.

What difference did it make? she asked herself. Someone had to be Arthur's mother. She knew she wasn't.

She just wished she were.

There. She'd admitted it. She'd put the thought into words, even though only she had heard them, acknowledged the truth of them.

Piran's apology yesterday had left her stunned. And aching. All the hopes, all the dreams, all the 'might have beens' wouldn't leave her alone. She hadn't been able to settle for the rest of the day. She'd done her best to look as if she was working. She'd felt a complete fraud.

She'd gone to bed early, hoping that tomorrow would be better, that she would have her equilibrium back. So far, it wasn't much of an improvement.

'Didn't she at least say why she was going to leave him with you?' she asked rather desperately.

'She didn't say much. Just some babble about her surprise making me take her seriously.'

'Well, it's certainly done that,' Carly said.

'Hasn't it just?'

They were silent for a long moment, each absorbed in his and her own thoughts.

Then, 'Damn!' Piran smacked his fist on the desktop. 'I wish to God I'd read those earlier letters!'

Before Carly had a chance to ask what good it would have done, Arthur, with a surprisingly well-developed sense of good timing, set up a wail from the bedroom.

Carly jumped out of her chair and hurried to pick him up.

'Swim time?' Piran asked when she came back after having changed and fetched him.

'Maybe I shouldn't take the time today,' Carly said.

'Why not?'

'I…haven't been getting a lot done. I've been… distracted.'

'You've been working flat out all day. We both have.'

'But we've only got a little more than a week and a half until it's due.'

'We'll make it. And do you honestly think we can work with him awake? Both of us?'

'Probably not,' Carly admitted. 'But one of us ought to.'

Piran nodded. 'Then I will.'

She was relieved that he wouldn't be coming with them. 'We won't be long,' she promised. 'Hold him, will you, while I change into my suit?'

She held out the baby and Piran showed no hesitation in taking him. He even dropped a kiss on Arthur's forehead.

Something in the area of Carly's heart suddenly seemed to squeeze tight. She hurried out the room and went in to her own, stripping off her shorts and shirt and pulling on her suit. Then she caught her hair up in a ponytail, slipped her feet into beach sandals and went back to get Arthur.

'Thanks.' She picked up two towels, scooped the baby out of Piran's arms and headed toward the door. 'See you in a while.'

'Yeah.'

She knew she'd promised not to take long, but once she

got down to the beach where the water was warm, the breeze was gentle, and Arthur clearly loved it—it was far easier to stay than to go back and be with Piran.

Because she wanted to be with Piran, heaven help her, and the more she was with him, the more tangled her emotions became.

She wanted things to happen that she knew would never happen—love, marriage, family, happily ever after. She'd told herself she'd outgrown that nonsense where he was concerned. And she'd even half believed it until yesterday.

And then, when he'd apologized, when he'd told her he'd been wrong about her—and her mother—all those years ago, all her hopes had come flooding back.

God, she was such a fool.

'Ah, da!' Arthur jumped in her arms, a wide grin spreading across his face as he waved his hands.

'Glad to see me, are you?'

Carly spun round in the water, almost falling as she did so. Piran was close enough to reach out and catch her, pulling both her and Arthur against him.

'See?' he said to Carly. 'I told you he could talk!'

'What are you doing here?'

He gave her a guilty grin. 'I have no willpower?'

'Piran, really—you need to—'

'Relax. I finished the chapter and I decided to reward myself with a swim. OK?'

He was still holding them and Carly didn't think it was OK at all. And there was no way she was going to be able to relax. Her body was responding even to that much contact. She tried to wriggle away. 'So go swim,' she said gruffly.

'In a minute. I think a reward from you would be nice, too.'

'What kind of reward?' Carly said suspiciously.

'A kiss?'

Her eyes narrowed. 'I never gave you a kiss for finishing any of the others!'

'Obviously we need to renegotiate.'

She gave him a shove. 'Go swim.'

He feigned hurt, but he let her and Arthur go, turning to plunge under an incoming wave and swimming with long, powerful strokes out toward the reef. Carly stood and watched him, her body still tingling, her heart still hammering.

'Ah, da,' Arthur said again.

'Oh, yes,' Carly agreed. 'Oh, yes.'

Piran swam almost to the reef, then turned and swam parallel to the shore. Carly walked in the water, keeping abreast of him, her eye always on his dark head as it dipped and rose with the movement of the waves. At last he turned and started swimming back and she turned too and stayed with him.

'Someday you'll swim like that,' she told Arthur.

Arthur giggled and gummed her shoulder, then tugged on her ponytail and grabbed her ear. 'Uh, da!' he chortled.

Carly hugged his small, slippery body close, cherishing these moments, knowing how soon the time would come when she would be missing him.

And Piran.

They had reached the spot where the trail led back up the hill toward the house now and Piran was swimming back toward her. As he reached the shallows and emerged, the water slid down his strong muscled chest, plastered his navy boxer-style trunks against his abdomen, against his groin. He looked like Neptune, Carly thought, rising from the sea. He was looking right at her, his eyes dark, his mouth smiling.

And then he looked beyond her up toward the beach,

and he stopped smiling. He hesitated, and she saw something flicker in his gaze. Then he came toward her more quickly and reached out to grasp her arm. He slipped his around her shoulder.

'What's the matter?' Carly said, because this touch was not quite the same as the earlier one. That one had been teasing and easy, albeit hungry. This one was pure leashed tension.

'Piran?' She slanted a glance at him, but he wasn't even looking at her.

His gaze was fixed on a woman who must have been standing at the bottom of the trail and was now coming across the beach. She had thick, honey-coloured hair that hung loose down her back. She wore white shorts and a flame-red halter-top. She was slightly curvier than the average model, but no less beautiful. She reminded Carly of exactly the sort of women who had swarmed around Piran all those years ago—the pretty, pouty ones who adored him and whom he had adored in turn.

'Piran!'

The woman was waving now, smiling broadly, and Piran muttered under his breath, 'Give me Arthur,' and promptly took him from Carly before she could even make a move. He strode doggedly out of the water holding the child, hauling Carly with him until he stopped to face the woman.

She wasn't smiling now. She looked apprehensive, confused as she looked from him to Arthur and Carly.

'Wendy,' Piran said curtly.

Carly's jaw dropped. *Wendy*?

This was Arthur's mother?

Wendy was regarding Piran nervously. 'You…got my letter?'

A corner of Piran's mouth lifted sardonically. 'Today.'

She blanched. 'Oh, dear. So you weren't expecting…'
Her voice wavered and faded away.

'No, my dear, I certainly wasn't expecting…' Piran
drawled, twisting the final word.

'So you're not…happy?'

'On the contrary,' Piran said, 'I'm quite happy, thank
you very much.'

Wendy brightened. 'You are?'

'Yes. I'm also married.'

She stared at him. So did Carly.

'Married?' Wendy echoed.

Married? Carly thought just as he hauled her forward
and said, 'This is my wife. Carlota. Carly, this is Wendy
Jeffries. You remember me telling you about her.' His grip
meant there was only one answer to that. He was going to
leave bruises for days.

'O-of course. How nice to meet you,' she stammered.

Wendy didn't say anything. She just stared—first at
Piran, then at Carly, and finally at Arthur.

'He's—' she started, but Piran cut her off.

'He's mine,' he said in a tone that brooked no argument.
'I'll admit it wherever it needs to be admitted. I'll take full
responsibility in the courts, wherever I have to. I fully
intend to provide for him; you don't have to worry.'

Wendy blinked. 'What?'

'I said, you don't have to worry about Arthur. Obviously
you don't want him. Fair enough. I don't blame you in the
circumstances. But Carly and I do want him.'

Wendy stared at him. So did Carly. Wendy opened her
mouth, then closed it again. Then she ran her tongue over
her lips as if she was considering what to say.

'Do you have a problem with that?' Piran demanded in
a tone that said she'd better not have.

'Piran, I—'

'Look, I don't know all the legal ins and outs. I've never had a kid before, believe me. Probably I owe you something—support, recompense, I don't know. Whatever it is, I'll do right by you as long as Carly and I can keep him.'

'Piran—'

'You can talk to my lawyer! We'll go back up to the house and I'll get you his number. I'll call him first and you can when you get back to the States. He'll straighten everything out, do the legal—'

'*Piran*!'

'What is it?'

'The baby—Arthur? He's…not mine.'

'*What*?' Piran yelled it. Carly thought it. They both stared at Wendy Jeffries. 'What did you say?'

Wendy shrugged helplessly. 'You seem to think that I…that we… Did someone leave you a baby?'

'Someone left me Arthur,' Piran said tersely. 'On the veranda a little over a week ago. I thought it was you! He's the right age, damn it. And you said…you wrote me all those letters! You wrote about a surprise!' He glared at her accusingly.

Wendy flushed deeply. 'I didn't mean…I was trying to reestablish what little relationship we'd begun. We didn't meet in the best of circumstances, as you might recall. It was a terrible time in your life.'

'I know. That's why I thought…'

'You were hurting badly. You talked about it a lot. To me. And then I didn't see you any more. But for one night we had been close. And I thought maybe it meant something. I hoped it meant something,' she admitted. 'I thought I'd see if things were better with you now. So I wrote. Lots. I was a fool, I guess. And I had some vacation coming and before Thanksgiving I saw Des and he said you were both going to be here over Christmas. So I thought I'd come down. He never said you were married!'

Piran's jaw set tight. The color on his face was at least as deep as it was on hers.

'Arthur couldn't be mine, Piran,' she said after a moment. 'We never even made love.'

Piran looked as if he wanted the ocean to come and swallow him up. He shook his head desperately. 'I couldn't—I didn't…remember it all. Like you said, I was a basket case back then. After Gordon died. I remember going back to your apartment and then—' he shrugged '—I don't remember what happened. When Arthur showed up, I just assumed—'

'No. You drank. You talked. You cried. And then you fell asleep in my bed,' Wendy told him. 'I thought we might have something eventually. As I said, I hoped. But we never made love.'

Piran bent his head. 'Oh, lord, I'm sorry,' he muttered. 'I never meant— Oh, geez, what a mess.'

'I shouldn't have come,' Wendy said.

Piran grimaced wryly. 'Probably better that you did, though maybe not as far as you're concerned. But now at least I know you're not his mother.'

'But you don't know who is.'

He sighed. 'No.'

Wendy looked from Piran to Carly, then back at Piran again, and shook her head. 'You have an understanding wife, Piran. You're lucky. She really must love you.'

'It's not a bad idea, you know,' Piran said that evening after they had seen Wendy on to the water taxi and Ben had given them a ride back home.

They hadn't had a moment alone to discuss anything until Ben left, and once he had Arthur had needed feeding and while Carly had done that Piran had disappeared down to the beach.

Carly hadn't called him back. She hadn't known what to say to him. She still didn't. And she didn't really know what he was talking about now.

She looked up from the manuscript she'd been trying to concentrate on. He was standing just inside the door, staring out the window into the darkness, not looking at her, one hand tucked into the pocket of his shorts, the other balled lightly into a fist. 'What are you talking about?'

'Getting married.'

'Getting married?' The words gave her stomach an odd roller coaster feeling when she said them.

'I thought about it while I was walking and I thought, Why not?' He gave her a sidelong glance. 'I mean, it's what you wanted, isn't it? That's what you said.'

'I didn't mean—'

He raked his fingers through his hair. 'I know you didn't mean like this, but let's be logical. Why the hell shouldn't we? God knows we've wanted each other for years!'

'For heaven's sake, Piran—'

'We have. You can't deny it. And we would have made love by now if you'd been willing, and you know it. You haven't been because you want marriage. So, OK, I'm offering marriage.' He looked right at her as he said it.

Carly felt a pain where the roller coaster had been. 'Such a charming proposal,' she said with as much lightness as she could muster.

Piran kicked at the rug underfoot. 'I'm sorry. But you must know by now that romantic is not really my style. And this whole mess hasn't exactly been charming, you have to admit. But it would work,' he went on a little desperately. 'Surely you must see that?'

'There's more to marriage than wanting each other,'

Carly said faintly, unsure exactly what she saw beyond a meshing of her wildest dream and her worst nightmare.

'We've got more. You like Arthur, don't you?'

'Of course I like Arthur!'

'And you like it here?' He looked at her for confirmation then went on. 'And you like to dive. You said you'd always wanted to dive. If we get married, you'll be able to dive all the time. Here. In Greece. Maybe in the Pacific if that business Des is looking into works out. And we're doing good together on the book, aren't we?'

'Yes,' Carly admitted, her throat tight.

'So, like I said, why not? We get married and Arthur has two parents. You get to dive. We can write books together all day and have sex together all night.' He looked positively pleased with himself.

Carly wanted to scream. 'What about Arthur's mother, whoever she is?'

'What about her?'

'When she shows up—'

'She can damned well leave again! She doesn't want him. She proved that. If she hasn't come by now, she hasn't got a chance in hell of getting him back from me. Especially if I'm married.' He looked at her now, his dark gaze intent. 'Come on, Carly. What do you say?'

Carly couldn't answer. Her tongue was glued to the roof of her mouth. Her mind spun. Her heart seemed to have stopped.

Marry Piran? Be Arthur's mother? Share their lives every day? Travel and dive and write books with Piran for years to come?

Just like that. It felt so right—and yet so wrong. So logical. So cold-blooded.

And yet Carly didn't feel cold-blooded at all. She yearned. She ached.

Piran didn't move. He waited.

'If I...if I say no?' Carly whispered after a moment. 'What then?'

He frowned. 'What do you mean, what then?'

'I mean, are you just going to go into town and ask the next woman you meet?'

'What do you think I am? I want you. It solves all our problems, doesn't it? You want marriage. I want a mother for Arthur. We both want to go to bed!' The smile he gave her had a wry, almost wistful quality to it. 'But if you say no I'm not just going to go looking for another warm body, I promise.'

As a marriage proposal, it left a lot to be desired. John's mere hinting had been considerably more romantic than Piran's flat suggestion. But Carly didn't want to marry John.

She'd never stopped wanting to marry Piran.

But, even acknowledging that, she hesitated to say yes. It seemed the height of folly to get into a marriage that was no more than a convenience.

But perhaps it was a bigger folly not to be willing to try.

She didn't believe that Piran would cheat on her. When he gave his word, he kept it. He tried to do the right thing. He was morally upright and judgmental almost to a fault. He also believed in duty. If he said marriage vows with her, Carly felt he would honor them.

Marriages had started with less.

She heard a whimper from the bedroom. And, of course, there was Arthur. She would have Piran. And she would have Arthur. Maybe she would have other children. A home. A family. Her childhood dreams come true.

Well, perhaps not quite.

But close.

She remembered her mother, leaping into marriage after marriage, always hoping for the best.

'You can't be afraid to risk, Carly,' she'd told her daughter time and time again, even when she'd got hurt.

Carly knew she could get hurt marrying Piran. But would she hurt less if she turned him down?

She looked at him, still waiting.

'All right,' she said slowly, lifting her gaze and meeting his levelly. 'I'll marry you. Yes.'

CHAPTER NINE

THEY got engaged, they fed and changed Arthur and put him to bed, and then they finished chapter eight.

'I'll get started on nine,' Piran said when he'd approved her corrections. 'The last chapter. You look tired. You can go on to bed.' His tone was brusque, not exactly that of a doting fiancé.

Carly gave him a wan smile and nodded. 'Yes, I am tired. I'll see you in the morning,' she said.

But Piran was already consulting his notes and pecking away at the keyboard. He didn't even turn around.

She hadn't really expected romance, she thought as she stripped off her clothes and got ready for bed. After all, their 'engagement' was not precisely a love match. Not on Piran's side, at least. On her own, no matter how much she might wish otherwise, she very much feared that it was.

She didn't admit it, of course. The only thing she had left, it sometimes seemed, was the dignity she was clinging to by not wearing her heart on her sleeve.

If Piran knew how much she loved him, she wouldn't even have that.

She washed her face and brushed her teeth and stared at her reflection in the mirror. 'You are engaged to Piran St Just,' she told herself out loud.

Years ago she had said those words to herself in the mirror, trying them out, and they'd made her smile secretly and hug her feelings for him close against her heart.

Now the smile wouldn't come, and the feelings that hugged her heart were tangled with feelings of worry.

Would it work? Would they be good parents for Arthur? Good spouses to each other?

Would Piran ever really care about her?

'Tune in tomorrow,' she advised her reflection, 'for the next exciting installment of the "Follies of Carly O'Reilly".'

'And what follies would those be?' asked a voice from just beyond the half-opened door.

Carly spun around, her mouth sounding a faint, 'Oh!' She stepped back, bumping into the sink, surprised.

Piran gave her a wry grin. 'You were expecting someone else?'

Carly shook her head, flustered. 'Of course not. What do you want?'

'To kiss you goodnight?'

Carly's eyes widened. She groped for the towel and held it in front of her thin nightgown, realizing even as she did so how foolish she was being. She scraped her dignity together.

'Fine,' she said, and leaned forward quickly and just far enough to brush her lips along the line of his jaw, then pulled back. 'Goodnight.'

Piran shook his head slowly. 'Not good enough.'

Still clutching the towel, Carly tried to move past him, but he didn't budge. 'Don't be silly, Piran. I'm going to bed and you've got to get to work on chapter nine.'

'No, I don't.'

'But you said—'

'I know what I said. I was being noble. I wasn't going to push. But—' he shrugged ruefully '—I have a very low nobility span, it seems.'

He didn't say anything else, offered no more arguments,

no convincing lines. He simply stood quietly, speaking and touching her only with his beautiful eyes.

Carly felt the heat of his gaze as if he'd made physical contact. A delicate frisson began at her shoulders and swept slowly down over her breasts, the curve of her hips, the tanned length of her legs. Everywhere Piran's eyes touched her, her body grew taut and seemed to hum with awareness.

'What follies, Carly?' he asked again, his voice barely more than a whisper. 'Follies like this?' He lifted his hand and touched her cheek, traced her jawline with one finger, then ran it along the line of her lips and finally leaned toward her to touch them with his own.

There was no demand in this kiss, no urgency, only a lazy, teasing playfulness, a hint, a promise. It was a nibble, no more.

'Was that a folly, Carly?' he asked softly. 'Is this?'

His lips met hers again. This kiss was longer. It touched, teased, tasted. Lingered. And then, just when Carly's breathing began to quicken and her toes to curl, it ended.

She'd been a part of him—fleetingly—and now she was alone again. She squelched a whimper. She couldn't quite uncurl her toes.

'I think it was,' Piran said raggedly. 'But I'm not sure. I think I'd better try that again, don't you?'

He didn't wait for her response, but instead ducked his head once more and melded his lips with hers. His hands came up this time, taking hold of her arms, drawing her into his, slipping around her and bringing her against him so that from lips to knees their bodies touched.

Carly felt a quiver run through her. Her own hands, which had been curled as tightly as her toes, slackened and came up around him, sliding under the cotton knit of his T-shirt to press against his hard, warm, muscular back.

Folly? Probably. Carly didn't know any more. All sense of self-protection, all rationality had deserted her. She was at the mercy of her need—and her love—for Piran St Just.

'It's not enough,' Piran said against her lips. 'It's so good, but it could be so much better.' She heard urgency in his tone now. The teasing was overlaid by a desire that sent tremors through him, but he made no move to steer her out the bathroom and toward the bed. 'Carly?'

'Wh-what?' Stop talking! she wanted to shout at him. Her nails dug into his back.

'Do you want me?'

'What do you think?'

He grimaced. 'I think you'd better. But if you don't I need to know now. I'll stop.' He gave her a rueful look. 'I can stop these days. I'll wait till we're married if that's what you want. It's up to you.'

She lifted her gaze to meet his. 'I want you,' she whispered. I love you, she told him in her heart.

He took her hand and drew her with him into the darkened bedroom, flipping off the bathroom light switch as he went. 'Here?' he asked. 'I've got a bigger bed in my room.'

'Do we need a bigger bed?'

Piran gave her a lopsided smile. 'No.'

'Then here's fine.'

There was a certain poetic rightness to it, she realized as she moved to lie down on the bed and reached for his hand to draw him down beside her. This had been her room during the times that she had come down here as a teenager. This had been the bed in which she'd lain while she'd entertained her adolescent fantasies.

She remembered how the moon had hung above the trellised bougainvillaea, spilling its cool light over her heated body as, night after night, she'd imagined loving Piran and Piran loving her.

And now he was here.

He was tugging his shirt over his head and tossing it on the floor. He was planting an arm on either side of her and settling his knees astride her thighs. His fingers were easing up the hem of her gown, exposing more of her thighs. She trembled at his touch, marveled at the intensity in his face.

She lifted her hands and touched his chest, raking her fingers lightly down through the dusting of dark hair that arrowed toward his navel. The muscles tightened at her touch. He bit down on his lip and she saw a shudder run through him.

'Careful,' he said, and his voice was unsteady. 'We're going to do this right.'

'Whatever you do will be right, Piran.' She touched him again, brushed her palm against his belly, slid her fingers just beneath the waistband of his cut-offs.

'Carly!' He sucked in his breath sharply.

She smiled. Folly? Oh, no doubt. But it was a dream come true to touch Piran like this, to make him quiver and hear the catch in his voice, the urgent strangled sound at the back of his throat.

He shifted again so that now his knees were between hers. His hands slipped beneath the sheer fabric and pushed it up past the thin barrier of her panties, across her belly, over her breasts. His thumbs grazed her nipples and a shiver skated down her spine. Her breath caught in her throat.

He urged her up so that he could slip the gown over her head and in the same motion tossed it to the floor to lie beside his shirt. His eyes never left hers until he hooked his thumbs in the elastic of her underwear. Then he bent his head, watching intently as he slowly stripped away this last garment and Carly lay naked before him.

Slowly, deliberately, he drew his hands down and cupped her breasts, traced circles on her skin, making her quiver and twist. With her fingers she grabbed handfuls of the sheet. He smiled. His hands moved on down, outlining the curve of her hips, then coming together at the downy apex of her thighs. His thumb teased her heated flesh. Her eyes widened. Her jaw clenched. He touched her again, stroked her.

'Piran!'

Her fantasies had never been this explicit. Oh, they'd been naked together, but somehow their clothes had melted away, not been removed with such exact care, such disturbing caresses. And, while they'd touched in her dreams, she'd never imagined a jolt like the one she felt when Piran's fingers actually touched her.

And besides his touch it was even more intimate because he was watching her reactions. Never in all her dreams had she and Piran looked at each other so hungrily; never had they devoured each other with their eyes.

'Not fair,' Carly whispered now, stunned at the shakiness of her voice. 'I want to see you too.'

Piran's mouth twisted. 'By all means.' His hands went to the buttons on his cut-offs, but Carly's reached out to still them.

'My turn.'

He looked for an instant as if he might protest. But then his mouth twisted further and he straightened up, kneeling tall between her legs. 'Whatever you say. Go ahead. Have your way with me.'

Carly smiled. 'I think I will.'

She couldn't believe she'd said it, let alone meant it.

But once the words were out she knew that when dreams came true, folly or not, a woman made the most of them.

Carly had dreamed for years of loving Piran right here in this bed. Now that she had the chance, she was going to enjoy every minute of it.

She took her time. She didn't start at once with the buttons. Instead, with a daring she hadn't known she possessed, she let her fingers drop down to his knees, then they drifted back up, tracing, teasing, touching lightly the hair-roughened insides of his thighs, brushed the scraggly cut-off fringe of his shorts, moved up briefly beneath it, then slid down and began their trip all over again.

As her hands made their upward journey, Piran's jaw tightened. He shifted slightly, spreading his legs a bit more, allowing her more access. She went higher, slid her fingers right beneath the hem of his briefs, touched him, caressed him with her fingers, traced him lightly with her nails.

He moaned. 'Carly!' Her name was an explosion of breath.

She looked at him worriedly. 'Aren't I doing it right?'

'Too damn right! You're torturing me.'

She laughed. 'And myself.'

'Then let's get on with it!' His hands went to the buttons again, but she forestalled him, easing them open herself, one by one, slowly, carefully. Her fingers felt the heat of him pulsing through the thin cotton of his briefs. He held very still until the last button came undone and she peeled the cut-offs down his hips. Then he practically scrambled out of them, yanking his briefs off with them and pitching them both aside.

She had seen Piran naked before—the first night she'd arrived and he'd hauled her up from the beach. That man had been fierce and intimidating. This man was beautiful.

She said so and was met with an embarrassed laugh.

'I think that's my line.' He nuzzled her between her breasts, suckled each in turn, driving her wild. She gripped his shoulders desperately. Her legs shifted against his. Then his fingers went once more between her thighs and touched the core of her.

'Piran!' She reached for him, touching him too, needing to kindle flames in him that burned as brightly as those he was stoking in her.

'Now?' His voice was ragged.

'If you—are you—?'

He gritted his teeth. 'God, yes!' And then he became part of her at last.

It was pain and pleasure, desire and fulfillment, fantasy and reality all rolled into one. There was, too, one instant in which Carly's body resisted and panic flared in Piran's eyes.

'Carly?' He gazed down at her, shocked.

She laced her fingers against his back and drew him deeper. That was her answer.

Apparently it was enough, for after a moment's hesitation Piran began to move, slowly at first, so slowly that she thought she would die of frustration. Then his movements became faster, his breathing quickened into short, shallow gasps and her own matched it. Her fingers dug into his back, her thighs locked against his hips. Even their hearts seemed to pound in unison.

Once years ago Carly had gone bodysurfing. She knew the powerful building of the surf around her. She knew the sensation of having her body lifted by the surge of the wave and remembered the thrill of becoming a part of that flow of energy. Mostly she recalled the joy, the excitement of her headlong fall over the crest into the rush of the wave on to the shore.

That memory was as near as she could come to what she felt as she and Piran moved and crested and fell together. It didn't even come close.

He collapsed against her and she held him tight, reveling in the weight of his body on hers, in the warmth of his breath against her cheek, in the dampness of his sweat-slick back beneath her hands.

I love you, she told him in her mind, in her heart. Heaven help me, I love you, Piran St Just.

He lifted his head and their eyes met in the moonlight. His expression was grave. 'Why didn't you say?'

She knew what he was asking, and it wasn't about love. 'That it was my…' She faltered.

'First time,' he finished for her. 'Why didn't you?'

'Are you angry?'

'Of course not. I mean… Hell!' He looked more upset than angry. 'I wouldn't have just—just— I would have taken more time,' he said finally. 'Tried to make it better for you.'

Carly smiled. 'It gets better?' There had been a moment's pain, but she certainly had no complaints about what had come after.

Piran gave a shaky laugh. 'Not for me. But I would…I could make it better for you.' He levered himself out of the bed. 'Wait right here.' He looked at her worriedly, as if she might vanish on him.

'I'm not going anywhere,' Carly assured him. A grin flickered over his face as he disappeared into the bathroom and came back moments later with a damp cloth and towel.

Gently—'The way I should have done if I'd known,' he muttered—he parted her thighs and bathed her, then dried her with equal care. His touch was so tender that it made her shiver with longing and she was astonished to find herself becoming aroused again.

She moved restlessly and Piran cocked his head, looking at her. 'Do you want…?' he began, then stopped, shaking his head doubtfully.

But Carly had no doubts.

'You. I want you,' she told him, and reached for him once more.

Carly awakened to the sun spilling across her bed. She sat bolt upright and stared at the clock. *Ten-forty*?

It couldn't possibly be. She *couldn't* have slept that late!

And then she realized that, yes, in fact she could have— because she remembered how she'd spent the night, and it hadn't been sound asleep.

But surely Arthur—?

She scrambled out of bed, starting toward his room, then realized something else: that she didn't have a stitch on.

Her nightgown lay on the floor where Piran had tossed it. Her panties were a few feet away from it. Piran's shorts and shirt—and Piran himself—were nowhere to be found.

Hurriedly Carly dressed in shorts and a sleeveless top. Then she washed her face and teeth and dragged a brush through her hair. She caught a glimpse of her face in the mirror and blushed. She looked so…so…*loved*.

Well, maybe that wasn't quite the right word. But her lips seemed somewhat fuller, felt slightly tender. Her breasts seemed sensitive against the sheer fabric of her bra. And the rest of her… Her color deepened and hastily she turned away, heading out to find out why Arthur hadn't roused her with his usual six-thirty babbling.

She found him in the living room sitting in Piran's lap, with Piran using Arthur's index fingers to type letters on the keyboard. At the sound of her feet on the plank floor, they both turned.

Arthur crowed cheerfully and Piran smiled.

'Sleeping Beauty has arisen,' he told Arthur.

Whatever color had vanished from Carly's cheeks came flooding back. 'I'm sorry. I didn't hear him,' she babbled. 'What time did he wake you?'

'A little after seven.'

'I should have—'

'No. You need your rest. You were very busy last night.' The smile turned into a grin.

'So were you,' Carly retorted, blushing.

Piran laughed. 'And I enjoyed every minute of it. Let's just say this morning was on me. Want some coffee?'

'Thanks. Yes.' What she really wanted was a refuge from the look in his eyes, which were already this morning warm with desire—which made her desire him again too. She went into the kitchen and poured herself a cup from the pot he'd made. 'Shall I bring you one?' she called, and was startled when he said from right behind her,

'Yes, but I'll drink it in here.' He was carrying Arthur and the similarity in their features seemed even more striking than usual this morning. Perhaps it was because Piran looked comfortable holding him now. Whatever it was, it made Carly smile.

'Is that for me or for him?' Piran asked her, taking the cup she handed him. Their fingers brushed. The electricity was still there.

'Is what for you?'

'The smile.' His eyes were hooded, but there was a gentleness in his expression that increased her self-consciousness.

'For both of you,' she said quickly. 'Of course.'

'Of course,' Piran said, his tone slightly mocking, and Carly wondered if she'd hurt his feelings. Surely not.

'How much have you done this morning?' she asked

him, wanting to talk about something else, something that wouldn't make her blush even more.

'A fair bit. It's all come together. I can probably finish if I get rid of my helper. Arthur doesn't type very fast.'

'You should have got me up.'

'You needed the sleep.' He smiled at her. 'And you looked beautiful.'

Embarrassed at his frankness, Carly looked away. 'You were very clever, entertaining him that way,' she said after a moment.

Piran laughed. 'Entertaining him, hell. He's got to earn his keep. I figure if I keep typing with him in five years he'll be able to do it on his own.'

'Good idea,' she said, taking Arthur out of his arms.

'I'm just full of good ideas,' Piran said. 'Want to hear a couple more of them?' There was enough suggestiveness in his tone to tell her what the ideas entailed even without explanation.

Carly blushed. 'I think we'd better get to work right now,' she said, settling Arthur on her hip. 'Or one of us should, anyway.'

'There's not much for you to do until I finish. Why don't you and Arthur decorate the Christmas tree?'

He nodded toward the table and for the first time Carly noticed the array of things lying on it.

Apparently he and Arthur had done more than type this morning. They'd laid out fishing flies and lures, some of which she remembered seeing Piran use when they'd come here years ago. There were seashells, including several that she and Arthur had brought back from their daily excursions to the beach. There were small portions of fishnet and the sea glass he'd given her the other day, which she'd set on the mantel in a place of honor. He'd also provided several bits of driftwood, some dried pods off one of the trees they passed on the way to the beach and, next to them, a carton filled with freshly picked deep red and coral and white hibiscus flowers.

'You'll have to change the flowers every day, but as far as the rest goes…' Piran hesitated. 'I know it's not exactly your garden variety Christmas decorations, but Arthur and I thought maybe you could use some of it.' He spoke off-handedly as he carried his coffee into the living room and went back to the computer.

Carly stared at his back, then at the assortment of decorations he'd so carefully provided. For a man who hadn't even wanted a tree, he'd done an awful lot. Her heart felt suddenly very full. She hugged Arthur close.

'Yes, I will,' she said to Piran. 'Who wants a garden variety Christmas tree? This is a wonderful idea.'

Hanging lures and net and such on the tree with Arthur in one arm wasn't easy, but Carly wasn't complaining. In fact she would have happily sung out loud if she hadn't thought that the noise would bother Piran as he worked. She tried to move quietly, talking to Arthur only in an undertone as they hung the various ornaments.

Piran typed as if possessed, stopping only rarely, but smiling at the tree—and at her and Arthur—when he did so.

'It looks great,' he told her when at last she was done and stepped back to consider it.

'It does,' Carly agreed, smiling. She loved it. She remembered thinking last year that the tree she and her mother and Roland and his girls had decorated with brightly painted wooden nutcrackers and glass bells and papier-mâché angels was the most wonderful tree in the world. But it didn't hold a candle to this one, with its tiny colored lights, its gaily feathered lures and flies, its bits of polished glass and curling shells and smooth pieces of driftwood.

Piran flicked on the printer and got to his feet. As the pages spewed forth, he came over to stand behind Carly who still held Arthur in her arms. Piran slipped his arms around both of them and bent his head forward so that his lips just brushed the back of Carly's ear.

'I like it,' he said.

'Yes.'

His lips nibbled her ear. 'I like you.'

Carly smiled. 'I'm afraid I'm getting rather fond of you, too,' she said. I love you, her heart said again. But still the words remained unspoken. They had a start. She was afraid to push for too much.

'Ouch,' Piran said as Arthur reached up and grabbed his nose. 'Hey, kid, behave yourself.'

'He wants to be included,' Carly said.

'He is,' Piran asserted, prying the baby's fingers off his face and nibbling them until Arthur giggled. 'After all,' he added gruffly, 'he caused it.'

Right after lunch Piran said to Carly, 'We're going Christmas shopping.'

She looked up from the chair where she'd just settled down with the last chapter. 'Now? But I can't. I've got to finish this.'

'I meant Arthur and me. You're staying here.'

'But I saw this darling little wooden toy sailboat in the hardware store. We could hang it on the tree and then when Arthur gets a little bigger he could take it in the bath.'

'I'll look at it,' Piran promised.

'But—'

'You work. And if you finish, then we can celebrate

tonight.' He waggled his eyebrows at her and she knew
what kind of celebrating he had in mind. He looked
pleased when the color rose in her cheeks. Carly wished
she knew if it was just the idea of making love or of making love with her that caused his eagerness.

She smiled at him. He bent down and kissed her lingeringly on the lips.

'In fact,' he said when he'd left her breathless, 'we can
take a few days off, then do the last run-through after
Christmas. How about it?' He took Arthur from her with
newly developed ease and started toward the door.

'I'd like that,' Carly admitted.

Piran nodded. 'It's a date.'

'You can leave Arthur with me this afternoon,' Carly
called after him. 'You don't have to take him along.'

He turned back. 'No. The book is going to get your
undivided attention. And Arthur is going to get mine.
Aren't you, sport?'

It was a sign of how much he'd changed, Carly realized,
that he seemed actually to be looking forward to it.

'A little male bonding?' Carly teased.

Piran grinned. 'You better believe it.'

The odd thing was, he meant it. And he was enjoying it.
It surprised him how much he was enjoying Arthur.

It didn't surprise him how much he was enjoying Carly.

Talk about bonding! He grinned now as he walked back
from town, carrying a sleeping Arthur, his thoughts busy
reminiscing about how well they had bonded last night.

He'd been shocked to find out that Carly was a virgin.
He was also pleased, though he knew very well he had no
right to be. Still, it made him feel more responsible than
ever to be considerate, attentive, the best lover she could
ever wish for. He wanted to make up to her in quality

what she would be lacking in quantity when she married him.

Well, actually, he thought with a grin, he'd be happy to provide the quantity too.

He was looking forward to doing a bit more bonding tonight after Arthur was tucked up in bed. They could go to bed right after he did. They'd have more time now that the book was pretty much under control. Just thinking about spending hours in bed with Carly made him hot. No surprise there.

What did surprise him was the fact that the longer he thought about it, marrying her made more and more sense.

It had been a spur-of-the-moment thing, what he'd told Wendy about being married to Carly. It had been stupid in the extreme. But once he'd said it the idea of actually marrying Carly hadn't seemed stupid at all.

It made sense. Piran had never really thought about getting married and having kids with her or anyone else. He'd known since he was a boy what he'd wanted to do with his life, and marriage and kids had never seemed a part of it. He wasn't against the idea. He'd just always been too busy.

Besides, what sort of examples had he had?

His own parents, from his earliest memories, had always seemed distant and preoccupied, their marriage a mystery. After their divorce, his mother had ceased to be part of his life, and Piran had expected his father to pursue his career with equally monkish fervor.

Arthur St Just's unexpected marriage to the very unsuitable Sue had rattled him thoroughly. It hadn't made sense and it had destroyed his rapport with his father. Marriage had seemed to him something to stay well away from.

When Carly had taken it for granted nine years ago that

if he wanted to make love to her he must want to marry her, he'd been aghast. And he'd rejected the notion—and Carly—out of hand.

Now he didn't.

Now he was mature. Ready to settle down. Plus he had a son who needed a mother.

Carly would be a good mother. She'd proved that. Besides, she liked to dive, she edited books and he loved to make love with her. What more could he possibly ask for?

Yes, marrying Carly now made a hell of a lot of sense.

He said as much to Arthur as he carried the child up the last few yards of the gravel road that led toward the house. Arthur sucked his thumb and sighed contentedly, nestling his head against Piran's shoulder. There was no doubt in Piran's mind that Arthur agreed with him.

As he approached the veranda he saw that Carly wasn't alone. There was a woman sitting on the swing. She had long, golden-brown hair and an island tan and looked vaguely familiar.

Across from Carly, he saw Des.

Piran's jaw tightened. Trust Des to show up the minute all the work was done.

At the sound of his footsteps they all looked up.

'You're back,' Carly said, and the expression on her face puzzled him. She looked as if she had sunstroke. Her eyes were dazed, her cheeks were flushed, yet there was a hint of white around her mouth.

The woman in the swing leaped to her feet and ran down the steps toward him. 'A.J.!' she cried, and if Piran hadn't hung on she would have snatched Arthur right out of his arms.

His eyes narrowed. 'Who the hell are you?'

'That's Angelica.' Carly smiled wanly. 'Arthur—er—A.J.'s mother.'

Piran stared at the tawny-haired woman. She was familiar, yes, but—

'Now wait a minute. I might have been round the bend for a while, but I know damned well I never slept with her!'

'No, you didn't,' Des said.

Piran's gaze jerked toward his brother who was getting to his feet.

'I did,' Des said.

'What are you talking about?'

But Des only had eyes for the child in Piran's arms, and his voice, when he spoke, was as soft as his smile. 'You're not his father—I am.'

CHAPTER TEN

PIRAN supposed that if he made them go over it again and again someday he might feel less betrayed, might even feel he'd been given a reprieve.

At least he might feel it made sense.

'I can't believe you would just abandon your child on a veranda!' he said to Angelica for the second time.

Carly would never do a stupid, irresponsible thing like that, and she wasn't even Arthur's—he couldn't bring himself to think of the baby as A.J.—mother.

'I didn't think I was abandoning him!' Angelica retorted hotly. 'I thought Des was here. He'd made such a point out of telling everyone this was where he *had* to be so you two could finish your damned book!'

Des looked decidedly uncomfortable at her words. Piran thought he ought to look as if he was being consumed by the fires of hell.

'How did I know you were going to leave me a baby?' Des demanded. 'It isn't like you ever told me we were going to have one!'

'I tried,' Angelica said. 'You were never where I could get hold of you! You were always off on some boat or running around the world. If you had a phone—or an office—like a normal person—'

'Sorry!' Des snapped. Then immediately his tone softened and he reached out and took her hand. 'Hey, we've been through all this.' He looked at his brother. 'I'm sorry about the mix-up. She did try. And then, when she got desperate, she came here.'

'And left him! She could have waited,' Piran pointed out. 'I'd have been happy to tell her you were off sailing the seven seas.'

'Yes, well, she was annoyed by then. She thought I was avoiding her, avoiding responsibilities. She thought maybe a little shock treatment might make me see the light.' He gave a wry grimace. 'So she left him and took off to crew for Jim. Imagine her surprise when, the day after Jim picked her up, he sent her down into the cabin to take care of the mate with the flu and she found out it was me!'

'Imagine,' Piran said drily.

'You should have heard her when she thought I was here learning how to be a father and I was actually half a world away with no idea what she'd done.' Des shook his head in dismay at the memory.

Piran didn't have to hear her. He could imagine that too. What he couldn't imagine was life without Arthur.

To be fair, the past few weeks didn't seem to have been easy for Angelica either. The way she was cuddling Arthur in her arms right now, as if she couldn't bear to put him down, he knew she must have gone spare when she'd realized there was no way for her to get off Jim's boat at once and fly halfway round the world to the child she'd left on the veranda.

And then she'd had to explain to Des why she was so frantic. That couldn't have been easy either. Nor could their plight have made poor, unsuspecting Jim's shake-down sail any easier for all concerned.

So what? Piran thought savagely. It served them right! It would have served them right if he and Carly had disappeared with Arthur and left no trace. He glared now at them both.

'We got married as soon as we could,' Des said. 'Somehow I never thought I'd spirit a woman off to Las Vegas, but I did. And then we came right on here. We're really grateful,' he added. 'To both of you.'

He turned his gaze directly on Carly. 'I'm sorry. I had no idea when I asked you,' he apologized. 'You must hate me. First the book, then Piran, then A.J.' He grimaced sympathetically.

Piran's teeth clenched. His gaze followed Des's to see Carly's reaction to that.

She was smiling wanly. 'It's…all right,' she said softly.

She didn't say anything else. She had said almost nothing at all since he'd come back almost an hour ago. Apparently she'd already heard the explanations before he got there. At least she'd had no questions this time through.

He'd had a thousand, all furious. And all the while he'd been asking them Carly had simply sat there, motionless, her hands folded in her lap, her eyes either on them or staring off unseeing at the horizon.

'I don't think you ought to have a baby,' he snarled at Des and Angelica now. 'An irresponsible pair like you!'

Angelica gasped, cuddling Arthur closer and looking fearfully to Des to defend them.

Des did. He bristled. 'And I suppose you're more responsible?' One brow lifted. 'Who thought Arthur was probably his?' he said mockingly.

Piran flushed, then felt a stab of surprise when Carly spoke up.

'He didn't,' she said in a low, firm voice. 'He never thought that. Not from the first.'

'Not *at* first,' Piran corrected her. 'But then…well, I

thought it was possible,' he conceded, glancing her way, wondering why in heaven's name he was arguing with her.

'Well, he's not yours,' Des said firmly. 'He's ours.' He reached out a hand and brushed it across Arthur's hair. 'Our son,' he repeated softly. His voice cracked on the words, but he didn't even seem embarrassed by the display of emotion, and that, finally, more than all the protestations he'd made so far, convinced Piran that his brother meant every word.

He sat in stunned silence and saw his future slipping away. No one else spoke either. In the distance he could hear the surf hitting the sand, a frog near by under a coconut tree.

Just like yesterday. But nothing was as it had been yesterday. Nothing at all. And Piran couldn't sit here any longer and pretend that it was. He shoved himself to his feet. 'Congratulations,' he said abruptly. 'I hope you're very happy. It was a long walk back from town and I'm hot. So if you don't mind I think I'll go for a swim.'

He left without another word.

It might not have been the shortest engagement on record, Carly thought, but it was close.

Probably she should have been brave enough to stick around until Piran got back from his swim and bid him a pleasant farewell.

But even though she knew she should, knew as well that there would be no end to Angelica and Des's speculations if she left at once, still she packed her bags and did just exactly that.

She couldn't stay around and pretend that nothing had happened. She couldn't even bring herself to follow him down to the shore.

He hadn't asked her. And if she went, what would he say to her that she could possibly want to hear? Would she have to endure awkward protestations that he would marry her anyway? Desperate mumblings that might get him out of an engagement he no longer wanted?

No, thank you. Carly didn't need to hear what she already knew.

She wanted to go home.

'Tonight?' Des demanded. 'You want to leave tonight?'

'Not tonight,' Carly said. 'Now. There's a plane at six. If I go now, I can catch it. I mean, why stay around?' she said desperately. 'The manuscript is, to all intents and purposes, finished. At least, Piran's part is. I can do my part in New York. Besides,' she lied, 'I miss the city. I miss my friends. It's Christmas, Des,' she added plaintively.

She didn't know which of her pleas convinced him, but finally he shrugged. 'If that's what you want. I owe you big. But what about saying goodbye to Piran?'

'He won't care.' She didn't know whether she hoped that was true or feared it was.

'OK,' Des said at last. 'Good thing I borrowed Sam's moke. I can run you to town in that.'

'I'll be ready in five minutes,' Carly said. She was ready in less.

Des waited with her in the Quonset hut terminal until the plane arrived. He looked as if he wanted to apologize again, to explain things that as far as Carly could see could never be explained. Or if they could she didn't want to hear them.

She avoided his gaze, shifting from one foot to the other, watching the clock and then the doorway to the terminal, half afraid that Piran would come through it at any moment—though rationally she knew there was no reason why he should.

Rationally she was sure he would be grateful to come back and find that she was gone and that they would never have to face each other again.

Still, by the time the plane arrived, she had bitten her thumbnail down to the quick and had Des asking anxiously, 'Are you sure you're all right?'

'Fine. Just eager to get home.' Carly gave a nervous little laugh. 'I think I must have island fever. You know, feeling too hemmed in. I just want to get away!'

Des frowned. 'Did you and Piran—?'

'No!' Carly leaned forward and kissed Des lightly on the cheek, then turned and bolted toward the door that the other three passengers had already gone through. 'Bye.'

She didn't say how lovely his son was or how much she was going to miss him or anything else irrelevant but oh, so true. She just ran for the plane and scrambled up the steps, hugging the carryall with the manuscript against her chest.

Diana would be pleased. So would Sloan. She'd done her job. And that was, after all, what she'd come for. Not for Des or Arthur. Or, God help her, Piran. She swallowed hard. Her throat ached. She felt a stinging behind her eyes.

Editors don't cry, she told herself fiercely as the plane began to rumble down the runway.

At least, she hoped they didn't.

'What do you mean, she left?'

'Just what I said. She said you'd finished the book—at least, you had finished your part—so there was nothing to wait around for. I guess she still had some revising to do, but—'

'What the hell has that got to do with anything?' Piran glared at his brother. He couldn't believe what Des had just told him, even though the knot that was tying itself in his stomach meant that his emotions seemed to know instinctively that it was true.

He'd been gone for three hours. It was already dark by the time he'd walked the length of the damned beach, trying to sort out what had happened, trying to figure out what to do next.

He'd wished Carly had gone with him, talked to him, listened to him, but as he'd walked he'd told himself that maybe it was better that she hadn't. Maybe they both needed a little time alone before they decided what to do together.

Or so he'd thought. Apparently Carly had made the decision for him.

'She said you wouldn't care. The book is why she came. That's what it was all about.'

'Was it?' Piran's tone was scathing. She'd said he wouldn't care? He kicked at the slats of the deck railing, then jammed his hands into the pockets of his shorts.

Des watched him without speaking for a long moment. Then, 'I thought it was,' Des said quietly. 'Did something happen between you?'

'None of your damned business!'

'I only thought—'

'Then stop thinking! You're no good at it.'

'Look, Piran, I'm sorry. Sorry for sticking you with Carly. Sorry for the whole mess. I've told you, it's not like I knew about A.J.'

'Who? Oh, you mean Arthur? This has nothing to do with Arthur.'

'Then what the hell are you so upset about?' Des paused

and considered his older brother narrowly. 'Did you do something to Carly?'

Piran hunched his shoulders. 'What the hell would I do to Carly?'

'Hurt her.'

'Of course not.' Unless you counted accusing her of being a gold digger, taking her virginity, and proposing a marriage of convenience so he'd have someone to take care of his bastard child.

Piran raked a hand through his hair. Hell, no wonder she'd wasted no time getting out of there!

Once Arthur's identity had been resolved and any obligation she might have felt toward him thus relieved, the weight of the world must have dropped from her shoulders.

Obviously Arthur had been the attraction, not him. She hadn't wasted any time dumping him. He felt a hard, heavy ache somewhere deep inside that he didn't wholly comprehend.

It didn't make sense. He told himself he should be feeling relieved as well. He was well off out of such a marriage of convenience.

It wasn't as if he really wanted to marry Carly O'Reilly. Was it?

Carly made herself buy a Christmas tree. It was the day before Christmas Eve and the tree was the last one sitting by the grocery on the corner of 92nd and Broadway, and it was really pretty dreadful-looking. She told herself she felt sorry for it, that she needed to give it a home for the holiday.

But she wasn't sure if she was feeling sorrier for the tree or for herself.

It's what you wanted, she reminded herself hourly. You

were the one who wanted not to have family around at Christmas. You could have gone to Roland's. You could still go to John's. He'd renewed his offer only the night before.

But she didn't want any of them.

She only wanted Piran.

She wanted the dream to go on, wanted to wake up and find herself in his arms, loving him, holding him, planning a future with him and with Arthur.

Ah, Arthur.

What a shock it still was whenever she thought about Des and Angelica's arrival, their startling revelation.

She thought about it all the time, mulled it over, wondered at the workings of providence. What would Piran have done if Des and Angelica had come later? Too late? After he and Carly had married?

Thank God that hadn't happened. She couldn't have borne it, knowing that he was trapped and it wasn't even his fault.

But she didn't seem to be bearing this much better.

'Hey, lady, you're gonna wreck that tree dragging it through the slush!'

Carly turned to see a rough-looking teenage boy leaning against a lamppost, watching her. He shoved himself upright as he spoke and came toward her. Carly glanced around nervously.

'How far you goin'?' he asked as he took it from her and hoisted it on his shoulder.

'Er, the other side of Amsterdam. Halfway up the block. It's fine, really. I—'

'Lead on.'

And what else could she do with him standing there with her tree on his shoulder?

He carried it all the way to her stoop and up the steps. There he stopped.

'I won't carry it in for you. Wouldn't want to make you too nervous.' He grinned and sketched her a quick salute. 'Merry Christmas.'

And before Carly could do more than stare after him he'd bounded down the stairs and headed back down the street.

'M-merry Christmas,' Carly called after him, still astonished at the uncalled-for good deed.

She thought about it. It made her smile—the first smile she'd managed since she'd got home three nights before.

'Things are looking up,' she promised herself. But by the time she had wrestled the tree up three flights of stairs she wasn't quite so sanguine.

Still, she did her best to muster some holiday spirit. She put on a CD of cheerful seasonal music—and if it didn't have any of the songs on the tape she'd left in Conch Cay that was all right too. Then she vacuumed her carpet using pine air-freshener beads in the vacuum. Finally she set up the tree in front of the window overlooking the garden four floors below.

She'd bought two strings of lights at the drugstore by the subway stop, and she was just getting them out of their boxes when the phone rang. She picked it up.

'Last chance,' a cheerful masculine voice said.

'Oh, John, I can't.'

'Of course you can. I'm leaving in a couple of hours. You've got time to get ready. What else are you doing? You're finished with the book.'

'I still have some work to do on it,' Carly hedged. She probably could have finished it already. Probably *should* have. But she couldn't bring herself to let it go.

She'd taken the manuscript out of her carryall when she'd arrived back in the apartment three nights ago. She'd set it on the counter between the living room and her tiny kitchen where she passed it fifty times a day. So she would remember that she still had it and that it needed work, she told herself.

As if she could forget.

Sometimes she picked it up, intending to go through it one last time. Instead she stood staring out the window, holding it against her chest and rocking back and forth, hugging it to her the way just days ago she had hugged Arthur.

Arthur. Piran.

If she didn't have the manuscript to hold, it would all seem like a dream now. Perhaps she should be trying to convince herself that it was.

But she couldn't. It was real—all of it—too real. And the manuscript was the only thing she had left to show for it.

Unless you counted her broken heart.

'Come on, Carly, what do you say?'

'Oh, John, really, I can't. If I came with you, your parents would get the wrong impression.'

'That I like you? That you like me?'

'That we're serious about each other.'

'I am serious.'

'But I'm...' She stopped herself before she said the word.

'Not?' John said it for her. He sighed. 'You couldn't maybe muster a little seriousness?'

Carly could tell he was hurt though he was trying to sound offhand. 'You're a wonderful friend,' she told him, and meant it.

'Damned by faint praise.'

'No, truly. I'm very fond of you.'

'Even worse.'

'Merry Christmas, John,' she said gently.

'Merry Christmas, Carly.'

She stood holding the receiver for a long moment before she finally set it down. She might have been able to forget if she'd gone with him. She might have started looking forward instead of back.

She told herself she was a fool. Piran didn't love her. If she gave him proper encouragement, someday John might.

Did she want to end up an old maid just because the one man she'd ever loved only needed her as a convenience?

How pathetic was she, for heaven's sake?

Still, when the buzzer rang an hour later and she knew it had to be John stopping on his way out of the city to give her one very last chance, she still couldn't bring herself to throw some clothes in a bag and go with him.

In fact she couldn't even bring herself to go downstairs. He would leave if he didn't get an answer, she assured herself even though the buzzer sounded once again.

'Don't do this, John,' she muttered, huddling into the sofa. 'Please don't.'

But John apparently wasn't taking nothing for an answer. At that moment she heard the buzzer blast again. And again.

Carly got up off the sofa and went into the bathroom, turned on the water and put her hands over her ears.

Finally, after ten minutes, she shut it off and came out. Silence. She breathed a sigh of relief.

There was a knock on the door.

Damn! He must have rung everyone in the building and

someone must have pressed the answering buzzer to let him in. Carly shoved her hands through her hair, then sighed and went to answer it.

'John, I told you, I'm not—'

It wasn't John.

'Piran?'

'In the flesh.' He had a duffel bag in his hand and he pushed past her into the room, scowling as he came. 'Who's John?' he asked her at the same moment that she asked,

'What are you doing here?'

They stared at each other, each waiting for the other to speak. Carly could have waited forever, so stunned was she at the sight of him.

Piran was far more impatient. He glared at her. 'Shut the damned door and tell me who John is.'

Numb, Carly did, then leaned against the door, grateful to have something to hold her up.

'Well?' Piran prompted.

'He's a friend,' she said faintly. What are you doing here? Tell me! she wanted to shout at him.

'A good friend?'

'Yes. Why?'

'Have you slept with him?'

'*What*?'

A dull red flush crept up Piran's neck. He shoved a hand through his hair. He dropped the duffel bag and paced around her small living room. 'Forget it,' he muttered.

'I will not forget it,' Carly said, incensed. 'How can you ask me that after you…after you and I…?'

'I know, I know!' He kicked at the carpet. 'That's why I said forget it!'

Carly wasn't likely to, but she pressed her lips together

in a tight line and composed herself. 'All right. I answered your question. Now you answer mine. Why did you come here? What do you want?'

'You left.' The bleak tone of his words surprised her. She looked at him closely.

'I thought you'd be glad.'

He frowned. 'Why should I be?'

'Well, once Des and Angelica showed up, you were free…of Arthur at least. But you still had me.' She shrugged awkwardly. 'I didn't want to hang around to listen to you tell me the engagement was off, thank you very much. I mean, it isn't as if you really wanted to marry me!' She blinked rapidly, hating the way her eyes were filling with tears.

'No,' he said softly. He bent his head, and whatever hope she'd held in one tiny corner of her heart that he might deny it died with that one word.

She swallowed painfully. 'So…what's the problem?'

Piran hesitated, then let out a harsh breath. 'The problem is I do now.'

The words were spoken so quickly that Carly wasn't sure she heard them—or, if she had, if she'd heard them right.

'What?' she asked after a moment.

'I want to marry you now.' A corner of his mouth lifted. 'Ironic, isn't it? Nine years ago you wanted marriage and I walked away. Then we agreed to it for Arthur's sake. And now, when Arthur doesn't need us any more, when he has his own set of parents at last, you walk away…and I can't.'

Carly just stared at him. 'Why can't you?' she said faintly. She wondered if she'd fallen asleep and started to dream. She looked around the apartment, trying to ground herself.

She saw the manuscript lying on the counter. She saw her scraggly Christmas tree still only halfway strung with lights. And she saw Piran St Just looking at her with a tormented expression in his eyes.

'Why do you think?' he said harshly.

Carly simply shook her head, not certain of anything now.

He gave a ragged half-laugh. 'You can't even imagine, can you, after all the good and sensible reasons for getting married that I gave you before?'

'Well, most of them seemed more to my benefit than yours,' Carly said cautiously. 'Besides Arthur and the editing. I mean, I'd get to go diving, travel, write books—'

'Make love?'

Carly felt her cheeks warm. 'That too,' she admitted.

'That too,' he echoed mockingly. 'God, you are well rid of me. I should never have come.' He started for the door, but she was blocking his way. 'Move.'

Carly stayed where she was.

'Why did you come, Piran?' she asked him quietly, barely daring to hope. 'Why do you want to marry me if not for Arthur?'

His throat worked. He rocked back and forward on his heels. 'For the time-honored reason, I suppose,' he said bitterly when the silence had dragged on far too long. 'Because I love you, damn it!'

He glared at her as if defying her to dispute it. She wasn't about to. She started to smile.

'That's right, go ahead and laugh,' he snarled. 'And then go off with this John character. I don't care. Just move out of my way!'

'No.' She met his gaze defiantly. 'And you do care. You just admitted it.'

'So now we're even.'

'Yes, we are.' Carly nodded slowly. 'Because I love you too.'

As she spoke the words she pushed away from the door at last and crossed the few feet that separated them. She slid her arms around him, and Piran groaned as her hands locked against his back and her lips lifted to touch his.

It was a kiss as hungry and eager and passionate as the ones they'd shared on her birthday nine years before. It was a kiss as sweet and tender as the ones he'd given her after they'd made love just days ago. It was ecstasy.

And it was agony when Piran finally broke it moments later to ask raggedly, 'You're not just saying that, are you?'

Carly laughed. 'Does it feel like it?'

'No, but—God, Carly, by rights you ought to hate me. Are you sure?'

'I think I'm the one who ought to be asking that question. I've loved you for years. You didn't love me last week.'

Piran smiled wryly. 'I did. I just didn't realize it. I never admitted it to myself. Not until after Des came and robbed me of my excuse for marrying you, that is.' He met her gaze and held it and Carly saw in his eyes everything she'd ever hoped to see.

She touched his cheek. 'Do you need an excuse?' she asked him softly.

'Not any more.' He kissed her again and showed her what he meant with his lips as well as his words. 'I have the best one of all and the only one that matters: I love you.'

'Oh, Piran!' She hugged him tightly, kissed him back, and didn't object in the least when his fingers fumbled open the buttons of her shirt and made quick work of sliding down the zipper of her jeans. As she led him into the bedroom, she was busy doing the same to him.

'Do you have a thing about Christmas trees?' Piran asked her late the next morning as she was making him toast and coffee. They were both in her tiny kitchen, stepping on each other's feet and getting in each other's way, but it really didn't matter because it simply gave them more excuses to touch and kiss.

'I like them. Why?'

'Well, you dragged that one home on Conch Cay. And I notice you've got one half dressed over there.' Piran nodded in the direction of the tree that Carly had never finished putting lights on the night before because she and Piran had had far more interesting things to do.

'Maybe I do have a thing about them,' Carly said now, considering the tree and the possibility. 'They remind me of the good things in life, the things people share—home and family and hope. I was having a hard time mustering it with this one, though,' she admitted, 'until you came.'

'I know what you mean.' He bent and fished in his duffel bag which sat beside the sofa, then he handed her a wadded-up beach towel. 'Open it.'

Carly set it down on the table and did just that. Inside it she found smaller towels. Carefully she opened each one. She found the fishing lures and flies that she'd hung on the tree in Conch Cay. She found the bits of sea glass, the shells, the pods, the fishnet and the driftwood.

She looked at him, amazed. 'You brought all the ornaments on the tree?'

'They were ours, not Des's and Angelica's. Our home and our family and our hope.' His voice was almost fierce in its intensity. He looked right at her. 'They have to make their own. They are. I told them how.'

Carly smiled. She laid her fingers against his cheek. His hand came up and wrapped around hers. He pressed a kiss into her palm.

'I didn't know what I was going to do with them when I took them,' he said after a moment. 'Des thought I was out of my mind. I was. It seemed a hell of a long shot bringing them here.' He hesitated, then asked, 'Can we put them on your tree?'

'Our tree,' Carly corrected him.

It took them most of the afternoon. And when they were finished Carly turned out the lights except for the ones on the tree, lit a pair of candles on the mantel, then curled up next to Piran on the sofa. 'Isn't it beautiful?'

'Beautiful,' he agreed. 'But I think it needs a little something right over there.' He pointed to a bare spot.

'I can move the driftwood.' Carly started to get up.

But Piran caught her hand and pulled her back down. He reached into the duffel bag again and handed her a small sack.

'You put these where they belong.'

'What?' She opened the sack. In it were two even smaller wrapped packages. She looked at Piran. He nodded. She opened the first one. It was a small black velvet box. It held a ring. A diamond solitaire ring.

'I said I was going Christmas shopping.'

She started. 'But that was…that was before…'

'It was, but even then I didn't want any question about this being a legitimate marriage. I couldn't have said, but somewhere inside I knew. Will you wear it, Carly?'

And this time Carly didn't even bother to blink back the tears. 'Forever,' she promised.

He slid the ring on her finger, then kissed her. 'Open the other one.'

She fumbled with the wrapping, then opened a small cardboard box to draw out a tiny wooden object.

'It...it's Arthur's sailboat!' She lifted wide eyes toward Piran. 'But surely you should have left this for him?'

'I did. Every little boy should have a boat. But before I left I bought another one. Call it foolishness. Call it desperation. Call it love. But I was hoping,' he said, drawing her into his arms, 'as only a desperate man dares hope, that someday somehow I might be able to talk you into having an Arthur of our own...'

Sally Wentworth was born and raised in Hertfordshire, where she still lives, and started writing after attending an evening class course. She is married and has one son.

Sally has been writing successfully for Mills & Boon® for over twenty years and has had her seventy novels translated into many languages—including Chinese, Russian and Yugoslavian!

CHRISTMAS NIGHTS
by
SALLY WENTWORTH

CHAPTER ONE

PARIS had been home for less than an hour when the police came. The flat was cold and unwelcoming. When she'd left to go to Budapest six weeks ago the weather had been mild and autumnal and it hadn't seemed worthwhile leaving the heating on. Now, a week before Christmas, it was freezing outside and the flat was not much warmer.

She'd turned the heating up as high as it would go, drawn the curtains across the frosted windows, fixed herself a drink, and kicked off her shoes as she sat on the settee and began to go through the piles of letters, Christmas cards and junk mail that she had found on the doormat.

When the buzzer sounded Paris frowned, of half a mind to ignore it, but it rang imperatively for a second time, and with a sigh she went over to the entry phone. The faces of two men she didn't know looked at her from the screen.

'Yes?'

'Miss Paris Reid?'

'Yes.'

'We're policemen, Miss Reid.' The nearest man held up an identity card. 'May we talk to you, please?'

'Has there been an accident?' Paris asked, immediately fearful for her parents.

'No, it's nothing like that, but we need to talk to you urgently.'

'You'd better come up, then.'

She waited by the open door for the lift to arrive at her floor. The flat, in the northern suburbs of London, was her own, the mortgage paid for out of her quite considerable earnings. There was only one bedroom, but that suited Paris fine; she had no intention of ever sharing it with a female flatmate—or anyone else, if it came to that.

The policemen had said that there hadn't been an accident but Paris was still uneasy as she greeted them and led the way into her sitting-room. 'It isn't one of my parents?' she asked anxiously.

'No, Miss Reid. It's about Noel Ramsay.'

For a moment it didn't mean anything, then she grew still. 'Noel Ramsay?' she repeated, to give herself time.

'Yes. You must remember that you were on the jury when he was tried for murder, nearly four years ago now.'

'Yes, of course.' She dredged her memory. 'He escaped, didn't he? I seem to remember reading about it in the papers some months ago.'

'That's right.' The policeman who'd introduced himself as a detective inspector gave her a pleased smile, as if she were a bright pupil in a classroom.

'But why on earth should you come to me about him? You did catch him again, didn't you?'

'No, I'm afraid we didn't,' the inspector admitted ruefully. He paused, then said, 'I don't want to alarm you, but you may remember that at the trial Ramsay swore to be revenged on everyone who put him away.'

For a brief, horrible moment the vision of Ramsay's face, twisted by hate, shouting threats and abuse as he was dragged away, came sharply back into Paris's mind. 'Yes, I remember,' she said tightly.

'Yes. Well—I'm afraid it's beginning to look as if he's carrying out his threat.'

'What do you mean?'

'Haven't you been reading the papers lately? The barrister who prosecuted Ramsay was killed by a hit-and-run driver about three months ago, and then one of the policemen who arrested him was very badly injured when the brakes on his car failed—a newish car that had always been well maintained.'

'Couldn't those things have been coincidental?'

'Possibly.' The inspector shrugged. 'But a month ago one of the prosecution witnesses just disappeared, and then a member of the jury was found dead in suspicious circumstances. Two incidents could possibly be coincidence, but hardly four. And so we—' He broke off. 'Are you all right, Miss Reid?'

Every last vestige of colour had fled from Paris's face and her throat didn't seem to work. Her whole being felt suspended in time, too frozen to breathe, but by a tremendous effort of will-power she somehow forced herself to say, 'Which—which member of the jury?'

'A Mrs Sheila Rayner. She was the foreman of the jury, if you remember,' he answered, looking at her curiously.

'Yes, of course.' Paris's heart started to beat again, relief to flow through her veins and bring the colour back to her cheeks. 'That—that's terrible. I'm so sorry.' Getting to her feet, she turned away. 'Would you like a drink?' Both men refused but she topped up her own glass and took a long swallow before she faced them again. 'I didn't know any of this. I've been away, in Hungary, and it wasn't easy to get English papers.'

'We know,' the inspector said with a small smile. 'We've been calling here hoping to find you for a week or so.'

'To warn me?'

'Partly that, but also because we're taking everyone who was involved in the trial to a place of safety. We don't want anyone else being hurt while we catch Ramsay again.'

Paris's eyes widened. 'You're taking *everyone* involved? Even the jurors?'

'Everyone,' he confirmed. 'The judge, barristers, witnesses, jurors, even the clerk of the court.'

'But surely the jurors' names were never stated in court; how could Ramsay possibly know who we are?'

A grim look came into the policeman's eyes. 'Unfortunately the records of the case have disappeared from the archives; we can only assume that Ramsay or an accomplice must have taken them. And if he has—' he shrugged expressively '—then Ramsay knows the names and addresses of everyone connected with the trial.'

'Don't you have any leads?'

'We're pursuing the matter with the utmost urgency, of course,' he told her, in what was plainly a stock police phrase for saying that they didn't have a clue. 'But he's already got one of you jurors and I'm not taking any chances. So if you'll pack a suitcase we'll get you to a place of safety tonight.'

Paris stared at him unseeingly, her mind whirling as she tried to take in the implications, decide what to do. 'Are all the people being taken to the same place or are you splitting them up?'

'No, you'll all be together. It makes it easier to protect you that way.'

That, of course, made her mind up fast. 'I'm sorry,' she said firmly, 'but I can't possibly go. Please don't worry about me. I shall be quite safe here and I—'

'You will *not* be safe.'

He spoke sharply but Paris didn't hesitate before saying, 'But of course I will. My old address may be on the records but I've moved three times since then. And I'm ex-directory. No one could possibly trace me.'

'We did,' the second policeman, a sergeant, pointed out with some irony.

'Yes, but you're the police; with all the resources you have you're supposed to find people.'

'You're on the electoral roll for this district. Anyone can walk into a library, look at it, and find your address. With a Christian name like yours it was simple.'

Paris bit her lip, not for the first time blaming her parents for giving her such a distinctive name. But she persisted, saying, 'I'm sorry, but I refuse to go. You can't make me.'

'No, we can't,' the inspector agreed. 'Is it because you've made plans for Christmas, or are you having guests to stay?'

'No,' she admitted. 'But I've already been away for over a month; there's loads I have to catch up on, at work as well as here.'

'I've already spoken to your employers and they quite understand the situation. They told me to tell you that they don't expect to see you again until Ramsay is caught.'

She gasped, amazed that the police had gone to those lengths before they'd even talked to her. 'I've been invited to several parties,' she said doggedly. 'If I didn't go to them my friends would worry and—'

'In that case you can phone and tell them you've changed your plans. Tell them you've had an unexpected invitation and that you'll be going away for Christmas instead.'

'But...' She sought for a convincing argument. 'But it could take weeks, months even, before you catch him. I can't possibly be away for that length of time.'

'We don't anticipate it taking anything like that long, miss.'

'Are you saying that you're close to catching Ramsay?'

'I don't want to commit myself, but just take my word for it that it won't be for very long.'

Paris didn't believe him but there was no point in saying so. Finishing her drink, she shoved her hands into the pockets of her jacket so that the men couldn't see the way they tightened into fists. 'Look,' she began, then stopped, not wanting to say this. But there was no help for it—the policemen were so very determined. 'There are reasons— very personal reasons—why I can't possibly go with you.'

'What reasons?'

'They needn't concern you,' she snapped. 'But I am *not* going.'

The middle-aged inspector, who looked as if he wouldn't be sorry when retirement came along, gave her a tight-lipped look. 'Very well, Miss Reid. In that case you leave me no choice.'

'What do you mean?' Paris asked warily.

'If you won't let us take you to a place of safety, then I shall have to give you police protection.'

To Paris that didn't sound at all bad but his voice had had a threatening note in it, so she said, 'Which means?'

'A woman police officer will have to be with you at all times, day and night, and there will also be a male constable at your door. We will turn this place into a fortress,' he threatened determinedly.

'But my neighbours would hate that—and besides, there isn't enough room here for two people to live,' Paris protested.

'No help for it, I'm afraid—if you're going to be obstinate.'

He had deliberately made the conditions impossible to accept, she realised, and burst out on a desperate note, 'Don't people's personal feelings matter to you?'

'Not when their lives are in danger, no. I can't let them matter,' the inspector answered emphatically.

She was cornered, and hesitated, wondering whether to throw herself on his mercy and explain just why it was impossible for her to go. But a glance at the inspector's set face, wearily patient but determined, made her decide it would be no use. He was too stolid to understand the trauma of seeing again an ex-lover, a man who had, quite literally, thrown her out of his life.

Clenching her fists till it hurt, Paris said, 'Are the other people already at this safe place?'

'Yes.'

'All of them? All the jurors?'

His assessing eyes met hers. 'All except the lady who was murdered, yes.'

Murdered. Such a dreadful word. It brought home to Paris for the first time the danger she was in. But she still said, 'Please, I can't go with—with all the others. I'll go somewhere else, if you like, but not with them.'

He nodded, in no way surprised. 'I see.'

She caught her breath, realising that there had been no need for any soul-searching; he already knew it all. 'Yes, very likely you do,' Paris said bitterly.

The inspector glanced at his colleague, hesitated, then said with a degree of sympathy that she hadn't expected, and which confirmed his knowledge, 'It probably won't be for long, perhaps just a week or so, and then you'll be able to come home. There will be a lot of people there, enough so you won't be thrown together with anyone you don't want to be with. You'll have your own room and be as private as you like. But I'm sorry, I can't arrange for somewhere else for you at this short notice. If it goes on for longer I might be able to arrange for you to go somewhere else after Christmas, though.'

When it would be a complete waste of time, Paris thought despondently. Her nightmare of the last three years had been that she might chance to meet the man she'd been so in love with, have to face him again and see the contempt in his eyes. Now it looked as if she was not only going to see him, but would have to spend an indefinite period in his proximity.

With a sigh, Paris said dully, 'If you'll promise to find

me somewhere else as soon as possible, then, all right, I'll
come. Where are we going?'

'I'm afraid we're not allowed to tell you that.'

She gave him a look that spoke volumes. 'I am going
to wash my hair,' she said forcefully. 'And then I'm going
to have something to eat, unpack, and make several phone
calls. *Then* I'll get ready to go. Is that all right by you?'
Her hands were on her hips and the last sentence was said
in a dangerous tone that dared him to argue.

The inspector, having got his own way by forceful coercion, could have been magnanimous, but all he said was,
'So long as you can do all that within the next two hours,
yes.'

They took her in a car and drove for quite some way, but
then, to Paris's surprise, the car stopped and they hurried
her into a station and onto a train where she was to share
a sleeping compartment with a policewoman. The blinds
were pulled down across the windows on both sides and
she couldn't see out. The door was locked and the light
turned low.

Paris's thoughts were far too full for her to want to sit
and chat with the policewoman, so she said that she was
tired, took off her shoes and coat and climbed into the
upper bunk, firmly closing her eyes.

Her heart was filled with a dread so deep that it was
almost like a physical fear. How would she bear it if Will
openly showed his hatred of her? Even now, after so long,
it was still sometimes hard to understand how it had all
gone so wrong—so horribly, humiliatingly wrong. Maybe
it was because of the circumstances in which they'd met:
at a murder trial, of all things. But there had been such
radiant happiness, too, at the beginning...

The train journeyed on through the night, swaying,
clanking along the rails, the rushing air loud outside, and

Paris's mind went back to the very beginning, when she had been sitting at breakfast with Emma, one morning in late spring.

'Jury service!' Paris gazed at the letter in her hand in consternation. 'But I can't possibly do it. I don't have the time.'

'When are you supposed to go?' Emma, her flatmate, reached over and took the letter from her. 'The seventh. That's only three weeks away. And at the Old Bailey, too; that's where they have the longest cases, isn't it?'

Paris's frown deepened into gloom. 'I know—and I'm supposed to be going to the conference in Brussels that week.'

'Perhaps you can get out of it,' Emma suggested languidly as she handed the letter back. 'Tell them you're going on holiday or something.'

Paris hesitated. 'Wouldn't that be against the law? Couldn't you be fined or something if you were found out?'

Emma gave an astonished laugh. 'For heaven's sake! Who's going to find out? People do it all the time.'

'Well, I can try, I suppose,' Paris said, still rather dubious, but she reflected that Emma, who was more than ten years older and worked for the same company, usually knew what she was talking about.

Later that morning, as soon as she arrived at her office at the cable network company for which she worked as a sales representative, Paris called the clerk of the court's office and asked to be released from doing the jury service. He asked for proof that she had booked a holiday, and when she lamely admitted that she had none he refused point-blank to let her off.

'Isn't it possible to postpone it indefinitely?' she begged.

'No, madam, it is not,' the man said shortly.

So there was no getting out of it. Paris had to go and see her boss, who arranged for Emma to attend the Brussels conference in her place. Paris was furious at her bad luck; she'd had this job for less than a year since leaving university and was putting everything she had into it. Representing the company at conferences, going abroad to promote their network strategies, being always available to visit potential clients constituted a big part of the job.

Paris had passed the training course with flying colours, was one of the brightest young reps, and knew that a good career lay ahead of her. Which she certainly intended to achieve. She was ambitious and wanted to get to the top just as soon as she possibly could. But there were always others with the same ambitions, the same aims. Having to sit through some criminal case for weeks on end, or even months, she thought with a groan, wouldn't do her career any good at all.

Angrily reluctant to serve as she was, Paris had to admit to a feeling of awe when she arrived at the Central Criminal Court—the Old Bailey as the building was commonly known—in the heart of the City of London. The courtroom was so old, the polished wooden benches and the judge's throne-like seat high on a dais so reminiscent of all the trial films she'd ever seen that she couldn't help but feel the solemnity and power of the place. Looking at the dock, she thought of all the people who had been tried there—murderers, rapists; she gave a shiver, her anger momentarily chastened.

Her fellow jurors seemed to have similar feelings. Earlier, they'd had to stand one by one and give their name and age and take the oath. Paris hated that, considering her age to be her own business. When it was her turn, her voice had a strong note of defiance as she said, 'Paris Reid. I'm twenty-two.'

A couple of the younger barristers smiled, as did one of the male jurors, she noticed. He was sitting on the end of the row and hadn't yet been called—a dark-haired man with a strong jaw and clean-cut features adding up to a good-looking face. He was the last to take the oath and did so in a firm voice.

'William Alexander Brydon. Twenty-nine. I swear by Almighty God that I will faithfully try the defendant and true verdict give according to the evidence.'

The oath, which Paris had hardly taken in, sounded very impressive when spoken in his deep, attractive tone, making her realise again the solemnity of the court. The judge must have been impressed too, because when he asked them to choose a foreman from amongst themselves he looked straight at William Brydon. But before the latter could speak a middle-aged woman stood up purposefully and volunteered herself, which pleased Paris; she was all for women sticking up for their rights. The judge merely raised his eyebrows slightly.

The case they were to hear was one of aggravated assault and murder. The prisoner, a man in his early forties named Noel Ramsay, was accused of beating up several people, one of whom—a man who had tried to steal Ramsay's girlfriend—had later died. The man in the dock was smartly dressed, had a boyishly good-looking face and a figure that was only just beginning to run to fat.

Paris found it difficult to imagine him hurting anyone. Perhaps it was the engaging, crinkly-eyed smile that he flashed at them all, the look of surprised innocence in his eyes, as if he still couldn't believe that he was there, that it was all happening to him.

That first morning it seemed to be all technical stuff. They broke for lunch, most of which time Paris spent on the phone, first to her office, trying to keep up with everything that was happening, and then to customers. She had just a few minutes left in which to grab a couple of bites from a sandwich before it was time to go back into the courtroom.

The jurors automatically sat in the same places as before. That afternoon they listened to a pathologist and had to look at photographs that made Paris's stomach turn over. If she hadn't really been aware of the seriousness of the case before, she certainly was after that.

At the end of the day, Paris rushed out of the building and drove to her office in a town to the north of London. There she spent three hours at her desk before driving home to a scratch supper and bed. She was young and healthy and could keep up the hectic pace for a while, but during the second week she began to feel the pressure. To add to everything the unpredictable English weather decided to have an early heatwave.

Paris overslept one morning and arrived just as the jurors were filing into their places. She gave a hasty apology to the clerk of the court, a man moved up for her, and she slipped in at the end of the row. Because she'd been so busy she had hardly talked to her fellow jurors and it took her a minute before she remembered that her neighbour's name was William Brydon. He gave her an amused smile which she met with a small shrug.

The evidence that morning was again technical. There was no air-conditioning in the court and it was very hot. The barristers were sweltering under their white wigs and several members of the jury took off their jackets.

Paris tried to concentrate but found her eyes drooping. She straightened in her seat, licked dry lips and wished she could have a drink. The police witness droned on— something about makes of cars that the accused had owned and sold. William Brydon's shoulder was invitingly close. Paris's head rested gently on it and she fell asleep.

'She seems to have fainted, my lord.'

The words, spoken loudly close by in a man's voice, woke her.

Paris blinked, came to guiltily, and would have jerked upright, but William Brydon was gently slapping at her cheeks, leaning over her so that she was hidden from everyone else. 'You fainted,' he murmured so that only she could hear. 'You don't want them to restart the whole trial, do you?' he added insistently.

Realising what he was doing, Paris gratefully fell in with the act. She gave a realistic moan and let him put her head down between her knees—none too gently, she noticed. The clerk and the woman foreman of the jury came over, the latter with some smelling salts which she insisted on holding under Paris's nose, making her sneeze.

'Perhaps if she could have some fresh air?' William Brydon suggested.

'We'll adjourn the court for lunch,' the judge decided.

Putting a strong arm round her, her neighbour escorted her out of the court, down the long corridor and out into the street. Not far away there was a small green oasis of trees surrounding the remains of a ruined church. When they reached its screening shade he immediately withdrew his arm. 'A heavy date last night?' he asked sardonically.

'No, I was working,' she retorted indignantly.

'After a day here? Are you self-employed or something?'

'No, I work for a cable network company. I'm a sales rep.'

Again his mouth, the lower lip fuller than the other, twisted with irony. 'Can't they manage without you?'

Paris's face hardened. 'I want to make sure they don't find out that they can,' she said shortly, adding, in a voice as scathing as his had been, 'You obviously don't have to worry about your job—if you have one.'

He looked amused. 'Oh, I have one. I'm a financial consultant, here in the City.'

Paris said moodily, 'Right now I should be in Brussels, representing my company at a medical conference, trying to persuade television and telephone companies to use our networks. It was to be my first time alone. And instead I'm stuck with this case. It's all so slow. And it could go on for weeks.'

'It might at that,' he agreed. 'So we'll just have to make the best of it, won't we?'

There was something in his voice, a note that immediately made her realise he was aware of her as a woman. Glancing quickly up at him, Paris saw that he was looking her over, from her short red-gold hair, down her slim figure, to her legs beneath the fashionably short skirt. 'Seen enough?' she said with a tilt of her chin, but not at all displeased.

He grinned. 'For now. My name's Will, by the way. Will Brydon.'

She smiled and shook the hand he held out to her. 'Mine's Paris Reid.'

'Yes, I know. An unusual name.'

'My parents went to Paris for a holiday; I was the result.' They began to stroll under the shade of the trees and she said, 'Thanks for helping me back there. I suppose I would have got into terrible trouble if they'd found out I'd fallen asleep. It's rather like being back at school with the teacher watching you all the time.'

They came to an ice-cream cart and Will bought her a cornet—one with a chocolate flake stuck into it. Paris ate it delicately, trailing her tongue along the chocolate, scooping a little of the ice cream and raising it to her mouth.

Will slowed as he openly watched her. 'You know,' he said with a sigh, 'you have the sexiest way of eating an ice.'

She laughed, her face lighting up. Glancing at him, she liked what she saw. His eyes were grey, clear and intelligent, under dark brows, the left one of which had a slight quirk, as if he raised it more than the other. His bone structure was good, his cheekbones high above the clean jawline, and there was a humorous look to his mouth.

He was tall, too—a definite plus in Paris's eyes because she was tall herself. Walking with him, she had to look up at him, which put him at about six feet two or three, she guessed. Perhaps it was his height that gave him such physical self-assurance, but there was an irresistible magnetism about him, as if he was full of energy that he could hardly contain.

'Don't you find having to do this jury service a bind?' she asked him.

'In some ways, of course, but I find the whole process of the law fascinating to watch; there's so much history behind it all. It's something that I'll probably have to do only once in a lifetime so I want to do it to the best of my ability. And I suppose we should be grateful that we don't live in a police state where there is no jury system.'

Paris wrinkled her nose at him. 'That sounds terribly po-faced. Is that really what you think?'

Will laughed. 'I think it's a damn nuisance, but I may as well get it over and done with.'

'That's better. I'm not looking forward to having to reach a verdict, are you? Suppose we don't all agree and have to stay in a hotel or something for days.' She looked at him from under her lashes. 'Your wife—or partner— would probably hate that.'

Will's lips curled in amusement. 'Fortunately I have neither, so there's no problem. But maybe you do?'

Paris shook her head. 'No, I'm single and unattached.' She added, 'At the moment,' to let him know that she wasn't hard up for boyfriends.

'Well, I'm glad that I've met you "at the moment",' Will remarked, and they both laughed. His eyes on her, he said, 'Maybe you'd better sit next to me when we go back in the court-room. Just to make sure you don't go to sleep again, of course.'

'Of course,' Paris agreed demurely. And as they walked back to the court they both knew that this could be the start of a very interesting friendship.

Emma came back from Brussels and told her off for trying to fit in her job with the trial. 'You can't possibly go on like this,' she remonstrated. 'Look, give me your customer list and I'll look after them for you until you're back at the office,' she offered.

'Oh, Emma, would you? It is rather getting me down,' Paris said gratefully.

Emma's kindness made Paris once again think herself extremely lucky that the older woman had taken a liking to her and more or less taken her under her wing. Her own parents had split up many years ago and both had remarried, but Paris didn't really feel at home with either of them, although they both always made her welcome and tried to include her in their new families.

When she'd first joined the company she'd lived in a bedsit quite nearby, but then Emma had become friendly with her and finally asked her if she'd like to share her flat. 'It's in the suburbs of London, mind,' Emma warned her. 'You'd have to drive into the office every day.'

But Paris hadn't minded that at all; the company had given her a car and the thought of living in London excited her.

At first, because of the difference in their ages, she'd been surprised that Emma had been so friendly, but she'd also been flattered by it too. Emma had quite a senior position in the sales department; it was her job to oversee and train the new recruits and to stand in when an emergency occurred, as in the case of the Brussels conference.

Because she was mostly based at head office, Emma was no longer entitled to a company car, and it didn't take Paris long to work out that one of the reasons why Emma had offered to let her share the flat was so that she could get a lift to and from work every day. But Paris was so grateful to her that she didn't mind in the least. And she was grateful to her again, now, for taking on her workload, especially now that she'd met Will and realised how pleasantly her lunch-hours could be if spent in his company instead of on the phone.

The heatwave continued and she and Will got into the habit of taking their sandwiches out to the old churchyard, where they sat on the grass beneath the trees to eat and talk. They talked as strangers do, telling each other about themselves, their likes and dislikes, asking questions, getting to know one another, until they weren't strangers any longer.

Instead of being reluctant to go to the court, Paris became eager to get there. She took care with her appearance and felt a thrill of pleasure when Will's grey eyes went over her admiringly. And he was so good-looking himself that she enjoyed being seen with him, liked walking along with him beside her, so tall and broad that he made her feel delicately feminine in comparison. From having lunch together, it took very little time before Will asked her to stay behind in town one evening and have dinner with him.

They went to see a film first, and afterwards had dinner at Topo Gigio—'The best Italian restaurant in Soho,' Will declared. He seemed very familiar with London—had lived there all his life, he told her, except for his years at university.

Paris envied him that; she had fallen in love with the city, with its pace and constant change, with its shops, cinemas and theatres. In London you got everything first—the new films and new fashions—and met people who were as ambitious as she was herself, and men who were eager to take out a pretty girl like Paris.

So there had been a lot of dates, but Will was the first man—the first real man, not someone of her own age—that Paris felt strongly attracted to.

After that first dinner date he insisted on taking her home in a cab, which must have cost the earth, and kept it waiting when he walked her to her door where he leant her against the wall, put his hands on her shoulders, and bent to kiss her. He merely touched her lips gently with his at first—small kisses that explored her mouth.

Paris, who wasn't that experienced, had been brainwashed by a thousand films and books and some equally inexperienced boyfriends into thinking that passionate clinches and devouring kisses were the bee's knees. But she found this light exploration, the soft, teasing kisses, both tantalising and sensuous. His breath was warm and she could smell the faint tang of aftershave that still clung to his skin.

It came to her that he was a very masculine kind of man, with a powerful aura of sensuality that excited her. He was the kind of man who knew what he wanted. And right now he wanted her.

Resting her hands against his chest, Paris closed her eyes. Opening her mouth, she felt him touch the tip of her tongue—a brief touch that she found incredibly erotic. She gave an involuntary sound of pleasure and Will's hands tightened a little on her shoulders.

Raising her hand, she caressed the back of his neck, his hair silky under her fingers, and she felt him give a small sigh as his hand came down to her waist and drew her against him. His kiss deepened, taking all her mouth, but it was still gentle, and she responded willingly.

It was a while before Will straightened. Pushing back his thick dark hair, he looked down at her with the heaviness of desire in his eyes, but then he gave a crooked grin. 'I think maybe I'd better go.'

'Mmm. Your taxi is waiting.'

But he bent to kiss her again before he drew away for a second time and said, 'See you in court.'

Then he waved and was gone, leaving Paris with an overwhelming feeling of physical excitement and a longing for him to kiss her again.

That kiss marked a new awareness of each other and was the start of an inevitable closeness between them. But just as Will had been in no hurry with that first kiss so they were in no hurry to become even closer, both of them recognising that this was something special and wanting to anticipate each phase of their relationship. Maybe Paris would have been more eager, but it was Will who set the pace, he who had the dominant role.

They didn't go out every night; Will worked out at a gym two nights a week and also spent time in his own office, but they were together with increasing frequency.

The trial lasted over a month and was drawing to its close. Although they talked a lot to each other, they seldom discussed the trial. It was bad enough having to listen to all the terrible details during the day without thinking about it during their time alone together. They wanted to put it out of their minds, to escape from it. But at last, on a Thursday, it came to the judge's summing-up, which lasted nearly a whole day. The judge was eminently fair, pointing out facts that they should remember, think about, but emphasising that they had heard everything and it was up to them to make up their minds now.

Leaving the court and going into the jury-room felt strange. They had used the room so many times before, but now they had come to make the decision, to give their verdict, to condemn a man to prison or to set him free. All twelve of them, without exception, felt the burden heavy on their shoulders.

They didn't all agree on all the counts the first time, which meant that they all had to spend the night in a hotel, closed off from their homes and families—twelve special people with an enormous responsibility.

A table had been set aside for them in the hotel restaurant and they ate together, but afterwards they were free, within limits, to do as they liked. Four of them began to play cards, others went to their rooms, and some to the bar. Paris and Will were among the latter, but they sat in a corner, apart from the others, who gave them indulgent looks.

The kisses they had exchanged had got hotter over the past weeks, and both of them were experiencing deep frustration, which was heightened by sitting next to each other every day in court and having to pretend that there was nothing between them. Their hands, hidden by the bench in front of them, had often touched, their knees brushed and not always by accident, but they hadn't dared to look directly at one another in case they gave themselves away to the beady-eyed judge. This secretiveness had added spice to their romance, but now it was coming to an end.

Nothing had been said, but both of them were awaiting the end of the court case with eager, excited anticipation. It was as if they had tacitly agreed that a man's trial was an entirely wrong background against which to form a relationship, and that they couldn't take their affair further until it was over, until they were free of it. And now that time was almost here.

'Hopefully we'll reach a verdict tomorrow and we won't have to stay here over the weekend,' Will remarked. His eyes, darkening a little, rested on her face. 'So, if we're free, will you come away with me for the weekend?'

'Away?' Paris felt her colour heighten. 'Where—where to?'

Will gave a sudden, almost rueful grin. 'I haven't really thought that far. All I can think of is being with you,' he admitted. 'Where would you like to go?'

Her blush deepened at his admission, but Paris said, 'I don't know. In the country somewhere, I suppose. You said you could ride a horse; how about teaching me?'

'Definitely not,' Will said positively.

'Why not?'

'You might get bruised and stiff. I think we should do something very, very gentle—during the day.' His eyes met hers, smiling and suggestive, promising so much.

Her voice strangely husky, and somehow knowing that he would make a good lover, Paris said, 'So what do you recommend?'

'Painting, archery. Or why don't we just play it by ear?'

'All right.' Her voice shook a little. 'We'll do that, then.'

Reaching out, Will took her hand and raised it to his lips. 'Thank you, my darling.'

It was quite late on Friday afternoon before the jury finally reached a verdict. Paris gave an inner sigh of relief when it was decided at last. All day she had been on ten-terhooks in case they lost their weekend together. Will, she knew, had felt the same. Their eyes had often met in exasperation and impatience; to them the verdict was cut and dried and it had been frustrating, to say the least, waiting for everyone else to agree.

They filed back into court, the judge came in and they were asked if they had reached a verdict. The foreman replied that they had and the prisoner stood up. He was a little pale, Paris saw, but there was still a jauntiness in his shoulders, the charming smile clung to his lips, and it came to her that he had the inescapable belief that they would acquit him.

When the verdicts were read out Ramsay changed completely. For a few moments he just stared as if he couldn't believe his ears. Then he shouted, 'No!' and grasped the front of the box.

The policemen on either side of him quietened him as the judge gave sentence. 'You are an evil and sadistic man, entirely unable to control your emotions, and your vindictiveness finally led to murder. I sentence you to life imprisonment.'

'No!' the prisoner shouted again. His face convulsed with fury. The boyish charm disappeared and his inherent cruelty was plain to see as he shouted, 'I'll get you for this. All of you!' His frenzied eyes swept round the court. 'Every last one of you.' His finger stabbed out like a stiletto blade at the judge, the officials and then the jury. 'Curse you, you filthy swine. I'll make you pay. I'll cut your throats. I'll make you beg to die.'

He went on swearing and screaming insults as the guards tried to overpower him and eventually managed to drag him out of the dock and down out of the court. When they'd gone and the door had banged after him, there was a terrible silence, everyone too shocked by Ramsay's hatred and venom to move or speak. It was the judge who broke it.

Wryly, speaking from long experience, he said, 'You must take no notice of his threats. You have done your duty and I will make it my concern to see that you are all exempted from further jury service for the next ten years. Thank you for your services. You may now leave the court.'

They did so numbly, as did everyone else: the judge, the barristers and clerks, the public up in the gallery, their ears still ringing with the curses that had been hurled at them.

Will collected his car from a nearby car park and drove Paris to her flat where she packed some clothes for the weekend, then to his place where he threw some things into a bag. Within an hour they were on the road and heading out of London, away from the court and the evils they'd had to listen to for the past month or so, away from the threats and curses that had shattered their peace.

It was quite late before they reached the country hotel where Will had booked a room for the weekend. There was no time even to look around; they were shown to their room and Paris took the bathroom first, showering and changing quickly. Then it was Will's turn, and immediately he was ready they went down to the dining-room for dinner.

Here, at last, they were able to relax, to enjoy a meal after having had little to eat all day, to drink a bottle of wine which helped to dispel the slight embarrassment that had been forced on them when they'd had to rush to change in each other's presence but when they weren't intimate enough for that yet. The meal also helped to ease the tension that Noel Ramsay's outburst had caused. As Will said, they had more pleasant things to think about.

Looking into his eyes, so warm and expressive, Paris felt her heart miss a beat then fill with the excitement of anticipation, an emotion mirrored in his gaze. 'What things?' she asked, being deliberately provocative.

He gave a slow smile. 'Do you really want me to tell you here and now?'

Again her heart leaped. 'Yes,' she said on an unsteady note.

'All right.' Taking her hand, he lifted it to his lips and kissed her fingers one by one. 'We could think of how I'm going to very slowly take off all your clothes and look at you and then tell you how beautiful you are. And about the way I'm going to carry on kissing you like this until there won't be a part of your body that I haven't touched and loved. And of how—'

Paris hastily reached out and put her fingers against his lips, silencing him. 'Don't,' she breathed, her eyes wide with awareness, her cheeks flushed. 'You mustn't.'

'Oh, but I must tell you how lovely you are, my darling.'

'No, I meant…'

'What? What did you mean?'

Her colour deepened and she looked suddenly shy. 'I meant that you mustn't make me feel this way—not here, in public.'

His grip on her hand tightened a little. 'Tell me how I make you feel.'

She hesitated, then said, 'So—wanton.'

Will smiled, the pleasure at her answer deep in his eyes. But he said warmly, 'And wanted too, my lovely one. You know that.'

'Yes.' Not trying to hide the desire she felt, she said, 'I feel that way too.' And, lowering her free hand below the table, she placed it on his thigh.

He gave a small gasp, her gesture completely unexpected, but then he laughed softly. 'Now who's turning who on?' Putting his hand over hers, he pressed it against himself, then said on a note of strong urgency, 'Let's go to bed.'

Paris gave him a demure look. 'You haven't finished your coffee.'

'To hell with the coffee,' he said emphatically.

His vehemence increased Paris's excitement; for someone who had been content to take things slowly up to now, he was showing a gratifying eagerness. Slipping her hand from under his, she picked up her own coffee-cup. 'Really?

I'm quite thirsty,' she said teasingly. And she took a deliberately casual drink.

An answering gleam came into Will's eyes and he looked around as if searching for a waiter. 'You'll probably want another cup, then. And perhaps a liqueur. And then we might as well have—'

He broke off as Paris put her hand on his arm. She looked at him for a moment, then shook her head. 'No,' she said softly but with firmness. 'I want you to take me to bed.'

Will's grey eyes filled with warmth and desire. He didn't ask if she was sure, didn't fuss; he merely stood up and drew her to her feet with him. They said goodnight to the waiter and he tucked her arm in his, keeping hold of her hand as they walked across to the stairs and up to their room.

He had said what he wanted to do, what he intended to do, and he did start by undressing her slowly, murmuring words of pleasure at her beauty, his lips caressing her skin as he did so. But Paris was shaking with awareness, her breath coming in unsteady gasps that caught in her throat, her hands gripping his shoulders as he bent before her to take off her stockings.

Her pleasure and anticipation were an aphrodisiac too powerful for him to resist; Will's own breathing quickened and he stood to kiss her fiercely, saying her name over and over against her lips. 'Paris. Oh, Paris. I want you! Oh, God, I want you.'

The rest of her clothes came off fast, Will's soon joining the scattered heap on the floor. And then she was lying in the bed and there was no time to look, no time for endearments. She was reaching out to him, her body opening for him eagerly.

The next moment he was over her, taking her with overwhelming passion, lifting her towards the thrust of his body, and groaning out his climactic pleasure. He carried her with him, lifting her to spiralling excitement, to gasping, crying physical fulfilment, and then into the long aftermath of exhausted peace.

Earlier Will had ordered a bottle of champagne to be sent up to the room. It stood resplendent in its ice-bucket, but they hadn't even noticed it. When they'd recovered a little, when Will had kissed her lingeringly and told her how wonderful she was, he noticed the wine and laughed ruefully. 'The champagne was supposed to come before, not after.'

'Were you going to seduce me with it?' Paris asked, kissing his shoulder.

'It was in case we needed it,' he admitted.

'Idiot.' She licked his tiny nipple and was amazed to see it harden.

'Hey,' he said, bending to kiss her eyes. 'Have mercy.'

She laughed and reached up to caress his cheek with the back of her fingers. 'I'm glad we didn't have a big seduction scene. It was so good as it was.'

'And will be again, I hope.'

'Oh, I *know* it will,' she said, so emphatically that Will laughed.

'You're an amazing girl, you know that?'

'Why, thank you, kind sir.' She sat up and pulled the sheet up over her breasts. 'Why don't you open the champagne now?'

'Not if you're going to cover yourself like that,' Will said positively. Reaching over, he jerked the sheet from her hold and pulled it down again. 'This, my darling, is no time for prudery. And besides,' he added, his voice thickening, 'you're much too gorgeous to hide yourself away.'

Kneeling up, he cupped her breasts in his hands, his mouth slowly parting with concentration and growing concupiscence as he watched the rose hue of the areolae darken and the nipples thrust against his exploring fingers. 'Look how beautiful you are,' he murmured thickly, his eyes wide with reawakened desire. 'Can you wonder that I can't resist you? Look. Look for yourself.'

Slowly, with almost reluctant shyness, Paris lowered her eyes to look at her breasts. His hands, his skin dark against the whiteness of hers, held her tenderly. Her breasts had the firm elasticity of youth, were still small and perfect, and yet they seemed to fill his hands, to fit them perfectly.

As she watched, fascinated now, he moved his thumbs to circle gently the tender area around her nipples, touching nerve-ends, sending fires of frustration deep into her body. She had heard of eroticism, knew that these were among the most sensitive parts of her womanhood, but she had never known such sensual delight as she felt now.

To watch him toying with her, to feel the growing need inside her, to let her panting breath become a long groan of frustration, and to know from the tension in his hands and the sweat on his skin that Will felt the same way was the most exquisitely sexy moment she had ever known.

Still kneeling, as if in adoration, Will bent to kiss her breasts, sending shock waves of sensuality pulsing through her. Throwing back her head, Paris let out a low, animal moan of tormented pleasure. Coming up on her own knees, she held his head against her, crying out with the wonder of it.

Will at last lifted his head and looked at her, his breath an unsteady, panting groan of almost uncontrolled expectation. Paris's face was flushed with heat, her mouth parted and her lips trembling, her eyes great green pools of eager desire.

'Paris.'

He said her name again on a note of wonder but she mistook it for a question and said, 'Yes. Oh, yes, yes!'

Putting his hands on her hips, he drew her towards him, onto his lap, onto his manhood. She let out a great cry and put her arms round him, wanting to be closer and yet closer still, wanting to be a part of him, to take the intense pleasure he gave her and to give in return.

Afterwards they slept exhaustedly, tangled in the sheets, their arms around one another. During the night Will woke her with kisses and they made love again, so that it wasn't until the morning that they finally got round to opening the champagne and had it with breakfast instead.

CHAPTER TWO

PARIS and Will returned to London on Sunday evening, parting reluctantly outside her flat. Their weekend of love, of satiated sexuality was still in the glow in her eyes, in her flushed cheeks. Emma saw it and recognised it at once.

Her finely arched brows rose. 'Don't tell me you've been considering your verdict all this time?'

'No, we reached a decision on Friday. I've—er—been away.'

'With a man, obviously.'

'Yes,' Paris admitted, unable to keep from smiling.

Emma looked amused. 'So what was the verdict?'

'Guilty on all counts.'

'I meant on the man.'

'Oh.' Paris glowed. 'Marvellous! Fantastic! *Incredible.*'

'Good heavens! This man I've got to meet.'

There was a slight edge to Emma's voice, but Paris was too happy to notice it. 'And I want you to meet him; I'm sure you'll like each other,' she said with happy optimism.

She was still happy the next day when she went back to the office, eager to resume her interrupted career. Will was due to work out at the gym that evening and she had lots of chores to catch up on, so they'd agreed not to meet, but they might just as well have done because they spent ages on the phone, already missing each other, whispering words of intimacy that tantalised them both.

The next evening Will came to collect her and she introduced him to Emma, confident that they would like each other. Emma was friendly enough—very friendly really, making Will welcome and telling him, with that amused

33

little smile she had, how Paris had described him. 'So of course I've been really looking forward to meeting a man with all these incredible attributes,' she finished.

But Will only gave her a polite smile that didn't reach his eyes, refused a drink and asked Paris if she was ready to leave.

'What did you tell her about me?' he asked as soon as they were outside.

'Only that I thought you were wonderful,' Paris admitted. 'I didn't go into details, if that's what you're thinking.'

'She certainly made it sound as if you had.'

'Emma was probably teasing you. I wouldn't tell anyone. You should know that.' She put her arm through his and lifted a glowing face. 'It's very, very special to me.'

Will smiled at that and kissed her, so she knew it was all right, but it was obvious that he didn't like Emma.

They didn't go out, instead spending the evening at his flat. Even though they had spent most of the previous weekend making love, it was still novel, still overwhelmingly exciting. Paris felt no shyness now as she undressed Will, doing it slowly, touching and kissing him, running her hands over his broad, smooth chest, along the muscles in his upper arms, so powerful, so male.

His waist was slim and his stomach had the tautness of an athlete's even when relaxed. But it tightened even more under her exploring fingers; she could feel the tension running through his body, the slow dew of expectation on his skin, hear the quickened beat of his heart. Paris let her hands move on in their exploration, stroking, caressing, until his arousal was complete and Will groaned with pleasure.

He would have taken her in his arms then, but she made him sit on a chair and watch as she took off her own clothes, doing so as coquettishly as she could imagine, watching with growing excitement as he gripped the edge of the chair until his knuckles showed white and he strove to control his need for her, then giving a cry of delight when he could stand it no longer and surged up to grab her and carry her to the bed in one long, eager stride.

Later, Will dragged himself from the bed, dressed, and went out for a Chinese take-away, which took a long time to eat because they kept stopping to kiss and, as Paris was wearing only a bathrobe, quite a lot of caressing went on as well. So it was inevitable that they just pushed the plates away and made love all over again.

Paris was on cloud nine hundred and ninety-nine, but they became rain clouds only a few days later. It was at work that things started to go wrong. During her time with the company Paris had worked hard to find new markets for their products and there were three new accounts that she was particularly proud to have won, having spent a great deal of time and effort in acquiring them.

They were, of course, among the accounts that Emma had been watching over for her during the trial, but when Paris went to contact the companies to tell them that she was back she was informed that they preferred to deal with Emma in future.

When Paris questioned her, Emma was most apologetic. 'Oh, dear, did they really say that? I kept in contact with them as you asked and I *was* able to help them over some queries they had. In fact I had to visit all three of the companies to sort out the problems.'

'Problems? There weren't any problems.'

'Well, they must have cropped up recently,' Emma said with a vague wave of her hand. 'But luckily I knew everything about the network systems involved so I was able to reassure them quickly. I thought that was what you would have wanted, Paris.'

'Well, yes, of course, but—'

'Maybe they realised I was more experienced,' Emma

suggested. 'They're new accounts; perhaps it gave them more confidence to deal with someone older. Why don't you talk to the people involved, explain the situation?' she suggested. 'Although, of course, buyers do like to deal with just one person, not be messed around.' She gave a worried frown. 'We don't want to lose the accounts, do we? If we did, the sales director would definitely want to know why. But you must go ahead and explain things to them, of course.'

'No, as you said, we don't want to lose them,' Paris said slowly, reluctantly. 'As long as it isn't too much extra work for you.'

'Oh, I can cope,' Emma said with a smile. 'But what a disappointment for you. Still, maybe you won't care so much now you're dating Will; you'll be able to spend more time with him.'

There was that, of course, but Paris went back to her office feeling unhappy and frustrated. Not only were those three accounts the most prestigious that she had won, they were also the most lucrative, and as she was paid only a small basic salary and depended on bonuses to make up her money it meant a considerable drop in income.

If she had been able to go to the Brussels conference she might have generated some more work, but that too had gone to Emma, who, it seemed, had flown the company flag with some success. Paris tried not to be envious, but it was hard not to feel anger at a loss that was no fault of her own. That damn trial! But then she remembered that if it hadn't been for that she would never have met Will.

Her love affair, at least, was still going strongly. She and Will saw each other as often as possible and she often stayed overnight at his flat. The sex was just as good—better. He didn't seem as if he would ever have enough of her and delighted in her body, just as she gloried in giving him pleasure.

It wasn't only the sexual side of the relationship that was good; Will was terrific company and Paris loved just being with him. He had a great sense of the ridiculous, often making her laugh—sometimes even when she was trying to be serious. Life with Will was not only exciting but fun as well.

When they were apart her thoughts were full of him, and she would turn small things that happened to her into amusing anecdotes, anticipating with pleasure the way his eyes would fill with amusement as he laughed at them. Her feelings for him were growing ever deeper, far more so than anything she had ever experienced before, and she knew that she was in love.

Paris felt pretty confident that Will felt the same way about her, and she was staying with him so often that she thought he might ask her to move in with him. But they hadn't known each other very long yet so perhaps he felt it was too soon for that kind of commitment, because he didn't ask her.

Emma was still trying to be friendly with Will, even inviting him round to the flat to dinner, but Will still behaved distantly, maybe because Emma had coerced him into doing a few odd jobs around the place. She was pretty good at using people like that, putting on a 'helpless little woman' act to get people to do things for her, and would have used Paris the same way if Paris hadn't seen through the act and resisted, pointing out that they were supposed to share the chores.

A couple of months after the trial Paris went to a conference in Manchester for a few days. When she got back Emma regretfully told her that the rent on the flat had been increased quite substantially so she would, in turn, have to put Paris's share up, naming a much higher sum.

Paris looked at her with some dismay. 'But I can't possibly afford that much at the moment, Emma.' Worriedly, she pushed her hair back from her head. She had managed to find one new customer but the income no way made up for what she had lost.

'Well, I'm sorry, Paris. I wish I didn't have to ask you, but this is quite a luxurious flat, you know.'

'Yes, of course. I'll—I'll look round for somewhere else, then.'

'All right. I'll give you a month,' Emma offered.

Paris was taken aback; she hadn't expected to have to leave so soon, and for a moment felt a surge of resentment; it surely wouldn't have hurt Emma to let her take her time to find somewhere else? But Paris immediately felt ashamed; she had no idea of Emma's financial circumstances or what the total rent of the flat was. Maybe Emma had been subsidising her all this while, although she, Paris, had always paid her share of the rent promptly, as well as half the bills, which hadn't left a lot for herself.

That evening she developed a headache—a really bad one—and had to cancel her date with Will.

'You poor darling,' he said sympathetically. 'Would you like me to come round and stroke your brow?'

'Would that be all you would stroke?'

'Possibly not,' he admitted.

She chuckled but said, 'Maybe you'd better not, then.'

The headache got worse and, the following morning, was so bad that Emma had to drive them to work, and the elder girl advised her to see her doctor.

'Oh, no, I'm sure it will soon go,' Paris replied. 'I don't usually get headaches.'

'You're not pregnant, are you?' Emma asked, giving her a swift glance.

'No, definitely not.'

'OK. OK. I only asked.'

'Sorry, Emma,' Paris said contritely. 'But I am on the Pill; you know that.'

The headache went away eventually but a few days later she had another that was even worse. 'It sounds like a migraine to me,' someone told her, and so she went to the chemist and got some pills to try and relieve it, and they helped.

Out with Will one evening, he asked her to go to see a new film with him the following night, but she said, 'I'm sorry, I can't tomorrow.'

'Got another date?' he asked, raising his eyebrow. He was teasing; he was supremely confident that she wasn't interested in anyone else, as he had the right to be.

So he looked really surprised when she said, 'Sort of. I've arranged to go and look at a bedsit.'

His eyes settled on her face. 'Is Emma throwing you out?'

'No, but her rent has been put up and I can't afford my share any more, not after losing those three accounts. She's given me a month to find somewhere.'

'Generous of her,' Will commented wryly. He was silent for a moment, then said, 'Maybe it will be better if you do leave; I don't like you living with Emma.'

She always liked to think that her friends would get on well together and Paris felt a little disappointed. But the animosity seemed to be mutual because only recently Emma had commented rather acidly, 'Will may be incredible in bed, but his manners leave much to be desired. Still, if he suits you...' And she had given an eloquent shrug.

Paris had wanted to jump to Will's defence, but held her tongue; the two of them had taken a dislike to each other and that was that.

Looking at her now, Will gave a crooked smile—the one he used when he was teasing her. 'As a matter of fact I know of someone who's looking for a flatmate.'

Her heart skipped a beat, but she said, 'Really? Is it a nice flat?'

'Pretty good. All mod cons. Only, you might have to share a room.'

'I don't think I'd like that very much. How much is the rent?'

'Oh, I think you'd be able to afford the rent.'

'Well, I don't know. Who is this girl?'

'Girl?'

'The one who wants a flatmate.'

Leaning on his elbow, Will reached to take her hand, his grey eyes warm and mischievous. 'Who says it's a girl?'

Her eyes widened in mock innocence. 'You want me to share a room with some man?'

'Yes, please.'

She laughed, abandoning the demure look. 'When can I move in?'

'Would tomorrow do?'

Paris kissed the hand that held hers, her eyes alight with laughter and happiness. 'Tomorrow would be fine.' But then she felt compelled to add, 'So long as you're sure.'

'Of course I'm sure.'

'I wouldn't want you to feel pushed into it just because I can't afford to stay on with Emma.'

'Paris?'

'Yes?'

'Don't be silly.' And he leaned to kiss her on the mouth.

Moving in with Will was one of the most exciting times in Paris's life—having pretend arguments about wardrobe space, having him groan that he expected the bathroom to be festooned with drying underwear.

'I can dry it at the launderette,' she offered.

'Hell, no! I'm not going to have other men looking at that sexy black underwear of yours going round in the machine. I want to fantasise about it all by myself.'

She flung her arms round him, and kissed him exuberantly. 'God, I'm crazy about you, Will Brydon.'

'The feeling's mutual, ma'am.'

For the next couple of months everything was perfect, except that the wretched migraine attacks returned with painful frequency. But Paris was too happy to take much notice; she just pumped in headache pills until they went away.

She had to go to Europe a few times, once to a big convention in Prague where she was lucky enough to find two new accounts which put her more or less back on the income level she'd been on before. So she was able to insist on paying for all the food bills at the flat, although Will protested. But she felt happier paying her share.

She still saw Emma at work, of course, and they went out to lunch together on a regular basis, remaining friends but tacitly not discussing Will.

He and Paris were sharing their lives almost completely; Paris had taken him to meet each of her parents and their families, and both visits had been successful. In return Will took her to meet his elder brother, Mark, his only close relative since his parents had died some time ago. Mark, with his wife and two young children, lived in a village near Cambridge, where they invited Paris and Will to spend the weekend with them.

They set out from London around mid-morning; the day was fine and they were both in high spirits, Paris in particular looking forward to the trip. She wasn't at all nervous about meeting Will's relations; he'd told her a little about them, that they both had careers centred on Cambridge, and they sounded her kind of people.

The couple lived in an old, detached house, all stuccoed walls outside and beamed ceilings within, with an inglenook fireplace framed with a garland of dried hops. The walls of the downstairs sitting-room were rag-painted and

then stencilled with an intricate flower design, as were all
the cupboards in the traditional farmhouse kitchen. The
house looked like something out of a country-living-style
magazine and Paris fell for the place at once.

Mark was seven years older than Will, and his wife,
Annabel, looked to be about thirty. Their greeting was
friendly enough, but both of them seemed a bit distracted.
Mark, who was dressed in old jeans and a grease-stained
T-shirt, gave them each a drink and said, 'You'll have to
excuse me a minute; I was in the middle of cutting the
grass when the damn mower broke down. Perhaps you
could come and take a look at it, Will; you're better at
mechanical things than I am.'

Will caught Paris's eye, gave a slight wink, and the two
men went into the garden.

Annabel, dressed similarly to her husband, was kneeling
before a four-oven Aga, almost in an attitude of worship,
an anxious frown on her face as she looked at some cakes
she was cooking. There seemed to be a lot of small cakes
around, either cooling or waiting in trays to be cooked.

'Are you fond of cakes?' Paris asked curiously.

'What?' Annabel laughed and stood up. 'No, the village
is having an open day tomorrow and I offered to make
some cakes to sell with the teas. I think it's so important
when you live in the country to take an active part in
village life. Don't you?'

Paris had never thought about it, but it seemed that the
question was merely rhetorical because Annabel glanced
at her watch, gave an annoyed sigh, and said, 'Oh, Lord,
I was supposed to pick up the girls from their dancing class
ten minutes ago. And then I have to dash into town so that
Olivia can buy a present for a friend's birthday. The party
is this afternoon and she insists on choosing the present
herself. Which is good, of course, don't you think? Children should have the right of choice. We were supposed

to buy the present some time last week but somehow there was just too much happening.'

She knelt again at the Aga, took a batch of cakes out and put another lot in.

When she straightened, Paris knew what was coming but didn't volunteer. Annabel said, 'I know it's an awful cheek, but would you be an absolute angel and cook the rest of these cakes for me while I get the girls? I'm sorry to land it on you but it's one of those days.'

'I'm not very good at cooking and I've never used one of those cookers before,' Paris warned her.

'Oh, good heavens, you don't need any skill. Just have a look now and again to see if they're done. Thanks a million; I must fly.'

Annabel dashed upstairs, came down again ten minutes later wearing a smart town outfit, and ran outside to her car.

Those first few minutes seemed to set the tone for the whole weekend. Annabel rang on her personal phone about an hour later, full of apologies and asked Paris to start lunch for her. By the time she rushed in with her two daughters the lunch was ready and waiting; Will, having found out what was the matter with the mower and bought a new part from the local garden centre to fix it, was now mowing the large area of grass, and Mark was watering the plants in the greenhouse.

Paris thought that they'd relax over lunch but it seemed that the girls had to go to their violin lessons, arranged at an earlier time than usual because of the friend's birthday party, and they were already late.

'I'm sorry, I'll just have to rush,' Annabel said, and then, remembering, added, 'Oh, dear, I haven't shown you your room yet, have I? Never mind; Will knows where it is.'

It was a nice room, with views looking out on two sides

over the garden and meadows beyond. But the bed hadn't yet been made up and they had to search for sheets and things and do it themselves. The walls were marked out for another stencil effect but were only partly done and there were no curtains on the windows.

'How long have they lived here?' Paris asked.

'About six years,' Will said laconically.

Paris was surprised; she'd have thought that Annabel would have finished the decorating by now.

When Annabel and her daughters hurried home an hour or so later, Olivia went up to have a bath and change into her party clothes and Charlotte, the younger child, immediately began to make a big fuss because she hadn't been invited.

'Never mind, darling. We'll do something really special together instead,' Annabel soothed.

'What? What will we do?' Charlotte naturally wanted to know.

'I'll think of something,' Annabel said, almost curtly, and she went to the stairs to yell at Olivia to hurry up. But when she took Olivia to the party, Annabel must have got sidetracked because she didn't come back, so it was left to Paris to try and amuse the younger child, but as Paris had no experience and Charlotte was grumpy it didn't work too well. Charlotte kept going to the window to look for her mother and when she didn't come went up to her room, locked herself in, and wouldn't come out or answer when Paris spoke to her.

Will, meanwhile was helping Mark to unblock some gutters; or, at least, Will was up the ladder doing so while Mark, who was supposed to be holding it, kept wandering off to dig his overgrown vegetable patch or to answer the phone, although most of the callers seemed to want Annabel.

That evening some friends had been invited to dinner,

which Annabel cooked herself. She wasn't a bad cook, but, by the time she'd given the girls their pizzas, put them to bed, done the preparations for the meal, made half a dozen phone calls and got herself ready, it was very late before they sat down to eat, and almost three in the morning before the other guests left.

Curling tiredly up to Will, Paris said, 'Is it always like this?'

'Always,' he said resignedly.

The next day they were both roped in to help with the village open day, Paris helping Annabel in the tea tent and Will directing cars into the field being used as a car park, so they hardly saw one another. The main Sunday meal, to which Annabel liberally invited several neighbours, wasn't ready until eight in the evening, and Paris found herself doing most of the clearing up, as she had that morning because Annabel had been too tired to do it the night before.

It was midnight before they were able to drive back to London, Paris feeling more exhausted than she had when they'd arrived, and afraid that one of the blinding migraines was about to take over her head.

'Are you all right?' Will asked her when she grew silent. And when she admitted that her head ached he said angrily, 'I'm hardly surprised after the last two days. They don't have to live like that. They could well afford for Annabel not to work, but she insists on combining the roles of wife, mother, career woman and active villager. And tries to be perfect at everything but with the result that everything suffers.

'She's forever torn between her job, her home and her family, and most of the time the job comes first. After school and in the holidays the girls are looked after by a child-minder or are farmed out to various friends. And when Annabel *is* home she's always trying to decorate the

place in the latest fashion, or she's out at some village
organisation committee meeting.'

There was disgust in his voice as well as anger, but Paris
felt compelled to stand up for her sex and say, 'I'm sure
she's doing everything for the best.'

'That's just it; her intentions might be good but she
doesn't have the sense to see that she's achieving nothing.
Her family is suffering and so is she. She just cannot manage that lifestyle.'

'What does Mark think about it?' Paris asked guardedly.

Will shrugged. 'He's tried to persuade her to give up
her job but she won't. She says she won't be fulfilled if
she does.' The disgust was heavy again in his voice. 'If
she was so wrapped up in her career she shouldn't have
gone in for a family in the first place.'

'Rubbish!' Paris said shortly. 'A woman has every right
to have both a family and a career. Men do, don't they?
And thousands of women have children and *have* to go
out to work. Annabel isn't very organised, that's all.'

Will gave a sarcastic snort. 'She tries to be all things to
all people and it doesn't work. You saw that for yourself.
And, the way I see it, bringing up children should be a
full-time job; they need all the help, education and training
they can to get to face today's problems.

'There wouldn't be half the juvenile crime and adolescents with psychological problems if they'd got more attention at home. Most of them are thrust in front of the
television screen to keep them quiet when they're babies
and can work a video before they can talk. They become
latchkey kids as soon as they go to school, and live off
junk food for the rest of their lives.'

'Annabel cooks,' Paris protested.

'Yes, when she has a dinner party; the children don't
often join in, and the rest of the week the girls live on
stuff they take from the freezer and heat up in the micro-

wave themselves. And there's virtually no consistency in their lives; they're often up till past midnight, are lucky if they have any clean and ironed clothes to wear, and are always rushing around to everything at the last minute. You saw them, Paris. There's no peace in that household; they never relax.

'And because Annabel insists on living in that big old house Mark spends every weekend doing repairs or working in the garden. And she's volunteered him for so many organisations that the poor chap is hardly at home during the week.'

'So maybe they should give up a few things,' Paris admitted, but added firmly, 'But she still has the right to work as well as have a family. Her career probably means a lot to her.'

'Nonsense. People shouldn't have children unless they are fully prepared to commit themselves to bringing them up properly. And anyway, her job is no big deal. She works in the computer department of a company that specialises in agricultural research, that's all. Hardly an indispensable position. Mark's job is far more important—and more lucrative.'

It might not seem much to a man, but Paris could well understand how much Annabel's job must mean to her. She'd probably trained and worked hard for it; she ought to be able to keep it if she wanted to. And although their life was hectic none of the family had appeared to be really unhappy. Mark seemed a little harassed, perhaps, but Annabel was warmly hospitable and they seemed to have loads of friends.

So Paris said stiffly, 'Why is it that men always think that women can't hold down a career and have children? Is it because men are so selfish or because they're afraid of the opposition, I wonder? Do they feel threatened by women and feel the need to do them down any way they can?'

Will threw her a surprised glance. 'Don't tell me you're a feminist.'

'And why not?' Paris retorted. 'You're obviously dead against married women having a career.'

'I'm against mothers working when they don't have to,' he returned shortly. 'Especially Annabel. She just can't cope, and there's going to be some sort of crisis in that household before long. It's inevitable. Charlotte has already had to see a child counsellor. I ask you—a kid of seven!'

'You can't blame that on Annabel. Charlotte is probably highly strung or something.'

'Rubbish!' Will exclaimed. 'She needs a full-time mother. It's Annabel who is completely selfish. If she wanted a career then she shouldn't have had children in the first place. I blame Mark; he ought to put his foot down and insist that Annabel stay at home. I told him so, too.'

Paris gave a gasp of consternation. 'How can you possibly be so bigoted? What happens when the children leave school and go out to work themselves? Annabel will be really stuck at home then. She'll have lost years out of her career and will be lucky if she gets another job.'

'So she could do voluntary typing for a charity or something, if she feels the need,' Will said shortly.

'Voluntary work!' Paris said in appalled disgust. 'That would really be a challenge, wouldn't it? How very fulfilling. Something easy and unstressful for the little woman to do in the odd moments when she isn't waiting hand and foot on her husband!'

Hearing the sarcasm in her tone, Will said curtly, 'This is a futile argument, and purely hypothetical anyway, because I doubt if Annabel will ever be persuaded to give it up.'

'Then good for her,' Paris said vehemently. 'If Mark has any sense he should encourage her, not—' A piercing pain shot through her head and she broke off, suddenly realising that they were doing more than just arguing. Biting her lip, she leaned back in her seat and closed her eyes tightly.

'A migraine?' Will asked, glancing at her.

She nodded silently, wincing as she did so.

'You're getting too many of them. You must go and see your doctor first thing tomorrow.'

'It will go; there's nothing to make a fuss about.'

'Aren't I allowed to worry about you, then? Is advising you to see your doctor interfering in *your* career?' Will said on an acerbic note.

For a moment they were both silent, both shocked that they were quarrelling, then burst out together:

'I'm sorry; I didn't mean that.'

'I want you to worry about me; of course I do.'

Will gave a rueful sigh and put his hand over Paris's. 'It's been a dreadful weekend, hasn't it?'

'Exhausting,' she admitted.

'Please, darling, go and see your doctor about these headaches.'

'All right, I promise.'

Paris went, and when she found out the probable cause wished she'd gone earlier, because her doctor said, 'It's more than likely that the contraceptive pill you're taking doesn't agree with you. I'll put you on a different one and see if it helps. Finish off your current month's pills, though.'

Paris didn't see much point in doing that if it was the darn pills that were giving her the migraines, so left them off at once and started on the new ones. She felt a bit odd and unwell for a couple of weeks but the symptoms finally settled down and then she felt fine and the headaches seemed to clear like magic.

It was because of the change over from one lot of pills to another that at first she took no notice when her period failed to arrive. But when nothing happened the following month she began to get worried and could no longer dismiss it.

Emma, at lunch one day, noticed her preoccupation and asked her straight out what was the matter. Paris hesitated, then told her. 'It can't be anything disastrous, of course,' she added, confidence in her voice. 'I've been on either one pill or the other the whole time.'

'Well, you'd better make sure,' Emma said practically. 'Buy one of those do-it-yourself pregnancy test kits.'

Paris laughed. 'I'll be wasting my money.' But a few days later, when still nothing happened, she bought one anyway—and was stunned when it showed up positive. Sure that there must have been a mistake, she tried the second test in the kit, and nearly died when she got the same result. A visit to her doctor confirmed the catastrophic fact that she was pregnant.

Will was away at the time; he had gone with some friends to the South of France, to sail a yacht that one of them had bought back in England.

'Trust a man to be away and out of contact when you most need him,' Paris said to Emma rather shakily.

They were round at Emma's flat, Paris having gone round there in a highly emotional state, badly needing to talk to someone. Emma was alone, not yet having found anyone to take Paris's place, even though it had been several months since she'd moved out.

Emma looked at her for a moment, then said deliberately, 'Maybe it's just as well. You'll be able to think about it logically. Things tend to get uptight when men are around.'

'I hope Will will be pleased,' Paris said nervously. 'I'm not at all sure how he feels about children.'

Emma gave a laugh of astonishment. 'You're surely not going to tell him about this?'

Paris frowned. 'But I'll have to tell him.'

'Why? What has it got to do with him?'

'Emma! It has everything to do with Will, surely?'

'Did he ask you to get pregnant?'

'No, of course not. But—'

'Then why tell him? Did *you* intend to?'

'No, but—'

'Then I hope that you're not going to let a slip like this ruin your whole life.'

Paris stared at her. 'What are you talking about?'

'Why, a termination, of course. You surely aren't even considering keeping it?'

'Well, yes. It's a baby,' Paris said in consternation.

'Rubbish. It's just a fertilised egg, that's all. Something that has happened by accident, at entirely the wrong time in your life. And in Will's. And it's up to you to be sensible and put things right, not get all sentimental and mawkish.'

'I'm not. But it would be wrong to—'

'Do you want to ruin Will's life?' Emma cut in bluntly.

Paris looked at her in dismay. 'No, of course not. But would it really be so terrible? I—I haven't really had time to think it through yet.'

'Of course it would. You'd have to give up your job for a start.'

'Not necessarily. I could hire—'

'Of course you would,' Emma interrupted vehemently. 'I've seen other girls in your position who've tried to go it alone. It never works. The company took you on because you're a free agent, didn't they? So how can you go flying off all over Europe and, in time, all over the world when you're saddled with a baby?'

'It wouldn't be just me,' Paris protested. 'It would be Will's baby too, and he would help take care of it.' But even as she said the words Paris had a vivid memory of their quarrel about working mothers after that disastrous visit to Will's brother, and her voice trailed off.

Emma burst into laughter. 'Oh, Paris, you innocent. Haven't you learned anything about men? Everything is lovely with Will now; of course it is. He has a mistress who looks after him like a wife *and* who pays her way. What more could a man ask for, for heaven's sake?

'But if a baby came along all that would change. He'd be expected to stay home and do chores, to provide for you both, and to watch you become more interested in the child than in him. And you'd lose your figure and always be too tired to be any good at sex any more.'

'You don't paint a very pleasant picture,' Paris said shakily.

'But a true one, I assure you.'

'What about married couples? They have children. If they didn't the world would come to an end.'

'When a man asks a woman to marry him, it means he's ready to settle down, to take on that commitment.' Emma saw Paris's head go down and made a shrewd guess. 'And Will hasn't asked you to marry him, has he?'

Paris shrugged, shook her head. 'We haven't known each other long enough for that yet.'

'But if you have this baby you'll be forcing him to make that commitment—whether he likes it or not. Do you really want to force him into that?'

Frowning, Paris shook her head. 'No, but he has a right to know so that we can discuss the—the choices together.'

'Rubbish! If you do that, you're giving him no choice

at all. He'll think you're putting the onus on him, making him take the decision. The responsibility, then, will be his.

'Think about it; if he says to keep the baby he will have to support you both for the rest of your life. And if he says have an abortion then he'll always feel guilty—and you'll always blame him for it. Every time you row you'll throw it in his face until he can't take it any more and walks out.'

Paris's face had paled, but she said, 'But what if Will says keep it and we get married?'

Emma laughed rather scornfully. 'Then, again, every time you have a row he'll blame you for trapping him, and it will go on forever more—or until he decides to go and look for the freedom he lost and walks out on you anyway.'

Appalled at the prospect, Paris said faintly, 'A no-win situation.'

'I'm afraid so, my dear.'

Feeling as if she was fighting a battle, Paris said, 'But lots of people have been caught this way in the past and have survived, have had happy marriages.'

'Oh, yes, in the past, but not so much nowadays. And especially when the girl wants to keep her career, as I'm sure you do. Perhaps if you were willing to give up everything and just become Will's wife, the baby's mother…' Emma shrugged. 'If you'd be satisfied with that, then maybe it might work out.'

Paris stared at her, remembering how scathing Will had been about Annabel keeping on with her career. He'd said quite definitely then that people shouldn't have children unless they were willing to commit themselves entirely to their upbringing. She felt a chill settle on her heart; she wasn't ready to give everything up. Not yet. Not so soon. But if it meant keeping the baby…

Emma was saying, 'Really, Paris, I think you'd be acting in Will's best interests if you didn't tell him. Unless you make up your mind to keep the baby, of course. But I really can't see any reason to do so. It was just a mistake. Anyone must realise that. I mean, you were behaving very responsibly, and it wasn't your fault that this happened.'

Paris thought guiltily about how she hadn't followed her doctor's instructions to the letter, but said desperately, 'I *have* to keep it. I have to go through with it.'

Emma shrugged. 'Of course. If you've made up your mind to as good as finish your life now. But don't expect Will to stand by you.'

'But he will. You don't know him!' Paris said almost on a sob.

Coming to put her arms round her, Emma said with a sigh, 'I'm sorry, Paris, but it's a fact of life. There are some men who just don't want children, and I'm very much afraid Will is one of them. As soon as he finds out, things will change completely between you. He'll either leave, or if he stays it will be out of a sense of duty. Is that really what you want?'

Paris shook her head wordlessly, horrified more by the latter prospect than by anything else.

'It would be a great shame to spoil both your lives because of a silly little thing like this. Now wouldn't it?' Emma went on persuasively. 'It would be quite devastating for Will, I know. It always is for a man. And, as you said, you haven't known each other long enough yet. So why rush into making the biggest mistake of your life? You want to go on learning about each other, taking your time, letting your love develop. And this silly mistake could be all put right so easily and with so little fuss. It's so commonplace now. Will—no one—need ever know. I know a clinic where you could go. And I'd come with you if you liked, to hold your hand, make sure you're OK.'

Paris was very pale, her hands balled into tight fists.

'But what about the—the baby?' She found it very hard to say the word.

Emma stood and put her hands on her shoulders. 'You mustn't worry about that. It's nothing yet. Nothing at all. But, I beg of you, Paris, if you want to go on with Will as you were, then get this mistake, *which is no fault of yours*, out of the way, and get on with your lives. Will would want that, I'm sure. You *must* do it, for his sake. You do see that, don't you? Don't you?' she said more forcefully when Paris didn't answer.

Slowly, reluctantly, Paris nodded.

'That's very sensible of you. And I know Will would love you even more for it.' She smiled at Paris. 'Sometimes we women have to be very strong for the sake of the men we love, you know.'

The next few days were the worst that Paris had ever known. She was constantly torn first one way and then the other, couldn't sleep, couldn't eat, and definitely couldn't concentrate at work, especially with Emma there continuously pushing her to have a termination quickly.

Pleading illness, Paris stayed at home, hoping for quiet, but Emma was immediately on the phone, telling her to make up her mind, not to leave it a day longer, and she even came round in the evening, pushing, all the time pushing her to have the operation. And always emphasising that, one way or another, she would lose Will if she didn't.

He was still away, and Paris alternately longed for his return and was afraid that he might come back before she'd had the abortion. *If* she had it.

Paris pressed her hands against her head in distress, not knowing what to do. If only Will wasn't so fiercely anti working mothers; then she wouldn't have had any hesitation in keeping the baby. But she would be miserable if she didn't work, she just knew it. She needed the challenge of looking for new markets, needed the highs of success—what else had she been training for all these years, for heaven's sake? She was too young to give everything up, and a future of just staying at home for the next twenty years looked bleak indeed.

After another stress-filled night of gazing sleeplessly into the darkness, Paris felt really ill and half-crazy with indecision. She dragged herself out of bed, still not finally decided but coming closer to contemplating having the termination.

It went against her conscience, against her beliefs, but she felt that she must do it for Will's sake, not for her own. Her mind was filled with a terrible dread of forcing him into a marriage that he didn't want, of seeing their happiness fade into misery, and love into hate. If he loved her.

Paris knew that she loved him utterly, but he had never come right out and said that he loved her, although she had been sure that he did—before this, before Emma's arguments had completely undermined her confidence. She convinced herself that her first concern must be for Will, to protect him from her terrible mistake, but even as the thought filled her mind she had to stifle not only her own guilt but also the knowledge that she would do anything not to lose him.

That morning she phoned Emma and said painfully, 'I—I'm thinking of going to the clinic today. Will you come with me?'

But the older girl was busy and unable to make it. 'I'm dreadfully sorry, but I'm taking a training course this morning, and this afternoon there's a meeting I just have to go to,' Emma said with concern. 'Can't you go another time? But no, better not. You really should have it done as soon as possible.'

'Yes. Don't worry. I'll—I'll go alone.'

'Isn't there anyone else who—?'

'No. Goodbye, Emma.' Paris put the phone down and bit her knuckles hard, fighting back tears. She had said that she would go alone but she wasn't at all sure that she had the courage, or that she was indeed going to go through with it. If ever she had needed a friend it was now. Unable to stay in the flat, Paris put on her coat and went out for a long walk in the park, striding along, trying desperately to make up her mind.

She came upon a group of young women pushing their small children along in modern Baby Buggies. The women didn't look particularly well dressed but they all looked happy, content. And the babies looked so sweet.

Paris hadn't taken much notice of babies before, but as she came to the group, which had stopped to feed the ducks on the pond, she slowed and looked at them. One in particular caught her eye—a boy, she was sure, with such soft skin, a pretty little nose and great blue eyes that looked up at her so trustingly. Suddenly he gave her a toothless smile and Paris knew then that there was only one course open to her, that there had never really been a choice at all.

Quickly, smiling to herself with relief, she turned and strode towards the park entrance and home. She was going to phone Will, tell him without another moment's delay.

There were several teenage boys in the park riding their mountain bikes, racing each other, swerving round the trees and bushes. As she hurriedly rounded a bend in the path, almost running in her eagerness, she found one boy coming straight at her.

Paris gave a cry of warning and the boy swerved. But Paris had jumped to avoid him and had gone the same way. He cannoned into her and she lost her footing, falling down a steep grassy bank, rolling over and over until she came to a stop with a thud, face-on to a tree. The boy, frightened, cycled away fast.

Two women walking their dogs came to help her up, brushing at her coat, saying that the cyclists were a menace, asking if she was hurt. Paris didn't feel hurt—her coat had saved her as she'd rolled—but she'd hit the tree hard across her waist and hips.

The accident had shaken her, so she stood for a few minutes, leaning against the tree, until she felt recovered enough to leave the women and walk on. But as soon as she left the park Paris took a taxi home, and laid down on the bed to rest. It was less than an hour later that she started to bleed, and the choice that she'd so agonised over was no longer hers.

When Emma phoned the next day Paris was still in bed, feeling weak.

'How are you? Have you had it done?'

The questions brought back all the torments of the last few days and Paris's voice was heavy with distress as she said, 'It's gone. The baby's gone.'

'Was it very bad? Would you like me to come over?'

'No! Just leave me alone. And I don't want to talk about it, Emma. Do you understand? Never, ever mention it again.' And she put down the phone, cutting the other girl off.

Will came home a few days later, but she told him nothing of what she'd been through. He was so happy, so pleased to be home that there was no way she was going to spoil it.

A week after the miscarriage she felt physically much the same as ever. Mentally—it was different. Paris tried to put it out of her mind, but that was very difficult. She was consumed by guilt, sure that if she hadn't contemplated a termination she would never have lost the baby. OK, it was the fall that had actually caused it, but if she hadn't been so stressed out, felt so wretched, she wouldn't have been in the park in the first place. Paris blamed herself; she should have followed her conscience, not listened to Emma.

Even the inner knowledge that there was now no fear of losing Will gave her no comfort. Emma, seeing her dejection, advised her to forget the whole thing and received an angry flash from Paris's green eyes that made her hastily drop the subject.

At home with Will it was easier; he was so full of his holiday with his friends, so eager for her that she soon began to feel happier. Sometimes, though, she was a little withdrawn, but when Will asked her what was the matter she just shrugged it off and tried to be again the laughing, uncomplicated girl he wanted.

It was a few weeks later when Paris became aware that people at work were talking about her. When she walked into the ladies' room one day there were some girls there who immediately stopped talking when she came in and gave her strangely shocked looks. It was the same look that she had noticed on a couple of other people's faces recently but had ignored. She found, too, that some of the older members of the staff were no longer so friendly, while one or two of the men, conversely, became much too friendly.

One of them, with a reputation as a womaniser, came into her office when she was alone and shut the door. Paris was standing at a filing cabinet and turned, giving her usual bright smile until she saw who it was. 'What can I do for you?' she asked coolly.

'Ah, what couldn't you do for me? How about coming out for a drink with me tonight for a start?'

'No, thanks.'

'Why not? You might enjoy it.' And the man put his hand on her hip.

Paris swung round furiously, knocking his hand away. 'How dare you touch me? Get out of here, or I'll report you for sexual harassment.'

He laughed in her face. 'Who's going to believe you— with your reputation? Besides, it wouldn't look good on your record, would it? And we all know you'd do anything to keep your job, to further your career.'

'What are you talking about?' she demanded angrily.

'As if you didn't know,' he jeered. 'But you wouldn't have to worry if you were with me; I'd make sure you didn't get pregnant and have to get rid of it.'

She stared at him, for a moment too shocked to speak. But then she felt a surge of the most terrible anger that she had ever felt in her life, far too forceful for her to bother to deny his accusation. Filled by it, too over-whelmed to stop and think, she bit out, 'A wimp like you wouldn't have the balls to make anyone pregnant!' Then she strode to the door and jerked it open. 'Now get out of here, you creep.'

If looks could have killed she would have been anni-hilated. 'You'll pay for that, you slut,' he gritted. But at least he walked away.

Paris sat down at her desk and put her head in her hands. So that was what was wrong: they all thought she'd had an abortion. And there was only one way they could have found out. From Emma. Emma, who was supposed to be her friend.

But had she been such a friend? Paris remembered the way the older girl had taken over her special accounts and kept them for her own. Was that from jealousy, because Paris had started to get really successful and show that she had a bright future in the company? Had Emma been afraid for her own job? And then there was the way she had kicked Paris out of the flat. That too had been more the action of an enemy than a friend. And now this.

Paris sat there for some time, and in that time lost a lot of her trusting nature. She supposed that she could go round the office and tell them all the truth. But would they believe her? To hell with them all, she thought suddenly. I don't give a damn what they think. So long as I have Will then nothing else matters. She came out of her office with her head high, and it stayed that way.

But she knew that she would have to tell Will that night—tell him everything. But she was held up in the traffic getting home, then had to rush to change because they were going out to dinner with another couple, so there wasn't a chance. And the next morning she was jetting off early to Milan for another conference, so she reluctantly decided to leave it until she got back. This sort of confession would need more time; they would need to talk it through.

While she was away, Paris rang Will every day as she always did. The first couple of days were fine; he was as warm towards her as always, telling her about his day and how much he missed her. But the third time she called, and the day after that, all she got was her own voice on the answering machine. It could have been that she'd missed him, of course, but Paris had a sense of foreboding and couldn't wait to fly home.

He didn't meet her at the airport and the minute she walked into the flat she knew that her world was in ruins. Her cases, all her things, were standing piled in the hall. Will was sitting in the armchair in the lounge, waiting for her. He didn't get to his feet. His face was granite, his eyes like the coldest sea, as he said, his voice as cutting as a razor blade, 'Had another abortion while you were away?'

She flinched as if he really had cut her, and went very pale. 'No! I suppose Emma told you,' she said bitterly.

'Emma? I might have known she'd have something to do with it. No, I found out that you'd destroyed my child from some filthy swine from your office who sought me out in a pub. He knew it all,' Will said with tormented bitterness. 'And he knew that I didn't know a thing about it. He laughed in my face as he told me, enjoyed doing it.'

'I hope you knocked his head off,' Paris said in helpless rage. He didn't answer and she took a step towards him, her hands reaching out to him like a supplicant's. 'I didn't have an abortion. I—'

'Are you saying that you weren't pregnant?'

'No, but—'

'And are you pregnant now?'

'No,' she admitted wretchedly. 'But you don't—'

'No, I know you're not—none better.' His voice suddenly rose as he lost control of his anger. 'How could you? How could you even contemplate having an abortion? And don't insult me by saying you didn't.'

Guilt made her admit defensively, 'Well, yes, in a way. But only because of you. I thought you'd want me to and—'

'How *dare* you?' Will shouted the words at her, leaping to his feet, his face filled with ungovernable rage. 'How dare you say that you did it for my sake? How dare you presume to know what I want? If you think I'm the kind of man who would encourage—or even *allow* you to do something like this then you know nothing about me. Nothing!'

The last word came out explosively, his face rigid with rage and disgust, his hands balled into white-knuckled fists. Paris stared at him in appalled dismay, too stunned by his anger to defend herself, to try and explain.

Striding towards her, Will caught hold of her and propelled her towards the door. 'Get out of here! Get out of my life!'

'Will, no! Please.' She tried to cling to him, but he dragged her towards the door and pushed her outside it.

She was crying now but he took no notice, just picked up her things and dumped them down in the corridor beside her. She grabbed his arm and hung on to it desperately, as if by holding him she could make him understand, make him realise how much she needed him. But he shook her off, pushed her roughly against the wall, then went back into the flat and slammed the door shut behind him.

Paris tried hammering on the door and calling through the letter box but he took no notice, and he had bolted the door so she couldn't get in. She sat on the floor outside, sobbing uncontrollably, repeating his name over and over like a prayer.

The front door of the building opened and a taxi driver came in. He came up the stairs, hesitated when he saw her, checked the number of the flat and looked at her uncomfortably before saying, 'I've been told to come and take you to a hotel, miss.'

It was then that Paris knew that it was over. If Will was this determined to be rid of her then it was finished. She gave up then, painfully, achingly aware that by not telling him everything she had lost him for ever.

Somehow she dragged herself to her feet and, her breath still coming in heartbroken sobs, helped the driver carry her things to the taxi. Outside on the pavement she turned and looked up at the window of the flat. Will was there, watching. But he immediately turned away and she was left, her heart desolated, to get into the cab and let it drive her away.

CHAPTER THREE

Now the train thundered on through the night, a harsh background to the tormented memories that filled Paris's mind. The inspector had said that she would be able to shut herself away, but there was no comfort in that; it was inevitable that she and Will would cross paths however much she tried to avoid him—and he her, of course. And for the life of her Paris didn't know how to play it, what to do, what to say if they came face to face.

She sighed and tried to put it out of her mind, dozed a little, only to wake with a start of fear as she remembered the ordeal that lay ahead of her. It was before dawn when they got out of the train at a small, deserted station. Another car, or rather a van, was waiting. Paris had to climb in the windowless back and it was almost half an hour later that she was helped out, feeling cold and cramped.

She was standing in the open courtyard of a very large stone building that looked much too big to be just a house. The stone was weather-beaten and looked old, as did the very high wall that surrounded the courtyard. For an astonished moment Paris thought that they'd brought her to a prison, but then she saw a discreet notice near the double wooden doors of the building: 'The Castle Hotel'. Some hotel!

Lifting her eyes, she took in the turreted towers at each corner, the heavy shutters that could be drawn across the windows on its four floors. The air felt much colder than in London and when she looked round Paris could make out the snow-capped peaks of some distant hills just showing over the wall. Some instinct told her that she was in Scotland, and that it must have been quite far north for such a long journey.

'Let's go in,' the policewoman said, catching her arm.

The driver followed with her cases and they went into the castle-cum-hotel, the door opened for them by a burly-looking man in jeans and a loose knitted sweater. He obviously knew her escort because he nodded and stood aside to let them in. 'The last one?' he asked.

'Yes, that's the lot. They're all yours,' the driver said.

The man turned to Paris, who was feeling resentful at being treated like a parcel. 'I'm Captain Waters,' he told her. 'Mike Waters.'

'Captain?' Paris didn't think they had that rank in the police force.

'Army,' he explained. 'We're helping out. First I must tell you the rules. You must not, in any way, try to communicate with anyone outside. Not by phone, letter or any other means. Do you understand?'

'Yes, of course.'

The captain gave her an assessing look, then nodded. 'OK. I'll take you up to your room and then I'll show you round the place.'

'Are you in charge?'

He nodded. 'Together with a chief inspector in the police.'

Her room was on the third floor at the back of the building, looking out over a huge expanse of forest—but the serrated ranks of a man-made forest of fir trees, not the natural variety. They shouldn't have much difficulty in getting a Christmas tree, Paris thought cynically as she unpacked yet again.

Luckily the clothes she'd taken on her European trip had been mainly her smart business wear, so she'd had enough left in her wardrobe to bring clean things with her. But

they were mostly casual clothes—jeans and sweaters, together with a few dresses. A rueful smile came to her lips
as she hung them up; unfortunately the monthly fashion
glossies didn't give any advice on what one should pack
for an indefinite period under police protection.

When she went down into the entrance hall Mike Waters
was waiting for her. He took her round the ground floor,
into the galleried dining-room containing a dozen round
tables, where a couple of waiters were setting places for
breakfast.

'The staff here…?' she questioned.

'The place is always closed in the winter so most of the
staff have gone home. Those that have stayed all live in.
They have worked here for years and have been completely vetted. Some of our own men have taken the places
of those that have gone.'

'There seem to be an awful lot of people here,' she said,
counting the place settings and multiplying by the number
of tables.

'Several people have had to bring their family with
them; they couldn't say they were going away for
Christmas and leave their family behind, could they?'

Paris hadn't thought of that. It gave her some comfort
to think that she could probably hide among so many.

Captain Waters took her on to see the television-room,
the bar—a room tarted up with too much tartan—the
lounge, the ballroom, the card-room, and told her that there
was a pool and a gymnasium in the basement. There
seemed to be no end to the place. Again she was thankful;
if she saw Will coming she would easily be able to slip
away somewhere else. Maybe this situation wouldn't be as
bad as she'd feared.

It was, though. It was far worse than she could have
imagined.

It wasn't yet seven o'clock—too soon for all the 'guests'

to come down—but because of her long journey Paris was offered an early breakfast. She accepted with alacrity, not only because she was hungry, but so that she could eat and be out of the room before Will came down.

She helped herself to orange juice and a cheerful waiter brought her a plate of scrambled eggs on toast and a pot of steaming coffee. Paris sat down at a table near the window to eat, thinking that she'd never had a meal in such circumstances before.

At the far end of the room a door opened but she took no notice and didn't glance in that direction, thinking that it was one of the waiters. But then some instinct, some primitive awareness, made her look up.

Will was standing just inside the door, staring across the room at her. It was a very large room and they were at opposite ends of it, but she could see the tension in his body and face, the grim hardness of his jaw, the coldness in his eyes. For a long—eternally long—moment they stared at each other, the atmosphere becoming taut, electric. But then Will abruptly turned, pulled out a chair at a nearby table, and sat down in it, his back very deliberately turned towards her.

Paris looked blindly down at her plate and went to eat but found that her hands were shaking. Damn! Damn!

But why damn fate? she thought bitterly. She ought to be used to the tricks it was continually playing on her by now. Reaching out, she managed to pick up the cup of coffee and took a drink. It was hot—too hot, really—but it made her feel a degree better.

So Will was going to ignore her. That was the way he wanted to play it. Well, OK, that would probably make life easier, physically. But it would do nothing to relieve this terrible tension that still filled the room even though they were no longer staring at each other. It was like a tangible thing, so strong that when the waiter came in Paris expected him to have to fight his way through it, and was amazed when he just got calmly on with his work and then went out again.

Will was wearing a tracksuit and she guessed that he must have been either working out in the gym or jogging. Not that he'd jogged early in the day when they'd been living together, but then they'd had far more interesting things to do in the mornings. Biting her lip, Paris pushed that thought away, afraid that Will might read her mind.

She tried to eat her eggs and could only pick at them, her hunger gone, but pride demanded that she didn't just get up and walk away. She must sit it out, not let him think that seeing him had made her a trembling wreck.

Thankfully, a few more early risers came in—some adults and several young children. They greeted Will and looked at Paris with open curiosity. Under cover of the noise they made Paris was able hurriedly to finish her breakfast and leave, her going hopefully hidden by the arrival of more people.

She kept her face averted so didn't know whether Will saw her go, but then realised from her own relief at being out of the room that, if nothing else, he would probably be aware of the lack of tension. Not bothering to wait for the lift, she ran up the wide staircase to her room and threw herself down in the armchair. She should never have let the police persuade her into coming here. Any danger would have been better than this.

It was impossible not to think of Will. He was alone, so did that mean that he wasn't married? But maybe he was and it was just that his wife didn't jog. Or maybe they'd made love last night and she was too tired.

Fighting a fierce surge of jealousy towards this unknown woman, Paris gripped the arms of the chair in torment. The frustration after Will had left her had been dreadful; she had longed for him with a deep ache that time had done little to assuage. It had been almost as bad as the pain that filled her heart and the guilt that was a constant torment.

No matter that she hadn't actually had a termination; she had been persuaded to think of it—think seriously. For the millionth time she wished that she'd acted on her own instincts and never listened to Emma's poison. But she'd been so young and unsure of herself, so gullible. And finding herself pregnant had so shocked her that her emotions had been all over the place. But if only—

Paris realised what she was doing and forcibly turned her mind from the subject. She had taught herself not to dwell on the past, to turn her mind to other things. She had succeeded to a large extent, but that had been when Will had no longer been there. Now, after seeing him this morning, it was almost impossible.

Paris had been determined not to skulk away but to face up to her loss and to try and find new interests to take her mind off it. Those new interests also included new men, but there had been no one else, although Paris had had offers enough.

Sometimes it angered her that men found her so attractive; she gave them no encouragement, was open in her lack of interest, but had come to wonder if it wasn't that very lack that drew men to her. Perhaps they were piqued by her indifference, felt that to win her over would be a challenge. Or perhaps they were drawn by the air of mystery that her coolness created.

Either way, they were doomed to disappointment. However nice, however good-looking they were themselves, whatever they did to try to attract her, they withered away when they were unable to light a flame in her cool green eyes. Paris watched them go without regret; why settle for the commonplace when you had known the best?

There was the sound of laughter outside. Going to the

window, Paris opened it and looked out. Some children were playing in the courtyard. Well wrapped-up against the cold, they were playing a chasing game, their shrieks of excitement echoing back from the stone walls.

Paris watched them, wondering what her and Will's child would have been like. Would he have had Will's dark hair or have been red-headed like herself? It was always like this: whenever she saw a child she would start to wonder, to imagine. And in her imagination the child was always a boy. In her dreams too—those recurring dreams in which she and Will were still together, married, in their own house with a garden, and so wonderfully happy with their son. Then Paris would slowly, reluctantly awaken, to realise again what she had lost, and face again the eternal loneliness that was to be her punishment. With a sigh, she pulled the window shut and made herself go downstairs again.

A well-rounded middle-aged woman was walking through the hall from the dining-room as she came down the staircase. 'Hello.' The woman stopped. 'You must be the last member of our party. We were starting to get worried about you.' The woman spoke as if this were just an ordinary house party, as if being worried meant being concerned that Paris might not turn up, certainly not fearing that she might have been injured or even murdered.

'I've been away,' Paris explained. 'I only got back yesterday.'

'Well, I'm glad you got here safely.' The woman held out her hand. 'I'm Gwenda Paston, the judge's wife.'

Mrs Paston took Paris under her wing, taking her into the big lounge and introducing her to many people she didn't know and recalling several members of the jury to her memory. Paris sat down with a woman juror who was there with her husband—both broad Londoners—and soon the woman was gossiping away at full tilt.

It seemed that most of the people involved in the case had already been at the Castle Hotel for nearly ten days and had got to know one another. Amusements had been thought up to while away the time: bridge tournaments, talks on a whole variety of subjects and professions, craft lessons—making Christmas cards had been a very popular one, Paris was told.

'But surely you couldn't send them from here, could you?' she asked.

'No, they were all taken down to London and sent from there.'

Everyone seemed to be very blasé about their loss of liberty and the threat imposed by Noel Ramsay to their lives, but then they'd already had time to get used to it and to feel safe amongst so many others. They'd had more time, too, to prepare themselves to come here and had brought their hobbies and other projects to work on: several women were doing some kind of needlework, a man sat in a corner patiently cataloguing his stamp collection, another was doing marquetry.

But mostly people sat around and chatted, enjoying getting to know one another better, which Paris found to be an advantage when she so casually said, 'Are all the jury members here with their wives and husbands?'

'Most of us, although there are one or two single people. One man is divorced now, and then there's Will Brydon— he's alone. You must remember him—didn't you used to have your lunch together when the trial was on?'

'Why, yes, I think I do remember,' Paris said, and added offhandedly, 'He's still single, is he?'

'It seems so, although he's got quite friendly with one of the witnesses this last week. One of the girls Ramsay used to go with.' The woman chuckled. 'Although I doubt whether Will Brydon will go on being so friendly when he sees that you've arrived.'

It was meant as a compliment, Paris knew, and she smiled her thanks as she wondered just how 'friendly' Will had become with the other girl. It was to her own advantage, of course: it would keep him busy, make it less likely for them to bump into each other. But even though she told herself this very firmly Paris couldn't avoid the stab of pain that pierced her heart.

'How about you, dearie?' the woman asked. 'Are you still single?'

'Oh, yes.' Paris smiled, but suddenly saw a way that she could protect herself a little. 'Although I do have a close friend,' she added impulsively, banking on the woman being such a gossip that this titbit of information would soon go the rounds and reach Will's ears.

They were joined by some other people and Paris made sure that she stayed with them through lunch, and afterwards went with them to watch a video film in the television-room. Later, however, the group broke up, most of them going up to their rooms to prepare for dinner, which Paris was told was served early, at seven o'clock.

There was a small crowd of people waiting for the lifts so Paris opted for the stairs. She was crossing the landing to go up the second flight when she met Will coming down the opposite way.

She kept her head down, was ready to walk past without looking at him, but he slowed, then said, his voice reluctant, 'Paris?'

Her hand gripping the wide banister rail tightly, she raised her eyes to look at him. At first she thought he looked no different, but then she saw that the three years had changed him. His cheeks were thinner, and his left eyebrow—the one that had had the humorous quirk—now seemed to have a cynical lift to it. His mouth, too, had a little twist at the corner, making him look as if he regarded the world with some derision, found it wanting. But his thick dark hair was the same, and she recognised the coldness in his eyes, even though she had only ever seen it there twice before: this morning—and on the night he had thrown her out of his life.

'Hello, Will.' She tried to speak calmly, to let no emotion show, but the words came out on an unsteady breath.

'Strange circumstances to meet in,' he commented. He was looking her over, taking in her tall, slim figure, her shoulder-length red hair, and the attractiveness of her face, dominated by her green eyes. Once there would have been admiration in his gaze; now his features were a stony mask.

'Yes, aren't they?'

There was a pause which grew heavy. Paris went to move on, but then Will said, 'Why did you take so long to get here?'

'I was away. Working.'

'Ah, yes, your precious job,' he said on a sardonic note. 'I suppose you're still with that company?'

'Yes, I still work for them,' she answered. There was a story to that—one that concerned him in a way, she supposed—but Paris wasn't about to tell him.

Will gave a mocking grin. 'And I suppose you're their blue-eyed girl, the leading light of the sales department by now?'

'I have my own team and my own area, yes,' she admitted, her chin coming up a little at his tone.

'Somehow I just knew you would have.' The contempt in his voice was more open now. 'After all, it always was the most important thing in your life, wasn't it?'

Will's face had hardened and his eyes were narrowed in scarcely suppressed scorn. After seeing him at breakfast Paris knew that there was still tension between them, but it still came as a shock to see how deeply he still cared about what had happened.

Picking her words, she said, 'It is *now*, yes.'

By saying it that way she wanted to let him know that he had once been the most important thing in her life, that there had been nothing but work since they had split up. A stupid thing to do, perhaps, in the face of his sarcasm, and probably much too subtle, although people who had been close could often read hidden messages in a tone of voice.

Again she was surprised by the look of incredible scorn that filled Will's eyes. 'Well, at least you don't pretend any more,' he said scathingly.

'Pretend?' She frowned in puzzlement.

'That this new man in your life means more to you than your damn job.'

Hell! She'd forgotten that invention. It must have got back to Will with the speed of light. Straight from the woman she'd confided in probably.

Before she could find anything to say, Will said sharply, 'Who is this man?'

'No one.'

He gave a harsh laugh. 'Well, at least that's honest enough. What do you do—use him for sex when you're not away drumming up business for the first love of your life, the company?'

Paris flushed. 'I meant that he's no one you know.' His contempt sparked a flame of anger. 'And just what do you think gives you the right to be so damn rude?'

He suddenly lunged across the landing and caught her wrist. 'I have every right,' he said fiercely. 'You of all people should know that.'

She stared into his face and her anger fled. She wanted to ask him why it still mattered so much, whether it was because *she* still mattered, but was afraid of what he would say, that he would misunderstand her question. Devastated by his vehemence, she could only say in a husky, unsteady voice, 'Let me go, Will.'

The grip on her wrist tightened and for a moment his eyes threatened her, but then he stood back, dropping her arm. 'Sure.' His lips curled in disdain. 'Why the hell should I care if you louse up some other man's life?'

Turning away, he went quickly on down the stairs. Paris, stunned by that last, so very revealing remark, stood for a moment before taking a deep breath, then ran up towards her room.

It seemed to be her day for bumping into people on the landings. At the next one she literally bumped into another man—not so young as Will, and a stranger this time. She had been glancing down to watch Will as he reached and crossed the hall and hadn't noticed him.

'Oh! I'm sorry,' she exclaimed.

'My fault.' The stranger, of average height and with a pleasantly open face, put out an arm to steady her. 'No harm done, I hope?' he asked with an easy smile.

'No, of course not.'

Paris went to move round him but he said, 'You must be our late arrival, the missing member of the jury. Miss— Reid, isn't it?'

'Yes, that's right. Paris Reid.'

He didn't make the usual comment on the singularity of her name—which was a plus—instead saying, 'We were beginning to wonder if Ramsay had got to you before the police found you.'

'Oh, no. I've been away on business.' She hesitated, but the man seemed in no hurry to move on so she said, 'I'm sorry, I don't know who you are.'

'Ben Lucas.' He shook her hand. 'You probably don't recognise me because the last time we met I was wearing a wig.'

'A wig?' She looked in puzzlement at his full head of fair hair, then her brow cleared and she laughed. 'Oh, you mean you're a barrister. The wig-and-gown-type wig.'

'That's right.'

'Were you for the defence or the prosecution?'

'One of the barristers for the prosecution, I'm afraid.'

'Oh.' Paris's face clouded. 'So it was your colleague who was killed.'

'Yes, I'm afraid so, poor chap.'

The hotel-like atmosphere of the place and seeing Will again had driven the reason for their being here from Paris's mind. Now, realising in just how much danger Ben Lucas must have stood brought it back again and she gave a small shiver.

Ben saw it and recognised the cause. 'Look, there's plenty of time before dinner; how about a drink?'

'The bar won't be open yet, will it?'

'No, but I've got a bottle of very good whisky in my suite.'

'Suite?'

'Yes. Judge Paston and I were the first here so we got the choice of rooms. Come and see. I'm in one of the turrets.'

Paris hesitated for a moment, but after that encounter with Will she could do with a drink, and Ben seemed harmless enough. So she smiled, nodded, and went with him. They went up the stairs to her own floor, along the corridor and up another short flight set at an angle, then he unlocked a door in a thick round wall.

His suite was on two floors, the sitting-room on the lower, with a stone spiral stair in the thickness of the wall leading up to the room above. It was all most sumptuously furnished, the comfortable-looking sofa and two armchairs being upholstered in a soft green tartan. There was a music centre, television, bar and, best of all, a log fire blazing in the open hearth.

'Wow!' Paris looked round admiringly. 'This was worth getting here first for.'

Ben went over to the bar. 'Will Scotch do?'

'Please. On the rocks.' She sat in one of the armchairs and he brought the drink over to her, then sat on the sofa. 'I haven't seen you around today, have I?'

'No.' He gestured towards a desk on which there was a laptop computer and piles of folders. 'I've been working. I've too much on to be idle.'

'How do you get it in and out?'

'The police take it for me.'

'I wonder if they'd do that for me?' she mused. 'It's really frustrating not to be able to use the phone.'

'It has its advantages; at least you can work in peace and quiet.'

'Yes, I suppose there is that.' The whisky felt good in her throat. She gestured with the glass. 'Double malt?'

Ben nodded. 'The best.'

'We're in Scotland, aren't we?'

'It's better not to guess.'

She gave a small smile because he hadn't denied it, then said pensively, 'It will be the strangest Christmas I've ever had.'

'For all of us. But we shouldn't be lonely among so many—even if we have had to leave people we care about behind.'

Paris was immediately sympathetic. Ben must be in his forties, she guessed, and would probably have a family. 'Are you missing someone you care about?'

'No, I wasn't referring to myself—I'm a free agent. I was thinking of you.'

'Me?' She looked at him in surprise, wondering how, if

he'd been here in his rooms all day, he could possibly have got to hear about her non-existent lover.

As if guessing her thoughts, Ben said, 'I'm afraid I overheard you talking to Will Brydon on the stairs. I thought I'd better not interrupt so I waited until you'd finished. You seem to have known him rather well.'

A tactful way of putting it, Paris thought. Momentarily she was angry that he had listened, but then gave a mental shrug; it was too late now, and what did it matter anyway? She said shortly, 'We were—we lived together for some time after the trial.'

'I see.'

'Do you?'

'I think so. You split up and now you've got someone else, but Brydon is still jealous.'

'Is that how it seemed to you?'

'Is that how it was?'

She raised an eyebrow. 'That sounds like a barrister's question.'

'Sorry.'

Swallowing her drink, Paris stood up and walked over to set her glass on the bar. 'Thanks for the whisky. I must go; I want to get ready for dinner.'

'Of course. I'll see you on your way.'

'I'm sure I can find it.'

But he insisted on coming with her. It would be just her luck, Paris though wryly, for Will to come along and find her coming out of Ben's room. But when Ben opened the door and led her out to the corridor it was empty; there was just a girl of about Paris's own age who was about to descend the far stairs.

Perhaps attracted by their voices, the girl glanced back. She was shorter than Paris, with a more curvy figure and curly dark hair. She hesitated for a moment as she glanced back at them, then went on her way.

Paris recognised her at once from the trial; she had been one of the witnesses for the prosecution—one of Ramsay's ex-girlfriends. Her name was Melanie Truscott—and something in the way she had looked at them made Paris instinctively aware that this was the girl whom Will had become friendly with. Turning to Ben, she saw the confirmation in his eyes, but still said, 'Her—and Will?'

He nodded. 'It would appear so.'

CHAPTER FOUR

PARIS went down to dinner at what she thought was the last minute, but she was still there before Will. He came in from the bar with Melanie Truscott and another couple when the first course had already started to be served, and the four sat together.

Glancing at them surreptitiously, Paris wondered just what Will saw in the other girl. Perhaps it was her availability; she had admitted to several affairs at the trial. Trying to recall the details, Paris remembered that the defence had tried to make out that the murder had been a crime of passion, caused by Ramsay finding out that Melanie had been unfaithful.

Surely Will couldn't be attracted to that kind of girl? Paris thought in amazement. He couldn't be that hard up. But then she bit her lip hard; it was none of her business whom he went with—not any more.

'Are you feeling unwell?'

The question came from a woman sitting on her left. Paris blinked and pulled herself back to the present. 'No, I'm fine, thank you.' She smiled. 'It's just that I was travelling nearly all last night and the day before and my lack of sleep is catching up with me.'

She used the same excuse to go straight to her room after dinner, but sat on the bed and watched television for some time before finally turning out the light and trying to sleep. After an hour of tormented wakefulness, Paris knew that there was no way she was going to sleep naturally, so took a couple of pills that put her out within minutes.

* * *

The next morning she woke feeling woolly-headed, as she always did after taking sleeping pills, but she managed to avoid Will that day, spending the morning writing Christmas cards—thoughtfully provided by the authorities—and the afternoon working out in the gym and swimming in the pool. The exercise made her feel much better, and she went up to her room to change for dinner with a far lighter step.

While she was changing the phone rang.

Paris stared at it; having been told not to use the phone she hadn't expected anyone to be able to call her. Tentatively she picked up the receiver. 'Yes?'

'Paris? This is Ben Lucas.'

She gave an inner laugh of rueful amusement at her own stupidity; she should have realised that this was also an internal phone. 'Hello, Ben.'

'Would you care to have a drink with me before dinner?'

'The malt hasn't run out yet, then?'

'No, but I thought maybe you'd prefer a drink in the bar.'

Paris hesitated, wondering why he'd suggested the bar. Was it, in the circumstances of their confinement, the equivalent of asking her for a date? So did she want to have a date with him, be seen with him by everyone else? And by everyone else, of course, she really meant Will. What would he think? And would he care when he was with the curvy Melanie? The thoughts raced through her mind, but then she told herself, What the hell! It's only a drink. So she said, 'Thanks. I'd like to. See you there in half an hour.'

The tartan bar in the hour before dinner proved to be a popular place. Nearly everyone seemed to be there.

Ben stood up and waved to her as Paris came into the room and she was aware of a great many eyes watching as she walked over to him. Probably because of the dark green velvet dress she was wearing, she thought. It had long sleeves but was cut low on her white shoulders, and it had a tight skirt that clung the way a skirt should. Her hair she had piled on top of her head above the chunky earrings that clinked a little when she moved. Quite why she had dressed up like this, Paris didn't know. Or maybe she did but didn't want to admit it to herself.

Ben's eyes went over her in satisfying admiration. 'Whisky again?' he asked.

'Somehow I don't think it would be as good as yours. I'll settle for gin and tonic, please.'

He went over to the bar and she sat down in the seat he'd saved for her at a small table for two, crossing her legs to show them to their best advantage. Looking round, she saw that Melanie was already there, sitting on one of the stools by the bar, but she was alone, or, at least, not with Will.

Wearing a red dress that stretched tight across her breasts, she was talking to some other women, three of whom Paris recognised as more of Ramsay's ex-girlfriends. Maybe they'd formed a mutual society, she thought flippantly.

Ben came back with her drink, looked her over again and said, 'Thank you,' as if he meant it.

She gave him an amused glance. 'For what?'

'For making my day.'

Paris smiled her acknowledgement of the compliment. 'Have you been working again?'

'Afraid so. How about you?' She told him, and he said with mock severity, 'You mean to say you didn't go to the talk this afternoon on making jewelry out of enamelled coins?'

There was such reproach in his voice that she laughed

aloud. 'Don't knock it. You might end up doing exactly that one day.'

He raised his eyebrows high. 'God forbid,' he said fervently.

They both laughed, leaning towards each other in amusement. And it was at that moment Will walked into the room.

Paris knew at once that he was there. She didn't have to notice Melanie, who had been watching the door, suddenly sit up straight and smile a welcome—Paris had already sensed the sudden electricity in the air. Without looking round, she leaned closer to Ben, still smiling, and said, 'So what are your hobbies?'

'I play cricket in the summer, squash in the winter, and bridge all the year.' He glanced round, saw Will going towards the bar and looked quickly back at Paris speculatively.

But she gave nothing away as she said, 'Well, at least you'll have plenty of bridge here, even if you haven't the others. Maybe you'll take up tatting or something.'

He gave her an old-fashioned look. 'I may be middle-aged compared with you, but I haven't got that far yet. What is tatting, anyway?'

'I've no idea,' Paris confessed. Will had come into her line of sight now and she deliberately let herself glance in his direction. For a moment their eyes met, but she let nothing show in hers before turning coolly away to resume her conversation. 'Are you good at bridge?'

'Fairly,' Ben admitted, having watched the little exchange.

'Oh.' She let disappointment show and sipped her drink.

'Why "Oh"?'

Paris gave a small shrug, then said with false reluctance, 'It was just that I don't know how to play bridge and I thought, if you had an odd half-hour to spare, you might teach me. But if you're good then you won't want to be bothered with a learner.'

Ben laughed. 'I'm afraid even someone as intelligent as you would find it difficult to pick up bridge in an odd half-hour. I've been playing for years and I'm still learning. But I'd be happy to try and teach you, of course.'

She had known that he would offer, but felt compelled to say, 'I don't want to take up too much of your time, especially when you're working during the day.'

'We'll start tonight,' he promised.

'I've lost track of the days. How many more to Christmas?'

'Five.'

'Five more shopping days to Christmas. I bet the high streets are doing a roaring trade right now,' she said on a wistful note.

'Having withdrawal symptoms?'

Paris laughed. 'Something like that. I didn't have much time for shopping while I was away.' Under her lashes she saw that Will had joined the group of women at the bar, buying them all a drink, and Melanie had a possessive hand on his arm as she talked to him, gesturing freely with the other.

Will seemed to be giving Melanie all his attention, but Paris knew that he was watching her too. It was a trick he had—seeming to concentrate on one thing but all the time being aware of what was going on around him. But he had never done that to her; when they'd been together she had had all his attention.

Turning to Ben, she saw that his eyes were on her face. 'Why did you invite me for a drink in here?' she asked abruptly.

'Isn't that what you wanted?'

'Why should it be?'

'So that you could let Brydon see that he isn't the only

fish in the sea. To make him even more jealous, perhaps.'
He smiled. 'And so that you could put on that dress and
look beautiful, show him just what he's missing.'

Her cheeks flushed a little. 'Those are—very acute ob-
servations.'

'True ones?'

'Perhaps. Partly.'

'Only partly?'

'I wore it for you too, and for myself.'

'What happened between you two? Did someone come
between you?'

'I suppose you could say that,' Paris admitted, thinking
of Emma and her poisonous tongue.

'Was it this man you're going with now?'

Paris hesitated, then said, 'There isn't another man. I
just said that. I wanted to protect myself, I suppose.'

Looking at her, seeing the vulnerability in her eyes, Ben
said, 'Now I understand.'

She smiled. 'Well, I'm glad someone does, because I
certainly don't understand myself.'

'Don't you?' He gave her a quizzical look. 'Well, if you
need a friend while you're here, I'm always available.'
Seeing her hesitate, he added, 'Just a friend, Paris, nothing
more. I don't want to complicate your life more than it is
already. And besides, I'm a confirmed workaholic bache-
lor, than which there is nothing worse.'

That made Paris laugh, and she gave him a look of gratitude. The dinner gong sounded, people finished their
drinks and made for the dining-room, the meal the high
spot of the day, as meals always are in any institution, on
any holiday.

They sat at a table with the judge and his wife and some
other lawyers. The conversation was good, on an entirely
different level from that of the table on which she'd sat
last night, and Paris enjoyed herself. Afterwards she and

Ben went to the card-room and Paris found out that it was going to take her a whole lot longer to learn bridge than she'd expected.

They didn't break up until gone midnight, when most of the others had gone to their rooms. Ben escorted her to her door but that was all; he merely said goodnight and headed for his turret.

Her brain exhausted by trying to take so much in, Paris slept like a log and woke feeling really refreshed. But she didn't hurry to get up, instead turning over lazily, only slowly becoming aware of the deadness of sound from outside. Usually sounds echoed round the courtyard but today there was nothing.

Getting out of bed, she went to the windows, drew back the curtains and found that it had snowed in the night. Quite heavily too—the wall looked to be several inches higher and the greenness of the distant fir trees was lost beneath their white caps.

Everyone was talking about the snow at breakfast. A snowman-building competition was organised for the children and people went off to their rooms after the meal to find scarves, pipes, hats and gloves to decorate them. Nearly everyone went out to watch and admire; somebody started a snowball fight and even quite elderly people joined in.

In the middle of the hilarity, during the most enjoyable time they'd had there, Captain Waters came into the courtyard, sought out a middle-aged couple who had been Ramsay's neighbours, and who had given evidence against him, and drew them back into the hotel.

A silence descended on all the other adults as they waited in trepidation to find out what had happened. They soon found out. The couple's house had deliberately been set on fire and petrol used to intensify the flames, destroying their home and their two beloved cats, which they had left behind to be looked after by their married daughter who lived nearby.

Lunch was a gloomy meal, especially after the merriment of the morning. Everyone was thinking about their own homes, wondering if they would be next. Captain Waters was besieged by people demanding protection for their houses, some even wanting to leave to go and guard the places themselves.

He calmed them as best he could, and pointed out that at least it proved that Ramsay was far away from the castle. Feeling overwhelmingly sorry for them, Paris went to her room and changed into jeans and sweater, boots and a thick jacket, then went outside.

The sun had come out, making the snow sparkle and crackle underfoot where it was still untrodden. The snowmen stood in a line, fat and jolly, given wide smiles by their proud creators.

The gates to the courtyard were locked, but through them she could see where an old moat had been partially filled in and the outline of shrubs and small trees planted on its edge. Beyond the moat there was a thicker wall and, at an angle, a gatehouse with rooms inside it, guarding another heavy wooden door. There was a light on in the gatehouse, which must always be gloomy with its small windows—sign of someone being on guard.

'Wishing you could leave?'

The snow had deadened his footsteps and she hadn't heard Will walk up to her. Paris caught her breath, then managed to shrug. 'There wouldn't be anything much to do.'

'The company's packed up for Christmas, has it?' he said with a definite sneer.

Paris hadn't meant that; she'd merely meant that she'd made no plans, that there wouldn't be much to do for a

Christmas spent alone. She didn't bother to explain, just turned and walked on.

Will came to walk alongside her, his usual brisk stride slowed by the snow. For a few moments they paced along in silence, then he said, 'You've grown your hair.'

She turned quickly and surprised him in the act of lowering his ungloved hand and shoving it into his pocket, almost as if he had been about to touch her hair, which was hanging loose, blown by the slight breeze.

'Yes.' There was nothing else to say.

'And you look thinner.' That came out almost as an accusation.

'So do you.'

That surprised him. He blinked, then shrugged it off and said curtly, 'I see you haven't wasted any time in finding a gullible fool to entrap.'

'Nor have you,' Paris retaliated.

His eyes met hers and he frowned, looked as if he was about to say something, but then his jaw tightened and he looked away.

'Did you move back in with Emma?' he asked after a few moments. 'After you—left.'

'After you kicked me out? Isn't that what you mean?' He didn't answer and she said, 'No, of course not. She was the last person I'd have moved in with. If it hadn't been for her—' She stopped, unwilling to go over old ground.

'What were you going to say?'

'It doesn't matter.'

'It might.'

She glanced at him, but Will's face was still set and hard. Paris gave a wry smile. 'I don't think so.'

It seemed strange that he had asked her that, especially after all these years. He hadn't taken the trouble to enquire after her when he'd thrown her out, so why ask now? If he hadn't cared enough at the time then he surely couldn't care less now. It was one of the things that had added to her hurt then, and it had taken a long while to get over it. Paris found that she didn't want to talk about that time; it opened too many old wounds.

They turned the corner of the building and came in sight of the turret where Ben had his suite. Paris glanced up at his window, wondering whether he was there, whether he was watching them. But she gave Ben no more than a passing thought.

Abruptly she said, 'Do you think they will catch Ramsay soon? Have the police told you anything?'

'Nothing they haven't told anyone else. I know what he did today was dreadful, but the more criminal acts he commits, the more likely he is to make a mistake and get caught. At least he didn't hurt anyone this time.'

'He killed those poor cats,' Paris pointed out.

'They hardly matter compared with a human being.'

'Of course they matter.'

Will's mouth twisted. 'To *you*?'

His tone implied so much. The colour fled from Paris's face. She swung round to go back inside, desperate to get away from him.

But Will caught her arm. 'No, wait.'

'Damn you, let me go!'

'What's the matter—afraid to face up to your own guilt?' he bit out scornfully. 'You little coward.'

Suddenly she was angry, and fervently grateful for it. 'What the hell would you know?' She pushed him away. 'I've lived with what happened for three long years. I know everything there is to know about guilt. And about a hell of a lot of other emotions, too.'

Again she turned and tried to hurry away but the snow slowed her down and Will quickly caught up with her and barred her way. 'What are you trying to say?'

'Nothing!' Anger had brought colour back into her cheeks, made her green eyes flash fire. 'I didn't ask to come here and I certainly didn't want to. If seeing me again brings it all back, then I'm sorry, but there's nothing I can do about it. So just leave me alone. Keep away from me.'

'I can't!' Will spoke the words as if they were forced out of him.

For a moment the intensity in his voice brought them both up short. Then Paris gave a bitter laugh. 'Why? Wasn't throwing me out enough? Must I be punished all over again, is that it? Maybe you're a sadist; have you thought of that? Maybe you're getting a kick out of this.'

'Don't be ridiculous.'

'Then why are you being like this? Why do you keep on about the past?'

His face taut with emotion, Will burst out, 'Because I can't help it, damn it!'

Paris stared up at him, seeing the harsh bleakness in his eyes, feeling despair fill her heart. 'Oh, God, no,' she said on a breath of desolate consternation.

There was the sound of voices and some children came into sight. They were rolling a ball of snow before them, making it ever larger as they went, and had already achieved a ball that was almost as high as they were. A group of fathers followed, trying not to appear too eager to take over as soon as it was too big for the youngsters. Will had been about to reach for her again but he let his arm fall and Paris took the opportunity to leave him and run back to the castle.

She was desperate to be alone and ran up to her room, but it was being cleaned. 'Will you be long?' she asked the elderly cleaner.

'I've only just started,' the woman pointed out, in a

Scots accent so broad that it would have left Paris in no doubt at all where they were if she hadn't already guessed.

She looked the kind of woman who was slow, thorough and not to be hurried. Abandoning the idea of finding solace in her room, Paris went to go downstairs again, but just couldn't face all the other people. So instead she went along the corridor to Ben's turret and climbed a narrow staircase that she'd noticed when she'd gone to his room for a drink. It was quite steep and there were no handrails.

At the top there was a narrow wooden door which was locked, but the key was hanging on a hook fixed in the wall. It was an old key, big and heavy, but turned easily in the lock. Opening the door, Paris found that it led outside again, onto the narrow parapet that encircled the roof.

She hesitated, and then, not wanting to get locked out, put the key in her pocket and went outside. The walkway was about two feet wide and a little slippery where the snow had melted in the sun. The parapet on her right, in the form of battlements, came up to her waist at the higher points, then only to her thighs, so she went carefully along. The roof to her left was of lead, its slope hidden from view below by the parapet.

Paris didn't know much about buildings and architecture, but it struck her that the construction of the roof didn't look that old and she realised for the first time that the building was a sham—Victorian Gothic masquerading as the real thing. It explained a lot: the good plumbing and the efficient central heating, the lack of draughts and the windows that gave plenty of light.

Continuing along the walkway, Paris came to the next turret with an identical door beside it. It was locked but her key fitted. Fascinated, she went inside, down another little staircase, round the curve of the turret, and found that to reach the next section of the roof she had to go up yet another staircase. How complicated. And just so that the architect hadn't had to break the line of his turrets at each corner of the building.

Instead of going on, Paris went back to her original walkway because it faced the sun. At least here she had found a hide-away, a place where she could be absolutely alone.

Looking down into the courtyard, she could see the place where she and Will had stood, the snow scuffed where he had come after her. She tried to remember the exact words of their conversation—no, confrontation had been more like it—but all she could remember was the intensity of it all.

Will should have forgotten by now. He had put the entire blame on her and got rid of her. So why hadn't he put it all out of his mind and started afresh? His vehemence had taken her aback; there had been a desperate kind of note in his voice that she couldn't fathom. But the guilt hadn't been his—in his eyes it had all been hers; so why should he feel like that? Paris found it impossible to understand him.

Only one thing was clear: if Will hadn't been able to forget what had happened after so long then he would definitely never be able to forgive her. In her heart maybe Paris had hoped that he would have relented by now, but it seemed that he still hated her. So there was nothing for it but to put Will out of her mind, out of her heart, to try and forget—but she had been trying to do just that for the last three years without any real success. So what hope was there for her? Paris thought tiredly.

She lifted her hands to press her temples, her head aching. The sun lost its battle with a dark grey cloud that suddenly took all the warmth out of the day. She shivered but stayed where she was, trying to work things out, wondering what she should do, wishing she was anywhere but there.

But then it began to snow again, so she turned and went back inside, remembering to lock the door behind her and hang the key on the hook where no inquisitive child could reach it.

After dinner that evening, Paris again had a bridge lesson, and this time another couple came to sit with them so that she could practise actually playing.

Numerate enough to count up to thirteen and blessed with a good memory, Paris took to the game like a duck to water. It had been years since she'd played any card game—not since before her parents had split up—but she enjoyed the challenge, and was grateful to concentrate entirely on the game and forget everything else. Or she did until she insisted that it was her turn to buy a round of drinks.

When she went into the bar she found Will sitting in a corner with Melanie. There were drinks on the table in front of them but it seemed that the other girl had already had quite a few because she was giggling and leaning heavily against Will.

Maybe she was the kind of woman who got amorous after she'd had several drinks and Will was taking advantage of it, Paris thought cynically. He certainly didn't seem to mind; his long-lashed grey eyes were laughing down at the girl in amusement. They both glanced up as Paris walked in, and Melanie's mouth creased into a definite smile of malicious triumph.

Paris looked quickly away, but there had been no mistaking that look; the other girl obviously knew that Will and she had had a relationship in the past. And there was only one person who could have told her.

Paris's first feeling was of betrayal; how *could* Will have told anyone else, let alone a girl like that? And what else had he told Melanie? Had he told her that he believed Paris to have had an abortion, too? Was that going to be passed round for everyone to gossip over?

'Yes, miss? Miss?' The bartender raised his voice and Paris realised that he was waiting for her order.

She gave it and took the drinks into the card-room on a tray, careful not to look in Will and Melanie's direction as she went out.

After that she didn't play so well and soon Ben said that he thought she'd had enough. The other couple went up to their room and Ben said, 'Would you like to go into the bar for a nightcap?'

'No, let's stay here.'

'I take it that means Will Brydon is in the bar?'

She didn't deny it, just leaned her elbows on the table, rested her chin on her hands and said, 'Tell me about yourself, Ben.'

'What do you want to know?'

'Do you believe in love?'

His eyebrows rose. 'I didn't expect that question. What makes you ask?'

'You're a criminal lawyer; you must have experience of life with a capital L, have met so many people, heard so many stories.'

'That doesn't necessarily mean I have all the answers. I certainly believe in the power of attraction, if that's what you mean.'

'No, I know there's that. I mean real love—the kind you read about that lasts for ever.'

'Oh, yes, I suppose I do. I've seen people who've stood by their loved one through the most terrible times. Take Noel Ramsay, for instance—he seemed to have the knack of making women fall in love with him. A couple of them were reluctant to testify against him, even though he'd got angry and beaten them up. They wouldn't say anything against him until they found out about his other women.'

'Was Melanie Truscott one of the reluctant ones?' Paris couldn't help asking.

'I think she was at first, yes,' Ben admitted, watching her.

'She seems to have got over him completely now,' Paris remarked on an unknowingly acid note.

Ben's eyes flicked to her face, then he said, 'Yes, most of the women have. Though I think they may have more reason to be afraid of Ramsay than most of us.'

'Why?'

'Ramsay has a warped mind; he probably thinks that they betrayed him, and so he would want to be revenged on them more than anyone else. Don't forget that one of the girls has completely disappeared. The police have found no trace of her and must be pretty convinced by now that Ramsay got to her and has killed her.'

'He's such an evil man,' Paris burst out. 'Why on earth were they stupid enough to let him get away?' They were silent for a moment, each thinking the same thoughts, but then she said, 'I wish they'd hurry up and catch him.'

'You're in a hurry to leave?'

'Yes. Aren't you?'

Ben shrugged. 'Not desperate, no. I'm getting a lot of work done and I've nowhere else much to go for Christmas, so I'm happy to spend it here, among friends. Although I know you don't agree.'

Paris sighed. 'I wouldn't mind at all if Will weren't here. But as it is…' She shrugged.

'Is there no hope of the two of you getting back together?'

'Oh, no, none.' Her answer was decisive.

'Why not?'

'There are too many old emotions standing in the way.'

'I see.' Ben yawned and got to his feet. 'I think it's time I turned in.'

They walked companionably up the stairs; avoiding the lift had become a habit now. Someone in the lounge was playing a Christmas song on the piano and people were joining in, forgetting their fears. The sound followed them, hid the noise of their step on the carpeted stairs. Maybe that was why Will and Melanie didn't hear them.

The two of them were standing just outside an open door a short way from the staircase on the second floor, locked in a close embrace. Paris came to an abrupt stop, not wanting to attract their attention by walking by. But she needn't have worried; Melanie broke away and with a slow, sex-filled laugh, caught hold of Will's arm and drew him into the room.

Paris immediately strode quickly to the next flight and began to climb it rapidly, Ben having to hurry to keep up. 'I take it that was Will's room?' she said shortly.

'No, I think it was hers.'

Paris frowned, something momentarily troubling her mind, but she pushed it aside, too angry and humiliated to care. Her goodnight to Ben was curt and she would have gone straight into her room, but he caught her hand.

'Maybe he's just doing it to make *you* jealous,' he suggested.

'No, he doesn't care enough for that.'

'Of course he does.'

She turned on him angrily. 'Are you so blind? Will doesn't care about me—he hates me. Hates me so much he can't leave it alone!' She bit her lip, her hand clenching within his, the pain she was feeling impossible to hide.

Ben stared at her, then said awkwardly, 'Look, don't try and bottle things up. That's no good, you know.'

His kindness made Paris angry with herself. She collapsed against the wall, saying, 'God, I'm being really rotten to you, aren't I? Just forget about me, Ben. I'm a lost cause.'

'Nonsense. You're a beautiful, intelligent woman. And maybe you deserve someone better than Will Brydon.'

She looked at him for a moment without really seeing him, then shook her head in infinite sadness. 'No, it's the other way round.' Ben went to speak but she raised her hand in a small gesture to silence him, turned and went into her room.

Again she lay awake, unable to stifle the jealousy that tore at her heart. She had no right to feel that way, she knew, but could do nothing about it.

Will certainly hadn't needed any persuading to go with Melanie. He had allowed her to pull him into her room without even the slightest hint of resistance. But then, why should he resist? When a pretty girl made it obvious that she was available he'd have to be a fool not to take what was offered.

Pictures of the two of them in bed together tortured her mind, became unbearable. Getting out of bed, Paris scrabbled for the bottle of sleeping pills. She ought not to take so many of these, she thought, but she just had to sleep; she couldn't stand her own vivid imagination any longer.

She took two, got back into bed again, but it was something else now that niggled at her mind, and it was just as she was fading into oblivion that she remembered. The first time she had seen Melanie the girl had been going downstairs from this floor. So if Melanie's room was on the second floor, what had she been doing on the third?

Waking late the next morning, Paris didn't bother to go down to breakfast, and she stayed in her room most of the day. When she finally went down just in time for dinner she found that a huge Christmas tree had been set up in the hall. Everyone seemed to have gone into the dining-room already, but she stopped to admire it. It was hung with colourful bows and decorations, and twinkled with flashing lights and tinsel. A masterpiece of a tree!

As she stood admiring it, Will came down the stairs and walked up to her. Paris saw him and forced herself not to walk away, not to show any emotion.

'The children did it this afternoon,' he told her. 'They had a wonderful time.'

'It's magnificent.'

Will was standing with his hands in his pockets, spoiling the line of his well-cut suit. Glancing at her, he said, 'You haven't been around today.'

Hiding her surprise at his noticing, Paris said as casually as she could, 'No, I've been catching up on some chores, writing letters, washing my hair. You know.'

'I like it longer.' This time he openly reached up to touch it.

Suddenly angry, Paris swung away from him, her hair swirling. 'I don't give a damn what you like or don't like,' she said forcefully.

Will gave a small gasp. 'What the hell was that for?'

'Concentrate on one girl at a time, why don't you?'

His eyes narrowed. 'Why should you care what I do, who I'm with?'

Angry with herself, she tried her best to retrieve the situation. 'I don't. I just want you to get away from me. Go back where you're welcome—more than welcome, by the looks of it.' And, to her consternation, she found herself adding, 'You and all her other men.'

'What's that supposed to mean?' Will's hands were out of his pockets now, were on his hips, and he was glaring at her. It was too late to take it back now, and anyway, she didn't want to. Lowering her voice, Paris said forcefully, 'You used to be more fastidious.'

'Fastidious? Because I chose to live with you—is that what you mean? Do you think yourself so moral, then?

What about the way you're going around with Ben Lucas when you already have a boyfriend tucked away somewhere?'

'Ben is just being friendly, and you know it. I only met him a few days ago, for heaven's sake. Not that knowing someone only a short time seems to have caused *you* any qualms,' she added nastily.

Will leaned towards her, his strong jaw jutting forward. 'Has it occurred to you that Melanie's morals might be a damn sight more honest than yours? OK, maybe she sleeps around and you don't, but does that make you better than her, after what you did? Well, does it?'

CHAPTER FIVE

So THEY were back to the same thing again, at the same point as they had been three years ago. The colour flooded from Paris's face as she realised that this was how it would always be whenever she saw Will, whenever they talked. Although, talking didn't really come into it, because all they'd done since she'd been here was tear each other to pieces.

She turned blindly and went to hurry away, but Will caught her elbow. 'The dining-room is the other way.'

'I'm not hungry.'

'You didn't come down to lunch. You've got to eat,' he said with a rough edge to his voice.

'No, what I need is a drink,' Paris said on an unnatural laugh. And, pulling herself free of his hold, she headed for the bar.

Will looked at her uneasily for a moment, then gave a small shrug and went into the dining-room.

The bar was completely empty, the grille pulled down over the bar counter and the barman gone to have his own meal, presumably. Paris didn't much care. She went into the card-room, picked up a pack and, sitting down at one of the tables, began to play patience. Her mind wasn't on it; she stared moodily down at the cards, wishing for what seemed like the millionth time that she could get away from Will, away from the castle.

There was a movement by the door and she looked up. It was Will. He paused in the doorway for a moment, his hand against the frame, then came into the room. In his other hand he carried a tray with a bowl of soup, a roll and a glass of wine.

'Here.' He brushed the cards aside and put the plate in front of her.

She gazed up at him for a moment, then said huskily, 'Thanks.'

Paris expected him to go then, but instead Will sat down next to her and broke and buttered the roll. She watched him, his long, deft capable hands. It reminded her of so many other times, when they'd been together, when she had watched him working at some task, fascinated by his efficiency. The memory was raw hurt and she almost hated him for bringing it back. 'Why?' she said shortly.

'Just eat, Paris.'

'I don't want your pity, damn you!'

'Good, because you're not getting it. All you're getting is a bowl of soup. So eat.'

Strangely she saw the funny side of that and gave a low chuckle. Picking up the spoon, she took a couple of mouthfuls, then said, almost conversationally, 'I thought I knew you. But I don't. I didn't when we were together and I still don't.'

'You certainly didn't know me then.'

She glanced at him. He was leaning back in his chair, one leg crossed over the other knee—the way men sit when they're relaxed—and his hands were in his pockets. His face showed no emotion, could have been that of a stranger, but it had seldom pulled at her heart so much.

The soup was Scotch broth, very thick, a meal in itself. Paris took another couple of spoonfuls before she said reflectively, 'I think I did know you better then—knew you instinctively—but I was persuaded otherwise.'

'Who by?'

She shook her head and picked up a piece of bread. 'It doesn't matter.'

'I suppose I needn't have asked; it was that bitch Emma, wasn't it?' Paris didn't answer and he said grimly, 'Are you still friendly with her? Do you see her?'

'Oh, no. I haven't seen her since I was instrumental in getting her fired.'

Will straightened, his eyes on her face. 'And just how did you do that—and why?'

Paris hesitated, then said on a rueful sigh, 'I didn't realise it for a long time, but Emma was frightened to death of getting old. It made her dreadfully jealous of any younger girl she saw as a possible threat to her own job, her position in the firm. So she used to get them to leave in a very subtle way.

'First she'd pretend to be very friendly and let them share her flat, offer to take over their best accounts for a while if they were on holiday—or serving on a jury, as I was. Then she'd lie and make up excuses so she could keep the accounts, then kick the girl out of the flat and make her life unbearable at work until she either left or got fired.'

Breaking off another piece of bread, Paris paused, remembering, then said on a small laugh, 'She'd done that to two other girls before me, only it didn't work with me because I had you. I moved in with you and I managed to find some new accounts. But then I was stupid enough to play into her hands by confiding in her about—about being pregnant.'

Paris bit her lip, but went on, 'Afterwards, she told everyone I'd had an abortion, made sure they talked about it. I think she even urged that disgusting man to find you, tell you.' She fell silent, looking down at her plate, no longer eating.

'So what happened?' Will demanded.

She flicked him a glance. 'After you—after we split up, work was hell—Emma saw to that. She—' Paris broke off;

she wasn't looking for his pity or even sympathy, so instead she said, 'But it was all I had left so I clung to it. I was determined not to let her win. Then I found out that she'd done the same kind of thing before, so I traced the other two girls and we got together, put our cases to the management and threatened to sue for harassment. That forced them to look into it for themselves.'

She began to eat again. 'It was surprisingly easy when it came to it. Maybe the management had become aware of what Emma was doing; maybe they just wanted to be rid of her. Anyway, one day she was there, the next she was gone.'

'How did she make your life such a hell at work?'

'That hardly matters now.'

'Doesn't it?'

'No, it's over. And it wouldn't matter to you anyway.'

But Will surprised her by saying, 'Yes, it would. I'm glad it happened, that you did it. She was a bitch.'

'You sound very certain.'

'I am. She tried to get me to take her to bed, one night when you were abroad at a conference.'

Paris turned to stare at him. 'Really? Why didn't you ever tell me?'

'Because she was supposed to be your closest friend. Because she threatened, if I said anything to you, to tell you that it had been the other way round; that *I'd* tried to make it with her.'

'Do you mean to say that she just came round to our place and asked you to go to bed with her?'

'No, she wasn't quite that blatant. She phoned late at night and said that something had gone wrong with her central-heating boiler, that it was making a terrible noise and she was afraid it was going to blow up. I told her to phone a plumber but she said she'd tried and no one would come out. So I didn't have much choice but to go round there.'

'And?' Paris said when he paused.

'Finish your soup.' She arched her brows impatiently but ate the last few spoonfuls, and only then did Will go on. 'When I arrived she greeted me at the door wearing a nightdress and negligée, all black lace and a lot of cleavage, and said the noise from the boiler had suddenly stopped. I went to go home but she begged me to stay for a while in case it started up again. I looked at the boiler but I couldn't find a thing wrong with it. It was then, just in case I hadn't already got the idea, that she began to come on strong.'

Paris picked up the glass of wine and sipped it slowly. 'What did you do?'

Will shrugged. 'What do you expect? I told her that even if I wasn't already living with you, with a girl I was crazy about, she'd be the last woman I'd ever want to go to bed with. Then I pushed her aside and walked out.'

At his description of her, Paris's fingers had tightened on her glass, but now she gave a sigh of surprised comprehension. 'Now I know why she hated me so much! I thought it was just because of work that she had it in for me, but I didn't know the ''woman scorned'' bit came into it as well. Maybe if I had I'd have been on my guard against her.'

'Are you saying I should have told you?' Will's lips thinned. 'That everything that happened was my fault?'

'No, of course not.' She gave a definite shake of her head. 'Anyway, it's all in the past now. Over. ''Might have beens'' and ''if onlys'' are just a waste of time—and heartache.'

His voice softening a little, Will said, 'Where did you go after we split?'

'Oh, I found a place. I got by,' she said lightly, and

quickly changed the subject. 'How about you? Are you still working for the same firm?'

'No, I got restless. I spent some time in America, Hong Kong, Tokyo, learning the foreign money markets, widening my field.'

'A good career move.'

His lips twisted into a cynical smile. 'That wasn't why I did it.'

She understood at once and raised troubled eyes to his. 'I wished we'd talked—before—before—'

'Before I threw you out?' Will stood up and picked up her tray. 'It wouldn't have made any difference. I couldn't bear to be near you after what you did.'

Her face shadowed and she looked away, trying to hide the pain that knifed into her heart. That hadn't been what she'd meant but she didn't correct him. After a long moment she said, 'Well, I'm glad we've talked now.'

Will laughed mirthlessly. 'At least for once we didn't tear into one another.'

He carried the tray back to the dining-room and Paris watched him go, thinking how very wrong he was.

Later she sat in the bar with Ben and some other people, but pleaded a headache as an excuse for not playing bridge.

'Maybe you're coming down with a cold or something,' one woman said sympathetically. 'You must have an early night and dose yourself up. You don't want to miss the party tomorrow.'

'What party?'

'Haven't you heard? A couple of people are sharing a birthday, and they decided they'd like to have a party followed by carol singing. Can you sing?'

'Definitely not,' Paris said firmly. 'So don't get any ideas.'

Ben laughed. 'You'll get roped into doing something

soon—you'll see. I've been asked to help accompany the singers on guitar.'

'You play the guitar?'

'Product of a misspent youth. Why are you so surprised?'

'I don't know; I suppose because you seem so wrapped up in your work.'

'Well, I won't be wrapped up in it tomorrow. It's the weekend and I'm taking a couple of days off.'

'Good for you.' Paris got to her feet, said goodnight, and left them as they pulled their chairs up to a table to start a rubber of bridge.

A film was being shown on the video, somebody had organised a debate on the government's controversial road-improvement schemes, and there were lots of people in the bar and lounge. The younger children, tired after another day of playing in the snow, were safely asleep in bed. It seemed that Paris was the only person going up to her room so early.

The lift was on the ground floor and for a moment she was tempted to take it, but she'd had no exercise that day so she went up the stairs instead. She saw no one until she reached her own floor, then a movement at the end of the corridor caught her eye. She came quickly up the last few steps and was in time to see a woman getting into the lift. Paris was pretty sure that it was Melanie Truscott; she recognised her figure, the dress she was wearing and the large handbag she always carried, although she didn't actually see her face.

She stood on the landing, remembering that she'd seen Melanie up here before. Was there some lone man on this floor that she visited? If so, it was a strange time to do so. Maybe it was one of their guards. Paris knew that Captain Waters had a room up here—perhaps some of the other men did too. She wouldn't have been at all surprised to know that Melanie had more than one man on a string, although how any woman would need another man when she had someone as virile as Will Paris couldn't think.

The familiar flame of jealousy hit her and she strode towards her room, but slowed as she noticed some marks on the carpet. Bending down, she touched them and found that they were wet. From someone's shoes, obviously. And Melanie had been the only person up here.

Gripped by curiosity, Paris followed the marks to the next corner turret along from the one with Ben's room in it and up one of the small staircases that led onto the roof. The wet marks were very definite here on the stone steps and looked to be from a woman's shoes; they were too small to be made by a man's, especially by the boots favoured by their police guards. But surely Melanie couldn't have gone outside tonight? It must be icily cold out there. Paris hesitated, then unlocked the door and opened it a little way.

Immediately the wind hit her, even before the cold caught at her breath. She gasped and began to shiver in her short-sleeved dress as she stepped onto the parapet. It was pitch-dark; the curtains of the windows of the castle were all drawn so there wasn't even any reflected light. She must be mistaken, Melanie couldn't possibly have come out here; she'd have frozen to death in no time.

Afraid that she'd freeze herself, Paris turned to go back inside just as a fresh gust caught her. Instinctively she put out a hand to steady herself against the turret wall—and gave a scream of fright as she touched something furry and warm.

Her cry was lost on the wind, which was just as well as only a second later she realised that what she had touched was only a coat. A very thick anorak with a hood was hanging from a nail in the wall, protected from the wind and rain by the overhanging circular roof of the tower. It was lined with fur that was still warm from human contact, and it was this that Paris had inadvertently touched. One of the guards must have left it here. Or Melanie.

That thought came uneasily into her mind. What could the other girl possibly want up here at night? But then it occurred to Paris that she too had come up here—looking for solitude, wanting to be alone. But that had been in daytime and because her own room hadn't been available. It all seemed strange, wrong.

Troubled, Paris went back inside and locked the door, then rubbed her arms to restore some warmth in them as she walked to her room. Once there, she went to pick up the phone to call Captain Waters, to tell him what she'd seen, but hesitated with her hand over the receiver.

What if there was some perfectly innocent explanation? There could be. Maybe Melanie was an amateur astronomer or something. She would look an absolute fool if that turned out to be the case. And, again, she hadn't actually seen the other girl's face, couldn't definitely swear that it was her, even though she was sure in her own mind.

But what finally made Paris decide not to phone was the thought that it might be put down to jealousy on her part because Will and Melanie were having an affair. All the other jurors would know that Will and she had been close at the time of the trial, and she was certain that the police had looked into their background and knew that they had once lived together. No, there were too many things against it; she would wait until tomorrow and perhaps talk it over with Ben first, see what he advised.

Paris woke early the next morning and, too restless to go to sleep again, went down to the gym to work out, and afterwards swam for half an hour in the pool. There were showers in the pool area which she used before going in

to the dining-room. Ben wasn't there, but that wasn't unusual; he seldom bothered with breakfast.

After the meal Paris hesitated, wondering whether to go
up to his room to see him, but not wanting to disturb him
if he was sleeping late. In the end she compromised by
writing a note saying that she wanted to see him which
she sealed in an envelope and pinned on the notice-board
in the hall, where he would be sure to see it when he came
downstairs. If the note was still there in an hour, she decided, she would phone his room and get him to come
down and talk to her.

As she pinned the note on the board, the front doors
were pushed open and three grinning policemen in plain
clothes came in, each carrying two large, heavy sacks.
They looked like new forms of Father Christmas in their
boots and duffel-coats and with the snow clinging to them.

'Post!' they called out. 'The mail has arrived.'

People gathered round them excitedly, adults as well as
children, all eager for this link with the outside world. The
policemen emptied the sacks onto a table in the hall, creating a great pile of letters and parcels which had been
held back at all their local sorting offices and collected for
them by the police. They sorted the parcels first and Paris
noted that there were two for her, but to everyone's surprise one of the men took them all away again, going
through the door into the kitchen area.

'We just have to check the parcels,' another man explained.

The letters were given out, most of them white-
enveloped Christmas cards—whole wads of them to some
people. The word had gone round and people were coming
from all directions, laughing and talking, the arrival of the
mail cheering them all.

Will walked in with Melanie at his side, and Paris tried
not to wonder if they'd spent the night together. Some

people took their post away to open but the majority were still gathered in the hall when there was the unmistakable sound of an explosion from the basement.

Some women screamed, others grabbed their children to them, and everyone grew tense, their faces full of alarm. Will had just gone forward to collect his mail; he took a step backwards, somehow placing himself between Paris and the door to the kitchens, whether accidentally or on purpose she didn't know. They were all gazing towards the door, appalled at what might have happened. The two policemen dropped the letters they were holding and ran out, followed closely by Captain Waters who came tearing across the hall. It was almost ten unbearably long minutes before he came back again, his face grave.

First he suggested that the mothers take the children away, and when they'd gone he said, 'I'm afraid there was a small bomb in one of the parcels. But no one has been hurt. The man who opened it was wearing gloves and protective clothing; he's quite all right. And no damage has been done downstairs.' He smiled at them and said in a falsely cheerful voice, 'Don't worry, you'll all get your Christmas dinner.'

One woman, her voice trembling, said, 'The—the parcel—who was it sent to?'

The captain hesitated, then said, 'It was addressed to Melanie Truscott.'

Paris's eyes swung swiftly to the other girl, saw the stunned amazement on her face, and then she swayed, about to faint. Several arms went out to her, but it was Will who stepped swiftly to her side and caught her as she fell.

Picking Melanie up in his arms, Will carried her into the lounge and laid her down on one of the sofas. Someone produced some smelling salts and soon Melanie was coming round. She sat up and seemed dazed, saying, 'I can't believe it. I can't believe it.' Then she started to cry and turned her head into Will's shoulder. He put his arms round her, comforting her as one would someone close.

Several people looked on sympathetically, but most people were still in the hall. They stood around, all of them talking about the letter bomb, their voices subdued, and some—mostly the parents—were looking angry, saying that the post should have been inspected before it was brought there.

One man who had three small children to whom several parcels had been addressed started to accuse Captain Waters of not taking sufficient care, of not guarding them properly. It was a natural reaction, Paris supposed; they'd all been scared, and what if the bomb had been bigger? What if someone had been killed?

Captain Waters called for silence and raised his voice to address them. 'I'm sorry that you've all had a scare. In future all the post will be checked before it's brought here.

'But can't you see what Ramsay is doing? He knows that you're all in a safe place. He can't get at you. So he's trying to make you panic, to make you worry about your homes, and perhaps scare you into going back to them. But you must trust the police to take care of them for you. If you leave here your lives will be in danger. I can't stress that enough. So please, try to forget this has happened. We're having a party tonight; let's look forward to that.'

It was sensible advice but not that easy to take, although they tried. The crowd began to break up, several people going into the ballroom to practise for the carol concert.

Paris turned away and saw Ben standing on the edge of the crowd. He was holding a guitar in one hand and her note in the other. She went over to him and by tacit consent they moved away from the hall and went to the empty card-room. As on most mornings, the sun was shining, the rays streaming through the windows. The cleaners must have been in here recently, because dust motes still danced in the air.

'Did you hear what happened?' Paris asked.

'Yes.'

'You said Melanie would be high on Ramsay's hit list.'

'Sending her letter bombs won't flush her out. It will make her all the more determined to stay here.'

'She seemed so amazed that she should have received it—completely stunned,' Paris said with a frown.

'Any one of us would have been.'

'Yes, I suppose so.'

Ben gestured with the note he was holding. 'What did you want to see me about that was so important?'

'Oh, that.' Paris pulled herself out of her abstraction. Her suspicions about Melanie now seemed incredibly silly. Whatever Melanie had been up to on the roof—if it had been her—it couldn't possibly have anything to do with Ramsay, not after the letter bomb. Her faint and the amazement afterwards had obviously been genuine; no one could be such a good actress that she could fake reactions like that. 'I just wondered if you'd give me another bridge lesson today,' she said lamely.

Ben looked surprised. 'Of course. But I have to practise with the carol singers this morning. In fact I'm late already.'

'I hardly think anyone will notice this morning.'

Ben went off but Paris didn't follow him, instead going to sit on the deep sill of one of the windows, her back against the wall, her legs stretched out before her, one knee bent a little.

She was still wearing the tight black leggings that she had worn in the gym, and over them a long white sweater, belted at the waist. Her hair was tied back in a pony-tail, but several tendrils had come loose to caress her cheeks and throat. Leaning her head back, Paris closed her eyes, soaking up the reflected sun, which was bright on her face.

Maybe she dozed a little; maybe she was in that dream-like state between sleeping and waking. When she opened her eyes, languidly lifting her lids, she certainly thought that she was dreaming. Will stood nearby, looking down at her with oh, such a look on his face. Tenderness, desire, regret—they were all written there and plain to read. His eyes were as she'd so often known them when they'd been together—so warm, so dark with open need.

Paris's lips parted and she sat up eagerly, blinking against the sun. And then everything was suddenly back to normal, back in focus. Will was there all right—she hadn't imagined that—but his face was withdrawn, cool, as it always was when he looked at her now. In his hands he carried her parcels, obviously having been opened and resealed with sticky tape.

'The rest of the parcels were brought up and everyone collected them except you.'

'Thanks for bringing them.'

'It was thought better not to leave them just sitting there; it would remind everyone of what happened.'

'Oh, I see.' She took the parcels from him, glanced at the writing on the labels and saw that they were from her parents. 'How's Melanie?' she asked a little stiffly.

'All right now, I think. She had a large brandy and went up to her room.'

Paris glanced at him from under her lashes, wondering why he hadn't gone with her. 'She seemed very shaken,' she remarked.

'Yes.' Will gave a small frown. 'Didn't she.' But then he shrugged. 'I suppose we all think that nothing could ever happen to us, that it's always the other person.'

'But she's had experience of Ramsay before,' Paris

pointed out, and couldn't help adding, 'Intimate experience.'

Will's mouth twisted slightly, but he said, 'Yes, the poor girl has really suffered at his hands. One has to feel sorry for her.'

'Perhaps she just has rotten judgement,' Paris pointed out tartly.

His smile became sarcastic as he looked down at her. 'We all make mistakes in judgement. You, above all, should know that.'

There was nothing to say to that. Paris's hands gripped the parcels and she looked away. Will turned to go but just then Gwenda Paston came into the room.

'Oh, there you are, Paris. I've been looking for you. We've had the most wonderful idea to take the children's minds off that stupid incident this morning. We're going to have a pantomime.'

'Really?' Paris tried to concentrate. 'Yes, that's a great idea. Which one?'

'*Snow White and the Seven Dwarfs*, so that the children can play the dwarfs. The others who want to take part can be villagers or fairies or something. There'll be lots of work to do and I shall need everyone's help.'

'Of course. I'll be glad to. But there's hardly any time left before Christmas; how will you be ready in time?'

'Oh, it won't be before Christmas; pantomimes are best as after-Christmas treats, don't you think? But we must start rehearsing and planning straight away.' She turned to Will. 'Now what are you good at? Carpentry, electrics, painting? Can you turn your hand to any of those?'

'I can try,' Will said in amusement at being press-ganged.

'He's good at painting,' Paris put in. 'He could do your scenery for you.'

Will gave her a look, but didn't argue when Mrs Paston

greeted the information with enthusiasm. 'That's marvellous; I was beginning to worry about that. You must get together with the people I'm organising to build the scenery, tell them what you want when you've read the script.'

'You already have a script?' Will asked with a grin of admiration.

'It's being worked on,' Mrs Paston said grandly, then laughed and said in an entirely different tone, 'Anyway, everybody knows the story of Snow White; all we have to do is remember and write it down.'

'How can I help?' Paris asked.

'Why, you're going to be the most important person in the pantomime. I took one look at your legs in those woollen tights this morning and knew at once that you must be our principal boy.' She appealed to Will. 'Doesn't she have the most gorgeous legs?'

To Paris's embarrassment they both looked assessingly at her legs. Will nodded. 'She certainly does—and long too. Ideal for a principal boy, I'd say.'

'Exactly,' Mrs Paston said with satisfaction.

'But I can't,' Paris objected.

'Nonsense. You'll be ideal. And you mustn't worry about not having acted or anything before; we're all amateurs, you know.'

'No, you don't understand—'

'She's probably worried that she'll have to sing,' Will broke in, imps of mischief dancing in his eyes. 'She can't, you see.'

'You sound very sure.'

'I am. I've heard her, especially in the bath, and, believe me, you wouldn't want her to try.'

Paris, her cheeks pink, gave him an indignant look, but said, 'It's quite true. I'm afraid you'll have to find someone else.'

Mrs Paston had been looking at Will in some surprise,

but turned again to Paris. 'No, I won't, because it doesn't really matter that you can't sing. One of the women has a wonderful voice but a terrible figure; she can sing the songs in the wings and you can mime to them. So that's settled. Now I have to persuade someone to play the wicked queen. I wonder…'

She went to turn away but Paris pushed her parcels aside and got quickly to her feet. 'No! I'm sorry, but you don't understand. I *can't* be in the pantomime.'

The sharpness of her tone made the older woman turn to look at her more closely. 'Are you shy or something?'

'No, it isn't that. I'll gladly help you with the preparations until Christmas, but I can't take part because I won't be here after that. I'm leaving.'

'Leaving? But you can't! I mean—what if Ramsay hasn't been caught?'

Paris was aware of Will staring at her intently. Ignoring him, she said, 'I shall still be leaving. I'm sorry. If I can help in any other way, I will, of course.'

Mrs Paston frowned, not understanding. 'But how can you possibly leave? The police—surely they won't let you?'

Unable to explain, especially with Will standing there, Paris said, 'It's all arranged.' She picked up her parcels. 'Excuse me.'

Will went to stop her as she hurried out of the room but Mrs Paston spoke to him and he had to turn back.

Carrying a parcel under each arm, Paris ran to the hall and up the stairs. She had no doubt that Mrs Paston was asking Will what she'd meant, and was also sure that he would try to find out. That was why she locked her door when she reached her room.

Sitting on the bed, she began to unwrap her parcels. There was a card and letter enclosed in the one from her mother, with lots of photographs of her family—of Paris's stepfather and her half-sister and brother, both quite a lot younger than herself. She began to read the letter, and when a knock sounded at the door she didn't answer it.

The knock came again, louder and more imperative this time, but still she ignored it. Then came Will's voice. 'Paris I know you're in there. Open the door.'

She sat silently. He banged impatiently on the panel, making the oak door rattle, then he must have gone away, because he didn't knock again. Two minutes later the phone rang. It went on ringing until at last she could stand it no longer. With a curse she picked up the receiver, fully intending to just lay it by the phone, but she heard Will's voice say loud and clear, 'Paris, if you don't speak to me I'll come up and break your door down.'

'All right! So I'm listening,' she said shortly.

'Why wouldn't you open your door?'

'Possibly because I don't want to talk to you.'

'You can't hide away for ever. What's this about you leaving?'

'You heard what I said.'

'I suppose it's some conference you feel you can't live without attending,' Will said in disgust.

'You can think what you like.'

'You mean it isn't?' he pounced.

'I'm not going to tell you, Will, so just drop it, will you?'

'No, I damn well won't! You're not going anywhere until Ramsay is caught, do you hear me?'

'Yes, I hear you,' Paris answered shortly. 'And anyone hearing you might just think that you cared.'

There was silence at the other end of the line as he was brought up short. She put down the phone and it didn't ring again.

Will was right, of course: she couldn't hide away for ever. She went down to lunch and found him hanging around in the hall, apparently glancing through a news-paper. But he put it down immediately when he saw her and took a firm hold of her arm. 'You've some explaining to do,' he said shortly, and steered her into the nearest empty room, shutting the door firmly behind them and then leaning on it.

'Now,' he said curtly, 'I want to know why you intend to leave here.'

'It's none of your business.'

'Don't try that one because it won't work. Why, Paris?'

Still defiant, she said, 'What's it to you? Why all this anxiety to know?'

But he'd had time to think up an answer to that one and said, 'It's of concern to us all, not just me. Don't you realise that if you leave here and Ramsay finds you then he'll make you tell him where we all are? And don't think that he wouldn't be able to find you, Paris, because the damn man has an uncanny knack of doing just that. Melanie said that she'd moved several times since the trial, but Ramsay still managed to find out her current address.'

'Maybe she's in the phone book,' Paris said flippantly.

He came away from the door in one stride and caught her shoulders to shake her. 'Be serious, can't you? This isn't a game.'

It wasn't the first time he'd touched her since she'd been at the hotel, but it was the first time that he had been really close. She could feel the strength of his hands through her clothes, could breathe in his warmth and masculinity. It unnerved her, left her weak. She put up her hands to push him away but they only rested against his chest. She felt him grow still and lifted her eyes to look into his face.

It was impossible to hide her awareness of him—it was there in her wide, vulnerable gaze, in her softly parted mouth and trembling lower lip. Will made a low sound deep in his throat; his fingers tightened for a moment as his eyes, too, became intense. Paris thought that he was going to kiss her, was sure of it, and her heart almost stopped beating in anticipation. But he abruptly let her go and turned away, shoving his hands in his pockets.

'I'm sorry,' he said shortly. 'But you seem to be able to rile me as no one else can.'

He was silent for a moment, then turned to face her. His voice cool again, he said, 'Perhaps you don't take the situation as seriously as the rest of us because you've been away and weren't able to follow the story in the newspapers.

'As soon as it was realised that Ramsay was out for revenge, most of the people involved in the case clamoured for police protection. Everyone was afraid that they would be next. But there were so many of us that the police hadn't the resources to guard us all individually; that's why it was decided to bring us all here together. But they had to be careful, to make sure that Ramsay wasn't watching.'

He paused, picking his words, before saying, 'We were brought here in small groups, a few at a time, and it was a great relief when people got here safely. Eventually we were all here—except you. We all wondered where you were, what had happened to you. The police said that you were out of the country, but we weren't sure that they weren't just fobbing us off and that you too hadn't disappeared.'

'You asked them?' It wasn't really a question; she knew that he had.

'We all did.'

He was being evasive, but Paris looked at him with the light of discovery in her eyes. 'You do care.'

His mouth tightened. 'We've become a close community; we all care about each other. Which is why I insist on knowing why you want to leave here.'

So he came neatly back to the original question and

avoided the main issue. Paris gave a small smile. 'I see. So you only want to know on everyone else's behalf?'

But he evaded that one too. 'So why?'

'I assure you that Ramsay won't find me and I won't be putting any of you in danger.'

'That isn't good enough.'

'It's all you're going to get.'

'I can ask Captain Waters.'

'Haven't you already?'

'Not yet, no, because…' He gave her an intent look, then said reluctantly, 'Is it because of this man you're involved with? Have you promised to go away with him or something?'

Again she had forgotten her imaginary lover, but Will obviously hadn't. 'Who told you I was involved with someone?'

He shrugged. 'Word got round. Well?'

'What if I am?' she temporised.

'You'd put yourself in danger just to be with him?'

'Maybe I care about him that much.'

A look of disgust came into Will's eyes. 'But he obviously doesn't care about you if he'd let you do it,' he said forcefully. 'No one who loved you would even contemplate it, let alone *urge* you to leave. What kind of man is he to suggest it?'

Paris looked at him for a moment, realising that he'd given away more than he intended, then shook her head. 'You're wrong; that isn't the reason.'

'You're not leaving to be with him?'

'No.'

'Is it because of your parents, your family?'

'Hardly. They don't need me.'

'It has to be a conference, then. Something to do with your job.'

She shook her head, walked to the door and reached for the knob.

But Will put his hand against the door, holding it shut. Angry now, he said, 'Damn you, Paris, stop making me play guessing games.'

'Just leave me alone, then. I'm not going to tell you and that's final.'

But he still held the door, and his voice grew harsh, his face set, as he said, 'Then I can think of only one other reason why you might want to leave.' Paris looked at him, her face wary, but didn't speak. 'It's because of me, isn't it?'

Her lashes came quickly down to hide her eyes, but not quickly enough; he saw that he was right. 'But...' He said the word on a gasp of realisation and surprise.

Paris gave him a hefty push, caught him off balance so that he had to step back, wrenched the door open and ran.

CHAPTER SIX

PARIS took refuge in the dining-room, losing herself in the queue of people waiting to serve themselves from the buffet, grateful for their noise and chatter. She was late in so it didn't take long to serve herself and go to find a seat next to Ben.

He smiled at her. 'Have you opened all your post?'

'Yes. I got a couple of presents from my parents.'

'Let's see. I bet your mother sent you something to wear and your father a book.'

Paris laughed. 'Is that what you always get?'

'Invariably. Was I right?'

'Close. But I think they must have colluded because my mother sent a chef's apron and oven gloves and my father a cookery book.'

'Can't you cook?'

She grimaced a little. 'Of course I can. I'm a whizz with a microwave. But they worry about me; they think I ought to settle down.'

'So, on the principle that the quickest way to a man's heart is through his stomach, they sent you the cookery gear.' Ben grinned. 'I think I'd like your parents; they seem to go for the direct, no-nonsense approach.'

Paris made a wry face. 'I suppose that is one way of saying that they have no subtlety.'

'And how about you—do you think it's time you settled down?'

Paris poured herself a glass of water. 'How did the carol rehearsal go?'

'Ouch!'

She raised her eyebrows as he winced. 'What's the matter?'

'I just bashed my head on your "Keep Off" sign.'

Smiling a little, Paris said, 'Does being ready to settle down depend upon age or circumstances?'

'Well, it is difficult to get married unless you meet someone you fall for, admittedly. But most men seem to reach an age when they feel that they've had enough of being on their own, that it's time to look around and choose someone to marry so that they can have a home and a family.' Ben gave her a sideways look. 'I suppose that sounds deadly boring to you, doesn't it?'

His words touched a raw spot so Paris hastily changed the subject by pushing her plate away and saying, 'Not boring—arrogant.'

'Arrogant?' He was astonished.

'The fact that men can think, because they've reached a certain point in their lives, that they can just go out and choose some girl to be their wife.'

'Ah, the feminist viewpoint.'

'Yes, exactly. Have there been girls in your past who've been really keen on you? Were they at an age when they were ready to settle down? What happened to them? Did you just say, "Well, thanks, but I'm not ready to commit myself yet."?'

'Something like that, yes,' Ben admitted. 'But it was a long time ago, when I was still training to be a barrister. I felt that I had to give that all my time and attention, which wouldn't have been fair on the girl. I would have been torn in two—my loyalties, my time divided—and probably would have failed in both my work and the relationship because of it. So I decided to concentrate on my career, get that under my belt first. Can't you identify with that?'

Paris had been looking at him rather belligerently, but

now she slumped. Yes, she could identify with that kind of ambition. God, could she. She pushed the thought aside, afraid of dwelling on it, afraid of looking into her soul. Somehow the conversation had become apposite to her own life and she couldn't face it.

Ben gave a frown of admonishment. 'I have just realised that you have avoided my question yet again. Are you a woman of mystery, Paris?'

'Oh, definitely,' she said in relieved amusement. 'And you haven't told me how the carol rehearsal went.'

This time he accepted her change of subject and they got onto safer ground. After lunch they took part in a bridge competition which required so much concentration that Paris was mentally shattered afterwards. They didn't do too badly, though, and Ben told her that he was proud of his pupil.

Being cooped up in the card-room all afternoon, Paris had seen nothing of Will—or Melanie, come to that—but both of them were in the bar when she came down after changing for dinner and the party. Paris had put on black evening trousers with a black and gold tunic-top. Elegant but casual. Melanie was in a silver lamé sheath that was so close-fitting that she couldn't possibly have had any underwear on beneath it.

The other girl was the centre of a small crowd of sympathisers, all talking of the letter bomb, and nearly everyone who came into the bar went over to ask how she was. Will, though, wasn't among those around her. He was sitting on a stool at the other end of the bar counter, talking to some other men about cricket. When he saw Paris come into the room, he broke off the conversation and stepped over to her.

'Buy you a drink?'

She gave him a searching look but could read nothing

in his face. Nodding, she said, 'OK. Thanks. A G and T, please.'

He gestured towards the stool he'd been using. Paris hesitated a moment then perched on it. The men he'd been talking to greeted her, but then moved aside a little, going on with their far more interesting views on the latest test match series in India.

'I didn't know you were a cricket buff,' she commented a minute later when he handed her a drink.

Will shrugged. 'One keeps up.' He leaned against the bar and took a swallow of his drink. 'How did you get on in the bridge tournament?'

'Fine. Ben's a good teacher.'

Paris glanced across at Melanie and the eyes of the two girls met momentarily. Paris gave her a sympathetic smile but only received a glare in return. Which was hardly surprising. Paris would have been angry herself if the man whom she was having an affair with invited an old flame to have a drink—and right in front of her eyes, too!

'I'd like to talk to you later,' Will was saying. He saw wariness come into her eyes and her face immediately close, so he said quickly, 'Nothing heavy. I just feel we need to talk, clear the air. I don't want you to feel that you have to get away from me.'

'I see.' She looked down at her drink.

'So will you?'

'Talk to you?' She raised her eyes to his, found him watching her intently. 'Perhaps.'

Will's mouth twisted a little. 'It's only to talk, not make a commitment.'

Paris took a drink, then said, 'Why aren't you with Melanie?'

'Why should I be with her?'

'Aren't you two an item?'

'No, we're not.' He said it with a definiteness that surprised her.

Her brows rose a little and she slid off the stool as she saw Ben and some other people stroll in. 'Maybe you ought to try telling Melanie that.' And she went over to join Ben and his friends.

The tension of their virtual imprisonment in the castle must have got on everyone's nerves, because they turned to the party that evening almost as a life-saver. Everyone had clubbed together to buy wine and beer, the hotel manager had donated a few bottles of Scotch, and one of the waiters turned out to be a virtuoso on the bagpipes. They danced reels, played silly party games, drank a little too much, and managed to forget where they were and why they were there.

It was midnight before they began to sing carols, and because they were still in a happy mood they started with the rousing ones, like 'Good King Wenceslas' and 'O, Come all ye Faithful'. Ben was playing his guitar so Paris stood against the wall, enjoying watching everyone letting their hair down, but definitely not singing.

She hadn't spoken to Will again that evening, although she'd seen him dancing and once they'd been in the same set for a Scottish reel. But their hands had touched as briefly as their eyes, and then they had gone back to their partners.

Paris had been dancing with Captain Waters at the time—he had been taking time off from his guardianship—and Will had been dancing with one of their fellow jurors, a middle-aged widow. Melanie too had joined in, but Paris hadn't seen her dancing with Will. So maybe what he had said was true.

But Paris had seen him go into the other girl's room with her own eyes, and could hardly think that their affair could have broken up so soon. And it was he who had rushed to Melanie's side when she had fainted earlier that day, although it already seemed ages ago.

Paris was sure that Will would never just ignore Melanie when they had been so close. Maybe it was Melanie, then? Had she got her eyes on someone else? But Paris could see no signs of it and, remembering the glare she'd got from the girl earlier, couldn't believe that it was Melanie's doing. So maybe something had happened between them.

A lot of wild reasons went through Paris's mind, but to conjecture was useless. And, after all, what did it matter? It would make no difference to Will's attitude to her. All right, he hadn't managed to conceal the fact that he still cared about her, but that was as far as it went—as far it would ever go.

He would never forgive her for what he thought she'd done; she knew that with absolute certainty. And there was little point in trying to tell him the truth because he wouldn't believe her and would only think worse of her for lying. But she was, anyway, to blame for losing the baby; it had been her responsibility. And there was no way that she could ever atone for it.

They were singing 'Silent Night' now, reducing everyone to misty-eyed pathos. Paris felt a touch on her arm and saw that Will had come up beside her.

'Our talk?'

She frowned. 'Now? Can't it wait till tomorrow?'

'I think it's best as soon as possible.'

Paris hesitated, then nodded. 'All right.'

Needing something to do with her hands, she picked up her glass and took it with her. They slipped out of the ballroom and walked down the carpeted corridor, found the television room empty and went inside.

She took only a few steps into the room and then turned to face him. 'So what do you want to say?'

'I was right this morning, wasn't I? The only reason you want to leave here is to get away from me.'

He didn't make it a question; he was already certain in his own mind, and Paris had little choice but to nod reluctantly. 'Yes.'

'I know I haven't made it exactly easy for you here, but I didn't think that—'

'It was already arranged before I came,' Paris broke in. She turned away from him. 'When the police came to collect me, I wouldn't go with them at first. I tried to make them take me somewhere else, some other safe house. But it was too near Christmas and they couldn't arrange it. The best they could promise was to find somewhere for me afterwards.'

Will was silent for a moment, then said tightly, 'You were so averse to seeing me again?'

She rounded on him indignantly. 'What else would you expect? We didn't exactly part on friendly terms. You threw me out! You said you were so disgusted that you couldn't bear to be near me. You—you looked at me as if I was dirt. Can you wonder that I didn't want to be cooped up in the same place as you for days, perhaps weeks on end?' Her voice broke and she took a hasty swallow of her drink.

'I wasn't exactly enthusiastic about coming here myself,' Will admitted. Then slowly, reluctantly, he added, 'Mostly, I suppose, because I'd never really got over you.'

She turned quickly to look at him at that, met his eyes for a brief instant and then looked hastily away again, her cheeks pale.

His voice became harsh as he burst out, 'I couldn't believe that you could go ahead and have an abortion. *And without even telling me.* The way I found out... I thought that was the worst part of it. But after you'd gone—that's when it really started to hurt.'

'I don't understand,' she said gropingly. 'You mean—because I wasn't there?'

'No. It was because I realised that I had been completely wrong about you—my thoughts, my hopes, my feelings—all of them wrong.'

He swung away from her, thumped his clenched fist against the back of a chair. Paris's hands tightened on her glass but she didn't speak, somehow knowing that what he would say next would be all-important to her.

Will gave a laugh of bitter self-mockery. 'For a start I thought that I meant more to you than your precious job.' She almost went to speak, then stopped, and was glad she had when he said forcefully, 'And don't tell me that I did, Paris, because I know darn well it isn't true. If you had loved me it would have been me you'd turned to when you were pregnant, not Emma. And if you'd loved me you would have wanted my child. OK, I know we weren't married, and that it was a mistake, but it was our child, for God's sake. Didn't that mean anything to you?' But then he answered his own question. 'But of course it didn't. I've asked myself that countless times, but it always comes back to the same thing. You were willing to destroy a life because it would have interfered with your ambition, with your career—'

'That isn't true,' Paris broke in, compelled to speak even though she knew it wouldn't make any difference.

Will looked as if he was going to argue, but then shrugged. 'So what is true?'

Her eyes widened and a wave of hope filled her. Might he believe her if she told him everything? But she couldn't just blurt it out, and there were things that needed to be brought out into the open first.

Paris paused for a moment, then said carefully, 'When I found out I was pregnant you were away. I needed someone—a woman—to talk to and Emma was the only friend

I had who was that close. My mother—we're too distant; I could never have confided in her.

'It came as a shock to find I was pregnant when I thought that I couldn't possibly be. I wasn't prepared for it, for even the possibility of it, and I wasn't sure how *I* felt about it, let alone how you would feel. I needed to sort things out in my mind, to talk them through, but you weren't there. So I went to Emma. I know now that it was a terrible mistake, but it seemed right at the time. She was a lot older than me, so much more experienced.'

'I can guess what she said to you; you don't have to tell me,' he said curtly.

'Can you? I suppose you think she told me that I'd lose my job, that it would ruin my career.'

'Well, didn't she?'

'Yes, she did,' Paris admitted. 'But that was almost incidental. What she told me first and foremost was that if I went ahead with the pregnancy then I would lose you.'

Will's head came up as he stared at her.

'She kept on and on about it. She said that if you'd been ready to accept a child you would already have asked me to marry you, that you would always blame me for getting pregnant, for ruining your life. And that if we did marry because of the baby and we ever quarrelled you would always accuse me of trapping you into marriage. She said that you would grow to hate me for it.'

Will shook his head in angry disbelief. 'And you let her convince you of all that rubbish?'

'Yes, because there were a couple of things that ran very true.'

'And they were?'

She paused, licked lips that had gone dry. 'That you only asked me to move in with you because I couldn't afford to stay with her. And that you hadn't asked me to marry you.' She raised her eyes to meet his. 'You hadn't even said that you loved me. Not in so many words. Although I thought you did.'

He gazed at her for a moment, moved his lips as if he couldn't speak, then jerked out, 'Of course I loved you. I loved you almost from the first moment I met you.'

'You never said.'

'I thought you knew. That it was the same for you. I thought it went so deep that it didn't have to be said.'

'But it does. A woman has to be told, to be sure. And I wasn't sure of your feelings, only of my own. I didn't want to lose you. I would have done anything not to lose you—' She broke off, realising how wrong an impression those last words would make. It was impossible now to tell him that she hadn't had an abortion; he would never believe her.

Angry with herself, she went on, 'But those weren't my only reasons for not telling you. You'd made it pretty clear just what you thought of working mothers. Well, my views are completely the opposite: I think it's perfectly possible for a woman to have a family as well as a career. But I felt torn apart because you were so adamant about it. I was almost glad you were away because I had to make up my mind whether to give up a job that I loved and live by your rules, or whether it would be possible to work out some sort of compromise.'

'But instead you took what was for you the easy way out. You little coward.'

'You asked me to tell you the truth and I'm trying to explain. If you'll just listen—'

But Will said acidly, 'So that's your version of what happened, is it?'

There was such scorn in his voice that her heart sank. 'I've told you the truth.'

'Rubbish! You've told yourself it's the truth, convinced yourself of it. But nothing—not Emma, no one— would have persuaded you to have an abortion if you hadn't wanted to—even if only subconsciously.'

She stared at him for a moment, then turned away, fighting a wave of terrible despair. In a few words he had exposed her own innermost fears—a dread that she had always been too afraid to face. It was true that she'd considered an abortion as a serious option, had thought about it for days, and, when she'd had the miscarriage, along with the sadness there had been an overwhelming feeling of relief.

Paris gripped the glass between her hands, held it so tightly that it shattered. What was left of the red wine inside it trickled over her fingers, red, like the blood of her gashed hand.

Without turning she said, 'Maybe you're right. I don't know. But it hardly matters now, does it?'

'Of course it damn well matters!'

She shook her head and walked forward to a table to set the broken glass down, her back still to him, blocking his view. She tried to press the vein in her palm but the blood was flowing freely now. 'No, it doesn't—because you don't trust me and you never will. You've convinced yourself of my guilt and nothing will change that. So I really don't think there's any point in prolonging this discussion, do you?'

'You cold-hearted little bitch.'

She flinched but only said, 'Yes, of course. Whatever you say. Shut the door on your way out, won't you?'

She heard Will move, stride to the door, but then he paused. 'We haven't yet settled the question of your leaving here. There's no need for it.'

'You mean that you wouldn't bring up this subject again? You wouldn't throw it in my face every time we met?'

He drew in his breath, then said, 'No.'

Paris laughed unsteadily. 'Liar! You can't leave it alone. You admitted that yourself, the first time we talked.'

'I give you my word.'

Her hand was starting to hurt—a throbbing pain that made her grit her teeth so that she didn't answer.

'It would be stupid for you to go, Paris. Promise me you won't.'

'Just get out of here, Will.'

'Not until you promise.'

Her voice rose hysterically. 'All right! All right, I promise. Now get out of here and leave me alone!'

'My pleasure,' he said in curt anger, and went out, slamming the door behind him.

She slumped when he'd gone, the stubborn pride that had held her upright draining away. There was blood all over her clothes, and it would drip onto the owner's tartan carpet if she didn't get her hand bound up quickly.

The manager had a first-aid box in his office, but the office would probably be locked and he would be in the ballroom with all the others. And there was no way that she was going to go back there and let everyone see how stupid she'd been. There were some sticking plasters in her own room, but she wasn't sure that they would be enough to stop the bleeding.

She tried to think what to do but her silly head felt as if it was packed with cotton wool and she found it difficult to concentrate. I must have had too much to drink, she decided. Come on, pull yourself together.

With a rush of determination, Paris swung round to go to the door, but must have turned too quickly because her head began to spin, and she stumbled. Wow! Someone must have spiked her drinks for her to feel this light-headed.

She put her good hand on the back of a chair to support herself—the chair that Will had hit in frustrated anger. The poor chair was really going through it tonight. She made another effort but before she could take more than a faltering step the door opened and Will came back in.

'We forgot to arrange which of us would tell Captain Waters that you're staying. I'll do it, if you—' He broke off and took a stride towards her, frowning. 'Paris? Are you all right?'

He caught her as she swayed. She laughed. 'It would seem to be your role in life: to catch fainting females.'

'Yes, but— My God, your hand! What have you done? Oh, Paris, you little fool, *what have you done*?'

'I cut my hand on the glass.' She said the words quite clearly but they didn't seem to come out that way. Then she looked into Will's face, saw the horror there and understood. 'No! The glass broke and I cut myself, that's all!'

He put her in an armchair and looked at her searchingly, then picked up the broken glass and saw the blood on the table. Reassured, he took a clean handkerchief from his pocket and bound it round her hand. 'Hold it up, and wait here. I'll be right back.'

A great lethargy filled her and she felt overwhelmingly tired. Leaning back in the chair, Paris was glad to close her eyes. Her hand hurt, at one with the painful thoughts that chased each other through her brain. Will would never believe her, never forgive her; she had ruined her own life and, it seemed, his too. There was nothing she could do— nothing. A stupid tear trickled down her cheek.

He was back with the first-aid box and she hastily wiped her face, leaving a smear of blood.

Will took hold of her hand, opened her fingers and swore softly. 'Why the hell didn't you tell me, you little idiot?' He didn't seem to expect an answer but worked quickly on her hand, using some kind of antiseptic that stung and made her quickly turn away as she winced.

'I'm sorry to hurt you even more. Soon be over.'

So he thought her tears were from the pain of her hand. Well, that was all right. Let him think that.

When her hand was bandaged Will leaned back on his heels to look at her, picked up a clean swab and used it to wipe the smear of blood off her face. Then he gently stroked her cheek with the back of his fingers. 'You always were a proud, stubborn little fool. Never admitting that you were hurt, never letting me see you cry.'

At the rough tenderness in his voice, Paris came very close to letting him see just how much she was hurting. But the hurt was all inside and that was where it had to stay. She managed a smile. 'It was a stupid thing to do. Would *you* have wanted anyone to know?'

His eyes troubled, Will said, 'I meant what I said, Paris. I won't refer to—to what happened again. It's over. Forget it.'

She gave a laugh that was more a sigh of despair. 'Oh, Will. How can you ever forget a thing like that?'

He frowned. 'But surely you…?'

She shook her head tiredly. 'No. It's there all the time. All the time.' Leaning forward, she said, 'I'd like to go up to my room now.'

But Will didn't get up out of the way. Instead he stayed where he was, looking intently into her face. 'Have I been wrong about you, Paris? Have I?'

Now, if ever, was her opportunity to tell him the truth, but somehow there now seemed little point in it. In her own mind she was almost as guilty as she would have been if she'd had the termination.

She pushed herself to her feet and Will rose easily with her, stepped back to give her space. She didn't look at him as she walked to the door; she went to open it, then paused, and said with difficulty, 'I know that nothing will make any difference now, but I wasn't ready for motherhood. I wanted to keep my job. OK, maybe that was a selfish attitude, but have you thought that maybe yours was too? It just wasn't the right time, Will. Not for me and probably not for you either.'

'Would it ever have been the right time for us, then?' he said heavily.

Paris didn't answer. She went to open the door with her injured hand, changed to the other one, and went out of the room.

The party had broken up; there were just a few stragglers saying prolonged goodbyes round the door of the ballroom or waiting for the lift. Paris avoided them, running as swiftly up the stairs as she could manage and was out of breath by the time she'd reached her own landing.

She hadn't locked her door; the key had a large and heavy metal number-tag on it that was too big for a pocket or her evening purse so she usually didn't bother with it. Tonight she wished she had, because as soon as she switched on the light Paris realised that someone had been in her room. The drawers in the dressing table and the doors of the wardrobe were open and clothes scattered on the floor. Her duvet had been pulled back and the mattress soaked in some liquid that absolutely stank.

Moving nearer, Paris took a tentative sniff and realised that it was bleach. Yes, the empty container had been thrown down onto the carpet, leaving a white stain.

With a cry of anger, she picked up one of her good evening dresses and found that it had been savagely torn— hacked at with a pair of scissors from the look of it. Looking in the open drawers, she saw that her bottles of nail varnish and perfume had been emptied all over the contents. It didn't take much guessing to know who had done this. Melanie! Whatever had happened between her and Will, she had evidently blamed Paris for it and had taken her revenge in this petty, spiteful way.

After all that had happened today this could have been the last straw that threw Paris into the depths of despair but, strangely, all it did was make her seething mad. She had a good mind to go straight to Melanie and face her with it.

She half turned to march down to the other girl's room, but then stopped; Melanie would be expecting something like that and would make darn sure that her door was locked. And she would deny everything, of course; that's why she had come here at night to take her sneaky revenge. On Paris, of course; she wouldn't have dared do anything like this to Will. OK, so facing Melanie would have to wait. And in the meantime, what was she going to do about the room?

Paris decided to abandon it. The smell was so bad that she couldn't possibly have slept there anyway.

Rescuing for the morning some clothes that had escaped Melanie's tender attentions, she went down the corridor to the cleaner's storeroom. The elderly cleaner habitually left it unlocked; that was how Melanie had got hold of the bleach. On the wall was a chart on which the numbers of the occupied rooms were marked off. Paris picked one that was unoccupied, helped herself to bedlinen and towels, and went to find it.

Because it wasn't being used, the central heating in the room had been turned low, so that it felt cold and inhospitable. Paris turned up the thermostat, remembering how she'd done the same thing when she'd got home to her own flat from Budapest. That seemed a lifetime ago now, although it was less than a week.

She went to the windows to close the curtains but paused for a moment to look out. The moon was out, silvering the snow, making it diamond-bright in the cold frostiness of the night. The wind had blown away the snow on the fir trees, so that they stood out like dark sentinels, straight and stark, their branches no longer bowed under the weight.

Soon they would be celebrating Christmas. And this landscape was a far different one from that of Bethlehem. There would not have been snow there, Paris imagined; it would have been warm for the new baby, the kings and the shepherds. Here the sheep would have been taken down from the hills weeks ago and would have a long wait for the grass to appear. And any pregnant woman in this area would be afraid of the snow, of being trapped in some highland croft and unable to get help. But was that so very different from the Nativity?

Pulling the curtains closed, Paris got ready for bed as quickly as she could with her bandaged hand, got in and pulled the duvet close around her for warmth.

Because she was cold it took a while for her to go to sleep, her thoughts drifting always back to that so-called talk with Will. It had been more of a full-scale fight, but she was strangely glad that it had taken place. And relieved too. At least she had faced her guilt—that terrible cancer that had been eating away at her soul—and in admitting the basic cause had found an inner peace. Nothing would make up for the miscarriage, of course, but she felt better able to live with it now.

She fell asleep at last but woke in the middle of the night. It wasn't from a bad dream or anything; she woke with a smile of realisation because the way to atone had come to her at last. And it was really so simple, so very simple. She smiled again, turned over and went back to sleep.

It was almost ten o'clock the next morning when Paris found that she had unknowingly created a crisis. The cleaner, thinking her at breakfast, had gone to her room and found the terrible state it was in, so had immediately called the manager. He had tried to find Paris and, when he couldn't, had in turn called Captain Waters. He and his police colleague were both in the room when she strolled in there to see what she could do about her clothes.

'Good morning. It's quite a mess, isn't it?'

They both swung round to stare at her. Captain Waters gave a sigh of relief. 'Are you all right? We'd started to worry about you.'

Paris put her injured hand, covered now with just a large sticking plaster, in her pocket. 'Yes, fine.'

'You'd better go and tell everyone to call off the search,' he said to the policeman. When he'd gone he said, 'How did this happen?' and gestured at the room.

'I don't know. I found it like this when I came up last night, so I slept in an empty room because of the smell.'

He gave her a shrewd look. 'Are you sure you have no idea who did it?'

'None,' she said blandly.

He looked as if he didn't believe her and was going to say so, but just then Will strode into the room.

Coming straight to Paris, he took hold of her arm in a firm grip. 'Where the hell have you been?' he demanded brusquely.

There was anger in his voice but it was the anger of relief, and she recognised it for what it was, what it meant, and her heart leaped.

'Er—if you'll excuse me for a moment.' Captain Waters went out, closing the door behind him.

'I thought you'd got lost again,' Will said curtly.

'Again?'

'When you didn't arrive here with the rest of us, and I thought Ramsay had got to you,' he explained. His eyes met hers, wry, rueful. 'It was hell then, waiting, wondering. The thoughts that kept going through my mind… And then to have it happen again this morning.'

She lifted a hand to touch his face gently. 'Will you do something for me?'

'What?'

'Will you kiss me?'

He froze, then raised a cynical eyebrow. 'For old times' sake?'

'No.' She shook her head. 'For now. For the me I am now.'

For a long moment Will didn't move and she thought that he was going to deny her, but his grip tightened on her arm and he drew her slowly towards him, his eyes holding hers. She could feel the tension in his hand, see it in his face. He lowered his head to hers, touched her lips with his mouth. For an instant it was as if time had stood still and he was kissing her for the very first time all over again. And yet it was so achingly familiar too—the searing heat of his lips, their firmness. But his lips had never quivered like this before, never been so hungry and yet so afraid.

Her mouth opened under his, soft and yielding. She felt his swift intake of breath, the undeniable tremor of emotion that ran through him. Desire suffused her like a burning ache deep in her body, but her overpowering emotion was one of excitement. It was possible—that resolve she had taken in the middle of the night. Now that he had kissed her it was surely possible.

His kiss deepened and Paris lifted her hand to his shoulder. But she brushed his neck as she did so, and it was as if her touch brought him back to reality, because Will suddenly let her go, stepping abruptly away. He stared at her, the hunger and need plain in his face but being subjugated to an even greater need to control his feelings.

'Paris, it's no good; I—'

But she held up a hand to silence him. 'It was only a kiss,' she said lightly, then walked to the door. 'I think I can hear someone outside.'

On opening it, she saw Mrs Paston and a couple of other women, come to see the wreckage of her room. Will slipped away while they were still exclaiming with horror. The women immediately began to help her to sort through her clothes, rescuing what could be washed and putting into a depressingly growing pile the number of things that were completely ruined.

'We all know who did this,' Mrs Paston said grimly. 'And she ought to be punished in some way. At the least she should be made to pay compensation for all this.'

'Nothing can be proved,' Paris pointed out. 'And I suppose it's my fault for not locking my door.'

She decided to keep to her new room and took the rest of her things along, then went down to the manager's office to get the key. He was on the phone, using the only line in the place that was connected to the outside world. Paris made signs for a key and he gestured to a board on the wall behind him.

Number 315, the one she wanted, was easy to find, but she noticed another key nearby with a plastic tag reading, 'Spare passkey. All floors.' With a small sigh of exhilaration Paris lifted that down as well and slipped it into her pocket.

After the party last night, most of the adults wanted to have a restful day, although some games were organised for the children. Everyone had heard of the attack on Paris's room and she was inundated with offers to lend her clothes, some of which she was glad to accept, although they weren't always the kind of thing that she would have chosen herself. But they were offered out of kindness and her acceptance was grateful, pleasing the donors.

Her delicate silk underclothes and night things had been

one of Melanie's prime targets and had been entirely ruined, so that night Paris had to wear a borrowed nightdress.
She waited until gone midnight, then put on a pair of light-
weight mules that hadn't been damaged, and slipped a borrowed dressing-gown, long and dark-coloured, over her
nightdress. This time she remembered to lock her door,
putting the heavy key in her pocket along with the passkey.

The corridor outside her room was lit only by two
dimmed wall-lights—one at the head of the stairs, the other
by the lift—but they were enough to see her way by.
Because she'd changed her room, Paris had further to go
to reach the stairs. She walked quietly along, letting the
excitement and anticipation take hold, praying that it
would all go right, this great adventure she was about to
set out on.

There was a soft whirr and the doors of the lift suddenly
opened. Paris quickly ducked into a doorway, afraid of
being seen. Whoever it was who came out must have been
alone; there was no sound of voices and the person was
very quiet.

Peeping out, Paris saw a woman walk along and stop at
the turret stair where Paris had followed the wet footprints.
When she reached it the woman glanced back and Paris
saw that it was Melanie. Surely she wasn't going to have
another go at her room? Paris thought indignantly. But
Melanie went up the stair, lighting her way with a torch.

Paris hesitated; she had important business of her own
tonight, but curiosity overcame her and she went quickly
to the staircase. The cold air from outside made her pull
the dressing gown closer around her, and again she hesitated, but then went up the stairs. The wooden door at the
top was ajar and she quietly pushed it further open, trying
to see outside. But the angle prevented her so she pushed
it wide and stepped cautiously out onto the roof.

The sky was black tonight, with dark clouds obscuring

the moon, and it was very cold and windy. There was no sign of Melanie, although a chimney-stack blocked her view of all the parapet.

Paris felt for the anorak but it wasn't there. She took another step forward to peer past the chimneys. There was a sudden noise from behind and above her, but before she could turn something hit her in the middle of the back and sent her flying towards the edge of the roof.

She felt herself falling but managed to twist sideways as she did so, avoiding the battlemented edge so that she ended up on the roof instead of overbalancing and pitching down to the ground so far below. She had fallen heavily and for a moment lay stunned, as much by fright as lack of breath. But then she realised that Melanie must have pushed her and got indignantly to her feet, having had about enough, prepared to do battle.

Groping her way to the door, Paris found the handle and turned it. Nothing happened. She turned it again and pushed against the door, but still it didn't move. With utter disbelief she realised that it was locked. Melanie had deliberately left her out here alone in the freezing cold.

CHAPTER SEVEN

'MELANIE! This isn't funny,' Paris yelled, banging her fist against the wood of the door. 'Come and unlock this door at once.'

She leaned her left ear against the panels, straining to hear, covering her other ear to try and cut out the noise of the wind that howled around the tower. But she could hear nothing, so banged on the door again.

'OK, you've had your fun; now let me in.' Nothing happened although she waited for several minutes. Paris shoved her hands into her pockets, already shivering with cold, then placed her mouth close to the door and shouted, 'You want me to apologise to you? All right, then—I'm sorry I followed you up here. Now, please, Melanie, let me in. It's really cold out here.'

She was angry at having to apologise, annoyed that she had to plead, but her teeth were chattering and the doorway gave little protection from the wind. The air was so cold that she might as well not have been wearing any clothes at all, they had so little warmth in them.

'Please, Melanie. I'm really sorry. *Please* open the door.' She could hear the begging note in her voice and despised herself for it, but was still confident that Melanie was standing on the other side of the door, hugely enjoying the silly prank she'd pulled, and would soon open it to see Paris's discomfiture for herself.

It was only when Melanie still didn't open it and let her back into the warmth that it dawned on Paris that maybe this wasn't just another vengeful trick, that maybe Melanie wasn't going to open the door at all and had left her out on the roof to freeze to death. But Paris wasn't about to be left out there to die tamely, so she decided she'd better do something about it.

The most obvious thing was to go along the parapet to the next turret and see if the door there was unlocked. It took a lot of courage to leave the comparative shelter of the doorway and go along the roof edge in the fierce wind.

The snow, which had melted a little and then frozen again several times, was treacherous under her slippered feet, and the wind constantly buffeted her, threatening to knock her off balance and make her slip over. Twice she almost fell, and with a curse realised that the only way she was going to get safely across was on her hands and knees. Anger kept her going along the long length of the building and when she reached the other turret at last she found, without surprise, that that door, too, was locked.

Paris leaned against it, her breath tight in her chest, her teeth chattering so loudly that she could hear nothing else. It was then that she screamed, knowing that she couldn't fight the cold much longer.

Across the courtyard she could make out a light in the gatehouse where the police guards were, but it might just as easily have been miles away, because the wind took her voice and made it just a shrill pipe in the howling cacophony. Paris screamed again, becoming really frightened now, but then huddled in the doorway and tried not to panic, tried to think, to find some way out of this.

Working out the plan of the hotel, she realised that this must be the turret where Ben had his suite, that he must be asleep in the bedroom only a few yards away from her. Leaning over the parapet as far as she dared, she yelled his name over and over again, but no light came on to shine in the windows, he didn't look out to see who called him.

She leaned back in the doorway again, knowing that she

couldn't last out much longer. Pressing herself against it, willing the door to open, she felt something press into her hip and realised that it was her doorkey with the heavy metal tag.

Feverishly she took it out of her pocket and tried it in the lock; then, when that didn't work, she tried the pass-key, but both were made for small Yale locks, not the locks on these heavy doors. She slumped again, hope gone. Her room key was freezing cold to her fingers, making them burn with the cold, and she almost dropped it. Then she had a sudden idea.

Going to the very end of the parapet, she leaned out as far as she could, gripping the last merlon with her left arm and swinging her right backwards and forwards; trying to take careful aim in the dark, trying to get as much impetus as she could. Then she hurled the heavy key at the nearest window with all the strength she had left.

She heard it smash even above the noise of the wind, the glass shattering. She waited breathlessly, petrified that Ben might have slept through it. But then light glimmered between the cracks in the curtains, they were pulled back and she could see Ben's silhouette against the light.

'Ben!' She screamed out his name with all the strength she had left. 'Ben, up here. Help me.'

He glanced up and the next second he was gone, but it seemed an age before the door behind her opened and he was helping her inside, exclaiming, asking questions. But she couldn't answer, could only cry with relief and cold.

Ben was magnificent; he carried her to his room, put her into his beautifully warm bed and gave her a slug of his whisky, before picking up the phone. Within minutes Captain Waters was there and then she found herself standing under a hot shower, nightdress and all, supported by both men who were getting as wet as she was.

Very gradually the terrible shivering eased and finally

stopped as warmth crept back into her veins. Then they
gave her towels and let her dry herself before she put on
a pair of Ben's pyjamas. There was hot coffee waiting,
strongly laced with whisky, which she drank gratefully as
she again sat in Ben's bed, the duvet held close around
her, while they each massaged one of her feet.

'Can you feel this?' Captain Waters asked.

'Yes, a little.'

'Good, hopefully you won't get frostbite, then. Now,
would you like to tell us what you were doing out there
in this weather and at this time of night?'

'She locked me out there.'

They exchanged glances. 'She?'

'M-Melanie.' Paris shivered again as she remembered.

'Oh, hell!' Captain Waters said feelingly. 'When she got
that letter bomb I thought she was in the clear. What happened?'

'I saw her going up to the roof again and—'

'What do you mean "again"? Had you seen her go up
there before?'

Paris nodded, then took another drink so that she could
go on. 'Yes. I saw her a few nights ago. At least, I was
pretty sure it was her.'

'Why didn't you tell me?' he said sharply.

'I wasn't absolutely sure. But I was going to tell you,
but the next morning the bomb came, so—so I didn't,' she
finished lamely.

'You were taken in as we all were,' he said ruefully.
'Sorry. Go on, please.'

'I didn't think she'd seen me tonight, but she must have
done. When I followed her she was hiding behind the door.
She pushed me out onto the roof and I fell down. Then
she went back in and locked the door. I—I thought it was
just revenge, the same reason for her making a shambles
of my room, ruining my clothes. I kept banging on the

door, expecting her to open it, but—but she left me out there. I yelled but no one heard because of the wind. And she'd taken the coat, so—'

'What coat?'

'The first time I went out on the roof, to have a look, there was a coat outside, by the turret. A thick anorak. I thought one of your men must have left it there.'

Captain Waters grimaced, stood up. 'Can you manage both feet for a while?' he said to Ben. 'I think I'd better go and make a few phone calls.'

When he'd gone, Paris said, 'Have I been abysmally stupid?'

'You and the rest of us too, by the sound of it. Have some more whisky.' He poured them both a generous helping. 'By the way, what were you doing out in the corridor anyway? Or needn't I ask?' Paris flushed a little and he said, 'I see that I needn't.' He began rubbing her feet again. 'Can you feel your toes yet?'

'Yes, but I'm quite enjoying having them rubbed.'

He laughed and went on for a while, but then found her his thickest pair of woollen socks to put on. They were bright red. 'A trendy aunt gave them to me for Christmas,' he explained. 'I was going to forget to take them home with me when we leave here.'

Captain Waters came back and pulled up a chair to sit beside her. He looked grim. 'I'd better come clean,' he said to them. 'We've been a bit suspicious of Melanie Truscott all along because she had some contact with Ramsay while he was in prison. However, we decided to let her come here with all of you but to keep a close eye on her until we were sure of her, one way or another. She seemed to take a fancy to your ex-boyfriend so we let him in on it and persuaded him to watch her for us.'

Paris stared. 'Will? You mean he wasn't keen on her himself?'

The captain shook his head. 'No. And at first he was very reluctant to help us. It took some persuasion to make him agree.'

'I suppose by "persuasion" you mean coercion,' she said shortly.

He grinned. 'I'm afraid so. He cut up rough until we promised him that we'd do everything in our power to get *you* here as soon as we possibly could.'

'Oh.' Paris could find nothing else to say.

'He kept his word, much against his will, but once the letter bomb arrived and we thought she was in the clear I'm afraid he dropped her like the proverbial hot cake.'

Paris, remembering Will being drawn into Melanie's room, was wondering just how close a watch on her they had considered it necessary for him to keep. She frowned. 'But I don't understand. Are you saying that you're now suspicious of Melanie again?'

'What reason could she possibly have for going out on the roof, unless she was sending Ramsay some kind of signal?'

'But the letter bomb? She didn't fake her shock at getting that. I swear it was genuine.'

'Yes, I'm sure it was. But what if Ramsay deliberately sent it to her to divert suspicion from her?'

'Without telling her, you mean?'

'Yes.'

They both looked at him with troubled eyes. 'But how would she signal to him?' Ben objected. 'With a torch or something?'

'No, much more simple than that. With a portable phone, of course. We went through her luggage when she arrived, the same way we went through everyone else's, but phones are so small nowadays, she might have been able to conceal it. We didn't body-search everyone. Her difficulty, though, is that we're surrounded by hills; portables don't work well here; that's one of the reasons why we chose the place. But they might up on the roof.'

'So you think Ramsay probably knows where we are?' Ben said slowly.

'I'm afraid I do, yes.'

'What will you do—move us somewhere else?'

Captain Waters shook his head. 'No, this has gone on long enough. I've spoken to my superiors and we've decided to try and trap him. But we'll need your help—both of you,' he said, looking at them intently.

'Of course,' Ben said at once.

But Paris looked at the captain warily. 'What sort of help?'

'Nothing very onerous. I want Melanie to think you're still out there on the roof, frozen stiff.'

'Oh, nice.'

'It's all right, you don't have to go out there again,' he said quickly, seeing the sudden alarm in her face. 'You can stay hidden here in Ben's suite. He can have breakfast served here, but he'll have to put in an appearance downstairs during the day, to allay any suspicion.'

'What about the cleaner, and the broken window?' Ben pointed out.

'That will be taken care of. No problem.'

'But surely I'll be missed,' Paris objected.

'Yes, but the police and I will naturally want to keep that quiet so as not to alarm everyone. But we'll look just worried enough for anyone who's watching us to notice.'

'You mean Melanie.'

'Of course.'

'But what's the point?'

'You following Melanie out onto the roof tonight must have stopped her from sending a message. Maybe she'll try again tomorrow night—and we'll be listening.'

'Can you do that?' Ben asked.

'Oh, yes, quite easily.'

Paris said, 'But other people might miss me, too.'

They both knew that she meant Will, but the captain said, 'We'll say that you've got a bad cold and are spending the day in bed.'

'Which will probably be true by tomorrow,' Paris said pessimistically. 'If Melanie notices that you're anxious and I'm not around, then Will might notice as well. Could you tell him that I'm all right?'

'No.'

'Why not?'

'Same reason as Ramsay didn't tell Melanie about the letter bomb: like hers, Will's reaction has got to be authentic.'

'But surely if you were searching everywhere for me you'd be bound to go out on the roof and look?'

'We'd have no reason to. And we'd be concentrating our search outside, questioning the tradesmen, looking in their vans, thinking that you'd run away on your own initiative. Now wouldn't we?'

Paris was silent, realising that he'd got it all worked out. She nodded, suddenly tired. 'All right; if there's no other way.'

Leaning back against the pillows, she fell instantly into a deep sleep and was unaware of Ben sitting in a chair beside her, watching over her, or of a policeman quietly replacing the broken window and clearing up the glass.

She woke late and found Ben still sitting patiently beside her, waiting to send for his breakfast. Some clothes had been brought from her room and by the time she'd dressed in the bathroom the food had arrived. Paris ate ravenously; she'd never felt so hungry in her life and food had never tasted so good. Even the thick porridge, which she usually avoided, tasted like manna from heaven this morning.

Ben watched her in grinning admiration. 'I pity the poor man who ever takes you on a skiing holiday,' he remarked.

She made a face at him and he laughed as he stood up, his own meal finished.

'I'd better go downstairs and look innocent as I mingle.'

'Do you have anything I can read? I shall be bored just watching television all day.'

'I've some law books; some of the cases make quite interesting reading.'

'Don't you have any novels or magazines?'

'No, but I'll try and bring you some up.'

'Oh, thanks. I like *Vogue* and *Cosmopolitan*—that kind of thing.'

'Sorry, but those are definitely out. If anyone saw me bringing that type of magazine up here they might get the wrong idea about me.'

Paris laughed richly. 'OK, just a book will do, then.'

When Ben had gone, she felt a strange mixture of emotions. For a start she felt lonely and out of place. Having to stay in Ben's suite was like visiting people you didn't know very well and being left to amuse yourself in a strange house. Only, this sitting-room, of course, was far more restricting.

She could see that outside it was snowing heavily again, which made her feel even more shut in. The door was locked and she had been warned not on any account to use or answer the phone, making the room like a prison, within a citadel that was no longer safe.

Because of Melanie's treachery and Ramsay's knowledge of their whereabouts, Paris should have felt afraid, but strangely she didn't. Instead, being still alive after coming safely through last night, she felt oddly elated, almost as if fate had forgiven her and allowed her to start again.

In her imagination she saw it almost as a sign that the

way which she had decided on had been approved and she was going to be allowed to carry it through. Not that she'd been able to last night. But there was tonight. And today was Christmas Eve, she remembered with a smile of satisfaction.

It was a couple of hours before Ben came back. He'd brought her a paperback from the hotel's library and yesterday's paper, but it was the news of what was happening downstairs not of the outside world that she really wanted to hear.

'Well, there's no panic or anything,' Ben told her. 'Captain Waters is playing it down, and nobody knows that you're missing.'

'Has—er—anyone asked for me?'

Ben grinned. 'I suppose by "anyone" you mean Will Brydon?' He shook his head. 'Not that I know of, but it's still early yet; for all anyone knows you could be sleeping late.'

He stayed with her till lunchtime, then went downstairs again, while Paris had to make do with soup and sandwiches that were smuggled up to her on the cleaner's trolley.

In the afternoon she read and watched television, whiling the hours away until Ben came again about five-thirty. Twice the phone had rung, and the first time she had automatically reached out to answer it, but had managed to stop herself in time.

Was it Melanie checking to make sure that she wasn't there? Paris wondered with a shiver. Just making certain she was lying up on the roof, dead and frozen? The thought brought the nightmare back again and she had to go and huddle against the radiator, so intense was the memory of the cold.

When Ben came she told him about the phone calls and he reported them to Captain Waters. Ben listened for a while as the captain talked to him, then said goodbye and put the phone down. Turning to her, he said, 'It seems there have been several calls to your room too. Will called you—twice, late in the morning—then went up there and banged on the door. When he didn't get any reply he went to see Mike Waters.'

'And?' Paris said impatiently.

'It seems you'd talked about leaving and he was afraid the police had spirited you away.'

'So what did Captain Waters tell him?' she asked, intensely interested now.

'Our good captain wouldn't commit himself either way. Which made Brydon somewhat angry evidently. He informed Mike Waters that if anything happened to you he would hold him personally responsible for it. He also demanded to be allowed to speak to you on the phone, and wasn't at all pleased when Mike refused.' He laughed. 'Mike says his desk won't ever be the same again after the fist-bashing it got.'

'Really?' She grinned widely, inordinately pleased.

Ben walked over to the spiral stair leading to the bedroom above. 'I'm going to change for dinner. It's special tonight. Venison soup and salmon fillets *en croûte*, and a whole range of puddings and cheeses to follow. I think they're going to do you proud too.'

'You mean they're sending some up for me?'

He gave her a sardonic grin. 'Not quite. You're having a ham sandwich instead of cheese.' Then he ran up the stairs as she indignantly threw a cushion at him.

It was Captain Waters himself who brought her food that evening and stayed with her while she ate.

'Melanie is safely downstairs in the dining-room,' he told her. 'She's being watched and if she makes a move I'll be informed.'

He had brought her a large tray and she was pleased to see that she was sharing the meal being served downstairs, and he had even brought her a bottle of wine.

'We searched her room today,' he added. 'We were right: she has got a portable phone—a very small one that she must have concealed on herself when she arrived.' Neither of them said anything but Paris's mind immediately went to Melanie's ample bosom, wondering if the phone had been concealed in her bra. 'It's quite likely that she'll try and make contact with Ramsay again tonight, and if she does we'll be waiting.'

'Won't she expect to see me up there?' she asked.

Captain Waters grinned. 'Yes, so we've made up a very lifelike—or perhaps I should say death-like—dummy which is now under several inches of fallen snow. Don't worry; her just going out onto the roof will be evidence enough, but we're hoping to listen in on her conversation with Ramsay so that we can get him in our net.'

'It will probably be late before she goes up there,' Paris observed. 'She'll have to wait until everybody goes to bed, won't she?'

'Probably. If you like, I'll let you know when she goes out there. Ben can answer the phone, just in case it's anyone else.'

'Thanks.'

He stood up to go, then held a key out to her. 'You may need this. We found it in the pocket of your dressing gown when we dressed the dummy in it last night.'

Paris took the passkey, blushed a little as she again said, 'Thanks.'

She had expected it to be really late before Ben came up to the suite, but he came in around midnight, saying that they had broken up early because of the children, who were excited because it was Christmas Eve. Their parents had been afraid that they either wouldn't get to sleep at all or would wake them at some unearthly hour in the morning to open the presents that a dozen 'Father Christmases' were covertly loading into stockings.

Ben had nothing much to report, but sat companionably with her as they finished off her bottle of wine. As the time passed they grew tense, waiting, both of them wondering if Melanie had changed her mind and hadn't gone up to the roof at all. But at one o'clock the phone rang and Ben answered it. He spoke only briefly, then put the receiver down and turned to Paris. 'They've got her. And they were able to listen. She was definitely talking to Ramsay.'

Paris went to ask him if Ramsay was nearby but stopped; she didn't want to feel any fear, not tonight.

'Well, I'm going to bed. Goodnight, Paris.'

'Goodnight.'

He went up the stairs, closing the door behind him, and ten minutes later Paris was out of the room and running lightly down the stairs, the passkey clutched in her hand. There was no one about; the whole hotel was asleep, waiting for Christmas Day. There was no one to see her in a borrowed nightdress, her hair loose, a light of eager anticipation in her green eyes.

The key turned easily in the lock of Will's door and she gave a small sigh of relief as she turned the handle and slipped inside. The room was in darkness but she made out the layout in the soft light from the corridor. It was a large room with a heavily carved four-poster bed dominating the centre. Paris didn't take any notice of anything else. She saw Will's sleeping figure and gently closed the door.

It made quite a loud click as the lock shot home, and Will stirred. She couldn't see him, but she heard the change in his breathing and guessed that he was awake.

Walking quietly on the soft carpet, her feet bare, Paris moved towards the bed.

There was a flurry of movement as Will turned over, and then came his voice, sharp and forceful. 'Get out of here, Melanie. I've already told you I'm not interested.'

Reaching the bed, Paris pulled back the covers and slid into it, encountering Will's hand as he reached for the bedside lamp.

'Damn it, Melanie, don't you listen? Get out of here before I darn well throw you out.'

'Well, if you really want me to go…' Paris murmured softly.

He was sitting up and had put one hand on her arm, was reaching past her for the light with the other. But when she spoke he immediately grew still. 'Dear God,' he said in little more than a whisper. 'Paris?'

She found his face with her hand and leaned forward to lightly kiss him on the mouth. 'Now do you know me?'

He didn't return the kiss, but went on with his original movement, found the light switch and turned on the lamp. Paris was disappointed but didn't let it show, instead smiling at him with imps of mischief dancing in her eyes.

She hadn't expected him to be angry, hadn't expected him to say harshly, 'Are you playing some kind of game, Paris? Disappearing and reappearing. I thought you'd broken your promise and got the police to take you somewhere else. Captain Waters as good as admitted that you'd gone.'

'No, I was here all the time. But it's a long story. Why don't I tell you about it later?' And she again leaned forward and would have kissed him, but he stopped her.

'Tell me now.'

'No, later.' She lifted her hands to the buttons of his pyjamas and began to undo them.

He caught her wrist, his eyes probing her face. 'Why are you here?'

'I came to give you your Christmas present,' she said lightly, and slipped her free hand inside his jacket. Finding his nipple, she caressed it gently.

Will stiffened, but said, 'And what makes you think I want you in my bed?'

Paris raised her brows. 'You don't? OK, we'll do it on the floor. I seem to remember we've had some pretty good times on the floor.' She kissed his throat. 'On the ground.' Her mouth moved to his ear. 'And in the car.' She bit gently. 'In that cave on the beach.' She traced his jawline and her tongue touched his lips, delicately tantalising. 'Then there was the hay barn out in the countryside when we got caught in that terrible thunderstorm. Now that was *really* something.'

'Are you trying to seduce me?' His voice had changed, sounded odd.

'You got it.' She freed her hand and carried on with the buttons. This time he didn't stop her, but when she raised her eyes to glance at him Paris found him watching her, a strangely rueful look in his eyes.

'Where did you get that terrible nightdress?'

She glanced down at the all-enveloping gown with its high neck and long sleeves, which was a dozen sizes too large for her. 'Mrs Paston lent it to me.'

'My God, no wonder the judge looks so frustrated.'

She smiled. 'You don't like it? I can always take it off.'

Heart beating, she waited. For a long moment Will didn't speak, then he said harshly, 'Are you protected, Paris?'

She had known that he would ask, was expecting it and had her answer ready. 'I don't make the same mistake twice.'

Grim lines showed round his mouth. 'That's what I thought. I don't know that I want this.'

'Why kick a gift-horse in the teeth?' she said pertly, and was pleased to see him smile despite himself.

Putting her hands on his chest, she let them rise caressingly to his shoulders, pushed off his jacket and drew it down his arms. Then she bent to kiss his nipples. He quivered, tried to control it, but couldn't. 'So do I take it off?' she breathed softly.

'No.' Her heart froze for agonisingly long seconds, until Will said, his voice thick, 'I'll take it off.'

He did so slowly, revealing to his gaze first her long, shapely legs, then the tempting loveliness of her slender body: the roundness of her breasts, the dark shadow of her thighs, the slimness of her waist—beauty concealed beneath prim and proper white flannel.

Will caught his breath, his eyes drinking her in. So a Victorian bridegroom must have felt when he saw his bride naked for the first time on their wedding night. 'God, I'd almost forgotten how lovely you are,' he murmured.

Lifting his hand, he let his fingertips touch her breast, so lightly, like the caress of a butterfly's wings. And yet it sent a great tremor of awareness running through her. Paris didn't try to hide it; there would have been no point—they both knew that she'd never been able to resist him. And anyway, she wanted him to know that she needed him—needed him desperately.

Pushing him gently back down on the pillow, Paris knelt over him as she drew back the duvet and tossed it aside. He was wearing pyjama trousers too, which made her smile. When they'd been together they had never worn anything in bed. But that had been a long, long time ago.

Undoing the button at his waist, she slowly pulled them down his legs, letting her nails run along his skin as she did so. Will made a hoarse sound deep in his throat, and again when she moved over him and let her hair trail across his broad chest.

Lowering herself a little until she was almost touching him, she let her nipple find his and rubbed herself teasingly against him. He groaned as his tiny nipple hardened and she felt the heat of anticipation on his skin. Her own breathing quickened and she felt her own breasts swell in awakened desire.

Will gripped her arms and she knew that he would soon become too excited and would take over, but she didn't want that—not yet. So Paris moved off him and knelt beside him, letting her fingers explore him instead. In the years since they had parted she had so often imagined herself in just this position, had thought that she knew every inch of his body, but seeing him naked now was an intense delight that no memory could compete with.

It was the contrasts in him that she saw anew: his whipcord muscles under the softness of his skin, the firmness of his features against the delicacy of his lashes, the strength in his hands and yet the gentleness of his touch. His broad chest was so powerful but his nipples so sensitive, his aroused manhood so hard and yet he trembled when she touched him there.

And yet in some ways it was almost as if time had stood still. She didn't have to try and remember what pleased him: her hands moved of their own accord, instinctively finding the places that made him catch his breath, that would make him groan if she stayed there. But she teased him, making him sweat but then moving on somewhere else until he grew tense again—playing with him, driving him mad with desire.

Then she bent and let her lips and tongue add to the game, circling his nipples, gently tugging at his ear, caressing him intimately until he groaned aloud and his hand found her shoulder, gripping it as tremor after tremor ran through him.

But then she was gone again, to trail her tongue along his arm, tasting the salt of his sweat, nuzzling his neck, feeling the tension in it, hearing his heart thudding in his chest, her senses full of the arrant masculinity of him. His body was trembling with almost uncontrollable need, was tense now, ready for love. She let her fingers brush his manhood again, lightly caress the heart of him, until he cried out and suddenly surged up and over her, unable to bear it any longer.

Will was so excited that he made no attempt to arouse her, instead taking her with a primitive hunger that wasn't to be denied. Fierce, almost savage hunger. But his need for her was more than enough for her to open to him willingly, to hold him tightly, exultantly inside her as he thrust with all his strength.

Her body rose to meet him, fuelling the flame of his passion, lifting them both to the heights of sexual ecstasy. Will cried out, then gasped out her name on a long groan that obliterated the long, empty years, the hurt and the mistrust. Her own moans joined his and she found that she was crying with happiness.

He seemed to be over her, holding her, taking her for ever, but then the shudders that ran through him slowly faded and his body relaxed. He lay down but still held her closely in his arms and, when his breathing had eased a little, drew her to him and kissed her.

'You're crying.' Putting up his hand, he clumsily wiped her tears.

'I know.' She laughed huskily. 'And so are you. Oh, *Will.*'

'I've wanted this so much, so much.' His voice was full of the remembered longing, but then grew rueful as he said, 'When I thought of you with your new lover, it nearly drove me crazy with jealousy. Although I had no right, I know, but—'

'There isn't anyone else,' she interrupted. 'I made him up. I'm sorry, but you were so antagonistic towards me when I arrived here that I felt I needed some kind of protection from you.' She put her hand against his chest. 'I thought you still hated me, you see.'

Will frowned, hesitated. 'I did. I convinced myself that I did. But when I saw you, looking lovelier than ever, all the old longing came back. I was angry, I'd hoped I was over you, so I took it out on you. But all the time—all the time—I was wanting this. Even though I told myself a thousand times that it was the last thing I wanted.'

Paris chuckled and kissed his chin. 'Well, it's a good job one of us did something about it, or I think we'd both have died of frustration.'

He smiled and cupped her breast possessively. 'It's the best Christmas present I've ever had. I just hope that Ramsay stays on the run for another couple of months at least.' He felt her tense and said quickly, 'Sorry! Sorry. I shouldn't have mentioned him when we're like this.'

'No, it's not that. It's just that he will probably be caught very soon now. Within a day or so, I imagine.'

'Why? How do you know?'

'Because your girlfriend has turned out to be the viper in our collective bosom.'

'What on earth are you talking about?'

'Melanie Truscott. It seems she's been in touch with Ramsay all along. He knows where we are.'

'So Mike Waters was right about her.' He glanced at Paris. 'She isn't my girlfriend; the police asked me to keep an eye on her.'

'I know; they told me. But did you have to keep such a *close* eye on her?'

'What do you mean?'

Paris lowered her head, watching her finger glide down his chest as she said in a detached tone, 'I saw you both going into her room one night.'

'Did you? And if you'd hung around for another ten minutes you would have seen me leaving.' Paris raised her eyebrows and he said, 'Melanie made some excuse about her hair-dryer not working properly. When I'd fixed it I ignored all the come-on signals and left.'

'You didn't go to bed with her?'

'No. I don't fancy Melanie, and I'm certainly not going to sleep with a woman I don't want.'

Paris smiled. 'Not even for Queen and country?'

'I'm no James Bond. I'm a one-woman man.'

'Really?' Her heart skipped a beat. 'Only one woman?'

A devilish look came into his eyes. 'Well—only one woman at a time.'

That made Paris laugh. Sitting up, she said, 'I ought to punish you for that and make you miss out a course.'

'A course?'

'Yes; because tonight is a banquet, and what you've had was just an appetiser. Now I'm going to give you the entrée—and I think you're just about ready for it.'

She moved over him, bent and kissed him until he groaned. 'Just—how many courses does this banquet have?' he gasped out.

Paris lifted her head and smiled. 'Why, just as many as you can manage.'

CHAPTER EIGHT

THE excited voices of children sounded through door panels as Paris hurried back to her own room in the morning. She could imagine them opening their presents, their eyes alight with excitement. Until last night, if she had seen children, thought of them, it would have been with guilt and sadness, but now those emotions were gone for ever, to be replaced with an exultant excitement.

She had left Will in a sleep of utter exhaustion; he had partaken deeply of his banquet, like a man starved for a long time and determined to eat his fill. And she had lured him along the way, making each time different, each course more erotic than the last, until his appetite had been sated and his strength spent.

Paris too ought to have been exhausted but had never felt more awake in her life, even though she had been carried with him to the peak of excitement many times. Her body was tired, yes, never having been loved or given so much love in one night before, but her mind was brilliantly alert, intensely happy.

For a while she sat on her bed, her chin on her knees, hugging the memory of the night to her. Later she showered and dressed, putting on a borrowed pair of tartan trews and a white cotton blouse, cinching them in with a wide black belt around her slim waist.

There were the dark shadows of a sleepless night around her eyes, but they were the radiant green of sparkling emeralds. As she fastened her hair back, Paris laughed aloud; anyone looking at her would know that she had been well and truly made love to. But would they guess who by?

She laughed again. As if there could possibly be anyone else but Will.

A ravenous hunger overcame her and she turned to go down to breakfast, but first she paused to look out of the window. It was a perfect Christmas Day; the snow lay thick and pristine again, but the sun was shining with that peculiarly clear luminescence of early morning out of a cloudless blue sky. Even the wind had died down. It was a golden morning.

Her thoughts went back to that first Christmas morning so long ago and she sent up a small but intense prayer for her own hopes and dreams. Then she laughed at her own lack of confidence; after last night nothing could go wrong. Life was going to be good again and she would have atoned at last.

The dining-room was already half-full of people, all of them wishing each other a merry Christmas, laughing and talking. Captain Waters had obviously kept his secret well because no one seemed to have heard about Melanie; Paris didn't hear her name mentioned once. Several people asked her how she was, whether her cold was better, and she replied that it must have been a twenty-four-hour bug, because she felt absolutely fine now.

'But you still look tired,' Mrs Paston remarked motheringly. 'You should rest for a while today. You don't want to overdo things and have to spend days in bed recovering, now do you?'

Somehow Paris managed to keep a straight face as she gravely agreed, her heart dancing inside.

None of the policemen seemed to be around this morning, which seemed strange; usually there were two or three of them having their meals at the same time as everyone else. Paris noticed but didn't think about it much. Ben came in and she waved to him. He helped himself to orange juice and porridge and came over to sit beside her.

He glanced at her face and sighed. 'Why don't the women I go to bed with look like that in the morning?'

'Never mind; you have a great way with feet,' she said consolingly.

'Feet! If that's all I might as well join a monastery.'

'Don't be silly; you've just got to find the right girl.' She leaned closer and lowered her voice. 'Have you heard anything more about you-know-who?'

'No. He-who-must-be-obeyed hasn't been in touch with me. Have you?'

She shook her head. 'No. What do you think is going to happen?'

Ben shrugged. 'I suppose it depends entirely on the gist of the call you-know-who made to someone-else-we-both-know.'

That made her giggle. 'What a ridiculous conversation.'

He grinned back, but said with a low forcefulness, 'I just wish to hell that it was all over and we could get away from here.' Paris didn't speak and he said, 'I suppose you don't, that now you want it to go on?'

She shook her head, not even having to think about it. 'No, I want it to be over too. I have a life to get on with.'

'With Will?'

Her eyes clouded a little, lost some of their inner glow. 'It hasn't been discussed.'

'I see.'

'No, you don't. Eat your porridge.'

Allowing her to change the conversation, Ben said, 'Do you know, I'm really getting to like this stuff? I thought it tasted like wallpaper paste the first time.'

'It certainly looks like it.'

'Yes, but it grows on you.'

'Puts hairs on your chest, huh?'

He groaned, pretending to be in pain at the joke, then looked up as the waiter paused by their table, ostensibly to give them a pot of coffee, but he also put a folded note down beside Ben's plate. Paris reached out for the coffee and poured it into their cups as Ben slipped the note beneath the table and quickly read it.

'Captain Waters wants to see us in my suite immediately after breakfast.'

'Both of us?'

'That's what he says.'

She frowned. 'I wonder what he wants.'

'Just to tell us what's happening, probably. Let's keep our fingers crossed that it's as good as over.'

They finished their breakfast and strolled out into the hall. There was a massive pile of parcels under the Christmas tree, in the most wonderful assortment of shapes and sizes; they looked the sort of presents that would intrigue a child and fill him with excitement. But they were all to stay under the tree until after the special lunch that was being prepared, when they would be given out by Santa Claus, alias one of the policemen.

'Ah, Ben, I've been looking for you.' A woman came up to him and drew him a little aside. 'We're having a sort of talent show this evening; you will take part, won't you? You play so well.'

Ben looked reluctant, was persuaded and profusely thanked.

'Flattery will get you anywhere,' Paris said with irony when he rejoined her.

'You're just jealous because you can't sing.'

They harangued each other amiably as they went up the stairs, unaware of the glances that came their way, and found Mike Waters already waiting for them in Ben's suite.

'What happened last night?' Paris asked eagerly.

'Melanie made the call, as we expected,' the captain replied. 'Only she went out by the stair on the other side of the turret. Evidently she didn't fancy coming across your dead body,' he said drily.

Ben, his voice sardonic, said, 'A sensitive murderess: that's something new.'

Captain Waters didn't smile; in fact he looked quite grave and Paris began to feel uneasy. 'Where is she now?' she asked.

'We took her away in the night and she's safely under lock and key. We taped her conversation. Here, I'll play it for you. You can hear Ramsay quite well because we put a minute bug in the phone, but Melanie's voice isn't that clear because of the wind. Not that she says much of any importance.'

He switched on a cassette-player and they heard the phone ringing then a man's voice say, 'Yes?'

'It's me,' Melanie replied.

'You were supposed to phone last night.'

'I couldn't. There was—there was someone around.'

'All right. Now listen. I'll come tomorrow night, Christmas night.'

'You've found where we are?'

'Yes. I've been watching the place. I can get over the outer wall all right, but I'll need you to let me in. You must be at that wine-cellar door you told me about at one in the morning, do you understand?'

'What if there's someone around?'

'Then wait till they go.' Ramsay sounded impatient. 'Use your common sense. Unlock the door earlier if you can, but I'll need you to guide me through the house.'

'What are you going to do?' Melanie's voice sounded husky, scared.

Ramsay laughed—a harsh and terrible sound that made Paris's blood run cold. 'Oh, I've got it all planned. The police have done me a favour getting everyone together; now I can deal with them all in one go.'

'What about me?'

'Don't do anything to make them suspicious. Don't pack or anything, but be ready to come with me when I leave.'

'All right. Will we really go to Spain?'

'Yes, I've said so. I've got the tickets and the false passports; there won't be any trouble. In two days we'll be there, and those bastards who put me inside will find out that I meant it when I said I'd make them pay.'

'I can't wait to see you again, Noel.'

It was difficult to understand what Melanie was saying and they realised that she must have been shivering with cold. Ramsay must have realised it too, because he cut her short and the call ended.

Ben looked grim. 'Thank God we found out in time. Now you'll be able to catch him easily. But I don't understand how he can be so confident of getting over the wall; it must be at least ten feet high.'

'It seems that Ramsay used to do some climbing in his younger days.'

'What do you think he means to do?'

The captain hesitated, and Paris said, 'I should have thought that that was pretty obvious. It sounds to me as if he intends to set fire to the place and burn us all to death.'

Ben gasped but didn't make any protest, and neither did Mike Waters try to deny it. Instead he slowly nodded and said gravely, 'I'm very much afraid you may be right.'

Ben said, 'But now you have this information you'll be able to catch him as soon as he comes within sight, so we have no need to worry. We'll all be able to sleep easy tonight.'

'It's quite possible that he'll have a gun,' Waters pointed out. 'And I don't want to run the risk of any of my men getting shot, or of Ramsay somehow getting away. So I want to take him when he comes inside.'

They both looked at him in trepidation. 'Isn't that risky?' Ben asked.

'He won't be expecting a trap.'

Paris, her voice tense, said, 'But he will be expecting Melanie to let him in. Will she do it?'

The captain shook his head. 'I couldn't risk her warning him.' Lifting his eyes, he gave Paris a direct look.

She understood at once and was immediately afraid. Her mind filled with dread; she had been unhappy for so long that she couldn't risk losing everything now, not when her dreams were within her grasp. Getting up from her chair, Paris said in great agitation, 'No. I can't. I'm sorry.'

'You'll be quite safe. My men will be all around and—'

She took a distressed step towards the door. 'No. You must get someone else.'

The captain, too, got to his feet. 'There isn't anyone else. You're the only one who knows about Melanie. The only one who—'

'Ramsay will see me. Recognise me.'

'It will be dark. And as soon as he comes inside we'll take him. You won't be in any danger. Please, Paris, for all our sakes.'

Clasping her arms defensively around herself, she shook her head vehemently. 'I'm sorry. You don't understand, but I can't—'

Her voice had risen in forceful refusal but immediately broke off as a sharp knock sounded at the door.

'You'd better answer it,' the captain said to Ben as he moved out of the line of the door. 'Get rid of whoever it is as quickly as you can.'

Ben nodded and walked over to the door, intending to open it just a few inches. But as soon as he turned the latch the door was sent crashing back on its hinges and he had to jump smartly out of the way to avoid it.

'Mind if I join the party?' Will said curtly as he strode

inside. His eyes went straight to Paris standing in the middle of the room and he gave her a tight look. 'What is it you can't do?' But then he saw the captain and he frowned. 'Just what's going on?' he demanded tersely.

Captain Waters quickly shut the door. He glanced at Paris but she was standing with her hands clenched, her face pale. 'Nothing's going on. We're just having a chat, that's all.'

'Is this something to do with Melanie betraying us?' Will demanded bluntly.

Mike Waters sighed. 'How much have you told him?' he said to Paris.

'Just—just that.'

'So now you tell me the rest,' Will said in a tone so forceful that the captain didn't even try to prevaricate. Briefly he told him about the illicit phone call.

'And now he's trying to get Paris to stand in for Melanie,' Ben broke in angrily. 'I don't know how you have the nerve to ask her after all she's been through.'

Will looked at him sharply. 'What are you talking about? What happened to Paris?'

Ben looked startled. 'Didn't you tell him?' he said to her.

'No—and it's of no importance.'

Looking at Will, she suddenly thought of him lying in his bed while Ramsay stole into the building and set it on fire. She could imagine the flames leaping up the staircase, Will being trapped or overcome by smoke, the children crying and screaming in fear. The thought of them being hurt, possibly killed was quite unbearable and in the face of it her earlier refusal to help seemed small and selfish.

'I've reconsidered,' she said shortly. 'I'll do what you want.'

'But you can't!' Ben exclaimed.

'Will someone damn well tell me what's going on?'

Will strode to Paris and took hold of her by the shoulders. 'What do they want you to do?'

'I told you—to take Melanie's place. To meet Ramsay and let him into the cellars,' Ben said when Paris didn't speak.

'No way.' Will turned and put himself between Paris and Captain Waters. 'I'm not going to let her do it.'

But this time the captain wasn't to be intimidated. 'Paris has already agreed. And she'll be quite safe; I've assured her of that.'

'You assured us that we would all be quite safe here until Ramsay was caught, but he fooled you into relaxing your watch on Melanie so that she was able to lead him here,' Ben said harshly. 'If he can fool you once he can fool you again.'

'No, he won't. Not this time. And it has to be Paris. I can't ask anyone else because I can't take the risk of starting a panic. If they all knew that Ramsay was near there would be uproar. I'd have all the men demanding that everyone be taken somewhere else, and all the women in hysterics. I need someone who can keep her head, the way Paris did two nights ago.'

'And just what happened two nights ago?' Will asked sharply. 'I insist that you tell me,' he said to her.

But she shook her head and it was Ben who said, 'I'll tell you. Paris saw Melanie going out onto the roof and went after her. But Melanie shut her out there in the freezing cold and left her to die.'

Will's face paled and he stared at her in appalled disbelief.

'Luckily Paris had her room key with her and she threw it through my window so I was able to go and let her in. But she couldn't have lasted much longer out there,' Ben finished.

His gaze fixed intensely on her face, Will reached out

to draw her to him. 'Why didn't you tell me?' he asked, his voice unsteady.

'It was over. There was no point.' Looking into his eyes, seeing the tender anxiety in them, her heart swelled. He'd said that when they had lived together he'd thought she'd always known that he loved her. Now she recognised that this was one of the times when there was no need for words, when his eyes said it all. She could read it now and know it for what it was; after last night she had the confidence to be sure without words.

Putting up a hand to touch her face, Will said, 'When I was outside the door I heard you say that there was something you couldn't do; was that to meet Ramsay?'

'No, of course not. It was something else entirely.'

But Ben immediately contradicted her. 'She's lying. She's scared and she doesn't really want to do it.'

Paris turned on him. 'Ben, will you please shut up? If I want to say something then I'll say it for myself. I don't need you to speak for me. I've decided to do it and that's final.'

'Oh, no, it damn well isn't,' Will said forcefully. '*I'll* let him in.'

Captain Waters soon torpedoed that idea. Giving him a scornful look, he said, 'Oh, yes, you really look like Melanie, don't you? Only about a foot taller and wider and one of the most masculine voices I've ever heard, but that doesn't matter, of course. Surely you can see that it has to be a woman?'

'Then get a policewoman to do it—someone trained to use a gun and capable of defending herself.'

'If I could, I would, but the nearest experienced woman couldn't possibly get here in time, even if I could get hold of one.'

'Then get one here by helicopter,' Will returned tersely.

'In the phone call Ramsay said that he'd been watching

the place. He'd be bound to smell a rat if he saw a heli-copter trying to land. Here, you'd better listen to the call for yourself.'

He switched on the cassette-player and again the men-acing words filled the room.

'It doesn't take much to guess that he intends to burn the place down with all of us inside it,' Mike Waters said when it finished. 'We have to catch him—and we need Paris to help us. I've already told her that there won't be any danger.'

Both Will and Ben started to argue, but Paris said im-patiently, 'Look, I've said I'll do it. You know there isn't any choice. So let's get this over and done with so that we can get on with our lives.'

'You don't *have* to do it,' Will said, coming to take her hand.

She smiled at him, but there was sadness in her eyes. 'Oh, yes, I think I have to. Don't you?'

He guessed what she meant and gave her a troubled look. 'Let's go somewhere and talk about this.'

'No.' She shook her head, afraid that he would dissuade her and that she would despise herself for being a coward forever more. 'I've made up my mind. I'm glad that you care, but this is something I have to do.'

Will looked as if he had a lot more to say, but she walked over to the door and opened it. 'It's Christmas Day; I'm going downstairs to join in the festivities. Are you coming, all of you?'

Ben came to join her but Will said, 'Shortly. I want a word with Mike first.' And he glared at the poor captain.

Downstairs there was great excitement among the children as they lined up for a fancy-dress competition on a winter and Christmas theme. The costumes, as ingenious as their parents could make them, ranged from a cotton-wool snowman to a miniature Santa Claus and a couple of delightful tree-fairies, to an amazing Christmas stocking that must have taken hours of work. This last won first prize but there was something for every child, and to Paris's amazement there was no crying or disappointment and they all behaved beautifully.

'It's all this quality time they've been having with their parents,' Ben remarked. 'They've probably never had so much attention lavished on them before in their lives.'

'You think coming here has done some good, then?'

'Must have done. And haven't you noticed how all the adults have pitched in together to think up things to pass the time? It's almost like the wartime spirit all over again.'

'How would you know about wartime spirit? You weren't even born.'

Ben grinned. 'I see I shall have to confess; I'm an old war-film groupie. I've got dozens of them on video.' He glanced at his watch. 'Would you like a pre-lunch drink?'

'Isn't it rather early?'

'Yes, but you look as if you need it.'

They went into the bar and that was where Will found them a short time later. He was looking a little grim, but his face lightened when he saw Paris. Coming over to them, he gave her a smile that was all in his eyes, that caressed and sent messages that brought last night vividly to her mind and colour to her cheeks.

Paris hastily looked away and took a sip of her drink, but Ben had noticed and said, 'I suppose you want me to go away and leave you alone?'

Will sat down with them, leaning comfortably back in the chair and crossing his legs. 'Not at all,' he said equably. 'After all, I have it on good authority that you two more than fancy each other. ''Quite smitten'' was the phrase the lady used when I asked where Paris was and she told me that you and Ben had gone up to his room.'

'So that was why you came charging in,' Ben said with a grin.

'It was. The dear lady didn't know whether to disapprove of your outrageous behaviour, be sentimental at the thought of you being in love, or get excited at thinking I might start a fight.'

'Who was it?'

'A gentleman never betrays a lady—even a gossip.'

Ben glanced round the bar and several curious pairs of eyes hastily turned away. He laughed. 'Well, the place would be even more boring for them without a bit of scandal.'

'Possibly. But I don't want Paris to be the cause of gossip, so to show that we're all friends I'll let you buy me a drink. A large Scotch.'

Ben went to the bar and Will said softly, 'Are you all right?'

She knew what he meant and nodded, the happiness returning to her eyes.

'You should have woken me.'

'I'm not sure I could have done; you were sleeping—very deeply.'

He grinned. 'Which is hardly surprising.' Reaching across the table, he took her hand. 'We must talk soon.'

'Tomorrow.'

'Not till then?'

'No.' She didn't want to talk about the future today, not when she had tonight hanging over her, not when she had to find the courage to face Ramsay, even if it would be for only a moment.

Will read her mind, and squeezed her hand in encouragement. Leaning forward so that only she could hear, he said, 'Don't worry, I'm not going to try and make you change your mind. I tried to persuade Waters to let me in on it, but he's refused, damn him.'

Paris gave a silent prayer of relief and deliberately sent their thoughts in another direction by saying with a co-quettish look, 'You'll be adding fuel for the gossips if you talk to me this close. They'll think you're murmuring sweet nothings.'

He gave a mock leer. 'There are several very definite somethings I would like to say. And I know a very good place where I could say them this afternoon.'

'I'm shocked.'

'Is that yes or no?'

She laughed, and didn't answer as Ben came back with a tray of drinks, but made it clear in their conversation that she wanted to watch the children open their presents that afternoon. Will looked disappointed but accepted it. But for the rest of that day he left her side only when they went up to change for dinner, making it quite clear to everyone that it was he who was with her and not Ben.

It was a wonderful day; Paris enjoyed it thoroughly, especially being with Will. It was just like the old days, before she'd ruined everything, only it was better now be-cause she had hope for the future. If the fates were kind then she would never again know the lonely emptiness of the last years. But first there was the night to face.

Will walked with her to her room just after midnight. There he kissed her long and tenderly and had to drag himself from her arms. 'Take care,' he said raggedly. 'Promise me you'll take great care.'

'I promise. You mustn't worry; I'll be fine.'

He left her and she stifled a small feeling of disappoint-ment; she'd thought that he would have been far more emotional and encouraging, seeing what she had to face in just a short time.

Paris pushed the thought aside and changed into a black tracksuit with a hood, which Mike Waters had found for her to wear. Under it she wore a thick sweater which, it was hoped, would make her figure look more like Melanie's, and she wore her flattest shoes to make her as short as possible. It probably wouldn't fool Ramsay for more than a few minutes, but then hopefully it wouldn't even take that long before he was captured.

A policeman came for her at a quarter to one and they went down together in the service lift to the kitchens. 'Everyone's in position,' he told her. 'They're all waiting by the outside door. As soon as he walks inside, they'll take him.'

Paris nodded and took the torch he handed her as they reached the door that led down to the large cellars that ran beneath the whole building. The original owner, who'd had the house built, had been a wine buff. Now most of the basement rooms had been altered to make a space for the gymnasium and swimming pool, but there were still several rooms that held racks of wine for the hotel guests.

The door was locked. The policeman unlocked it and gave her a thumbs-up sign. 'Use the torch. Don't put on any lights. And if he makes a lunge for you shine the torch in his face.'

Paris frowned, puzzled, but nodded again. Switching on the torch, she went through the door. It closed behind her and she immediately wanted to turn and bang on the panels, to demand to be let out. For a terrible moment it was like being out on the roof all over again. Somehow she fought back the panic and went on down the steps.

She had expected it to be very cold but the central heating must have been installed here too, although it was several degrees lower than upstairs. To keep the wine at an even temperature, presumably.

Pulling the hood over her hair and forward over her face, she went on her way. Mike Waters had taken her down there earlier that day, so she knew which direction to take.

Will had come with her, although the captain hadn't been very pleased. He'd pointed out the door that Ramsay would come through, shown her the wooden cases they'd stacked nearby, where the policemen would be hidden.

Now, although she walked quietly, Paris's footsteps still echoed around the corridor. It was one of the reasons why she had to do this part alone—just in case Ramsay was at a window, watching, listening. If he heard two sets of footsteps he would immediately take alarm and they might lose him again.

The corridor came to an end. To reach the outer door, she now had to unlock another door and go through a series of cellars, first passing rooms that had once been used as laundries, lamp-room, boot-room—all the workplaces that had been needed when the castle had been a private house and which now were largely obsolete.

There was time yet and it wasn't easy walking by the light of the torch, but she went as quickly as she could. There was a faint noise and her scalp prickled, her heart standing still for a moment, but the noise didn't come again and she thought of mice. Lord, she was scared to death of mice.

One of the doors, marked mysteriously 'Fish-Room', stood open. Paris went to walk past it and caught a definite whiff of tobacco smoke. Was one of the policemen hiding there? She took another step and then a low voice said, 'Melanie.'

She froze, then swung round. And there, in the light of the torch, grinning at her, stood Noel Ramsay.

He put up an arm to shield his face from the light. 'Don't shine it on me. Here, give it to me and let me look at you.'

Paris instantly turned off the torch and threw it as far away as possible. Then she raised her voice to a squeal that wasn't far short of a scream, praying that the police would hear. 'You frightened me!'

'Sorry, darling.' But he didn't sound it. 'Where's the torch?'

Trying to make her voice as nasal as possible, Paris said, 'You gave me such a start, I dropped it.'

'Damn!'

She felt him grope for her and he found her arm and held it before she could move away. Without warning he pulled her into his arms and kissed her. There was no finesse about it; he pressed his mouth hard against her own, bruising her lips, at the same time taking her breast in his hand and squeezing. He had grown a beard and it felt like wire on her skin.

'There, that's what you've been missing. And there's plenty more to come.' He laughed, plainly pleased with himself.

He let go of one of her arms and Paris rubbed her hand across her mouth, feeling ill. She wanted to wrench herself away from him, to run back towards the light and warmth and peacefulness of the hotel, but she knew that somehow she must let the police know that he was already inside.

'Why aren't you waiting by the door, like we said? How did you get in?'

His hand tightened a little. 'Your voice sounds different.'

Trying desperately to sound like Melanie, Paris said in an accusing tone, 'I caught a cold out on the roof, calling you.'

'Now she tells me,' Ramsay said in distaste. But he let her go, saying, 'Search around; see if you can find the torch.'

'Was the door open already?'

'No, but I got here early and it was too damn cold to

wait outside, so I broke a window and got in that way. I would have tried to get up to your room and surprise you there if the door out of here hadn't been locked. Then I could have given you what you really want, couldn't I, my sweet?' he said lasciviously.

Paris shuddered but managed a pretty good attempt at a coquettish giggle. 'We'd better go along to the door, make sure it's unlocked and ready for us to get away quick.'

But Ramsay said, 'There's no point; we can get out of any door. Have you found the torch?'

'No. It must have rolled.'

'You should have had enough sense to hold onto it.'

'You made me jump,' she responded in an aggrieved tone. She had found the wall of the corridor and was moving along it in the direction of the outer door, raising her voice, desperately hoping that the sound would carry and someone would hear.

'Where are you going?'

'I'm looking for the torch.'

'Forget it. Did you leave the door you came through open?'

'Yes. And the one in the kitchen that leads down here,' Paris said without thinking.

Ramsay's voice filled with satisfaction. 'Good. Come here. We can find our way up; my eyes have got used to the dark now.'

Paris's hand felt something on the wall and she realised it was a light switch; hastily she moved her hand away; the last thing she wanted now was light. In the distance she thought she heard a noise, very soft, but it sent a wave of hope to her heart. To cover it, afraid that Ramsay might also have heard it, she said loudly, 'What about the torch? It must be round here somewhere.'

His voice sharpened. 'I said forget it. Come over here.'

Perhaps he had heard or had become suspicious of her

voice again. To lull him, praying that the noise wasn't just mice, Paris said, 'Have you got the passports, like you said? How will we get to Spain?'

'Don't worry about that; it's all taken care of. Come here, darling.'

There was no help for it; he would become really suspicious if she didn't do what he wanted. With an inner sob, Paris turned and groped her way back to him. 'Here I am.'

'That's my girl. You sure those doors are unlocked?'

'Yes, I've said so, haven't I?'

'Just making sure.' Suddenly he laughed, the sound echoing horribly in the darkness. 'Just making sure I don't need you any more, you silly cow. Do you really think I'd take a cheap tart like you with me? No, you gave evidence against me and you're going to die with the rest of them.'

She tried to pull away but he grabbed her and held her close against him, so that she could smell the stink of tobacco and drink on his breath, the unwashed odour of his skin.

'And you'll be the first to go, and you'll know what's coming to you. You'll—'

His voice broke off with a gasp as she brought her knee up as hard as she could. He let go of one of her arms and she hit him in the face, wrenching herself free and turning to run blindly along the corridor towards the police, screaming for help as she went.

Behind her Ramsay gave a grunt and then she heard his footsteps pounding after her. Her outstretched hand brushed a wall and she guessed that she must have gone through the archway into the first of the wine cellars. If she could only hide! She turned to her left, hoping to find the wine racks, but tripped over something on the floor and went crashing down.

It must have been a barrel; it went skittering across the

floor and landed against another rack. There was light! She
gave a moan of thankfulness, thinking that it must be the
police at last, but then realised that it was coming from
behind her.

The light flickered and grew brighter as Ramsay came
nearer, and she realised that he must have a cigarette
lighter. Paris was leaning against a wine rack and hastily
used it to pull herself to her feet as he came into the cellar.
He laughed when he saw her, enjoying himself, knowing
that she was trapped, but swore when she grabbed a bottle
and turned to throw it at him.

He ducked and the lighter went out, plunging them into
even deeper darkness. With a terrified sob, Paris pulled out
more bottles and hurled them in his direction. Suddenly he
was on her and she screamed again. Desperately she hit
out, trying to break free, but he was so strong, so strong.
His hands went to her throat and he began to squeeze. His
laugh filled her ears as the blackness began to grow even
deeper.

Suddenly there was light again—the dark-destroying
glare of a powerful electric bulb. The grip on her throat
relaxed as Ramsay reacted with surprise. Paris opened her
eyes and looked into his startled eyes as he saw her face
for the first time. Then a hand caught his shoulder and he
was wrenched away from her as Will's voice said, 'Try
fighting a man instead of a woman, you murdering swine.'

Putting her hands up to her throat, Paris leaned limply
against the wine rack and watched. Ramsay, knowing that
he had walked into a trap, fought desperately and dirty.
But Will was in a cold, implacable rage. Though the two
men were of similar height and build it was obvious from
the start that Ramsay didn't stand a chance. A lot of hard
blows were exchanged but then Will hit him good and
hard, and when Ramsay, knowing that he was beaten, tried

to get a revolver from his pocket Will just smashed his hand against the wall until he dropped it.

Paris became aware that the police were there, that Captain Waters was trying to stop the fight, but Will pushed him out of the way too and went on grimly hitting Ramsay until he fell to the ground.

Then Will stood there, legs braced, chest heaving, hands still clenched into bruised fists, staring down at their enemy, almost as if daring him to get up so that he could hit him again. Only when the captain stooped to put handcuffs on Ramsay did Will straighten up, then stride over to take Paris in his arms.

'How did you get here? Oh, how did you get here?' she said with a sob, her head against his shoulder.

'Did you really think I'd let you come down here alone? Never in a million years.'

Will insisted on carrying her up to her room and would have stayed with her, but his face was bruised and bleeding and she insisted he be attended to, asking instead for Mrs Paston to come and sit with her. The older lady came bustling in wearing a quilted red dressing gown and held Paris's hand for the rest of the night.

Tomorrow everyone would be told that Ramsay had been caught and that they were free to go, but only a few would ever know just how close he had come to gaining his revenge.

Early in the morning, before anyone else was about, Paris dressed and packed what was left of her clothes, then went to find Captain Waters. He wouldn't agree to what she wanted at first, but she was adamant, and shortly afterwards Paris climbed into a Range Rover that drove her away.

As they went through the gatehouse archway, Paris glanced back at the castle. So much had happened there, both unbelievably good as well as indescribably terrible. Somehow she must try to forget the bad and remember only the good. There was the future to look forward to now and she was full of hope.

They went through the archway and the building was lost from sight. She had done everything she could to atone; now she must wait and see if she had been forgiven and fate would be kind to her.

The daffodils were in bud before Will found her. Paris had bought some from the local market along with a basket of groceries. It was Saturday and the sun was shining, bringing the first promise of spring.

She had got over the trauma of Ramsay's attack and no longer woke in shuddering fear as she went through it in her dreams. Now she knew an inner contentment and was able to face the world on equal terms again.

Will was waiting outside her building, leaning against his car and reading a newspaper. He saw her first and tossed the paper through the window of the car, then walked purposefully to meet her. Paris stood still, her heart giving a great leap of thankfulness. When he came up to her, they just stood and gazed at each other for long minutes. There was a guarded look about Will's eyes and he didn't attempt to kiss her.

Reaching down, he took her basket from her. 'You have been extremely difficult to track down,' he commented as he fell into step beside her.

'Have I?' Her voice was unsteady.

'You're not in the phone book, your company refused to give me your address, and Captain Waters wouldn't tell me it even when I threatened to spill the beans on his cock-up over catching Ramsay. In the end I had to go through all the electoral registers for most of London before I found you. And then, of course, you weren't here. "Gone abroad," your neighbour said.'

They reached the entrance to the building. Paris punched in her code number, they went inside and took the lift to her floor. Once inside the flat, Will at last took her in his arms and kissed her.

When he finally raised his head, he said raggedly, 'Are you going to go on disappearing from my life, making me go through hell until I find you? Because I warn you, Paris, I don't think I can take it again.'

'You—you can't?'

'No, I think it would be much better if we got married so that I can tie you down if necessary.'

She smiled but said, 'Is that why you want to marry me, then?'

His arms tightened around her and he looked down at her with intense tenderness. 'No, you idiot, it's because I love you most dearly, and because I know I can't live without you. And we'll do it on your terms, have it any way you want.'

She knew that he was referring to her work and loved him the more for it, but it was incidental now. 'I've waited a long time to hear you say that,' she said huskily.

Drawing a little away from her, Will gave her a searching look. 'Why did you leave the castle so soon, without seeing me? I went searching for you but Mike Waters said you'd insisted on leaving.'

Paris moved away a few steps, then turned to face him again. 'It was so that—this could happen. I wanted you to be sure that you really loved me, that you'd forgiven me. I knew that if you came to find me then you would still care, that the past would no longer be between us.'

'It isn't,' he said instantly. 'And I was as much to blame; I've realised that now. If you'd been confident of my feelings for you, you would have come to me instead of

Emma. I let you down when you needed me, and it never occurred to me that you might have done it for my sake. I think it was the fact that you hadn't told me, that I'd had to learn it from someone else that made me go over the top and react the way I did. I was a damn fool not to listen to you then; I wasted those years when we could have been together.'

'Yes, you should have listened,' she agreed. 'Because I never had an abortion.'

He stared at her. 'But I don't understand.'

'I'd decided to keep the baby, but I had an accident. Oh, nothing major,' she added as he gave her a startled look. 'Just a fall, but I lost it. I should have told you, I know, but I wanted everything to be the same between us. But it couldn't be, because I felt so guilty.'

'But if it wasn't your fault...'

She swung away from him. 'But I'd thought about an abortion, considered it as an option. And when I had the miscarriage—' her voice filled with pain '—I wasn't altogether sorry, because I'd been so afraid of losing you.'

'Oh, Paris,' Will said wretchedly. 'Why didn't you tell me this when we were at the castle?'

Turning to face him, she said, 'Would you have believed me? Every time I saw you, you threw the abortion in my face. You were still so angry—' She broke off, biting her lip.

'I'm sorry. I'm so sorry.' Reaching for her, he said urgently, 'Will *you* forgive *me*, my love?'

'There's nothing to forgive.' Lifting her hands to either side of his face, Paris gazed at him for a long moment, her eyes alight with happiness. 'I love you—love you with all my heart.' Then she reached to gently kiss his lips.

'And I you,' he said softly. 'I shall go on telling you that for the rest of my life.' His expression changed. 'That's if you ever get round to saying yes, of course.'

Paris dropped her eyes, took a step away from him.

Something in her manner made Will say sharply, 'What is it?'

'There—there's something you ought to know.' Lifting her head, she looked at him directly, her gaze serious. 'I lied to you.'

His face set, grew tense, as if expecting a blow. 'Lied? How?'

'That night we spent together at the castle, you asked me if I was protected. Well, I wasn't.'

Will stared at her, his face slowly changing as he realised. 'You mean, you…?'

Paris nodded, imps of happy devilment in her eyes. 'Yes, if you marry me you'll have to take on our child as well.'

He gave a disbelieving shake of his head. 'But this is—wonderful! Incredible! But what about your career?'

'Maybe I'll put that on hold for a while.'

Catching hold of her hands, he held them tightly. 'Are you sure?'

'Oh, yes, I've seen a doctor.'

'No. I meant, are you sure this is what you want? Why did you do it? What if I hadn't come to find you?'

'It wouldn't have made any difference. I knew that this was the only way I could atone for what happened, and I want this baby—want it desperately. Almost as much as I want you,' she added softly.

Putting his arms round her, Will gave her an exuberant hug, sweeping her off her feet, a huge grin on his face. 'I'm going to be a father! Can you beat that?' Then he set her on her feet and said, 'Don't just stand there; we've got to go out and find a house for the three of us.' Taking her hand, he pulled her towards the door, then stopped. 'You still haven't said it,' he complained.

Paris laughed. 'Well, OK, I suppose I'd better make an honest man of you.'

'Is that the best you can do?'

Her voice softened. 'No—the best is yet to come, my love...'

MILLS & BOON®

Makes
any time
special

Enjoy a romantic novel from
Mills & Boon®

Presents...™ *Enchanted*™ TEMPTATION.

Historical Romance™ MEDICAL ROMANCE™

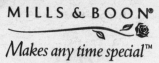

MILLS & BOON®

MISTLETOE *Magic*

Three favourite Enchanted™ authors
bring you romance at Christmas.

Three stories in one volume:

A Christmas Romance
BETTY NEELS

Outback Christmas
MARGARET WAY

Sarah's First Christmas
REBECCA WINTERS

Published 19th November 1999

*Available at most branches of WH Smith, Tesco,
Martins, Borders, Easons, Volume One / James Thin
and most good paperback bookshops*

THE

Regency

COLLECTION

Where rogues find romance

Look out for the ninth volume in this limited
collection of Regency Romances from
Mills & Boon® in January 2000.

Featuring:

A Biddable Girl?
by Paula Marshall

and

The Wolf's Promise
by Alice Thornton

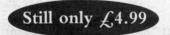

Still only £4.99

MILLS & BOON®

Makes any time special™

MILLENNIUM

Celebrate the Millennium with your favourite
romance authors. With so many to choose from,
there's a Millennium story for everyone!

Presents...™
> *Morgan's Child*
> *Anne Mather*
> On sale 3rd December 1999

Enchanted™
> *Bride 2000*
> *Trisha David*
> On sale 3rd December 1999

TEMPTATION.
> *Once a Hero*
> *Kate Hoffmann*
> On sale 3rd December 1999

> *Always a Hero*
> *Kate Hoffmann*
> On sale 7th January 2000

√ **MEDICAL ROMANCE**™
> *Perfect Timing*
> *Alison Roberts*
> On sale 3rd December 1999

MILLS & BOON®

Makes any time special™